USA TODAY

Bre

"Brenda Jackson writes ... that sizzles and
characters you fall in love with."
—*New York Times* and *USA TODAY* bestselling author
Lori Foster

"Jackson's trademark ability to weave multiple
characters and side stories together makes
shocking truths all the more exciting."
—*Publishers Weekly*

"There is no getting away from the sex appeal and
charm of Jackson's Westmoreland family."
—*RT Book Reviews* on *Feeling the Heat*

"Jackson's characters are wonderful, strong, colorful
and hot enough to burn the pages."
—*RT Book Reviews* on *Westmoreland's Way*

"The kind of sizzling, heart-tugging story
Brenda Jackson is famous for."
—*RT Book Reviews* on *Spencer's Forbidden Passion*

"This is entertainment at its best."
—*RT Book Reviews* on *Star of His Heart*

* * *

The Secret Affair
is part of The Westmorelands series: A family bound by
loyalty...and love! Only from *New York Times* bestselling
author Brenda Jackson and Mills & Boon® Desire™!

M X

THE SECRET AFFAIR

BY
BRENDA JACKSON

Published in Great Britain 2014
by Mills & Boon, an imprint of Harlequin (UK) Limited,
Eton House, 18-24 Paradise Road, Richmond, Surrey, TW9 1SR

© 2014 Brenda Streater Jackson

ISBN: 978-0-263-91488-7

51-1214

Harlequin (UK) Limited's policy is to use papers that are natural, renewable and recyclable products and made from wood grown in sustainable forests. The logging and manufacturing processes conform to the legal environmental regulations of the country of origin.

Printed and bound in Spain
by CPI, Barcelona

Brenda Jackson is a die "heart" romantic who married her childhood sweetheart, Gerald, and still proudly wears the "going steady" ring he gave her when she was fifteen. Their marriage of forty-one years produced two sons, Gerald Jr. and Brandon, of whom Brenda is extremely proud. Because she's always believed in the power of love, Brenda's stories always have happy endings, and she credits Gerald for being her inspiration.

A *New York Times* and *USA TODAY* bestselling author of more than one hundred romance titles, Brenda is a retiree from a major insurance company and now divides her time between family, writing and travel. You may write Brenda at PO Box 28267, Jacksonville, Florida 32226, USA, by e-mail at authorbrendajackson@gmail.com or visit her website at www.brendajackson.net.

To the man who will always and forever be the love of my life, Gerald Jackson, Sr.

Special thanks to Dr Dorothy M. Russ of Meharry Medical College for your assistance in providing information on medical schools and residency programs.

In whom are hid all the treasures of wisdom and knowledge.
—*Colossians* 2:3

Prologue

Jillian Novak stared across the table at her sister, not believing what she'd just heard.

Jillian placed the glass of wine she'd been holding on the table, barely keeping the drink from spilling. "What do you mean you aren't going with me? That's crazy, Paige. Need I remind you that you're the one who planned the trip?"

"A reminder isn't needed, Jill, but please understand my dilemma," Paige said in a rueful tone, her dark brown eyes shaded with regret. "Getting a part in a Steven Spielberg movie is a dream come true. You can't imagine what I was feeling—happiness at being chosen one minute, and then disappointment the next, when I found out that shooting starts the same week I was supposed to be on the cruise with you."

"Let me guess, your happiness overpowered your disappointment, right?" Jillian felt a pounding pressure in her head and knew why. She had been looking forward to the Mediterranean cruise—for many reasons—and now it appeared she wouldn't be going.

"I'm sorry, Jill. You've never gone on a cruise and I know it's one of the things on your bucket list."

Paige's apology only made Jillian feel worse. She'd

made her sister feel awful for making a choice Jillian would have made herself if given the chance. Reaching across the table, she grabbed Paige's hand.

"I'm the one who should be apologizing, Paige. I was only thinking of myself. You're right. Getting that part in the movie is a dream come true and you'd be crazy not to take it. I'm truly happy for you. Congratulations."

A bright smile spread across Paige's lips. "Thanks. I wanted so much for us to spend time together on the cruise. It's been ages since me, you, Pam and Nadia have had sister time."

Nadia, a senior in college, was their youngest sister. At twenty-one she was two years younger than Paige and four years younger than Jillian. Pamela, their oldest sister—who Jillian, Nadia and Paige were convinced was the best older sister anyone could ever have—was ten years older than Jillian. A former actress, Pam had given up the glitter of Hollywood to return home to Gamble, Wyoming, and raise them when their father died. Now Pam lived in Denver. She was married, the mother of two and the CEO of two acting schools, one in Denver and the other in Gamble. Paige had followed in Pam's footsteps and pursued an acting career. She lived in Los Angeles.

With Pam's busy schedule, she'd said accompanying them on the cruise would have been close to impossible. Nadia had wanted to go but finals kept her from doing so. Jillian had wanted sister time with at least one of her siblings. And now that she had completed medical school, she needed those two weeks on the cruise as a getaway before starting her residency. But there was another reason she wanted to take that two-week cruise.

Aidan Westmoreland.

It was hard to believe it had been a little over a year since she'd broken things off with him. And every time she remembered the reason she'd done so her heart ached. She needed a distraction from her memories.

"You okay, Jill?"

Jillian glanced up at Paige and forced a smile. "Yes, why do you ask?"

"You zoned out on me just now. I was talking and you appeared to be a million miles away. I noticed you haven't been yourself since I arrived in New Orleans. More than once you've seemed preoccupied about something. Is everything okay?"

Jillian waved off Paige's words. The last thing she wanted was for her sister to start worrying and begin digging. "Yes, everything is okay, Paige."

Paige didn't look convinced. "Um, I don't know. Maybe I should forget about being in that movie and go on that cruise with you after all."

Jillian picked up her wineglass to take a sip. "Don't be silly. You're doing the right thing. Besides, I'm not going on the cruise."

"Why not?"

Jillian was surprised at her sister's question. "Surely you don't expect me to go without you."

"You need a break before starting your residency."

Jillian rolled her eyes. "Get real, Paige. What would I do on a two-week cruise by myself?"

"Rest, relax, enjoy the sights, the ocean, the peace and quiet. And you might luck up and meet some nice single guy."

Jillian shook her head. "Nice single guys don't go on cruises alone. Besides, the last thing I need right now is a man in my life."

Paige laughed. "Jill, you haven't had a guy in your life since you dated Cobb Grindstone in your senior year at Gamble High. I think what's missing in your life is a man."

Jillian bristled at her sister's words. "Not hardly, especially with my busy schedule. And I don't see you with anyone special."

"At least I've been dating over the years. You haven't. Or, if you have, you haven't told me about it."

Jillian schooled her expression into an impassive facade. She'd never told Paige about her affair with Aidan, and considering how it had ended she was glad she hadn't.

"Jill?"

She glanced up at her sister. "Yes?"

A teasing smile spread across Paige's lips. "You aren't keeping secrets, are you?"

Jill knew Paige had given her the perfect opportunity to come clean about her affair with Aidan, but she wasn't ready. Even after a year, the pain was still raw. And the last thing Jillian needed was for Paige to start probing for more information.

"You know the reason I don't have a man in my life is because of time. My focus has been on becoming a doctor and nothing else." Paige didn't have to know that a few years ago Aidan had wiggled his way past that focus without much effort. That had been a mistake that cost her.

"That's why I think you should go on that cruise without me," Paige said. "You've worked hard and need to rest and enjoy yourself for a change. Once you begin your residency you'll have even less time for yourself—or anything else."

"That's true," Jillian said. "But—"

"No buts, Jillian."

Jillian knew that tone. She also knew that whenever Paige called her by her full name she meant business. "If I were to go on that cruise alone I'd be bored stiff. You're talking about two weeks."

Paige gave her a pointed look. "I'm talking about two weeks that I believe you need. And just think of all the fabulous places you'll get to see—Barcelona, France, Rome, Greece and Turkey." Now it was Paige who reached out to take hold of Jillian's hand. "Look, Jill, there *is* something going on with you, I can feel it. Whatever it is, it's tearing you apart. I picked up on it months ago, the last time I came to visit you."

A wry smile touched Paige's lips when she added, "Perhaps you *are* keeping secrets. Maybe there's some doctor in medical school that caught your eye and you're not ready to tell me about him. One who has blown your mind and you don't know how to handle the intensity of such a relationship. If that's the case, I understand. All of us at some time or another have issues we prefer to deal with alone. That's why I believe two weeks on the open seas will be good for you."

Jillian drew in a deep breath. Paige didn't know how close she was to the truth. Her problem *did* center on some doctor, but not one attending medical school with her.

At that moment the waitress returned with their meal, and Jillian appreciated the interruption. She knew Paige would not be happy until Jillian agreed to go on the cruise. She'd heard what Paige had said—Paige knew something was bothering Jillian. It would only be a matter of time before Pam and Nadia knew as well, if they didn't already. Besides, Jillian had already taken those two weeks off. If she didn't go on the cruise, the family would expect her to come home and spend that time with them. She couldn't do that. What if Aidan came home unexpectedly while she was there? He was the last person she wanted to see.

"Jill?"

Jillian drew in another deep breath and met Paige's gaze. "Okay, I'll do it. I'll go cruising alone. Hopefully, I'll enjoy myself."

Paige smiled. "You will. There will be plenty for you to do and on those days when you feel like doing nothing, you can do that, too. Everybody needs to give their mind a rest once in a while."

Jillian nodded. Her mind definitely needed a rest. She would be the first to admit that she had missed Aidan— the steamy hot text messages, the emails that made her adrenaline surge and the late-night phone calls that sent heat sizzling through her entire body.

But that had been before she'd learned the truth. Now all she wanted to do was get over him.

She sighed deeply while thinking that Paige was right. Jillian needed that cruise and the time away it would give her. She would go on the cruise alone.

Dr. Aidan Westmoreland entered his apartment and removed his lab coat. After running a frustrated hand down his face, he glanced at his watch. He'd hoped he would have heard something by now. What if...

The ringing of his cell phone made him pause on his way to the kitchen. It was the call he'd been waiting for. "Paige?"

"Yes, it's me."

"Is she still going?" he asked, not wasting time with chitchat.

There was a slight pause on the other end and in that short space of time knots formed in his stomach. "Yes, she's still going on the cruise, Aidan."

He released the breath he'd been holding as Paige continued, "Jill still has no idea I'm aware that the two of you had an affair."

Aidan hadn't known Paige knew the truth, either, until she'd paid him a surprise visit last month. According to her, she'd figured things out the year Jillian had entered medical school. She'd become suspicious when he'd come home for his cousin Riley's wedding and she'd overheard him call Jillian *Jilly* in an intimate tone. Paige had been concerned this past year when she'd noticed Jillian seemed troubled by something that she wouldn't share with Paige.

Paige had talked to Ivy, Jillian's best friend, who'd also been concerned about Jillian. Ivy had shared everything about the situation with Paige. That prompted Paige to fly to Charlotte and confront him. Until then, he'd been clueless as to the real reason behind his and Jillian's breakup.

When Paige had told him of the cruise she and Jillian had planned and had suggested an idea for getting Jillian on the cruise alone, he'd readily embraced the plan.

I've done my part and the rest is up to you, Aidan. I hope you can convince Jill of the truth.

Moments later he ended the call and continued to the kitchen where he grabbed a beer. Popping the top, he leaned against the counter and took a huge gulp. Two weeks on the open seas with Jillian would be interesting. But he intended to make it more than just interesting. He aimed to make it productive.

A determined smile spread across his lips. By the time the cruise ended there would be no doubt in Jillian's mind that he was the only man for her.

Moments later, he tossed the empty can in the recycle bin before heading for the shower. As he undressed, he couldn't help but recall how his secret affair with Jillian had begun nearly four years ago....

One

"So, how does it feel to be twenty-one?"

Jillian's breath caught in her throat when Aidan West-moreland's tall frame slid into the seat across from her. It was only then that she noticed everyone had gone inside. She and Aidan were the only ones on the patio that overlooked a beautiful lake.

This birthday party had been a huge surprise and Aidan's attendance even more so since he rarely came home from medical school. She couldn't imagine he'd come home just for her birthday. With her away at college most of the time as well, their paths rarely crossed. She couldn't recall them ever holding what she considered a real conversation during the four years she'd known him.

"It feels the same as yesterday," she said. "Age is just a number. No big deal."

A smile touched the corners of his lips and her stomach clenched. He had a gorgeous smile, one that complemented the rest of him. If there was such a thing as eye candy he was certainly it. She had the hots for him big-time.

Who wouldn't have the hots while sitting across from

this hunk of sexiness? If his lips didn't grab you then his eyes certainly would. They were deep, dark and penetrating. Jillian's heart missed beats just looking into them.

"Just a number?" He chuckled, leaning back in his chair, stretching long legs in front of him. "Women might think that way but men think differently."

He smelled good. When did she start noticing the scent of a man?

"And why is that, Aidan?" she asked, picking up her glass of lemonade to take a sip. It suddenly felt hotter than usual. It had nothing to do with the temperature and everything to do with her body's heated reaction to him.

She watched him lift a brow over those striking dark eyes. A feral smile edged his lips as he leaned forward. "Are you sure I'm Aidan and not Adrian?"

Oh, yes she was sure he was Aidan. She'd heard about the games he and his identical twin would play on unsuspecting souls, those who couldn't tell them apart. "I'm sure."

It was Aidan and not Adrian who stirred her in places she'd rather not think about at the moment.

He leaned in even closer. So close she could see the pupils in his dark eyes. "And how are you so certain?" he asked.

Was she imagining things or had the tone of his voice dropped to a husky murmur? It was rumored that he was a big flirt. She had seen him in action at several Westmoreland weddings. It was also a fact that he and his twin were womanizers and had developed quite a reputation at Harvard. She could certainly see why women were at their beck and call.

"Because I am," she replied. And that's all she intended to say on the matter.

There was no way she would tell him the real reason, that from the moment her brother-in-law Dillon had introduced her to Aidan, before he'd married Pam, she had developed a full-blown crush. She'd been seventeen at the time, a senior in high school. The only problem was the crush hadn't lessened much since.

"Why?"

She glanced back up at Aidan. "Why what?"

"Why are you so certain? You still haven't said."

She inwardly sighed. Why couldn't he leave it alone? She had no intention of telling him. But since she had a feeling he wouldn't let up, she added, "The two of you sound different."

He flashed another sexy smile, showing the dimples in his cheeks. Her hormones, which always acted out of control around him, were erratic now. "Funny you say that. Most people think we sound a lot alike."

"Well, I don't think that."

There was no way she could think that when it was Aidan's voice, and not Adrian's, that stroked her senses. Deciding it was time to take charge of the conversation to keep his questions at bay, she inquired, "So how is medical school going?"

He didn't let on that he suspected her ploy, and as she took another sip of her lemonade, he began telling her what she had to look forward to in another year or so. Becoming a neurosurgeon had been a lifelong dream of hers ever since her mother died of a brain infection when Jillian was seven.

Aidan told her about the dual residency program at hospitals in Portland, Maine, and Charlotte, North Carolina, that he planned to pursue after completing medical school. His dream was to become a cardiologist. He was excited about becoming a doctor and she could hear it in his voice. She was thrilled about becoming a doctor one day as well, but she had another year left before she finished her studies at the University of Wyoming.

While he talked, she nodded as she discreetly gave him a slow, appreciative appraisal. The man was too handsome for words. His voice was smooth as silk, with just enough huskiness to keep her pulse rate on edge. Creamy caramel skin spread across the bridge of a hawkish nose, sharp cheekbones, a perfect sculptured jaw and a mouth so sensual she enjoyed watching it in motion. She could imagine all the things he did with that mouth.

"Have you decided where you're going for medical school, Jillian?"

She blinked. He had asked her a question and was waiting on an answer. And while he waited she saw that sexy mouth ease into another smile. She wondered if he'd known she was checking him out.

"I've always wanted to live in New Orleans so working at a hospital there will be at the top of my list," she said, trying to ignore the eyes staring at her.

"And your second choice?"

She shrugged. "Not sure. I guess one in Florida."

"Why?"

She frowned. Why was he quizzing her? "I've never been to Florida."

He chuckled. "I hope that's not the only reason."

Her frown deepened. "Of course that's not the only reason," she said defensively. "There are good medical schools in Louisiana and Florida."

He nodded. "Yes, there are. How's your grade point average?"

"Good. In fact my GPA is better than good. I'm at the top of my class. In the top ten at least."

Getting there hadn't been easy. She'd made a lot of sacrifices, especially in her social life. She couldn't recall the last time she'd gone out on a date or participated in any school activities. But she was okay with that. Pam was paying a lot of the cost for her education and Jillian wanted to make her sister proud.

"What about the entrance exam—the MCAT—and admission essays? Started on them yet?"

"Too early."

"It's never too early. I suggest you prepare for them during your free time."

Now it was her turn to smile. "Free time? What's that?"

The chuckle that erupted from his throat was smooth and sexy and made her pulse thump. "It's time you should squeeze in regardless of whether you think you can or not. It's essential to know how to manage your time wisely, otherwise you'll get burned-out before you even get started."

She grudgingly wondered what made him an expert. Then she pushed her resentment aside. He *was* giving her sound advice and he had gone where she had yet to go. And from what she'd heard, he was doing pretty well at it. He would graduate from Harvard Medical School at the top of his class and then enter a dual residency program that any medical student would die for. He would get the chance to work with the best cardiologists in the United States.

"Thanks for the advice, Aidan."

"You're welcome. When you get ready to knock them out of the way, let me know. I'll help you."

"You will?"

"Sure. Even if I have to come to you to do it."

She lifted a brow. *He would come to her?* She couldn't imagine him doing such a thing. Harvard was in Boston and that was a long way from her university in Laramie, Wyoming.

"Hand me your phone for a second."

His request jarred her thoughts back into focus. "Why?"

"So I can put my numbers into it."

Jillian drew in a deep breath before standing to pull her cell phone from the back pocket of her jeans. She handed it to him and tried to ignore the tingling sensation that flowed through her when their hands touched. She watched him use deft fingers to key in the numbers. Surgeon's fingers. Long, strong, with precise and swift movements. She wondered how those same fingers would feel stroking her skin. She heated just thinking about it.

Moments later his phone rang, interrupting her thoughts. It was then that she realized he'd called himself to have her number, as well. "There," he said, handing her phone back to her. "You now have my number and I have yours."

Was she jumping to conclusions or did his words hold some significance? "Yes, we have each other's numbers," she agreed softly, shoving the assumption out of her mind.

He stood, glancing at his watch. "Adrian and I are meeting up with Canyon and Stern in town for drinks and to shoot pool, so I best get going. Happy birthday again."

"Thanks, Aidan."

"You're welcome."

He walked away but when he got to the French doors he turned and looked back at her, regarding her through his gorgeous dark eyes. The intensity of his gaze made her stomach quiver and another burst of heat swept through her. She felt something…passion? Sexual chemistry? Lust? All three and more, she decided. She'd thought all the Westmoreland males she'd met since Pam married Dillon were eye candy, but there was something about Aidan that pulled at everything female inside of her.

She cleared her throat. "Is anything wrong?" she asked when the silence began to stretch.

Her question seemed to jar him. He frowned slightly before quickly forcing a smile. "Not sure."

As he opened the French door to go inside, she wondered what he meant by that.

Why, of all the women in the world, have I developed this deep attraction for Jillian Novak?

The first time he'd noticed it was when they'd been introduced four years ago. He'd been twenty-two, and she only seventeen, but still a looker. He'd known then that he would have to keep his distance. Now she was twenty-one and still had the word innocent written all over her. From what he'd heard, she didn't even have a boyfriend, preferring to concentrate on her studies and forgo a love life.

And speaking of life, Aidan was fairly certain he loved every part of his, especially his family. So why was he allowing himself to be attracted to Pam's sister? He didn't want to cause any trouble for Dillon.

Pam Novak was a jewel and just what Dillon needed. Everyone had been shocked when Dillon announced he had met a woman who he intended to marry. That had been the craziest thing Aidan had ever heard.

Dillon, of all people, should have known better. Hadn't his first wife left him when he'd refused to send the youngest four members of the Westmoreland family—namely him, Adrian, Bane and Bailey—to foster care? What had made Dillon think Pam would be different? But it didn't take Aidan, his siblings and cousins long to discover that she *was* different.

As far as Aidan was concerned, she was everything they'd *all* needed; she knew the value of family. And she had proven it when she'd turned her back on a promising acting career to care for her three teenaged sisters when her father passed away.

To say the Westmorelands had undergone a lot of family turmoil of their own was an understatement. It all started when Aidan's parents and uncle and aunt died in a plane crash, leaving his cousin Dillon in charge of the family, along with Aidan's oldest brother, Ramsey, as backup. Dillon and Ramsey had worked hard and made sacrifices to keep the family together—all fifteen of them.

Aidan's parents had had eight children: five boys—Ramsey, Zane, Derringer and the twins, Aidan and Adrian—and three girls—Megan, Gemma and Bailey. Uncle Adam and Aunt Clarisse had had seven sons: Dillon, Micah, Jason, Riley, Canyon, Stern and Brisbane.

It hadn't been easy, especially since he, Adrian, Brisbane and Bailey had been under the age of sixteen. And Aidan would admit the four of them had been the most challenging of the bunch, getting into all sorts of mischief, even to the point that the State of Colorado ordered they be put in foster homes. Dillon had appealed that decision and won. Lucky for the four youngest Westmorelands, Dillon had known their acts of rebellion were their way of handling the grief of losing their parents. Now Aidan was in medical school; Adrian was working on his PhD in engineering; Bane had joined the navy and Bailey was taking classes at a local university while working part-time.

Aidan's thoughts shifted back to Jillian, although he didn't want them to. The birthday party yesterday had been a surprise, and the shocked look on her face had been priceless—adorable and a total turn-on. If he'd had any doubt about just how much he was attracted to her, that doubt had been dispelled when he saw her.

She had walked out onto the patio expecting a going-away party for his sister Gemma, who had married Callum and was moving to Australia. Instead it had been a surprise birthday party for her. After shedding a few happy tears, which he would have loved to lick away, she had hugged Pam and Dillon for thinking of her on her twenty-first birthday. From what he'd heard, it was the first time Jillian had had a party since she was a little kid.

While everyone had rushed over to congratulate her, he had hung back, checking her out. The sundress looked cute on her and it was obvious she wasn't the seventeen-year-old he'd met four years ago. Her face was fuller, her features stunning and her body…

Where had those curves come from? There's no way he would have missed them before. She was short compared with his six-foot-two-inch height. He figured she stood no taller than five feet three inches in bare feet. And speaking of her feet, her polished toes, a flaming red, had been another turn on. Pam might not want to hear it, but her sister was Hot with a capital *H*.

When he realized he had been the only one who hadn't wished her a happy birthday, he was about to do so when his phone rang. He had slipped off the patio to take the call from a friend from college who was trying to fix him up on a blind date for next weekend.

When he returned to the patio after finishing his call, everyone else had gone inside to watch a movie or play cards, and she'd been alone. She would never know how hard it had been for him to sit across from her without touching her. She looked good and smelled good, as well.

Jillian Novak had definitely caught his eye.

But Dillon and Pam would pluck out that same eye if he didn't squash what he was feeling.

Everybody knew how protective Pam was when it came to her sisters. Just like everyone knew Aidan wasn't one to take women seriously. And he didn't plan to change his behavior now. So the best thing for him to do while he was home for the next three days was to keep his distance from Jillian as he'd always done.

So why did I get her phone number and give her mine, for crying out loud?

Okay, he reasoned quickly, it had been a crazy moment, one he now regretted. The good thing was he doubted she would ever call him for help and he would make it a point never to call her.

That was a good plan, one he intended to stick to. Now, if he could only stop thinking about her that would be great. Glancing down at the medical journal he was supposed to be reading, he tried to focus on the words. Within a few minutes he'd read one interesting article and was about to start on another.

"Will you do me a *big* favor?"

Aidan glanced up to stare into the face of his sister Bailey. She used to be the baby in the Denver Westmoreland family but that had changed now that Dillon and Pam had a son, and Aidan's brother Ramsey and his wife, Chloe, had a daughter.

"Depends on what the favor is?"

"I promised Jill that I would go riding with her and show her the section of Westmoreland Country that she hasn't seen yet. Now they've called me to come in to work. I need you to go with Jillian instead."

"Just show her another day," he said, quickly deciding that going horseback riding with Jillian wasn't a smart idea.

"That was my original plan but I can't reach her on her cell phone. We were to meet at Gemma Lake, and you know how bad phone reception is out there. She's already there waiting for me."

He frowned. "Can't you ask someone else?"

"I did but everyone is busy."

His frown deepened. "And I'm not?"

Bailey rolled her eyes. "Not like everyone else. You're just reading a magazine."

He figured there was no use explaining to Bailey that his reading was important. He just so happened to be reading about a medical breakthrough where the use of bionic eyes had been tested as a way to restore sight with good results.

"Well, will you do it?"

He closed the medical journal and placed it aside. "You're positive there's no one else who can do it?"

"Yes, and she really wants to see it. This is her home now and—"

"Her home? She's away at school most of the time," he said.

"And so are you, Adrian, Stern and Canyon, and this is still your home. So what's your point?"

He decided not to argue with her. There were times when his baby sister could read him like an open book and he didn't want her to do that in this instance. It wouldn't take her long to figure out the story written on his pages was all about Jillian.

"Fine. I'll go."

"Act a little enthused, will you? You've been kind of standoffish with Jillian and her sisters since Dillon married Pam."

"I have not."

"You have, too. You should take time to get to know them. They're part of the family now. Besides, you and Jill will both become doctors one day so already you have a common interest."

He hoped like hell that would remain their only common interest. It was up to him to make sure it did. "Whatever," he said, standing and walking toward the door, pausing to grab his Stetson off the hat rack.

"And Aidan?"

He stopped before opening the door and turned around, somewhat annoyed. "What now?"

"Try to be nice. You can act like a grizzly bear at times."

That was her opinion. Deciding not to disagree with her, because you could never win with Bailey, he walked out of the house.

Two

Jillian heard the sound of a rider approaching and turned around, using her hand to shield her eyes from the glare of the sun. Although she couldn't make out the identity of the rider, she knew it wasn't Bailey.

The rider came closer and when her heart began pounding hard in her chest, she knew it was Aidan. What was he doing here? And where was Bailey?

Over breakfast she and Bailey had agreed to go riding after lunch. Because the property was located so far from Denver's city limits and encompassed so much land, the locals referred to it as Westmoreland Country. Although Jillian had seen parts of it, she had yet to see all of it and Bailey had volunteered to show it to her.

Dropping her hand to her side, Jillian drew in a deep breath as Aidan and his horse came closer. She tried not to notice how straight he sat in the saddle or how good he looked sitting astride the horse. And she tried not to gawk at how his Stetson, along with his western shirt, vest, jeans and boots, made him look like a cowboy in the flesh.

When he brought the horse to a stop a few feet from where she stood, she had to tilt her head all the way back to look up at him. "Aidan."

He nodded. "Jillian."

His irritated expression and the cutting sound of his voice made her think he was upset about something. Was she trespassing on a particular part of Westmoreland land where she had no business being?

Thinking she needed to give him an explanation, she said, "I'm waiting for Bailey. We're going riding."

"Yes, those *were* your plans."

She lifted a brow. "Were?"

He nodded. "Bailey tried reaching you but your phone is out of range. She was called in to work and asked that I take her place."

"Take her place?"

"Yes, take her place. She indicated you wanted to tour Westmoreland Country."

"I did, but…"

Penetrating dark eyes held hers. "But what?"

She shoved both hands into the pockets of her jeans. There was no way she could tell him that under no circumstances would she go riding anywhere with him. She could barely be around him for a few minutes without becoming unglued…like she was becoming now.

The reason she had placed her hands in her pockets was because they were already sweaty. And then there was that little ball of fire in her stomach that always seemed to burst into flames whenever he was around. Aidan Westmoreland oozed so much sexiness it was driving her to the edge of madness.

"Jillian?"

She blinked when he said her name. The sound of his voice was like a caress across her skin. "Yes?"

"But what? Do you have a problem with me being Bailey's replacement?"

She drew in a deep breath. She couldn't see him being anyone's replacement. It was easy to see he was his own man, and what a man he was. Even now, the weight of his penetrating gaze caused a heated rush to cross her flesh. So, yes, she had a problem with him being Bailey's replacement, but that was something she definitely wouldn't tell him.

"No, I don't have a problem with it," she lied without even blinking. "However, I would think that you do. I'm sure you have more to do with your time than spend it with me."

He shrugged massive shoulders. "No, in fact I don't, so it's not a problem. Besides, it's time for us to get to know each other better."

Why was her body tingling with awareness at his words? She was sure he didn't mean them the way they sounded, but she thought it best to seek clarification. "Why should we get to know each other better?"

He leaned back in the saddle and she couldn't help noticing the long fingers that held the reins. Why was she imagining those same fingers doing things to her, like stroking her hair, splaying up and down her arms, working their way across her naked body? She tried to downplay the shiver that passed through her.

"Dillon married Pam four years ago, and there's still a lot I don't know about you and your sisters," he said, bringing an end to her fantasizing. "We're all family and the Westmorelands are big on family. I haven't been home to get to know you, Paige and Nadia."

With him naming her sisters his earlier statement felt less personal. It wasn't just about her. She should be grateful for that but for some reason she wasn't. "Because of school I haven't been home much, either, but we can get to know each other another time. It doesn't have to be today," she said.

She doubted she could handle his closeness. Even the masculine scent of him was overpowering.

"Today is just as good a day as any. I'm leaving to go back to Boston tomorrow. There's no telling when our paths will cross again. Probably not until we come home for Christmas or something. We might as well do it now and get it over with."

Why did she get the feeling that getting to know her was something he felt forced to do? She took offense at that. "Don't do me any favors," she all but snapped at him while feeling her pulse pound.

"Excuse me?" He seemed surprised by her remark.

"There's no need to get *anything* over with. It's obvious Bailey roped you into doing something you really don't want to do. I can see the rest of Westmoreland Country on my own," she said, untying her horse and then mounting it.

When she sat astride the mare she glanced back over at him. "I don't need your company, Aidan."

He crossed his arms over his chest and she could tell by the sudden tensing of his jaw that he hadn't liked her comment. She was proven right when he said, with a degree of smoldering intensity that she felt through her clothes, "I hate to tell you this, Jillian Novak, but you have my company whether you want it or not."

Aidan stared hard into Jillian's eyes and couldn't help but feel they were waging a battle. Of what he wasn't sure. Of wills? Of desire? Passion? Lust? He rubbed his hand down his face. He preferred none of those things but he had a feeling all of them were fighting for the number one spot right now.

He all but saw steam coming from her ears and figured Jillian didn't like being ordered around.

"Look," he said. "We're wasting time. You want to see the land and I have nothing better to do. I apologize if I came across a little gruff earlier, but by no means did I want to insinuate that I am being forced into showing you around or getting to know you."

There was no need to tell her that Bailey had asked him to be nice to Jillian and her sisters. He'd always been cordial and as far as he was concerned that was good enough. Getting too close to Jillian wasn't a good idea. But then, he was the one who had suggested she call him if she needed help preparing for medical school. He now saw that offer had been a mistake. A big one.

She studied him for a moment and he felt something deep in his gut. It was a lot stronger than the kick in his groin he'd experienced when he'd watched her swing her leg over the back of the horse to mount it. He'd taken a long, explosive breath while fighting the sexual hunger that had roared to life inside of him. Even now, with those beautiful full lips of hers frowning at him, a smoldering spike of heat consumed him. One way he knew he could put a stop to this madness was to get her out of his system, since she seemed to have gotten under his skin.

But the way he would do that wasn't an option...not if he loved his life.

"You're sure about this?"

Hell no, he wasn't sure about anything concerning her. Maybe the main reason behind his attraction to her, in addition to her striking beauty, was that he truly didn't

know her that well. Maybe once he got to know her he'd
discover that he didn't like her after all.

"Yes, I'm sure about this, so come on," he said, nudg-
ing his horse forward to stand beside hers. "There's a lot
to see so I hope you're a fairly good rider."

She gave him a smile that made him appreciate the
fullness of her mouth even more. "Yes, I'm a fairly good
rider."

And then she took off, easing her horse into a canter.
He watched in admiration as she flawlessly jumped the
horse over a flowing creek.

He chuckled to himself. She wasn't a fairly good rider;
she was an excellent one.

Jillian slowed her pace and glanced over her shoulder
to see Aidan make the same jump she had. She couldn't
help but be impressed at his skill, but she shouldn't be
surprised. She'd heard from Dillon that all his brothers
and cousins were excellent horsemen.

In no time, he'd caught up with her. "You're good,"
he said, bringing his horse alongside hers. The two animals eased into a communal trot.

"Thanks," she said, smiling over at him. "You're not
bad yourself."

He threw his head back and laughed. The robust sound
not only floated across the countryside, but it floated
across her, as well. Although she'd seen him smile before,
she'd never seen him amused about anything.

"No, I'm not bad myself. In fact there was a time I
wanted to be a bronco rider in the rodeo."

For some reason she wasn't surprised. "Dillon talked
you out of it?"

He shook his head, grinning. "No, he wouldn't have

done such a thing. One of Dillon's major rules has been for us to choose our own life goals. At least that was his rule for everyone but Bane."

She'd heard all about Aidan's cousin Brisbane West-moreland, whom everyone called Bane. She'd also heard Dillon had encouraged his baby brother to join the military. He'd said Bane could do that or possibly go to prison for the trouble he'd caused. Bane had chosen the navy. In the four years that Pam had been married to Dillon, Jillian had only seen Bane twice.

"So what changed your mind about the rodeo?" she asked when they slowed the horses to a walk.

"My brother Derringer. He did the rodeo circuit for a couple of summers after high school. Then he got busted up pretty bad. Scared all of us to death and I freaked out. We all did. The thought of losing another family member brought me to my senses and I knew I couldn't put my family through that."

She nodded. She knew about him losing his parents and his aunt and uncle in a plane crash, leaving Dillon—the oldest at the time—to care for all of them. "Derringer and a few of your cousins and brothers own a horse-training business right?"

"Yes and it's doing well. They weren't cut out to work in the family business so after a few years they left to pursue their dreams of working with horses. I try to help them out whenever I come home but they're doing a great job without me. Several of their horses have won important derbies."

"Ramsey resigned as one of the CEOs as well, right?" she asked of his oldest brother.

He glanced over at her. "Yes. Ramsey has a degree in agriculture and economics. He'd always wanted to be a sheep farmer, but when my parents, aunt and uncle died in that plane crash he knew Dillon would need help at Blue Ridge."

Jillian knew that Blue Ridge Land Management was a Fortune 500 company Aidan's father and uncle had started years ago. "But eventually he was able to pursue his dream, right?"

Aidan nodded. "Yes. Once Dillon convinced Ramsey he could handle things at the corporation without him. Ramsey's sheep ranch is doing great."

She nodded. She liked Ramsey. In fact, she liked all the Westmorelands she had gotten to know. When Pam married Dillon, the family had welcomed her and her sisters with open arms. She'd discovered some of them were more outgoing than the others. But the one thing she couldn't help but notice was that they stuck together like glue.

"So how did you learn to ride so well?" he asked.

"My dad. He was the greatest and although I'm sure he wanted at least one son, he ended up with four girls. He felt we should know how to do certain things and handling a horse was one of them," she said, remembering the time she'd spent with her father and how wonderful it had been for her.

"He evidently saw potential in me because he made sacrifices and sent me to riding school. I competed nationally until he got sick. We needed the money to pay for his medicine and doctor bills."

"Do you regret giving it up?" he asked.

She shook her head. "No. I enjoyed it but making sure Dad got the best care meant more to me…more to all of us…than anything." And she meant it. There had been no regrets for any of them about giving up what they'd loved to help their father.

"Here we are."

She looked around at the beauty of the land surrounding her, as far as her eyes could see and beyond. Since Dillon was the oldest, he had inherited the main house along with the three hundred acres it sat on. Everyone else, upon reaching the age of twenty-five, received one hundred acres to call their own. Some parts of this area were cleared and other parts were dense with thick foliage. But what took her breath away was the beautiful waterway that branched off into a huge lake. Gemma Lake. She'd heard it had been named after Aidan's great-grandmother.

"This place is beautiful. Where are we exactly?"

He glanced over at her and smiled. "My land. Aidan's Haven."

Aidan's Haven, she immediately decided, suited him. She could see him building his home on this piece of land one day near this huge waterway. Today he looked like a cowboy, but she could see him transforming into a boat captain.

"Aidan's Haven. That's a nice name. How did you come up with it?"

"I didn't. Bailey did. She came up with all the names for our one-hundred-acre plots. She chose names like Stern's Stronghold, Zane's Hideout, Derringer's Dungeon, Ramsey's Web and Megan's Meadows, just to name a few."

Jillian had visited each of those areas and all the homes that had been built on the land were gorgeous. Some were single-story ranch-style designs, while others were like mansions with several floors. "When do you plan to build?"

"Not for a while yet. After medical school I'll probably work and live somewhere else for a while since I have six years of residency to complete for the cardiology program."

"But this will eventually be your home."

A pensive look appeared on his face. "Yes, Westmoreland Country will always be my home."

She'd always thought she would live in Gamble, Wyoming. Although she knew she would leave for college, she figured she would return one day and work in the hospital there before setting up a practice of her own. After all, she had lived there her entire life; all her friends were there. But after Pam married Dillon things changed for her, Paige and Nadia. They were close to their oldest sister and decided to leave Wyoming and make their homes close to Pam's. It had worked out well for everyone. Nadia was in her last year of high school here in Colorado and Paige was in California attending UCLA.

"What about you? Do you ever plan to return to Gamble, Wyoming, to live, Jillian?"

Again, she wondered why her stomach tightened whenever he said her name. Probably had something to do with that deep, husky voice of his.

"No, I don't plan to return to Gamble. In fact, Nadia and Paige and I talked a few weeks ago and we plan to approach Pam about selling the place. She would have done so already, but she thinks we want to keep it as part of our legacy."

"You don't?"

"Only because we've moved on and think of Denver

as home now. At least Nadia and I do. Paige has made a life for herself in Los Angeles. She's hoping her acting career takes off. We're hoping the same thing for her. Pam has done so much for us already and we don't want her to feel obligated to pay more of our college tuition and expenses, especially when we can use the money from the sale of the house to do so."

He nodded. "Let's take a walk. I want to show you around before we move on to Adrian's Cove."

He dismounted and tied his horse to a nearby tree. Then he turned to help her down. The moment he touched her, awareness of him filled her every pore. From the look in his eyes it was obvious that something similar was happening to him.

This was all new to her. She'd never felt anything like this before. And although her little lovemaking session with Cobb Grindstone on prom night had appeased her curiosity, it had left a lot to be desired.

As soon as her feet touched the ground, she heard a deep moan come from Aidan's throat. Only then did it become obvious that they'd gotten caught up in a carnal attraction that was so sharp it took her breath away.

"Jillian…"

He said her name again and, like all the other times, the deep, husky sound accentuated his sexiness. But before she could respond, the masculine hand planted around her waist nudged her closer and then his mouth lowered to hers.

Three

All sorts of feelings ripped through Aidan, making him totally conscious of the woman whose lips were locked to his. Deep in the center of his being he felt a throb unlike any he'd ever felt before—an intense flare of heat shooting straight to his loins.

He knew he had to stop. This wasn't any woman. This was Jillian Novak, Pam's sister. Dillon's sister-in-law. A woman who was now a part of the Westmoreland family. All that was well and good, but at the moment the only thing his mind could comprehend was that she had desire clawing at his insides and filling his every cell with awareness.

Instead of yielding to common sense, he was captivated by her sweet scent and her incredible taste, and the way her tongue stroked his showed both boldness and innocence. She felt exquisite in his arms, as if she belonged there. He wanted more. He wanted to feel her all over, kiss her all over. Taste her. Tempt her with sinful enticements.

The need for air was the only reason he released her lips, but her flavor made him want to return his mouth to hers and continue what they'd started.

The shocked look in her eyes told him she needed time to comprehend what had just happened between them. She took a step back and he watched as she took a deep breath.

"We should not have done that."

Aidan couldn't believe she had the nerve to say that while sultry heat still radiated off her. He might have thought the same thing seconds ago, but he couldn't agree with her now. Not when his fingers itched to reach out and pull her back into his arms so he could plow her mouth with another kiss. Dammit, why did her pouty lips look so inviting?

"Then why did we do it?" he countered. He might have made the first move but she had definitely been a willing participant. Her response couldn't lie. She had enjoyed the kiss as much as he had.

"I don't know why we did it, but we can't do it again."

That was easy for her to say. "Why not?"

She frowned at him. "You know why not. Your cousin is married to my sister."

"And?"

She placed her hands on her hips giving him a mind-boggling view of her slim waist line. "And we can't do it again. I know all about your womanizing reputation, Aidan."

Her words struck a nerve. "Do you?"

"Yes. And I'm not interested. The only thing I'm interested in is getting into medical school. That's the only thing on my mind."

"And the only thing on mine is getting out of medical school," he countered in a curt tone. "As far as Dillon being married to Pam, it changes nothing. You're still a beautiful woman and I'm a man who happens to notice such things. But since I know how the situation stands between us, I'll make sure it doesn't happen again."

"Thank you."

"You're welcome. Glad we got that cleared up. Now I can continue showing you around."

"I'm not sure that's a good idea."

He watched her and when she pushed a lock of hair away from her face, he again thought how strikingly beautiful she was. "Why not? You don't think you can control yourself around me?" he asked, actually smiling at the possibility of that being true.

Her look of anger should have warned him, but he'd never been one to heed signs. "Trust me, that's definitely not it."

"Then there's no reason for me not to finish showing you around, is there, Jillian? Besides, Bailey will give me hell about it if I don't. There's a lot of land we still have to cover so let's get started."

He began walking along the bank of the river and figured that after cooling off Jillian would eventually catch up.

Jillian watched Aidan walk ahead and decided to hang back a moment to reclaim her common sense. Why had she allowed him to kiss her? And why had she enjoyed it so much?

The man gave French kissing a whole new definition, and she wasn't sure her mouth would ever be the same.

No one had ever kissed her like that before. No one would have dared. To be honest, she doubted anyone she'd ever kissed would know how. Definitely not Cobb. Or that guy in her freshman year at Wyoming University, Les, that she'd dropped really quickly when he wanted to take her to a hotel and spend the night on their first date. He might have been a star on the school's football

team, but from the couple of times they had kissed, compared to what she'd just experienced with Aidan, Les
had definitely dropped the ball.

But then, regardless of how enjoyable Aidan's kiss
had been, she was right in what she'd told him about
not repeating it. She had no business getting involved
with a guy whose favorite sport was messing around.
She knew better. Honestly, she didn't know what had
come over her.

However, she knew full well what had come over him.
More than once she'd overheard Dillon express his concern to Pam that although the twins were doing well at
Harvard, he doubted they would ever settle down into
serious relationships since they seemed to enjoy being
womanizers. That meant Aidan's interest in her was only
because of overactive testosterone. Pam had warned Jillian numerous times about men who would mean her no
good, and her oldest sister would be highly disappointed
if Jillian fell for the ploy of a man like Aidan. A man
who could take away her focus on becoming a doctor
just to make her his plaything.

Feeling confident she had her common sense back on
track, she began walking. Aidan wasn't too far ahead
and it wouldn't take long for her to catch up with him. In
the meantime she couldn't help but appreciate his manly
physique. His faded jeans emphasized masculine thighs,
a rock-solid behind, tight waist and wide shoulders. He
didn't just walk, he swaggered, and he did it so blatantly
sexily, it increased her heart rate with every step he took.

Moments later he slowed and turned around to stare
at her, pinning her with his dark gaze. Had he felt her
ogling him? Did he know she had been checking out his
rear big-time? She hoped not because his front was just

as impressive. She could see why he was in such high demand when it came to women.

"You coming?"

I will be if you don't stop looking at me like that, Jillian thought, getting closer to where he stood. She felt the heat of his gaze on every inch of her. She came to a stop in front of him. She couldn't take looking into his eyes any longer so she glanced around. In addition to the huge lake there were also mountains surrounding the property. "You have a nice mountain view in this spot and can see the lake from here," she said.

"I know. That's why I plan to build my house right here."

She nodded. "Have you designed it yet?"

"No. I don't plan on building for several more years, but I often come here and think about the time when I will. The house will be large enough for me and my family."

She snapped her head around. "You plan on getting married?"

His chuckle was soft but potent. "Yes, one day. That surprises you?"

She decided to be honest. "Yes. You do have a reputation."

He leaned one broad shoulder against a Siberian elm tree. "This is the second time today that you've mentioned something about my reputation. Just what have you heard about me?"

She took a seat across from him on a huge tree stump. "I heard what hellions you, Adrian, Bailey and Bane used to be."

He nodded solemnly. "Yes, we were that. But that was a long time ago, and I can honestly say we regretted our actions. When we grew older and realized the impact we'd had on the family, we apologized to each one of them."

"I'm sure they understood. You were just children and there was a reason you did what you did," she said. She'd heard the full story from Pam. The deaths of their parents, and aunt and uncle, had been the hardest on those youngest four. Everyone had known that their acts of rebellion were their way of handling their grief.

"Sorry I mentioned it," she said, feeling bad that she'd even brought it up.

He shrugged. "No harm done. It is what it is. It seems the four of us got a reputation we've been trying to live down for years. But I'm sure that's not the reputation of mine that you were really referring to."

No, it wasn't. "I understand you like women."

He chuckled. "Most men do."

She raised a brow, not in the least amused. "I mean you really like them, but you don't care about their feelings. You break their hearts without any concern for the pain it might cause."

He studied her for a long moment. "That's what you heard?"

"Yes. And now you want me to believe that you're seriously considering settling down one day, marrying and having a family?"

"Yes. One doesn't have anything to do with the other. What I do now in no way affects any future plans. I need to clarify something. I don't deliberately set out to break any woman's heart. I tell any woman I date the truth up front—my career as a doctor is foremost. However, if she refuses to take me at my word and assumes that she can change my mind, then it's not my fault when she finds out otherwise."

"So in other words…"

"In other words, Jillian, I don't intentionally set up any woman for heartbreak or lead her on," he answered curtly.

She knew she should probably leave well enough alone and stop digging, but for some reason she couldn't help herself. "However, you do admit to dating a *lot* of women."

"Yes, I admit it. And why not? I'm single and don't plan to get into a committed relationship anytime soon. And contrary to what you believe, I don't date as many women as you might think. My time is pretty limited these days because of medical school."

She could imagine. How he managed to date at all while in medical school was beyond her. He was definitely into multitasking. She'd discovered most relationships demanded a lot of work and it was work she didn't have time for. Evidently he made things easy by not getting serious with any woman. At least he'd been honest about it. He dated women for the fun of it and didn't love any of them.

"I have one other question for you, Aidan," she said, after drawing in a deep breath.

"What's your question?"

"If all of what you said is true, about not getting serious with any woman, then why did you kiss me?"

Now that was a good question, one he could answer but really didn't want to. She did deserve an answer, though, especially after the way he had plowed her mouth earlier. She was twenty-one, five years younger than him. And although she'd held her own during their kiss, he knew they were worlds apart when it came to sexual experience. Therefore, before he answered her, he needed to ask a few questions of his own.

"Why did you kiss me back?"

He could tell by her expression that she was surprised by his counterquestion. And, as he'd expected, she tried to avoid giving him an answer. "That's not the issue here."

He couldn't help but smile. Little did she know it *was* the issue, but he would touch on that later. "The reason I kissed you, Jillian, is because I was curious. I think you have a beautiful pair of lips and I wanted to taste them. I wanted to taste you. It's something I've wanted to do for a while."

He saw her jaw drop and had to hold his mouth closed for a second to keep from grinning. She hadn't expected him to answer her question so bluntly or to be so direct. That's something she needed to know about him. He didn't sugarcoat anything. *Straightforward* could be his middle name.

"So now that you know my reason for kissing you, what was your reason for kissing me back?"

She began nibbling on her bottom lip. Watching her made him ache, made him want to take hold of those lips and have his way with them again.

"I—I was…"

When she didn't say anything else, he lifted a brow. "You were what?"

Then she had the nerve to take her tongue and lick those same lips she'd been nibbling on moments ago. "I was curious about you, too."

He smiled. Now they were getting somewhere. "I can

understand that. I guess the reason you asked about the kiss is because I told you I'm not into serious relationships when it comes to women. I hope you don't think a deep kiss constitutes a serious relationship."

From the look on her face, which she quickly wiped off, that's exactly what she'd thought. She was more inexperienced than he'd assumed. He wondered just how inexperienced she was. Most twenty-one-year-old women he knew wore desire, instead of their hearts, on their sleeves.

"Of course I knew that."

If she knew that then why were they having this conversation? If she thought he was looking for something serious just because he'd kissed her then she was so far off the mark it wasn't funny.

"How many boyfriends have you had?"

"Excuse me?"

No, he wouldn't excuse her. There were certain things she needed to know. Things experience had nothing to do with. "I asked how many boyfriends you've had. And before you tell me it's none of my business, I'm asking for a reason."

She lifted her chin in a defiant pose. "I can't imagine what reason you would have for needing to know that."

"So you can protect yourself." He thought she looked both adorable and sexy. From the way her curly hair tumbled down her shoulders to the way the smoothness of her skin shone in the sunlight.

She lifted a brow. "Against men like you?"

"No. Men like me would never mislead you into thinking there was anything serious about a kiss. But there are men who would lead you to think otherwise."

She frowned. "And you don't think I can handle myself?"

He smiled. "Not the way I think you should. For some reason you believe you can avoid kisses until you're in a serious relationship and there are certain kisses that can't be avoided."

He could tell by her expression that she didn't believe him. "Take the kiss we shared earlier. Do you honestly think you could have avoided it once I got started?" he asked her.

Her frown deepened. "Yes, of course I could have."

"Then why didn't you?"

She rolled her eyes. "I told you. The only reason I allowed you to kiss me, and the only reason I participated, is because I was curious."

"Really?"

She rolled her eyes again. "Really. Truly."

"So, you're not curious anymore?"

She shook her head. "Nope, not at all. I wondered what kissing you was like and now I know."

Deciding to prove her wrong and settle the matter once and for all, he moved away from the tree and walked toward her.

Figuring out his intent, she stood with a scowl on her face. "Hold it right there, Aidan Westmoreland. Don't you dare think you're going to kiss me again."

When he reached her, he came to a stop directly in front of her and she refused to back up. Instead she stood her ground. He couldn't help but admire her spunk, although in this case it would be wasted.

"I do dare because I don't just think it, Jillian, I know it. And I also know that you're going to kiss me back. *Again*."

Four

Jillian doubted she'd ever met a more arrogant man. And what was even worse, he had the nerve to stand in front of her with his Stetson tipped back and his legs braced apart in an overconfident stance. How dare he tell her what she would do? Kiss him back? Did he really believe that? Honestly?

She tilted her head back to glare up at him. He didn't glare back, but he held her gaze in a way that was unnerving. And then his eyes moved, slowly raking over her from head to toe. Was that desire she felt rushing through her body? Where had these emotions inside of her come from? Was she getting turned on from the way he was looking at her? She tried to stiffen at the thought but instead she was drawn even more into the heat of his gaze.

"Stop that!"

He lifted a brow. "Stop what?"

"Whatever you're doing."

He crossed his arms over his chest. "So, you think I'm responsible for the sound of your breathing? For the way your nipples have hardened and are pressing against your shirt? And for the way the tip of your tongue is tingling, eager to connect with mine?"

Every single thing he'd pointed out was actually happening to her, but she refused to admit any of them. She crossed her arms over her own chest. "I have no idea what you're talking about."

"Then I guess we're at a standoff."

"No, we're not," she said, dropping her hands to her sides. "I'm leaving. You can play this silly game with someone else."

She turned to go and when his hand reached out and touched her arm, sharp spikes of blood rushed through her veins, filling her pores, drenching the air she was breathing with heated desire. And what on earth was that hunger throbbing inside of her at the juncture of her thighs? And what were those slow circles he was making on her arm with his index finger? She expelled a long deep breath and fought hard to retain control of her senses.

Jillian wanted to snatch her arm away but found she couldn't. What kind of spell had he cast on her? Every hormone in her body sizzled, hissed and surged with a need she'd never felt before. She couldn't deny the yearning pulsing through her even if she wanted to.

"You feel it, don't you, Jillian? It's crazy, I know, and it's something I can't explain, but I feel it each and every time I'm within a few feet of you. As far as I'm concerned, Pam and Dillon are the least of our worries. Figuring out just what the hell is going on between us should be at the top of the agenda. You can deny it as long as you want, but that won't help. You need to admit it like I have."

She did feel it and a part of her knew there was real danger in admitting such a thing. But another part knew he was right. With some things it was best to admit there was a problem and deal with it. Otherwise, she would lay awake tonight and regret not doing so.

His hand slowly traveled up her arm toward her lips. There he cradled her mouth in the palm of his hands. "And whatever it is has me wanting to taste you and has you wanting to taste me. It has me wanting to lick your mouth dry and you wanting to lick mine in the same way."

He paused a moment and when he released a frustrated breath she knew that whatever this "thing" was between them, he had tried fighting it, as well. But he had given up the fight and was now ready to move to the next level, whatever that was.

"I need to taste you, Jillian," he said.

As much as she wished otherwise, there was a deep craving inside of her to taste him, too. Just one more time. Then she would walk away, mount her horse and ride off like the devil himself was after her. But for now she needed this kiss as much as she needed to breathe.

She saw him lowering his head and she was poised for the exact moment when their mouths would connect. She even parted her lips in anticipation. His mouth was moving. He was whispering something but instead of focusing on what he was saying, her gaze was glued to the erotic movement of his lips. And the moment his mouth touched hers she knew she had no intention of turning back.

Nothing could have prepared Aidan for the pleasure that radiated through his body. How could she arouse him like no other woman could? Instead of getting bogged down in the mystery of it all, he buried his fingers in her hair, holding her in place while his mouth mated hungrily with hers.

And she was following his lead, using her tongue with the same intensity and hunger as he was using his. It was all about tasting, and they were tasting each other with a greed that had every part of his body on fire.

He felt it, was in awe of it. In every pore, in every nerve ending and deep in his pulse, he felt it. Lowering his hand from her hair he gently gripped her around the waist and, with their mouths still locked, he slowly maneuvered her backward toward the tree he'd leaned against earlier. When her back rested against the trunk, her thighs parted and he eased between them, loving the feel of his denim rubbing against hers.

Frissons of fire, hotter than he'd ever encountered, burned a path up his spine and he deepened the kiss as if his life depended on him doing so. Too soon, in his estimation, they had to come up for air and he released her mouth just as quickly as he'd taken it.

He tried not to notice the thoroughly kissed look on her face when she drew in a deep breath. He took a step back so he wouldn't be tempted to kiss her again. The next time he knew he wouldn't stop with a kiss. He wouldn't be satisfied until he had tasted her in other places, as well. And then he would want to make love to her, right here on his land. On the very spot he planned to build his house. Crap! Why was he thinking such a thing? In frustration, he rubbed a hand down his face.

"I think we need to move on."

Her words made him look back at her and an ache settled deep in his stomach. She was beautiful and desire escalated through him all over again. Giving in to what he wanted, he took a step forward and lowered his mouth to hers, taking a sweep of her mouth with his tongue. His groin swelled when she caught his tongue and began sucking on it.

He broke off the kiss and drew in a ragged breath. "Jillian! You're asking for trouble. I'm within two seconds of spreading you on the ground and getting inside of you." The vision of such a thing nearly overpowered his senses.

"I told you we should go. You're the one who kissed me again."

He smiled. "And you kissed me back. Now you understand what I meant when I said there are some kisses that can't be avoided. You didn't want me to kiss you initially, but then you did."

She frowned slightly. "You seduced me. You made me want to kiss you."

His smile widened. "Yes, to both."

"So this was some sort of lesson?"

He shook his head. "Not hardly. I told you I wanted to taste you. I enjoyed doing so."

"This can't become a habit, Aidan."

"And I don't intend to make it one, trust me. My curiosity has more than been satisfied."

She nodded. "So has mine. Are you ready to show me the other parts of Westmoreland Country?"

"Yes. We're headed for Adrian's Cove next and then Bailey's Bay and Bane's Ponderosa."

He backed up to give her space and when she moved around him, he was tempted to reach out and pull her back into his arms, kiss her some more, until he got his fill. But he had a feeling that getting his fill would not be possible and that was something he didn't want to acknowledge.

* * *

"So, how did the tour go with Aidan yesterday?"

Jillian glanced up from her breakfast when Bailey slid into the chair next to her. Pam had shared breakfast with Jillian earlier before leaving for the grocery store, and had asked her the same thing. It had been hard to keep a straight face then and it was harder to do so now.

"It went well. There's a lot of land in Westmoreland Country. I even saw the property you own, Bailey's Bay."

Bailey smiled. "I can't claim ownership until I'm twenty-five so I have a couple years left. But when I do, I plan to build the largest house of them all. It will even be bigger than this one."

Jillian thought that would be an accomplishment because Dillon and Pam's house was huge. Their house was three stories and had eight bedrooms, six bathrooms, a spacious eat-in kitchen, a gigantic living room, a large dining room with a table that could seat over forty people easily, and a seven-car-garage.

"I can't wait to see it when you do." Jillian liked Bailey and had from the first time she'd set foot in Westmoreland Country to attend Pam's engagement party. And since there was only a couple years' difference in their ages, with Bailey being older, they had hit it off immediately. "What happens if you meet and marry a guy who wants to take you away from here?"

"That won't happen because there's not a man alive who can do that. This is where I was born and this is where I'll die."

Jillian thought Bailey sounded sure of that. Hadn't Jillian felt the same way about her home in Wyoming at one time? Although it hadn't been a man that had changed her mind, it had been the thought of how much money Pam would be paying for three sisters in college. Although her older sister had married a very wealthy man, it still would not have been right.

"Besides," Bailey said, cutting into her thoughts. "I plan to stay single forever. Having five bossy brothers and seven even bossier male cousins is enough. I don't need another man in my life trying to tell me what to do."

Jillian smiled. When she'd heard the stories about all the trouble Bailey used to get into when she was younger, Jillian had found it hard to believe. Sitting across from her was a beautiful, self-confident woman who seemed to have it going on. A woman who definitely knew what she wanted.

"I hope Aidan was nice and didn't give you any trouble."

Jillian lifted a brow. "Why would you say that?"

Bailey shrugged. "Aidan has his moods sometimes."

"Does he?"

"Yes, but if you didn't pick up on them then I guess he did okay."

No, she hadn't picked up on any mood, but she had picked up on his sensual side. And he had definitely picked up on hers. She was still in a quandary as to exactly what had happened yesterday. It was as if she'd become another person with him. She'd discovered that being kissed senseless wasn't just a cliché but was something that could really happen. Aidan had proven it. Even after brushing her teeth twice, rinsing out her mouth and eating a great breakfast Pam had prepared, the taste of him was still deeply embedded on her tongue. And what was even crazier was that she liked it.

Knowing Bailey was probably expecting a response,

she said. "Yes, he was okay. I thought he was rather nice."

Bailey nodded. "I'm glad. I told him he needed to get to know you and your sisters better since he's rarely home. And we're all family now."

All family now. Bailey's words were a stark reminder of why what happened yesterday could never be repeated. They weren't just a guy and a girl who'd met with no connections. They had deep connections. Family connections. And family members didn't go around kissing each other. Why of all the guys out there did she have to be attracted to one with the last name Westmoreland?

"So, besides Bailey's Bay where else did he take you?"

To heaven and back. The words nearly slid from Jillian's lips because that's where she felt she'd actually been. Transported there and back by a kiss. Amazing. Pulling her thoughts together, she said, "First, we toured Aidan's Haven."

"Isn't it beautiful? That's the property I originally wanted because of the way it's surrounded by Gemma Lake. But then I realized it would have been too much water to deal with. I think the spot where Aidan plans to build his house is perfect, though, and will provide an excellent view of the lake and mountains, no matter what room of the house you're in."

Jillian agreed and eradicated the thought from her mind that Aidan's wife and kids would one day live there. "I also saw Adrian's Cove. That piece of property is beautiful, as well. I love the way it's surrounded by mountains."

"Me, too."

"And from there we visited Bailey's Bay, Canyon's Bluff and Stern's Stronghold."

"Like the names?"

Jillian smiled. "Yes, and I heard they were all your idea."

"Yes," Bailey said, grinning. "Being the baby in the family has its benefits. Including the opportunity to play musical beds and sleep at whatever place I want. I was living with Dillon full-time, but after he married I decided to spread myself around and check out my brothers', sisters' and cousins' abodes. I like driving them crazy, especially when one of my brothers or cousins brings his girlfriend home."

Jillian couldn't help but laugh. Although she wouldn't trade her sisters for the world, it had to be fun having older brothers and male cousins to annoy.

"What's so funny?"

Jillian's heart skipped a beat upon hearing that voice and knowing who it belonged to. Aidan leaned in the kitchen doorway. Wearing a pair of jeans that rode low on his hips and a muscle shirt, he looked too sexy for her peace of mind. She couldn't help studying his features. It was obvious he'd just gotten out of bed. Those dark eyes that were alert and penetrating yesterday had a drowsy look. And she couldn't miss the dark shadow on his chin indicating he hadn't shaved yet. If he looked like that every morning, she would just love to see it.

"I thought you'd already left to return to Boston," Bailey said, getting up and crossing the room to give him a hug. Jillian watched the interaction and a part of her wished she could do the same.

"I won't be leaving until tomorrow."

"Why did you change your plans?" Bailey asked, surprised. "Normally, you're in a rush to get back."

Yes, why? Jillian wondered as well and couldn't wait for his answer.

"Because I wasn't ready to go back just yet. No big deal."

"Um," Bailey said, eyeing her brother suspiciously, "I get the feeling it is a big deal and probably has to do with some woman. I heard you, Adrian and Stern didn't get in until late last night."

Jillian turned her gaze away from Bailey and Aidan and took a sip of her orange juice. The spark of anger she suddenly felt couldn't be jealousy over what Bailey had just said. Had Aidan kissed Jillian senseless, then gone somewhere last night and kissed someone else the same way? Why did the thought of him doing that bother her?

"You ask too many questions, Bay, and stay out my business," Aidan said. "So, what's so funny, Jillian?"

Jillian drew in a deep breath before turning back to Aidan. "Nothing."

Bailey chuckled. "In other words, Aidan, stay out of *her* business."

Jillian heard his masculine grunt before he crossed the room to the coffeepot. The kitchen was huge, so why did it suddenly feel so small now that he'd walked in? And why did he have to walk around with such a sexy saunter?

"Well, I hate to run but I promised Megan that I would house-sit for a few hours so I'm headed for Megan's Meadows. Gemma is decorating the place before leaving for Australia and is sending her crew over to hang new curtains."

Megan and Gemma were Bailey and Aidan's sisters,

whom Jillian liked tremendously. Megan was a doctor of anesthesiology at one of the local hospitals and Gemma was an interior designer who owned Designs by Gem.

Bailey turned to Jillian. "You're here until tomorrow, right?"

"Yes."

"Then maybe Aidan can show you the parts of Westmoreland Country that you missed yesterday."

Jillian could feel Aidan's gaze on her. "I wouldn't want to put him to any trouble."

"No trouble," Aidan said, "I don't have anything else to do today."

Bailey laughed. "Until it's time for you to go and hook up with the woman who's the reason you're staying around an extra day."

"Goodbye, Bay," Aidan said in what Jillian perceived as an annoyed tone.

Bailey glanced over her shoulder at him while departing. "See you later, Aidan. And you better not leave tomorrow before telling me goodbye." She swept out of the kitchen and Jillian found herself alone with Aidan.

She glanced over at him and saw him leaning back against the counter with a cup of coffee in his hand, staring at her.

She drew in a deep breath when Aidan asked, "How soon can we go riding?"

Five

Aidan couldn't help staring into Jillian's eyes. He thought she had the most beautiful eyes of any woman he'd ever seen. And that included all those women who'd thrown themselves at him last night.

"I'm not going anywhere with you, Aidan. Besides, I'm sure the reason you changed your plans to remain in Denver another day has nothing to do with me."

Boy was she wrong. It had everything to do with her. He had spent three hours in a nightclub last night surrounded by beautiful women and all he could think about was the one he considered the most beautiful of all. Her.

A possibility suddenly hit him. Was she jealous? Did she actually believe that crap Bailey had just spouted about him changing his schedule because of some woman? He didn't know whether to be flattered or annoyed that she, or any woman, thought they mattered enough that they should care about his comings and goings. But in all honesty, what really annoyed him was that she *was* beginning to matter. And the reason he had decided to hang in Denver another day was because of her.

Instead of saying anything right away, for fear he might say the wrong thing, he turned and refilled his coffee cup. Then he crossed the room and slid into the chair across from her. Immediately, he sensed her nervousness.

"I don't bite, Jillian," he said, before taking a sip of coffee.

"I hope not."

He couldn't help but smile as he placed his cup down. He reached out and closed his fingers around her wrist. "Trust me. I prefer kissing you to biting you."

She pulled her hand back and nervously glanced over her shoulder before glaring at him. "Are you crazy? Anyone could walk in here!"

"And?"

"And had they heard what you just said they would have gotten the wrong impression."

He leaned back in his chair. "What do you think is the *right* impression?"

Her hair was pulled back in a ponytail and he was tempted to reach out, release the clasp and watch the waves fall to her shoulders. Then he would run his fingers through the thick, black tresses. He could just imagine the light, gentle strokes on her scalp and the thought sent a sudden jolt of sexual need through him.

"I don't want to make any impression, Aidan. Right or wrong."

Neither did he. At least he didn't think he did. Damn, the woman had him thinking crazy. He rubbed a frustrated hand down his face.

"It was just a kiss, nothing more."

He looked over at her. Why was he getting upset that she thought that way when he should be thinking the same thing. Hadn't he told her as much yesterday?

"Glad you think that way," he said, standing. "So let's go riding."

"Didn't you hear what I said?"

He smiled down at her. "You've said a lot. What part in particular are you asking about?"

She rolled her eyes. "I said I'm not going anywhere with you."

His smile widened. "Sure you are. We're going riding because if we don't, Bailey will think it's because I did something awful and got you mad with me. And if she confronts me about it, I will have to confess and tell her the truth—that the reason you wouldn't go riding with me is because you were afraid I might try to kiss you again. A kiss you can't avoid enjoying."

She narrowed her gaze at him. "You wouldn't."

"Trust me, I would. Confessing my sins will clear my conscience but will they clear yours? I'm not sure they would since you seem so wrapped up in not making any right or wrong impressions."

She just sat there and said nothing. He figured she was at a loss for words and this would be the best time for him to leave her to her thoughts. "Let's meet at the same place where we met yesterday in about an hour," he said, walking off to place his cup in the dishwasher.

Before exiting the kitchen he turned back to her and said, "And just so you know, Jillian, the reason I'm not leaving today to return to Boston has nothing to do with some woman I met at the club last night, but it has everything to do with you."

It has everything to do with you.

Not in her wildest dreams had Jillian thought seven little words could have such a huge impact on her. But they did. So much so that an hour later, she was back in the same place she'd been yesterday, waiting on Aidan.

She began pacing. Had she lost her mind? She wasn't sure what kind of game he was playing but instead of putting her foot down and letting him know she wanted no part of his foolishness, somehow she got caught, hook, line and sinker.

And all because of a kiss.

She would have to admit, it had been more than just a kiss. The fact that he was a gorgeous man, a man she'd had a secret crush on for four years, probably had a lot to do with it. But she'd always been able to separate fact from fiction, reality from fantasy, good from bad. So what was wrong with her now? An association with Aidan would only bring on heartache because not only was she deceiving her sister and brother-in-law, and no doubt the entire Westmoreland family, but she was deceiving herself, as well. Why would she want to become involved with a man known as a womanizer?

But then, she really wasn't involved with him. He was taking her riding, probably he would try to steal a few kisses and then nothing. Tomorrow he would return to Boston and she would return to Wyoming and it would be business as usual. But she knew for her it wouldn't be that simple.

She turned when she heard his approach. Their gazes connected and a luscious shiver ran through her body. He rode just like he had yesterday and looked basically the same. But today something was different. Now she knew he had the mouth of a very sensual man. A mouth he definitely knew how to use.

"I was hoping you would be here," he said, bringing his horse to a stop a few feet from her.

"Did you think I wouldn't after what you threatened to do?"

"I guess not," he said, dismounting.

"And you have no remorse?"

He tipped his Stetson back to gaze at her. "I've heard confession is good for the soul."

"And just what would it have accomplished, Aidan?"

"Putting it out there would have cleared your conscience, since it obviously bothers you that someone might discover I'm attracted to you and that you're attracted to me."

She started to deny what he'd said about her being attracted to him, but decided not to waste her time. It was true and they both knew it. "A true gentleman never kisses and tells."

"You're right. A true gentleman doesn't kiss and tell. But I don't like the thought of you cheapening what happened yesterday, either."

She placed her hands on her hips and leaned in, glaring at him. "How is it cheapening it when the whole thing meant nothing to you anyway?"

Jillian's question stunned Aidan. For a moment he couldn't say anything. She had definitely asked a good question, and it was one he wasn't sure he could answer. The only response he could come up with was that the kisses should not have meant anything to him, but they had. Hell, he had spent the past twenty-four hours thinking about nothing else. And hadn't he changed his plans so that he could stay another day just to spend more time with her?

She was standing there, glaring at him, with her arms crossed over her chest in a way that placed emphasis on a nice pair of breasts. Full and perfectly shaped. He could just imagine running his hands over them, teasing the nipples before drawing them in his mouth to…

"Well?"

She wanted an explanation and all he wanted to do was erase the distance separating them, take her into his arms and kiss that glare right off her face. Unfortunately, he knew he wouldn't stop there. Whether she knew it or not, Jillian Novak's taste only made him want more.

"Let's ride," he said, moving toward his horse. Otherwise, he would be tempted to do something he might later regret.

"Ride?" she hissed. "Is that all you've got to say?"

He glanced back over at her as he mounted his horse. "For now."

"None of this makes any sense, Aidan," she said, mounting her own horse.

She was right about that, he thought. None of it made any sense. Why was she like a magnet pulling him in? And why was he letting her?

They had ridden a few moments side by side in total silence when she finally broke it by asking, "Where are we going?"

"Bane's Ponderosa."

She nodded. "Has he built anything on it?"

"No, because legally it's not his yet. He can't claim it until he's twenty-five."

"Like Bailey. She told me about the age requirement."

"Yes, like Bailey."

He wished they could go back to not talking. He needed the silence to figure out what in the hell was happening to him. She must have deciphered that he was not in a talkative mood because she went silent again.

Aidan glanced over at her, admiring how well she handled a horse. He couldn't help admiring other things, as well. Such as how she looked today in her jeans and western shirt, and how the breasts he had fantasized about earlier moved erotically in rhythm with the horse's prance.

"There is a building here," Jillian said, bringing her horse to a stop.

He forced his eyes off her breasts to follow her gaze to the wooden cabin. He brought his horse to a stop, as well. "If you want to call it that, then yes. Bane built it a while back. It became his and Crystal's secret lovers' hideaway."

"Crystal?"

"Yes. Crystal Newsome. Bane's one and only."

Jillian nodded. "She's the reason he had to leave and join the navy, right?"

Aidan shrugged. "I guess you could say that, although I wouldn't place the blame squarely on Crystal's shoulders. Bane was as much into Crystal as Crystal was into Bane. They were both sticks of dynamite waiting to explode."

"Where is she now?"

"Don't know. I'm not sure if Bane even knows. He never says and I prefer not to ask," Aidan said, getting off his horse and tying it to the rail in front of the cabin.

He moved to assist her from her horse and braced himself for the onslaught of emotions he knew he would feel when he did so.

"You don't have to help me down, Aidan. I can manage."

"I'm sure you can but I'm offering my assistance anyway," he said, reaching his arms up to her.

For a minute he thought she would refuse his offer, but then she slid into his embrace. And as expected the moment they touched, fire shot through him. He actually felt his erection throb. He didn't say anything as he stared into her face. How could she arouse him to this degree?

"You can let go of me now, Aidan."

He blinked, realizing her feet were on the ground yet his arms were still around her waist. He tried to drop his arms but couldn't. It was as if they had a mind of their own.

Then, in a surprise move, she reached up and placed her arms around his neck. "This is crazy," she whispered in a quiet tone. "I shouldn't want this but I'm not thinking straight."

He shouldn't want it, either, but at that moment nothing could stop him. "We're leaving tomorrow. When we get back to our respective territories we can think straight then."

"What about right now?" she asked, staring deep into his gaze.

"Right now all I want to do is taste you again, Jillian. So damn bad."

She lifted her chin. "Then do it."

He doubted she knew what she was saying because her lips weren't the only thing he wanted to taste. He lowered his mouth to hers, thinking that she would find that out soon enough.

At that particular moment, Jillian couldn't deny herself the enjoyment of this kiss even if her life had depended on it.

She was getting what she wanted in full force—Aidan Westmoreland–style.

She stood with her arms wrapped around his neck and their lips locked, mesmerized, totally captivated, completely enthralled. How his tongue worked around in her mouth was truly remarkable. Every bone, every pore and every nerve ending responded to the way she was being thoroughly kissed. When had she become capable of such an intense yearning like this, where every lick and suck of Aidan's tongue could send electrical waves through her?

"Let's go inside," he whispered, pulling back from the kiss while tonguing her lips.

"Inside?" She could barely get the question past the feeling of burning from the inside out.

"Yes. We don't need to be out here in the open."

No they didn't. She had gotten so caught up in his kiss that she'd forgotten where they were. But instead of saying they shouldn't even be kissing, in the open or behind closed doors, she didn't resist him when he took her hand and tugged her toward the cabin.

Once the door closed behind them she looked around and was surprised at how tidy the place was. Definitely not what she'd expected. It was a one-room cabin with an iron bed. The colorful bedspread matched the curtains and coordinated with the huge area rug.

She turned to Aidan. "This is nice. Who keeps this place up?"

"Gemma promised Bane that she would and of course she had to put her signature on it. Now that she's getting married and moving to Australia, Bailey will take over. This place is important to Bane. He spends time here whenever he comes home."

Jillian nodded. "How's he doing?"

Aidan shrugged. "Okay now. It was hard for him to buckle down and follow authority, but he has no other choice if he wants to be a SEAL."

She'd heard that was Bane Westmoreland's goal. "So no one usually comes out this way?" She needed to know. There would be no turning back after today and she needed to make sure they didn't get caught.

"Rarely, although Ramsey uses this land on occasion for his sheep. But you don't have to worry about anyone showing up if that's what you're worried about."

She turned to face him. "I don't know why I'm doing this."

He touched her chin and tilted her head back to meet his gaze. "Do you want me to tell you?"

"Think you got it all figured out?"

He nodded. "Yes, I think I do."

"Okay then, let's hear it," she said, backing up to sit on the edge of the bed.

He moved to sit down on a nearby stool. "We're attracted to each other."

She chuckled slightly. "Tell me something I don't know, Aidan."

"What if I say that we've sort of gotten obsessed with each other?"

She frowned. "*Obsessed* is too strong a word, I think. We've only kissed twice."

"Actually three times. And I'm dying for the fourth. Aren't you?"

She knew she had to be honest with him and stop denying the obvious. "Yes, but I don't understand why."

He got up from the stool and stood. "Maybe it's not for us to understand, Jillian."

"How can you say that? How do you think our family would react if they knew we were carrying on like this behind their backs?"

He slowly crossed the room to stand in front of where she sat. "We won't know how they'd react because you're determined to keep this a secret, aren't you?"

She tilted her head to look up at him. "Yes. I couldn't hurt Pam that way. She expects me to stay focused on school. And if I did get involved with a guy, I'm sure she wouldn't want that guy to be you."

He frowned. "And what is so bad about getting involved with me?"

"I think you know the answer to that. She thinks of us as one big family. And there's your reputation. But, like you said, we'll be leaving tomorrow and going our separate ways. What's happening between us is curiosity taking its toll on our common sense."

"That's what you think?" he asked, reaching out and taking a lock of her hair between his fingers.

"Yes, that's what I think." She noticed something in the depths of his eyes that gave her pause—but only for a second. That's all the time it took for her gaze to lower from his eyes to his mouth.

She watched as he swept the tip of his tongue across his lips. "I can still taste you, you know," he said in a low, husky tone.

She nodded slowly. "Yes, I know." Deciding to be honest, she said, "And the reason I know is because I can still taste you, as well."

Six

Aidan wished Jillian hadn't said that. After their first kiss, he'd concluded she had enjoyed it as much as he had. When they'd gone another round he'd been sure of it. Just like he was sure that, although her experience with kissing had been at a minimum, she was a fast learner. She had kept up with him, stroke for stroke. And now, for her to confess that she could still taste him, the same way he could still taste her, sent his testosterone level soaring.

He took a step closer, gently pulled her to her feet and wrapped his arms around her waist. He truly didn't understand why the desire between them was so intense but he accepted that it was. The thought of Dillon and Pam's ire didn't appeal to him any more than it did to her, but unlike her, he refused to believe his cousin and cousin-in-law would be dead set against something developing between him and Jillian.

But he didn't have to worry because *nothing* was developing between them. They were attracted to each other; there was nothing serious about that. He'd been attracted to women before, although never to this degree, he would admit. But after today it would be a while before they saw each other again since he rarely came home. This would be a one-and-done fling. He knew for certain that Pam and Dillon would definitely *not* like the thought of that. They would think he'd taken advantage of her. So he agreed they did not need to know.

"I won't sleep with you, Aidan."

Her words interrupted his thoughts. He met her gaze. "You won't?"

"No. I think we should get that straight right now."

He nodded slowly. "All right. So what did you have in mind for us to do in here?" To say he was anxious to hear her answer was an understatement.

"Kiss some more. A lot more."

Evidently she didn't think an intense kissing match could lead to other things, with a loss of control topping the list. "You think it will be that simple?"

She shrugged. "No. But I figure if we both use a reasonable degree of self-control we'll manage."

A reasonable degree of self control? Jillian had more confidence in their abilities than he did. Just being here with her was causing a hard pounding in his crotch. If only she knew just how enticing she looked standing in front of him in a pair of jeans and a white button-up blouse that he would love to peel off her. Her hair was pinned up on her head, but a few locks…like the one he'd played with earlier…had escaped confinement.

"Is there a problem, Aidan?"

He lifted a brow. "Problem?"

"Yes. You're stalling and I'm ready now."

He fought to hide his grin. Was this the same woman who only yesterday swore they would never kiss again? The same woman who just that morning had refused to go riding with him? Her enthusiasm caused something within him to stir, making it hard to keep his control in check. His body wouldn't cooperate mainly because her scent alone was increasing his desire for her.

And she thought all they would do was some heavy-duty kissing?

Deciding not to keep her waiting any longer, he slanted his mouth over hers.

When had she needed a man's kiss this much? No, *this* much, she thought, leaning up on her toes to become enmeshed in Aidan's kiss even more. Jillian felt his arms move from around her waist to her backside, urging her closer to the fit of him, making her feel his hard erection pressing against her middle. She shouldn't like how it felt but she did.

The tips of her nipples seemed sensitized against his solid chest. When had she become this hot mass of sexual desire?

When he intensified the kiss even more, she actually heard herself moan. Really moan. He was actually tasting her. Using his mouth to absorb hers as if she was a delectable treat he had to consume. She was losing all that control she'd told him they had to keep and she was losing it in a way she couldn't define.

When he groaned deep in his throat and deepened the kiss even more, it took all she had to remain standing and not melt in a puddle on the floor. Why at twenty-one was she just experiencing kisses like these? And why was she allowing her mind to be sacked with emotions and sensations that made it almost impossible to breathe, to think, to do anything but reciprocate? Their tongues tangled greedily, dueling and plowing each other's mouths with a yearning that was unrelenting.

When she noticed his hands were no longer on her

backside but had worked their way to the zipper of her jeans, she gasped and broke off the kiss, only to be swept off her feet into Aidan's strong arms.

Before she could ask what he was doing, he tumbled them both onto the huge bed. She looked up into his dark eyes as he moved his body over hers. Any words she'd wanted to say died in her throat. All she could do was stare at him as intense heat simmered through her veins. He leaned back on his haunches and then in one quick movement, grasped her hips and peeled the jeans down to her knees.

"What—what are you doing?" she managed to ask, while liquid fire sizzled down her spine. She was lying there with only bikini panties covering her.

He met her gaze. "I'm filling my entire mouth with the taste of you." And then he eased her panties down her legs before lifting her hips and lowering his head between her thighs.

The touch of his tongue had her moaning and lifting her hips off the bed. He was relentless, and he used his mouth in a way that should be outlawed. She wanted to push his head away, but instead she used her arms to hold him in place.

And then she felt a series of intense spasms spread through her entire body. Suddenly, he did something wicked with his tongue, driving her wild. She screamed as a flood of sensations claimed her, tossing her into an earth-shaking orgasm. Her very first. It was more powerful than anything she could have imagined.

And he continued to lap her up, not letting go. His actions filled her with more emotions, more wanting, more longing. Her senses were tossed to smithereens. It took a while before she had enough energy to breathe through her lungs to release a slow, steady breath. She wondered if she had enough energy to even mount her horse, much less ride away from here.

Aidan lifted his head and slowly licked his lips, as if savoring her taste, while meeting her eyes. "Mmm, delicious."

His words were as erotic as she felt. "Why? Why did you do that?" she asked, barely able to get the words out. She felt exhausted, totally drained. Yet completely and utterly satisfied.

Instead of giving her an answer, he touched her chin with the tip of his thumb before lowering his lips to hers in an open-mouth kiss that had fire stirring deep in her stomach. Tasting herself on his lips made her quiver.

When he finally released her lips, he eased back on his haunches and gazed down at her. "I did it because you have a flavor that's uniquely you and I wanted to sample it."

She lifted her hips off the bed when he pulled her jeans back up. Then he shifted his body to pull her into his lap. She tilted her head back to look at him. "What about when we leave here tomorrow?"

"When we leave tomorrow we will remember this time with fondness and enjoyment. I'm sure when you wake up in your bed in Wyoming and I wake up in mine in Boston, we will be out of each other's systems."

She nodded. "You think so?"

"Yes, I'm pretty sure of it. And don't feel guilty about anything because we haven't hurt anyone. All we did was appease our curiosity in a very delectable way."

Yes, it had been most delectable. And technically, they hadn't slept together so they hadn't crossed any lines. She pulled away from him to finish fixing her clothing, tucking her shirt back into her jeans.

"Um, a missed opportunity."

She glanced over at him. "What?"

"Your breasts. I had planned to devour them."

At that moment, as if on cue, her breasts began to ache. Her nipples felt tight, sensitive, pulsing. And it didn't help matters when an image of him doing that very thing trickled through her mind.

"We need to go," she said quickly, knowing if they remained any longer it would only lead to trouble.

"Do we?"

He wasn't helping matters by asking her that. "Yes. It's getting late and we might be missed." When he made no attempt to move, she headed for the door. "I can find my way back."

"Wait up, Jillian."

She stopped and turned back to him. "We don't have to go back together, Aidan."

"Yes, we do. Pam knows of our plans to go riding together."

Color drained from Jillian's face. "Who told her?"

"I ran into her when I was headed to the barn and she asked where I was headed. I told her the truth."

At the accusation in her expression, he placed his hands in the back pockets of his jeans. "Had I told her I was going someplace else and she discovered differently, Jillian, she would have wondered why I had lied."

Jillian nodded slowly upon realizing what he said made sense. "What did she say about it?"

"Nothing. In fact I don't think she thought much about it at all. However, she did say she was glad you were about to start medical school and she would appreciate any advice I could give you."

Jillian swallowed tightly. He'd given her more than advice. Thanks to him, she had experienced her first orgasm today. "Okay, we'll ride back together. I'll just wait outside."

She quickly walked out the door. He'd claimed what they'd done today would get them out of each other's systems. She definitely hoped so.

When the door closed behind Jillian, Aidan rubbed a hand down his face in frustration. He couldn't leave Denver soon enough. The best thing to do was put as much distance between him and Jillian as possible. She felt uncomfortable with the situation and now he was beginning to feel the same. However, his uneasiness had nothing to do with Dillon and Pam finding out what they'd been up to, and everything to do with his intense attraction to Jillian.

Even now he wanted to go outside, throw her over his shoulders and bring her back inside. He wanted to kiss her into submission and taste her some more before making nonstop love to her. How crazy was that?

He'd never felt this much desire for any woman, and knowing she was off-limits only seemed to heighten his desire for her. And now that he'd gotten an intimate taste of her, getting her out of his system might not be as easy as he'd claimed earlier. Her taste hadn't just electrified his taste buds, it had done something to him that was unheard of—he was no longer lingering on the edge of wanting to make love to her but had fallen off big-time.

Every time his tongue explored her mouth, his emotions heated up and began smoldering. And when he lapped her up, he was tempted to do other things to her, as well. Things he doubted she was ready for.

Drawing in a deep breath, he straightened up the bed-covers before heading for the door. Upon stepping outside, he breathed in deeply to calm his racing heart. She stood there stroking his horse and a part of him wished she would stroke him the same way. He got hard just imagining such a thing.

He didn't say anything for a long moment. He just stood there watching her. When his erection pressed uncomfortably against his zipper, he finally spoke up. "I'm ready to ride."

She glanced over at him and actually smiled when she said, "You have a beautiful horse, Aidan."

"Thanks," he said, walking down the steps. "Charger is a fourth-generation Westmoreland stallion."

She turned to stroke the horse again and didn't look up when he came to stand next to her. "I've heard all about Charger. I was warned by Dillon to never try to ride him because only a few people could. It's obvious you're one of those people."

Aidan nodded. "Yes, Charger and I have an understanding."

She stopped stroking Charger to look at him. "What about you and me, Aidan? Do we have an understanding?"

He met her gaze, nor sure how he should answer that. Just when he thought he had everything figured out about them, something would happen to make his brains turn to mush. "I assume you're referring to the incidents that have taken place between us over the past two days."

"I am."

"Then, yes, we have an understanding. After today, no more kissing, no more touching—"

"Or tasting," she interjected.

Saying he would never again taste her was a hard one, but for her peace of mind and for his own, he would say it. "Yes, tasting."

"Good. We're in agreement."

He wouldn't exactly say that, but for now he would hold his tongue—that same tongue that enjoyed dueling with hers. "I guess we need to head back."

"Okay, and I don't need your help mounting my horse."

In other words, she didn't want him to touch her. "You sure?"

"Positive."

He nodded and then watched her move away from his horse to get on hers. As usual, it was a total turn-on watching her. "I want to thank you, Aidan."

He took his gaze away from the sight of her legs straddling the horse to look into her face. "Thank me for what?"

"For introducing me to a few things during this visit home."

For some reason that made him smile. "It was my pleasure." And he meant every word.

Seven

"You're still not going home, Jillian?"

Jillian looked up from eating her breakfast to see her roommate, Ivy Rollins. They had met in her sophomore year when Jillian knew she didn't want to live in the dorm any longer. She had wanted an apartment off campus and someone to share the cost with her. Ivy, who had plans to attend law school, had answered the ad Jillian placed in the campus newspaper. They'd hit it off the first time they'd met and had been the best of friends since. Jillian couldn't ask for a better roommate.

"I was home last month," she reminded Ivy.

"Yes, but that was a couple of days for your birthday. Next week is spring break."

Jillian didn't want to be reminded. Pam had called yesterday to see if Jillian would be coming home since Nadia had made plans to do so. Paige, who was attending UCLA, had gotten a small part in a play on campus and needed to remain in Los Angeles. Guilt was still riding Jillian over what she and Aidan had done. She hated deceiving her sister about anything. "I explained to Pam that I need to start studying for the MCAT. She understood."

"I hate leaving you, but—"

"But you will," Jillian said, smiling. "And that's fine. I know how homesick you get." That was an understatement. Ivy's family lived in Oregon. Her parents, both chefs, owned a huge restaurant there. Her two older brothers were chefs as well and assisted her parents. Ivy had decided on a different profession than her parents and siblings, but she loved going home every chance she got to help out.

"Yes, I will," Ivy said, returning her smile. "In fact I leave in two days. Sure you'll be okay?"

"Yes, I'll be fine. I've got enough to keep me busy since I'm sitting for the MCAT in two months. And I need to start working on my essays."

"It's a bummer you'll be doing something other than enjoying yourself next week," Ivy said.

"It's okay. Getting into medical school is the most important thing to me right now."

A few hours later Jillian sat at the computer desk in her bedroom searching the internet. She had tossed around the idea of joining a study group for the MCAT and there appeared to be several. Normally, she preferred studying solo but for some reason she couldn't concentrate. She pushed away from the computer and leaned back in her chair knowing the reason.

Aidan.

It had been a little over a month since she'd gone home for her birthday, and Aidan had been wrong. She hadn't woken up in her bed in Wyoming not thinking of him. In fact she thought of him even more. All the time. Thoughts of him had begun interfering with her studies.

She got up and moved to the kitchen to grab a soda from the refrigerator. He should have been out of her system by now, but he wasn't. Memories of him put her to sleep at night and woke her up in the morning. And then in the wee hours of the night, she recalled in vivid detail his kisses, especially the ones between her legs.

Remembering that particular kiss sent a tingling sensation through her womanly core, which wasn't good. In fact, nothing about what she was going through was good. Sexual withdrawal. And she hadn't even had sex with Aidan, but she hadn't needed sex to get an orgasm. That in itself showed the magnitude of his abilities.

Returning to her bedroom she pushed thoughts of him from her mind. Sitting back down at her desk, she resumed surfing the net. She bet he hadn't even given her a thought. He probably wasn't missing any sleep thinking of her, and he had probably woken up his first day back in Boston with some woman in his bed. Why did that thought bother her?

She had been tempted to ask Pam if she'd heard from Aidan, but hadn't for fear her sister would wonder why Jillian was inquiring about Aidan when she hadn't before.

Jillian turned around when she heard a knock on her bedroom door. "Come in."

Ivy walked into the room, smiling. "I know you have a lot to do but you've been in here long enough. Come grab a bite to eat at the Wild Duck. My treat."

Ivy wasn't playing fair. She knew the Wild Duck was one of Jillian's favorite eating places. They had the best hamburgers and fries. "You've twisted my arm," she said, pushing away from the desk.

Ivy chuckled. "Yeah. Right."

Jillian stood, thinking she did need a break. And maybe she could get Aidan off her mind.

* * *

"How are you doing, Dr. Westmoreland?"

Aidan smiled over at the doctor who'd transferred in to the medical school during the weekend that he'd gone home. He really should ask her out. Lynette Bowes was attractive, she had a nice figure, and she seemed friendly enough. At times almost too friendly. She enjoyed flirting with him and she'd gone so far as to make a few bold innuendos, which meant getting her into his bed probably would be easy. So what was he waiting on?

"I'm fine, Dr. Bowes, and how are you?"

She leaned over to hand him a patient's chart, intentionally brushing her breasts against his arm. "I would be a lot a better if you dropped by my apartment tonight," she whispered.

Another invite. Why was he stalling? Why wasn't he on top of his game as usual? And why was he thinking that the intimate caress she'd purposely initiated just now had nothing on the caresses he'd experienced with Jillian?

"Thanks, but I have plans for tonight," he lied.

"Then maybe another night?"

"I'll let you know." He appreciated his cell phone going off at that moment. "I'll see you later." He made a quick escape.

Later that night while at home doing nothing but flipping TV channels, he couldn't help wondering what the hell was wrong with him. Although he'd asked himself that question, he knew the answer without thinking.

Jillian.

He'd assumed once he was back in Boston and waking up in his own bed that he would eradicate her from his mind. Unfortunately, he'd found out that wasn't the case. He thought about her every free moment, and he even went to bed thinking about her. And the dreams he had of her were double X-rated. His desire for her was so bad that he hadn't thought twice about wanting anyone else.

And it hadn't helped matters when he'd called home earlier in the week and Dillon mentioned that Jillian wasn't coming home for spring break. She told Pam she had registered to take the MCAT and needed the time to study and work on her admissions essays. He applauded her decision to make sacrifices to reach her goal, but he was disappointed she hadn't reached out to him liked he'd suggested. He'd made a pretty high score on the MCAT and could give her some study pointers. He'd even keyed his contact information into her phone.

Yet she hadn't called to ask him a single question about anything. That could only mean she didn't want his help and had probably pushed what happened between them to the back of her mind. Good for her, but he didn't like the fact that she remained in the center of his.

Tossing the remote aside he reached for his cell phone to pull up her number. When her name appeared he put the phone down. They'd had an agreement, so to speak. An understanding. They would put that time in Denver behind them. It had been enjoyable but was something that could not and would not be repeated. No more kissing, touching…or tasting.

Hell, evidently that was easy for her to do, but it was proving to be downright difficult for him. There were nights he woke up wanting her with a passion, hungering to kiss her, touch her and taste her.

The memories of them going riding together, especially that day spent in Bane's cabin…every moment of that time was etched in Aidan's mind, making his brain cells overload.

Like now.

When he'd pulled down her jeans, followed by her panties, and had buried his head between her legs and tasted her...the memory made his groin tighten. Need for Jillian clawed at him in a way that made it difficult to breathe.

Aidan stood and began pacing the floor in his apartment, trying to wear down his erection. He paused when an idea entered his mind. He had time he could take off and he might as well do it now. He'd only been to Laramie, Wyoming, a couple of times, and maybe he should visit there again. He would take in the sights and check out a few good restaurants. And there was no reason for him not to drop in on Jillian to see how she was doing while he was there.

No reason at all.

Three days later, Jillian sat at the kitchen table staring at the huge study guide in front of her. It had to be at least five hundred pages thick and filled with information to prepare her for the MCAT. The recommendation was that students take three months to study, but since she was enrolled in only one class this semester she figured she would have more time to cram and could get it done in two months. That meant she needed to stay focused. No exceptions. And she meant none.

But her mind was not in agreement, especially when she could lick her lips and imagine Aidan doing that very same thing. And why—after one month, nine days and twenty minutes—could she still do that? Why hadn't she been able to forget about his kisses and move on? Especially now when she needed to focus.

The apartment was empty and felt lonely without Ivy. It was quiet and just what she needed to get some serious studying done. She had eaten a nice breakfast and had taken a walk outside to get her brain and body stimulated. But now her mind wanted to remember another type of stimulation. One that even now sent tingles through her lower stomach.

She was about to take a sip of her coffee when the doorbell sounded. She frowned. Most of her neighbors were college students like her, and the majority of them had gone home for spring break. She'd noticed how vacant the parking lot had looked while out walking earlier.

Getting up from the kitchen table she moved toward the front door. She glanced through her peephole and her breath caught. Standing on the other side of her door was the one man she'd been trying not to think about.

Shocked to the core, she quickly removed the security chain and unlocked the door. Opening it, she tried to ignore the way her heart pounded and how her stomach muscles trembled. "Aidan? What are you doing here?"

Instead of answering, he leaned down and kissed her. Another shock rammed right into the first. She should have pushed him away the moment their mouths connected. But instead she melded her body right to his and his arms reached out to hold her around the waist. As soon as she was reacquainted with his taste, her tongue latched onto his and began a sensuous duel that had her moaning.

In all her attempts at logical thinking over the past month, not until now could she admit how much she'd missed him. How much she'd missed this. How could a man engrain himself inside a woman's senses so deeply and thoroughly, and so quickly? And how could any woman resist this particular man doing so?

She heard the door click and knew he'd maneuvered her into her apartment and closed the door behind him. Noticing that, she almost pulled back, and she would have had he not at that moment deepened the kiss.

This had to be a dream. Is that why the room felt as if it was spinning? There was no way Aidan was in Laramie, at her apartment and kissing her. But if this was a dream she wasn't ready to wake up. She needed to get her fill of his taste before her fantasy faded. Before she realized in horror that she was actually kissing the short and bald mailman instead of Aidan. Had her fascination with him finally gotten the best of her?

The thought had her breaking off the kiss and opening her eyes. The man standing across from her with lips damp from their kiss was definitely Aidan.

She drew in a deep breath, trying to slow the beat of her heart and regain control of her senses.

As if he'd known just what she was thinking, he said, "It's really me, Jillian. And I'm here to help you study for your MCAT this week."

She blinked. *Help her study?* He had to be kidding.

Aidan wanted nothing more than to kiss the shocked look off Jillian's face. But he knew that before he could even think about kissing her again he had a lot of explaining to do since he'd gone back on their agreement.

"I talked to Dillon a few days ago and he mentioned you wouldn't be coming home for spring break and the reason why. So I figured I could help by giving you a good study boost."

She shook her head as if doing so would clear her mind. Looking back at him, she said, "There's no way you could have thought that. And what was that kiss about? I thought we had an understanding."

"We did. We still do. However, based on the way you responded to my kiss just now, I think we might need to modify a few things."

She lifted her chin. "There's nothing for us to modify."

That response irritated him to the core. "Do you think I want to be here, Jillian? I have a life in Boston, a life I was enjoying until recently. Ever since the kisses we shared on your birthday, I've done nothing but think about you, want you, miss you."

"That's not my fault," she snapped.

"It is when you're not being honest with yourself. Can you look me in the eyes and tell me that you haven't thought of me? That you haven't been wanting me? And be honest for once because if you deny it then you need to tell me why your kiss just now said otherwise."

He watched as she nervously licked her tongue across her lips and his gut clenched. "Tell me, Jillian," he said in a softer tone. "For once be honest with me and with yourself."

She drew in a long breath as they stared at each other. After several tense moments passed between them, she said, "Okay, I have been thinking of you, missing you, wanting you. And I hated myself for doing so. You're a weakness I can't afford to have right now. It's crazy. I know a lot of guys around campus. But why you? Why do I want the one guy I can't have?"

Her words softened his ire. She was just as confused

and frustrated as he was. "And why do you think you can't have me?"

She frowned. "You know why, Aidan. Pam and Dillon would be against it. In their eyes, we're family. And even if you were a guy she would approve of, she would try to convince me not to get involved with you and to stay focused on becoming a doctor."

"You don't know for certain that's how she would feel, Jillian."

"I do know. When Pam was in college pursuing her dream of becoming an actress, I asked her why she didn't date. She told me that a woman should never sacrifice her dream for any man."

"I'm not asking you to sacrifice your dream."

"No, but you want an involvement during a time when I should be more focused than ever on becoming a doctor."

"I want to help you, not hinder you," he stressed again.

"How do you think you can do that?"

At least she was willing to listen. "By using this week to introduce you to study techniques that will help you remember those things you need to remember."

She nervously licked her tongue across her lips again. "It won't work. I won't be able to think straight with you around."

"I'll make sure you do. I'm not asking to stay here, Jillian. I've already checked into a hotel a mile or so from here. I'll arrive every morning and we'll study until evening, taking short breaks in between. Then we'll grab something to eat and enjoy the evening. Afterward, I'll bring you back here and then leave. Before going to bed you should review what was covered that day, making sure you get eight hours of sleep."

She looked at him as if he was crazy. "I can't take time from studying to enjoy the evening. I'll need to study morning, noon and night."

"Not with me helping you. Besides, too much studying will make you burned out, and you don't want to do that. What good is studying if that happens?"

When she didn't say anything, he pushed harder. "Try my way for a couple of days and if it doesn't work, if you feel I'm more of a hindrance than a help, I'll leave Laramie and let you do things your way."

As she stared at him, not saying anything, he could feel blood throb through his veins. As usual she looked serious. Beautiful. Tempting. He wanted her. Being around her would be hard and leaving her every night after dinner would be harder. He would want to stay and make love to her all through the night. But that wasn't possible. No matter how hard it would be, he needed to keep his self-control.

"Okay," she finally said. "We'll try it for a couple of days. And if it doesn't work I intend for you to keep your word about leaving."

"I will." He had no intention of leaving because he intended for his plan to work. He had aced the MCAT the first time around, with flying colors. Once he'd gotten his act together as a teenager, he'd discovered he was an excellent test taker, something Adrian was not. Determined not to leave his twin behind, he'd often tutored Adrian, sharing his study tips and techniques with his brother. Aidan had also done the same with Bailey once she was in college. Unfortunately, he'd never gotten the chance to share his techniques with Bane since his cousin hadn't been interested in anything or anyone but Crystal.

"Now let's seal our agreement," he said.

When she extended her hand, he glanced at it before pulling her into his arms again.

He was taking advantage again, Jillian thought. But she only thought that for a second. That was all the time it took for her to begin returning his kiss with the same hunger he seemed to feel. This was crazy. It was insane. It was also what she needed. What she'd been wanting since leaving Denver and returning to Laramie.

Kissing was something they enjoyed doing with each other and the unhurried mating of their mouths definitely should be ruled illegal. But for now she could handle this—in the safety of her living room, in the arms of a man she thoroughly enjoyed kissing—as long as it went no further.

But what if it did? He'd already shown her that his definition of kissing included any part of her body. What if he decided he wanted more than her mouth this time? Her hormones were going haywire just thinking of the possibility.

He suddenly broke off the kiss and she fought back a groan of disappointment. She stared up at him. "Okay, where's the study guide?" he asked her.

She blinked. Her mind was slow in functioning after such a blazing kiss. It had jarred her senses. "Study guide?"

He smiled and caressed her cheek. "Yes, the MCAT study guide."

"On my kitchen table. I was studying when you showed up."

"Good. And you'll study some more. Lead the way."

* * *

Aidan leaned back in his chair and glanced over at Jillian. "Any questions?"

She shook her head. "No, but you make it seem simple."

He smiled. "Trust me, it's not. The key is to remember that you're the one in control of your brain and the knowledge that's stored inside of it. Don't let retrieving that information during test time psych you out."

She chuckled. "That's easy for you to say."

"And it will be easy for you, as well. I've been there, and when time allows I tutor premed students like yourself. You did well on the practice exam, which covers basically everything you need to know. Now you need to concentrate on those areas you're not so sure about."

"Which is a lot."

"All of them are things you know," he countered. He believed the only reason she lacked confidence in her abilities was because the idea of failing was freaking her out. "You don't have to pass on the first go-round. A lot of people don't. That's why it's suggested you plan to take it at least twice."

She lifted her chin. "I want to ace it on the first try."

"Then do it."

Aidan got up from his chair and went over to the coffeepot sitting on her kitchen counter. He needed something stronger than caffeine, but coffee would have to do. He'd been here for five hours already and they hadn't stopped for lunch. The key was to take frequent short breaks instead of one or two long ones.

She had taken the online practice exam on verbal reasoning and he thought she'd done well for her first time. He'd given her study tips for multiple-choice exams and gone over the questions she had missed. Personally, he thought she would do fine, although he thought taking the test in two months was pushing it. He would have suggested three months instead of two.

"Want some coffee?" he asked, pouring himself a cup.

"No, I'm okay."

Yes, she definitely was. He couldn't attest to her mental state with all that she'd crammed into that brain of hers today, but he could definitely attest to her physical one. She looked amazing, even with her hair tied back in a ponytail and a cute pair of reading glasses perched on her nose. He was used to seeing her without makeup and preferred her that way. She had natural beauty with her flawless creamy brown skin. And she looked cute in her jeans and top.

He glanced at his watch. "Jillian?"

She glanced up from the computer and looked over at him. "Yes?"

"It's time to call it a day."

She seemed baffled by his statement. "Call it a day? I haven't covered everything I wanted to do today."

"You covered a lot and you don't want to overload your brain."

She stared at him for a moment and then nodded and began shutting down her computer. "Maybe you're right. Thanks to you, I did cover a lot. Definitely a lot more than I would have if you hadn't been here. You're a great tutor."

"And you're a good student." He glanced at his watch again. "What eating places do you have around here?"

"Depends on what you have a taste for."

He had a taste for her, but knew he had to keep his promise and not push her into anything. "A juicy steak."

"Then you're in luck," she said, standing. "There's a great steak place a few blocks from here. Give me a few minutes to change."

"Okay." He watched her hurry off toward her bedroom.

When she closed the door behind her, he rubbed a hand down his face. Jillian was temptation even when she wasn't trying to be. When he'd asked about her roommate she'd told him that Ivy had gone home for spring break. That meant...

Nothing. Unless she made the first move or issued an invitation. Until then, he would spend his nights alone at the hotel.

Eight

Jillian glanced across the table at Aidan. It was day three and still hard to believe that he was in Laramie, that he had come to give her a kick-start in her studying. Day one had been frustrating. He'd pushed her beyond what she thought she was ready for. But going to dinner with him that night had smoothed her ruffled feathers.

Dinner had been fun. She'd discovered he enjoyed eating his steaks medium rare and he loved baked potatoes loaded with sour cream, bacon bits and cheddar cheese. He also loved unsweetened tea and when it came to anything with chocolate, he could overdose if he wasn't careful.

He was also a great conversationalist. He engaged her in discussions about everything—but he deemed the topic of medical school to be off-limits. They talked about the economy, recent elections, movies they had enjoyed, and about Adrian's plans to travel the world a few years after getting his PhD in engineering.

And Aidan got her talking. She told him about Ivy, who she thought was the roommate from heaven; about Jillian's decision two years ago to move out of the dorm; and about her first experience with a pushy car salesman. She told him about all the places she wanted to visit one day and that the one thing she wanted to do and hadn't done yet was go on a cruise.

It occurred to her later that it had been the first time she and Aidan had shared a meal together alone, and she had enjoyed it. It had made her even more aware of him as a man. She'd had the time to look beyond his handsome features and she'd discovered he was a thoughtful and kind person. He had been pleasant, treating everyone with respect, including the waitress and servers. And each time he smiled at her, her stomach clenched. Then he would take a sip of his drink, and she would actually envy his straw.

After dinner they returned to her apartment. He made her promise that she would only review what they'd covered that day and not stay up past nine, then he left. But not before taking her into his arms and giving her a kiss that rendered her weak and senseless—to the point where she was tempted to ask him to stay longer. But she fought back the temptation. Knowing she would see him again the next day had made falling asleep quick and easy. For the first time in a long time, she had slept through the night, though he'd dominated her dreams.

He arrived early the next morning with breakfast, which she appreciated. Then it was back to studying again. The second day had been more intense than the first. Knowing they couldn't cover every aspect of the study guide in one week, he had encouraged her to hit the areas she felt were her weakest. He gave her hints on how to handle multiple-choice questions and introduced her to key words to use when completing her essays.

For dinner they had gone to the Wild Duck. She had been eager to introduce him to her favorite place. A dinner of hamburgers, French fries and milk shakes had been wonderful. Afterward they went to Harold's Game Hall to shoot pool, something she had learned to do in high school.

When he'd brought her home, like the night before, he took her in his arms and kissed her before he left, giving her the same instructions about reviewing what they'd covered that morning and getting eight hours of sleep. Again, she'd slept like a baby with him dominating her dreams.

She enjoyed having him as a study coach. Most of the time she stayed focused. But there were a few times when she felt heat simmering between them, something both of them tried to ignore. They managed it most of the time but today was harder than the two days before.

Aidan was tense. She could tell. He had arrived that morning, like yesterday, with breakfast in hand. Since he believed she should study on a full stomach and not try eating while studying, they had taken their meal outside to her patio. It had been pleasant, but more than once she'd caught him staring at her with a look in his eyes that she felt in the pit of her stomach.

He wasn't as talkative today as he'd been the past two days, and, taking a cue from his mood, she hadn't said much, either. On those occasions when their hands had accidentally touched while he'd been handing her papers or turning a page, she wasn't sure who sizzled more, her or him.

That's why she'd made up her mind about how today would end. She wanted him and he wanted her and there was no reason for them to suffer with their desires any longer. She'd fallen in love with him. After this time to-gether, she could admit that now. That little crush she'd had on him for years had become something more. Something deeper and more profound.

The thought of Pam and Dillon finding out was still an issue that plagued her. However, since Aidan didn't feel the same way about her that she felt about him, she was certain she would be able to convince him to keep whatever they did a secret. He was doing that now anyway. He'd told her that neither Pam nor Dillon knew where he was spending this week. That meant Jillian and Aidan were already keeping secrets from their family, and she would continue to do so if it meant spending more time with him.

That night they went to a restaurant she had never visited because of its pricey menu. The signature dishes had been delicious and the service excellent. But the restaurant's setting spoke of not only elegance but also romance. Rustic wood ceilings with high beams, a huge brick fireplace and a natural stone floor. Beautiful candles adorned the tables and even in the dim light, each time she glanced over at Aidan he was looking back at her.

Getting through dinner hadn't been easy. They conversed but not as much as they had the previous two nights. Was she imagining things or did his voice sound deeper, huskier than usual? His smiles weren't full ones but half smiles, and just as sexy.

Like he'd done the previous two nights, he walked through her apartment, checking to make sure everything was okay. Then he gave her orders to only review what she'd studied that morning and get into bed before nine because at least eight hours of sleep were essential.

And then, as had become his habit, he pulled her into his arms to kiss her goodbye. This is what she had anticipated all day. She was ready for Aidan's kiss. Standing on tiptoe she tilted her open mouth toward him, her tongue ready. He closed his full mouth over hers and their tongues tangled, almost bringing her to her knees.

The kiss lasted for a long, delectable moment. It was different than any they'd shared before and she'd known it the moment their mouths fused. It was hot, heavy and hungry. He wasn't letting up or backing down—and neither was she.

Jillian felt herself being lifted off her feet and she immediately wrapped her legs around his waist while he continued to ravish her mouth in a way that overwhelmed her and overloaded her senses. His hunger was sexual and greedy. She could tell he was fighting hard to hold it together, to stay in control, to keep his sanity in check. But she wasn't. In fact, she was deliberately trying to tempt him every way that she could.

She felt the wall at her back and knew he'd maneuvered them over to it. He broke off the kiss and stared at her, impaling her with the flaming fire in his eyes. "Tell me to stop, Jillian," he said. "Because if you don't do it now, I won't be able to stop later. I want to tongue you all over. Lick every inch of your body. Taste you. Make love to you. Hard. Long. Deep. So tell me to stop now."

Her pulse jumped. Every single cell in her body sizzled with his words. Hot, sparks of passion glowed in his gaze and when a powerful burst of primal need slammed through her she didn't want to escape.

"Tell me to stop."

His plea made the already hot sexual tension between them blaze, and she knew of only one way to put out the fire.

"Stop, Aidan!"

His body went still. The only thing that moved was the pulse throbbing in his throat. He held her gaze and she was convinced she could hear blood rushing through both of their veins.

When she felt him about to untangle her legs from around his waist and lower her feet to the floor, she said, "Stop talking and do all those things you claim you're going to do."

She saw the impact of her words reflected in his eyes. While he seemed incapable of speaking, she released her arms from around his neck and tugged at his shirt, working her hands beneath to touch his bare chest. She heard the groan from deep in his throat.

"If you don't take me, Aidan Westmoreland, then I'll be forced to take you."

That was the last thing Aidan had expected her to say. But hearing her say it intensified the throbbing need within him. His crotch pounded fiercely and he knew of only one way to remedy that. But first…

He lowered her to her feet as a smile tugged at his lips. Only for a moment, he gazed down at her shirt, noticing the curve of her breasts beneath the cotton. In an instant, he tugged the shirt over her head and tossed it aside.

He drew in a deep breath when his eyes settled on her chest, specifically her skin-tone colored bra. Eager beyond belief, he touched her breasts through the lace material. When his fingers released the front clasp, causing the twin globes to spring free, the breath was snatched from his lungs.

Mercy. He eased the bra straps from her shoulders to remove it completely from her body and his mouth watered. Her breasts were one area that he hadn't tasted yet, and he planned on remedying that soon.

Deciding he wanted to see more naked flesh, he lowered to his knees and slid his fingers beneath the elastic waistband of her skirt to ease it down her legs. She stepped out of it and he tossed it aside to join her shirt and bra. His gaze raked the full length of her body, now only covered by a pair of light blue bikini panties. His hands actually trembled when he ran them down her legs. He felt as if he were unveiling a precious treasure.

She stepped out of them as she'd done her skirt and she stood in front of him totally naked. He leaned back on his haunches while his gaze raked her up and down, coming back to her center. He was tempted to start right there, but he knew if he did that, he wouldn't get to taste her breasts this time, either, and he refused to miss the chance again.

Standing back on his feet, Aidan leaned and lowered his head. He captured a nipple between his lips, loving how the tip hardened in his mouth as his tongue traced circles around the rigid bud. She purred his name as she cradled the back of his head to hold his mouth right there.

He continued to taste her breasts, leaving one and moving to the other, enjoying every single lick and suck. Her moans fueled his desire to possess her. To make love to her. And what he loved more than anything else was the sound of her moaning his name.

Aidan eased his lips from her breasts and moved his mouth slowly downward, tasting her skin. As he crouched, his mouth traced a greedy path over her stomach, loving the way her muscles tightened beneath his lips.

A slow throbbing ache took hold of his erection as he eased down to his knees. This was what he'd gone to bed craving ever since he'd first tasted her between her thighs. He'd fallen asleep several nights licking his lips at the memory. Her feminine scent was unique, so irresistibly Jillian, that his tongue thickened in anticipation.

Knowing she watched him, he ran his hands up and down the insides of her legs, massaged her thighs and caressed the area between them. His name was a whisper on her lips when he slid a finger inside of her. He loved the feel of her juices wetting him. He stroked her.

Hungry for her taste, he withdrew his finger and licked it. He smiled before using his hands to spread her feminine core to ready her for an open-mouth kiss.

Jillian released a deep, toe-curling moan the moment Aidan latched his hot tongue onto her. She grabbed his head to push him away, but he held tight to her legs while his tongue went deep, thrusting hard. Then she pressed herself toward his mouth.

She closed her eyes and chanted his name as spasms ripped through her, making her thighs tremble. He refused to let go, refused to lift his mouth, as sensations overtook her. Her body throbbed in unexpected places as an orgasm shook her.

When the last spasm speared through her, she felt herself being lifted into strong arms. When she opened her eyes, Aidan was entering her bedroom. He placed her on the bed, leaned down and kissed her, sending rekindled desire spiking through her.

When he ended the kiss and eased off the bed, she watched as he quickly removed his clothes. She could only lie there and admire his nakedness. He was a fine specimen of a man, both in and out of clothes. Just as he'd appeared in her dreams. Thick thighs, muscular legs and a huge erection nested in a patch of thick, curly black hair.

How will I handle that? she asked herself when he pulled a condom packet from his wallet and quickly sheathed himself. He took his time and she figured it was because he knew she was watching his every move with keen interest.

"You have done this before right?" he asked her.

"What? Put on a condom? No. One wouldn't fit me."

He grinned over at her. "Funny. You know what I'm asking."

Yes, she knew what he was asking. "Um, sort of."

He lifted a brow. "Sort of?"

She shrugged slightly. "I'm not a virgin, if that's what you're asking," she said softly. "Technically not. But…"

"But what?"

"I was in high school and neither of us knew what we were doing. That was my one and only time."

He just stood there totally naked staring at her. She wondered why he wasn't saying anything. What was he thinking? As if he'd read her mind, he slowly moved toward her, placed his knee on the bed and leaned toward her. "What you missed out on before, you will definitely get tonight. And Jillian?"

She swallowed. He'd spoken with absolute certainty and all she could do was stare back at him. "Yes?"

"This will not be your only time with me."

Her body reacted to his words and liquid heat traveled through her body. He hadn't spoken any words of love but he'd let her know this wasn't a one-time deal with them.

She didn't have time to dwell on what he'd said. He pulled her into his arms and kissed her. She closed her eyes and let herself be liquefied by the kiss. Like all the other times he'd used his expertise to make everything around her fade into oblivion, the kiss was the only thing her mind and body could comprehend. His hands were all over her, touching her everywhere. She released a deep moan when she felt his knees spreading her legs.

"Open your eyes and look at me Jillian."

She slowly opened her eyes to look up at the man whose body was poised above hers. He lifted her hips and his enlarged sex slid between her wet feminine folds. He thrust forward and her body stretched to accommodate his size. Instinctively, she wrapped her legs around him and when he began to move, she did so, as well.

She continued to hold his gaze while he thrust in and out of her. Over and over he would take her to the edge just to snatch her back. Her inner muscles clamped down on him, squeezing and tightening around him.

As she felt new spasms rip through her, he threw his head back and let out a roar that shook the room. She was glad most of her neighbors had gone away for spring break; otherwise they would know what she was doing tonight.

But right now, all she cared about was the man she loved, and how he was making her feel things she'd never felt before.

He kissed her again. Their tongues dueled in another erotic kiss and she couldn't help but remember the words he'd spoken earlier.

This will not be your only time with me.

She knew men said words they didn't mean to women

they were about to sleep with, and she had no reason to believe it was any different with Aidan.

Besides, considering that she needed to stay focused on her studies, it was a good thing he wasn't serious.

Aidan watched the naked woman sleeping in his arms and let out a frustrated sigh. This was not supposed to happen.

He wasn't talking about making love because there was no way such a thing could have been avoided. The sexual tension between them had been on overload since the day he'd arrived at her apartment and neither of them could have lasted another day.

What was *not* supposed to happen was feeling all these unexpected emotions. They had wrapped around his mind and wouldn't let go. And what bothered him more than anything else was that he knew he was not confusing his emotions with what had definitely been off-the-charts sex. If he hadn't known before that there was a difference in what he felt for Jillian, he definitely knew it now.

He had fallen in love with her.

When? How? Why? He wasn't sure. All he knew, without a doubt, was that it had happened. The promise of great sex hadn't made him take a week's vacation and travel more than fifteen hundred miles across five states to spend time with her. Sex hadn't made him become her personal test coach, suffering the pains of being close to her while maintaining boundaries and limits. And sex definitely had nothing to do with the way he felt right now and how it was nearly impossible for him to think straight.

When she purred softly in her sleep and then wiggled

her backside snugly against his groin he closed his eyes and groaned. It had been great sex but it had been more than that. She had reached a part of him no woman had reached before.

He'd realized it before they'd made love. He'd known it the minute she told him she'd only made love once before. As far as he was concerned that one time didn't count because the guy had definitely done a piss-poor job. The only orgasm she'd ever experienced had been with Aidan.

But in the days he'd spent studying with her he'd gotten to know a lot about her. She was a fighter, determined to reach whatever goals she established for herself. And she was thoughtful enough to care that Pam not bear the burden of the cost of sending Jillian to medical school. She was even willing to sell her family home.

And he liked being with her, which posed a problem since they lived more than a thousand miles apart. He'd heard long-distance affairs could sometimes be brutal. But he and Jillian could make it work if they wanted to do so. He knew how he felt about her but he had no idea how she felt about him. As far as he knew, she wasn't operating on emotion but out of a sense of curiosity. She'd said as much.

However, the biggest problem of all, one he knew would pose the most challenge to the possibility of anything ever developing between them was her insistence on Pam and Dillon not knowing about them.

Aidan didn't feel the same way and now that he loved her, he really didn't want to keep it a secret. He knew Dillon well enough to know that if Aidan were to go to his cousin and come clean, tell Dillon Aidan had fallen in love with Jillian, Dillon would be okay with it. Although

Aidan couldn't say with certainty how Pam would feel, he'd always considered her a fair person. He believed she would eventually give her blessing…but only if she thought Jillian was truly in love with him and that he would make Jillian happy.

There were so many unknowns. The one thing he did know was that he and Jillian had to talk. He'd given her fair warning that what they'd shared would not be one and done. There was no way he would allow her to believe that her involvement with him meant nothing, that she was just another woman to him. She was more than that and he wanted her to know it.

She stirred, shifted in bed and then slowly opened her eyes to stare at him. She blinked a few times as if bringing him into focus—or as if she was trying to figure out if he was really here in her bed.

Aidan let her know she wasn't seeing things. "Good morning." He gently caressed her cheek before glancing over at the digital clock on her nightstand. "You woke up early. It's barely six o'clock."

"A habit I can't break," she said, still staring at him. "You didn't leave."

"Was I supposed to?"

She shrugged bare shoulders. "I thought that's the way it worked."

She had a lot to learn about him. He wouldn't claim he'd never left a woman's bed in the middle of the night, but Jillian was different.

"Not for us, Jillian." He paused. "We need to talk."

She broke eye contact as she pulled up in bed, holding the covers in place to shield her nakedness. Aidan thought the gesture amusing considering all they'd done last night. "I know what you're going to say, Aidan. Although I've never heard it before, Ivy has and she told me how this plays out."

She'd made him curious. "And how does it play out?"

"The guy lets the woman know it was just a one-night stand. Nothing personal and definitely nothing serious."

He hadn't used that particular line before, but he'd used similar ones. He decided not to tell her that. "You weren't a one-night stand, Jillian."

She nodded. "I do recall you mentioning that last night wouldn't be your only time with me."

He tightened his arms around her. "And why do you think I said that?"

"Because you're a man and most men enjoy sex."

He smiled. "A lot of women enjoy it, as well. Didn't you?"

"Yes. There's no need to lie about it. I definitely enjoyed it."

A grin tugged at Aidan's lips. His ego appreciated her honesty. "I enjoyed it, as well." He kissed her, needing the taste of her.

It was a brief kiss and when he lifted his lips from hers, she seemed stunned by what he'd done. He found that strange considering the number of times they had kissed before.

"So, if you don't want to say last night was a one-night stand, what is it you want to talk about?" she asked.

He decided to be just as honest as she had been, and got straight to the point. "I want to talk about me. And you. Together."

She raised a brow. "Together?"

"Yes. I've fallen in love with you."

Nine

Jillian was out of the bed in a flash, taking half the blankets with her. She speared Aidan with an angry look. "Are you crazy? You can't be in love with me. It won't work, especially when I'm in love with you, too."

Too late she'd realized what she'd said. From the look on Aidan's face, he had heard her admission. "If I love you and you love me, Jillian, then what's the problem?"

She lifted her chin. "The problem is that we can't be together the way you would want us to be. I was okay with it when it was one-sided and I just loved you and didn't think you could possibly return the feelings, but now—"

"Hold up," Aidan said, and her eyes widened when he got off the bed to stand in front of her without a stitch of clothes on. "Let me get this straight. You think it's okay for me to sleep with you and not be in love with you?"

She tossed her hair back from her face. "Why not? I'm sure it's done all the time. Men sleep with women they don't love and vice versa. Are you saying you love every woman you sleep with?"

"No."

"Okay then."

"It's not okay because you're not any woman. You're the one that I *have* fallen in love with."

Why was he making things difficult? Downright complicated? She had to make him understand. "I could deal with this a lot better if you didn't love me, mainly because I would have known it wasn't serious on your end."

"And that would not have bothered you?"

"Not in the least. I need to stay focused on my studies and I can't stay focused if I know you feel the same way about me that I feel about you. That only complicates things."

He stared at her as if he thought she was crazy. In a way she couldn't very much blame him. Most women would prefer falling in love with a man who loved them, and if things were different she would want that, too. But the time wasn't right. Men in love made demands. They expected a woman's time. Her attention. All her energy. And being in love required that a woman give her man what he wanted. Well, she didn't have the time to do that. She was in medical school. She wanted to be a doctor.

And worse than anything, an Aidan who thought he loved her would cause problems. He wouldn't want to keep their relationship a secret. He was not a man to be kept in the closet or denied his right to be seen with her. He would want everyone to know they were together and that was something she couldn't accept.

"I still can't understand why you think me loving you complicates things," Aidan said, interrupting her thoughts.

"Because you wouldn't want to keep our affair a secret. You'll want to tell everyone. Take me out anyplace you want. You wouldn't like the thought of us sneaking around."

"No, I wouldn't." He gently pulled her into his arms. She would have pushed him away if he hadn't at that moment tugged the bedcovers from her hands leaving her as naked as he was. The moment their bodies touched, arousal hit her in the core. She was suddenly reminded of what they'd done last night and how they'd done it. From the way his eyes darkened, she knew he was reliving those same sizzling memories.

"Jillian."

"Aidan."

He drew her closer and closed his mouth over hers. She was lost. For a long while, all she could do was stand there feeling his body plastered to hers, feeling his erection pressed against her, feeling the tips of her nipples poking into his chest while he kissed her. Frissons of fire raced up her spine.

And when she felt herself being maneuvered toward the bed, she was too caught up in desire to do anything about it. The same urgency to mate that had taken hold of him had fused itself to her. As soon as her back touched the mattress she slid from beneath him and pushed him back. She had flipped them and was now on top of him. He stared up at her with surprise in his eyes.

She intended to play out one of her fantasies, one of the ways they'd made love in her dreams—with her on top. But first she needed him to know something. "I take the Pill…to regulate my periods. And I'm safe," she whispered.

"So am I."

She maneuvered her middle over his engorged shaft, which stood straight up. Every hormone inside her body sizzled as she eased down onto him, taking him inside inch by inch. He was big, but like last night her body stretched to accommodate his size.

"Look at me, Jillian." Obeying his command, she held his gaze.

"I love you, whether you want me to or not and it's too late for you to do anything about it."

She drew in a deep breath and continued to ease him inside of her, not wanting to dwell on the problems love could cause. They would talk again later. But for now, this is what she wanted. This is what she needed. And when she had taken him to the hilt, she moved, riding him the way she'd been taught to ride years ago. From the look reflected in the depths of his eyes, she was giving him a ride he would remember for a long time.

She liked the view from up here. Staring down at him, seeing his expression change each time she shoved downward, taking him deeper. His nostrils flared. His breathing was choppy. Was that a little sweat breaking through on his brow?

Riding him felt good. Exhilarating. He definitely had the perfect body to be ridden. Hard, masculine and solid. She had her knees locked on each side of his strong thighs. Her inner muscles clenched, gripping him in a hold that had him groaning deep in his throat.

She loved the sound. Loved being in control. Loved him. The last thought sent her senses spiraling, and when he shouted her named and bucked his entire body upward, she felt his massive explosion. He drenched her insides with thick semen. And she used her muscles to squeeze out more.

Perspiration soaked her head, her face, their bodies… but she kept on riding. When another explosion hit him, she nearly jerked them both off the bed when she screamed in pleasure.

He held her tight and she held him and she wished she never had to let him go.

Aidan pushed a damp curl out of Jillian's eyes. She was sprawled on top of him, breathing deeply. He figured she had earned the right to be exhausted. He'd never experienced anything so invigorating or stimulating in his entire life.

"Don't ask me not to love you, Jillian," he finally found the strength to say softly, and the words came straight from his heart. For the first time in his life, he'd told a woman he loved her and the woman wished that he didn't.

When he felt her tears fall on his arm, he shifted their bodies so he could look at her. "Is me loving you that bad?"

She shook her head. "No. I know it should be what I want but the timing… There is so much I still have to do."

"And you think I'd stop you from doing them?"

"No, but I'd stop myself. I'd lose focus. You would want to be with me and I would want to be with you. In the open. I know you don't understand why I can't do that, but I can't."

She was right, he didn't understand. He believed she was all wrong about how Dillon and Pam, or the entire Westmoreland family, would handle them hooking up. He doubted it would be a big deal. But it didn't matter what he thought. She thought otherwise and that's what mattered.

"What if I agree to do what we're doing now? I mean, keeping things between us a secret."

She lifted her head. "You would agree to that, Aidan? I'm not talking about a few weeks or a few months. I'm talking about until I finish medical school. Could you really wait that long?"

That was a good question. Could he? Could he be around Jillian at family gatherings and pretend nothing was going on between them? And what about the physical distance between them? She wasn't even sure what medical school she would attend. Her two top choices were Florida and New Orleans, both hundreds of miles away from Boston, Maine or North Carolina.

And what about his family and friends? Like Adrian, Aidan had quite a reputation around Harvard. What would his friends think when he suddenly stopped pursuing women? They would think he'd lost his ever-loving mind. But he didn't care what anyone thought.

It didn't matter. Wherever Jillian was, he would get to her, spend time with her and give her the support she needed to be the doctor she wanted to be.

What Jillian needed now more than anything was for him not to place any pressure on her. Her focus should be on completing the MCAT and not on anything else. Somehow he would handle the distance, he would handle his family and friends and their perceptions.

He held her gaze. "Yes, I can wait. No matter how long it takes, Jillian. Because you're worth waiting for."

Then he tugged her mouth down to his for another one of their ultrapassionate, mind-blowing kisses.

Ten

The present

"This is Captain Stewart Marcellus," a deep voice boomed through the intercom in Jillian's cabin. "My crew and I would like to welcome you aboard the Princess Grandeur. For the next fourteen days we'll cruise the Grand Mediterranean for your enjoyment. In an hour we'll depart Barcelona for full days in Monte Carlo and Florence and two days in Rome. From there we'll sail to Greece and Turkey. I invite you to join me tonight at the welcome party, which kicks off two weeks of fun."

Jillian glanced around her cabin. *A suite.* This was something she definitely hadn't paid for. She and Paige had planned to share a standard stateroom, definitely nothing as luxurious and spacious as what she'd been given. When she'd contacted the customer service desk to tell them about the mistake, she was told no mistake had been made and the suite was hers to enjoy.

No sooner had she ended the call than she'd received a delivery—a bouquet of beautiful mixed flowers and a bottle of chilled wine with a card that read, "Congratulations on finishing medical school. We are proud of you. Enjoy the cruise. You deserve it. Your family, The Westmorelands."

Jillian eased down to sit on the side of the bed. *Her family.* She wondered what the Westmorelands would think if they knew the truth about her and Aidan. About the affair the two of them had carried on right under their noses for three years.

As she stood to shower and get dressed for tonight's festivities, she couldn't help remembering what that affair had been like after they'd confessed their love for each other. Aidan had understood and agreed that it was to be their secret. No one else was supposed to know—unless the two of them thought it was absolutely necessary.

The first year had been wonderful, in spite of how hard it had been to engage in a long-distance love affair. Even with Aidan's busy schedule juggling dual residencies, he'd managed to fly to Laramie whenever he had a free weekend. And because their time together was scarce, he'd make it special. They would go out to dinner, see a movie, or if it was a weekend she needed to study, they would do that, too. There was no way she would have passed the MCAT the first time around without his help. She had applied to various medical schools and when she was notified of her acceptance into the one she wanted in New Orleans, Aidan had been the first person with whom she'd shared her good news. They had celebrated the next time he'd come to Laramie.

It was during that first year that they agreed to bring Ivy in on their secret. Otherwise, her roommate would have been worried when Jillian went missing because she was staying with Aidan at the hotel.

Jillian had fallen more and more in love with Aidan

during that time. Although she'd had a lot to keep her busy, she missed him when they were apart. But he'd made up for it when he came to town. And even though they'd spent a lot of time in bed making love, their relationship wasn't just about sex. However, she would have to say that the sex was off the chain, and the sexual tension between them was still so thick you could cut it with a knife. Ivy could attest to that and had teased Jillian about it all the time.

It was also during that first year that their control had been tested whenever they went home for holidays, weddings or baby christenings. She would be the first to admit she had felt jealous more than a few times when Aidan's single male cousins, who assumed he was still a player on the prowl, would try setting him up with other women.

Everything had gone well between them as they moved into their second year together. Aidan had helped her relocate to New Orleans after she bid a teary goodbye to Ivy. Jillian leased a one-bedroom efficiency apartment not far from the hospital where she would be working. It was perfect for her needs, but lonely.

It was during the third year that it became harder for Aidan to get away. The hospitals demanded more of his time. And her telephone conversations with him had been reduced from nightly to three times a week. She could tell he was frustrated with the situation. More than once he'd commented that he wished she would have applied to a medical school closer to Maine or North Carolina.

Jillian tried to ignore his attitude but found that difficult to do. Although Aidan didn't say so, deep down she knew the secrecy surrounding their affair was getting to him. It had begun to get to her, as well. And when it seemed Aidan was becoming distant, she knew she had to do something.

When Ivy came to visit Jillian in New Orleans one weekend, she talked to her best friend about the situation. Even now Jillian could remember that time as if it was yesterday…

"So, how is Aidan?" Ivy asked, after placing her order with their waitress.

Jillian had to fight back tears. "Not sure. We haven't talked in a few days and the last time we did, we had an argument."

Ivy raised a brow. "Another one?"

"Yes." She'd told Ivy about their last argument. He'd wanted her to fly to Maine for the weekend for his birthday. She had been excited about doing so until she'd checked her calendar and discovered that was the same weekend of her clinicals. Something she could not miss. Instead of understanding, he'd gotten upset with her and because of his lack of understanding, she'd gotten upset with him. Their most recent argument had started because he told her his twin now knew about them. He'd gotten angry when she'd accused him of breaking his promise and telling Adrian. He'd explained that he didn't have to tell his brother anything. He and his twin could detect each other's moods and feelings sometimes.

"I'm tired of arguing with him, Ivy, and a part of me knows the reason our relationship is getting so strained."

Ivy nodded. "Long-distance romances are hard to maintain, Jillian, and I'm sure the secrecy surrounding your affair isn't helping."

"Yes, I know, which is why I've made a few decisions."

Ivy lifted a brow. "About what?"

Jillian drew in a deep breath. "I've decided to tell Pam about us. The secrecy has gone on long enough. I believe my sister will accept the fact that I'm now an adult and old enough to decide what I want to do in my life and the person I want in it."

"Good for you."

"Thanks. I know she's been concerned about Aidan's womanizing reputation, but once she realizes that I love him and he loves me, I believe she will give us her blessing."

Jillian took a sip of her drink and continued, "But before I tell Pam, I'm flying to Maine to see Aidan. Next weekend is his birthday and I've decided to be there to help him celebrate."

"What about your clinicals?"

Jillian smiled. "I went to my professor and told her I desperately needed that weekend off. She agreed to work with me and arrange for me to do a makeup the following weekend."

"That was nice of her."

"Yes, it was. She said I was a good student, the first to volunteer for projects and my overall attendance is great. So now I'm set to go."

Ivy grinned. "Did you tell Aidan?"

"No. I'm going to surprise him. He mentioned that since I wouldn't be there to celebrate with him that he would sign up to work that day and then hang around his place, watch TV and go to bed early."

"On his birthday? That's a bummer."

"Yes, and that's why I plan to fly there to help him celebrate."

"You're doing the right thing by being there. I think it's wonderful that you're finally letting your sister know about you and Aidan. When she sees how much he adores you she will be happy for the two of you."

A huge smile touched Jillian's lips. "I believe so, too."

Jillian stepped out on the balcony to look at the ocean as she recalled what happened after that. She had been excited when she'd boarded the plane for Portland, Maine. She couldn't wait to tell Aidan of her decision to end the secrecy surrounding their affair and to celebrate his birthday with him.

Due to stormy weather in Atlanta, her connecting flight had been delayed five solid hours and she didn't arrive in Portland until six that evening. It had been another hour before she'd arrived at his apartment complex, anxious to use the door key he'd given her a year ago for the first time.

The moment she'd stepped off the elevator onto his floor she knew a party was going on in one of the apartments. Loud music blasted and boisterous voices made her ears ache. She hadn't known all the noise was coming from Aidan's apartment until she'd reached the door, which she didn't have to unlock since it was slightly ajar.

Jillian walked in and looked around. The place was crowded and there were more women in attendance than men. The women were wearing outfits that probably wouldn't be allowed out on the streets.

Jillian wondered what had happened to Aidan's decision to come home from work, watch TV and go to bed. It seemed he'd decided to throw a party instead and it was in full swing. In the center of the room Aidan sat in a recliner while some scantily dressed woman gave him a lap dance. And from the look on his face, he was enjoying every single minute of it. Some of the guys on the sidelines, who she figured must be Aidan's friends, were egging on both him and the woman, which prompted the woman to make the dance even more erotic.

When the woman began stripping off her clothes, starting with the barely-there strap of material covering her breasts, Jillian was shocked. She knew she'd seen enough when the woman's breasts all but smothered Aidan's face while she wiggled out of her panties.

Not able to watch any longer, a shaken Jillian had left, grateful Aidan hadn't even noticed her presence. What hurt more than anything was that he'd appeared to be enjoying every single minute of the dance. Aidan Westmoreland had seemed in his element. She couldn't help wondering if they had stopped with the dance or if he and the woman had ended up doing other things later.

When he'd called her a few days later he hadn't mentioned anything about the party at his apartment and she hadn't said anything about being there to witness what had gone on. And when she asked how he'd spent his birthday, he angered her even more when he gave her a smart aleck answer, asking, "Why do you care when you didn't care enough to spend it with me?"

He was wrong. She had cared enough. But he hadn't cared enough to tell her the truth. It was then that she'd made the decision to end things between them, since it was apparent that he missed his life as a womanizer. When he called later in the week and made another excuse for not flying to New Orleans to see her as he'd planned, she decided that would be a good time to break things off with him. She would give him his freedom, let him go back to the life he missed.

Deciding the less drama the better, she told him the secrecy of their affair was weighing her down, making her lose focus and she couldn't handle it any longer. She didn't tell him the true reason she'd wanted to end things.

Her declaration led to a huge argument between them. When he told her he was flying to New Orleans to talk to her, she told him she didn't want to see him. Then she ended the conversation.

He had called several times to talk to her but she'd refused to answer and eventually blocked his number. She knew that was the reason for the angry looks he'd given her when she'd attended the last couple of Westmoreland weddings. The last time she'd seen him was a few months ago at Stern's ceremony.

There had been no reason to tell Pam about the affair that had been a secret for so long, so she hadn't. The last thing Jillian needed was for her sister to remind her that just like a tiger couldn't change its stripes neither could a womanizer change his ways.

It had been a year since their breakup. At times she felt she had moved on, but other times she felt she had not. It was so disappointing and painful to think about the future they could have been planning together now that she'd finished medical school, if only things had worked out the way she'd hoped they would.

Jillian wiped the tears from her eyes, refusing to shed any more for Aidan. She was on this cruise to have fun and enjoy herself, and she intended to do just that.

"Yes, Adrian?"

"I'm glad I was able to reach you before ship left port.

I just want to wish you the best. I hope everything works out the way you want with Jill."

Aidan hoped things worked out the way he wanted, as well. "Thanks."

Like Paige, Adrian and Aidan's cousin Stern had figured out something was going on between him and Jillian a couple of years ago. "I will do whatever I have to do to get her back. When this ship returns to port, my goal is to have convinced Jillian to give me another chance."

"Well, Trinity and I are cheering for you."

"Thanks, bro." Trinity was Adrian's fiancée and the two would be getting married in a couple of months.

After ending his phone call with Adrian, Aidan crossed the suite to step out on the balcony. Barcelona was beautiful. He had arrived three days ago and taken a tour of what was considered one of the busiest ports in the Mediterranean. He had eaten at the finest restaurants, some in magnificent buildings etched deep with history. He had walked through the crowded streets wishing Jillian had been by his side. Hopefully when they returned to this port in fourteen days she would be.

He could just imagine what Jillian had assumed when she'd seen that woman giving him a lap dance last year. He had worked that day, as he'd told her he would, but he hadn't known about the surprise birthday party a few of his fraternity brothers had thrown for him.

And he definitely hadn't known about the lap dancer or the other strippers they'd invited until the women arrived. He couldn't get mad at his frat brothers for wanting to make his birthday kind of wild. All they knew was that for the past few years, the man who'd once been one of the biggest womanizers in Boston had taken a sabbatical from women. They'd had no idea that the reason for his seemingly boring lifestyle was because he was involved in a secret affair with Jillian.

So, thinking he'd been working too hard for too long and hadn't gotten in any play time, they thought they were doing him a favor. He would admit that after a few drinks he'd loosened up. But at no time had he forgotten he was in love with Jillian. The lap dance had been just for fun, and after the party all the women had left.

Yes, he'd made a mistake by not mentioning the party to Jillian. And he would be the first to admit his attitude had been less than desirable for the last year of their relationship. But he knew why. He'd had the best of intentions when he thought he could keep their secret without any problems, but as time went on, he'd become impatient. While she hadn't wanted anyone to know about them, he had wanted to shout the truth from the highest mountain.

It hadn't helped matters when some of his siblings and cousins began falling in love and getting married. It seemed as if an epidemic had hit Westmoreland Country when five of his relatives got married in a two-year period. And some had been relatives he'd thought would never marry. It had been hard being around his happily married kinfolk without wanting to have some of that happiness for himself. He would admit he'd spent too many months angry with himself, with Jillian, with the world. But at no time did he doubt his love for her.

Nothing had changed his feelings. He was still in love with her, which was why he was here. To right a wrong and convince her that she was the only woman he wanted.

He knew he had his work cut out for him. But he

intended to stay the course and not fail in his task. She wouldn't appreciate seeing him and she probably wouldn't like it when she found out about Paige's involvement. Or Ivy's for that matter. If Ivy hadn't told Paige the truth, he would still be angry, thinking the reason Jillian had broken up with him was because they were at odds regarding the secret of their affair.

He went back inside when he heard the cabin phone ring. He picked it up. "Yes?"

"I hope you find your quarters satisfactory."

Aidan smiled. That was an understatement. "It's more than satisfactory, Dominic."

This ship was just one of many in a fleet owned by Dominic Saxon. Dominic was married to the former Taylor Steele, whose sister Cheyenne was married to Aidan's cousin, Quade Westmoreland. Once Aidan discovered Jillian had booked her cruise on one of Dominic's ships, his friend had been all too eager to assist Aidan in getting back the woman he loved. Years ago Dominic had found himself in a similar situation.

"Taylor sends her love and we're all rooting for you. I know how misunderstandings can threaten even the most solid relationships, and I think you're doing the right thing by going after her," Dominic said. "I'm going to give you the same advice a very smart woman—my mother—gave me when I was going through my troubles with Taylor. *Let love guide you to do the right thing.* I hope the two of you enjoy the cruise."

"Thanks for the advice, and as for enjoying the cruise, I intend to make sure that we do."

After ending his call with Dominic, Aidan glanced around the cabin. Thanks to Dominic, Aidan had been given the owner's suite. It was spacious with a double balcony. There were also separate sleeping quarters with a king-size bed and a seventy-inch flat-screen television and a second wall-to-wall balcony. The sitting area contained a sofa that could convert into a double bed, another wall television and a dining area that overlooked yet another balcony. Other amenities he appreciated were the refrigerator, wet bar and huge walk-in closet. The bathroom was bigger than the one he had in his apartment, with both a Jacuzzi tub and a walk-in shower. He could just imagine him and Jillian using that shower together.

He walked back out on the balcony to see that people had gathered on the docks to watch the ship sail, waving flags that represented all the countries they would visit on the cruise. He expected Jillian to attend the welcome party tonight and so would he. Aidan couldn't wait to see Jillian's face when she discovered he was on board with her and would be for the next fourteen days.

He headed for the bathroom to shower.

Tonight couldn't get here fast enough.

"Welcome, senorita, may we assist with your mask?"

Jillian lifted a brow. "Mask?"

The tall crewman dressed in a crisp white uniform smiled down at her. "*Si*. Tonight's theme is a Spanish masquerade ball," he said, offering a red feathered mask to her.

She took it and slid it across her face. It was a perfect fit. "Thanks."

"Your name?" he asked.

"Jillian Novak."

"Senorita Novak, dinner will be served in a half hour

in the Madrid Room; someone will come escort you to your table."

"Thanks."

She entered the huge lounge that had beautiful rosettes hanging from the ceiling and several masquerade props in the corners of the room for picture taking. Flamenco dancers encouraged participation in the middle of the floor and several men dressed as dashing bullfighters walked around as servers. When a woman wearing a gorgeous *quinceañera* gown offered her a beautiful lace fan, Jillian smiled and took it.

"Would the senorita like a glass of rioja?"

"Yes, thanks," she responded to one of the servers.

Jillian took a sip and immediately liked the taste. It wasn't too tart or tangy but was an excellent blend of fruits. As she sipped her wine she looked around the room. It was crowded and most of the individuals were coupled off. Immediately, she felt like a loner crashing a party, but forced the feeling away. So what if there were a lot of couples and she had no one? She'd known it would be like this but had made the decision to come anyway.

"Excuse me, senorita, but someone asked me to give you this," the woman wearing the *quinceañera* gown said, while handing her a single red rose.

"Who?" Jillian asked, curiously glancing around.

The woman smiled. "A *very* handsome man." And then she walked off.

Jillian felt uneasy. What kind of *very* handsome man would come cruising alone? She'd seen a movie once where a serial killer had come on a cruise ship and stalked single women. No one had known just how many women he'd killed and thrown overboard until the end of the cruise. For crying out loud, why was she remembering that particular movie now?

She drew in a deep breath knowing she was letting her imagination get the best of her. The man was probably someone who'd seen her alone and wanted to state his interest by giving her a rose. Romantic but a total waste of his time. Even the woman's claim that he was *very* handsome did nothing for Jillian since she wasn't ready to get involved with anyone. Even after a full year, she compared every man to Aidan. That was the main reason she hadn't dated anyone since him. On the other hand, she would bet any amount of money Aidan was dating someone and probably hadn't wasted any time doing so.

She drew in a deep breath, refusing to let her mind go there. Why should she care in the least what Aidan was doing or who he was doing it with? Deciding not to think of an answer for that one, she glanced around the room, curiosity getting the best of her. She tried to find any single men but all she saw were the bullfighters serving drinks.

Jillian glanced at her watch. She'd deliberately arrived a little late so she wouldn't have long to wait for dinner. She'd grabbed breakfast on the run to catch her plane and because she'd come straight from the Barcelona airport to the ship, she had missed lunch altogether.

After taking another sip of her wine, she was about to check her watch again when suddenly her skin heated. Was that desire floating in her stomach. Why? And for who? This was definitely odd.

Jillian searched the room in earnest as a quiver inched up her spine. Declining a server's offer of another drink, she nearly dismissed what was happening as a figment of her imagination when she saw him. A man wearing a teal feathered mask stood alone on the other side of the room, watching her. So she watched back, letting her gaze roam over him. Was he the one who'd given her the rose? Who was he? Why was she reacting to him this way?

As she studied him she found him oddly familiar. Was she comparing the man to Aidan to the point where everything about him reminded her of her ex? His height? His build? The low cut of his hair?

She shook her head. She was losing it. She needed another drink after all. That's when the man began walking toward her. She wasn't going crazy. She didn't know the when, how or why of it, but there was no doubt in her mind that the man walking toward her—mask or no mask—was Aidan. No other man had a walk like he did. And those broad shoulders…

He was sex appeal on legs and he walked the part. It was a stroll of self-confidence and sinful eroticism. How could he have this effect on her after a full year? She drew in a deep breath. That's not the question she should be asking. What she wanted to know was why he was on the same cruise with her? She refused to believe it was a coincidence.

Her spine stiffened when he came to a stop in front of her. Her nostrils had picked up his scent from five feet away and now her entire body was responding. Sharp, crackling energy stirred to life between them. And from the look in his eyes he felt it, as well. Hot. Raw. Primal.

She didn't want it. Nor did she need that sort of sexual attraction to him again. She blew out a frustrated breath. "Aidan, what are you doing here?"

* * *

Aidan wasn't surprised that she had recognized him with the mask on. After all, they'd shared a bed for three solid years so she should know him inside out, clothes or not…just like he knew her. Case in point, he knew exactly what she was wearing beneath that clingy black dress. As little as possible, which meant only a bra and thong. And more than likely both were made of lace. She had the figure to handle just about anything she put on— or nothing at all. Frankly, he preferred nothing at all.

"I asked you what you're doing here."

He noted her voice had tightened in anger and he figured it best to answer. "I've always wanted to take a Mediterranean cruise."

She rolled her eyes. "And you want me to believe you being here is a coincidence? That you had no idea I was here on this cruise ship?"

"That's not what I'm saying."

"Then what *are* you saying, Aidan?"

He placed his half-empty wineglass on the tray of a passing waiter, just in case Jillian was tempted to douse him with it. "I'll tell you after dinner."

"After dinner? No, you will tell me *now*."

Her voice had risen and several people glanced over at them. "I think we need to step outside to finish our discussion."

She frowned. "I think not. You can tell me what I want to know right here."

In anger, she walked into the scant space separating them and leaned in close, her lips almost brushing his. That was too close. His bottom lip tingled and his heart beat like crazy when he remembered her taste. A taste he'd become addicted to. A taste he'd gone a year without.

"I wouldn't bring my mouth any closer if I were you," he warned in a rough whisper.

She blinked as if realizing how close they were. Heeding his warning, she quickly took a step back. "I still want answers, Aidan. What are you doing here?"

He decided to be totally honest with her. Give her the naked truth and let her deal with it. "I came on this cruise, Jillian, with the full intention of winning you back."

Eleven

Jillian stared at Aidan as his words sank in. That's when she decided it would be best for them to take this discussion to a more private area after all. She removed her mask. "I think we need to step outside the room, Aidan."

When they stepped into a vacant hallway, she turned to him. "How dare you assume all you had to do was follow me on this cruise to win me back?"

He pulled off his mask and she fought back a jolt of desire when she looked into his face. How could any man get more handsome in a year's time? Yes, she'd seen him a couple of times since their break-up, but she had avoided getting this close to him. He appeared to have gotten an inch or so taller, his frame was even more muscular and his looks were twice as gorgeous.

"I have given it some thought," he said, leaning back against a railing.

"Evidently, not enough," she countered, not liking how her gaze, with a mind of its own, was traveling over him. He was wearing a dark suit, and he looked like a male model getting ready for a photo shoot—immaculate with nothing out of place.

"Evidently, you've forgotten one major thing about me," she said.

"What? Just how stubborn you are?" he asked, smiling, as if trying to make light of her anger, which irritated her even more.

"That, too, but also that once I make up my mind about something, that's it. And I made up my mind that my life can sail a lot more calmly without you." She watched his expression to see if her words had any effect, but she couldn't tell if they had.

He studied her in silence before saying, "Sorry you feel that way, Jillian. But I intend to prove you wrong."

She lifted a brow. "Excuse me?"

"Over the next fourteen days I intend to prove that your life can't sail more calmly without me. In fact, I intend to show you that you don't even like calm. You need turbulence, furor and even a little mayhem."

She shook her head. "If you believe that then you truly don't know me at all."

"I know you. I also know the real reason you broke things off with me. Why didn't you tell me what you *thought* you saw in my apartment the night of my birthday party?"

She wondered how he'd found out about that. It really didn't matter at this point. "It's not what I *thought* I saw, Aidan. It's what I saw. A woman giving you a lap dance, which you seemed to enjoy, before she began stripping off her clothes." Saying it made the memory flash in her mind and roused her anger that much more.

"She was a paid entertainer, Jillian. All the ladies there that night were. Several of my frat brothers thought I'd been living a boring and dull life and decided to add some excitement into it. I admit they might have gone a little overboard."

"And you enjoyed every minute of it."

He shrugged. "I had a few drinks and—"

"You don't know what all you did, do you?"

He frowned. "I remember fine. Other than the lap dance and her strip act…and a couple other women stripping…nothing else happened."

"Wasn't that enough?" she asked, irritated that he thought several naked women on display in his apartment were of little significance. "And why didn't you tell me about the party? You led me to believe you'd done just as you said you were going to do—watch TV and go to bed."

He released a deep breath. "Okay, I admit I should have told you and I was wrong for not doing so. But I was angry with you. It was my birthday and I wanted to spend it with you. I felt you could have sacrificed a little that weekend to be with me. I hadn't known you changed your mind and flew to Portland."

He paused a moment and then continued, "I realized after we'd broken up just how unpleasant my attitude had been and I do apologize for that. I was getting frustrated with the secrecy surrounding our affair, with my work and how little time I could get off to fly to New Orleans to spend with you."

As far as Jillian was concerned, his attitude had been more than unpleasant; it had become downright unacceptable. He wasn't the only one who'd been frustrated with their situation. She had, too, which was the reason she had decided to confess all to Pam.

"Now that you're finished with medical school, there's no reason to keep our secret any longer anyway," he said, interrupting her thoughts.

She frowned. "And I see no reason to reveal it. Ever," she said. "Especially in light of one very important fact."

"And what fact is that?"

"The fact that we aren't together and we won't ever be together again."

If she figured that then she was wrong.

They *would* be together again. He was counting on it. It was the reason he'd come on the cruise. The one thing she had not said was that she no longer loved him. And as long as she had feelings for him then he could accomplish anything. At this point, even if she claimed she didn't love him, he would have to prove her wrong because he believed she loved him just as much as he loved her. Their relationship was just going through a few hiccups, which he felt they could resolve.

"If you truly believe that then you have nothing to worry about," he said.

She frowned. "Meaning what?"

"Meaning my presence on this ship shouldn't bother you."

She lifted her chin. "It won't unless you become a nuisance."

A smile spread across his face. "Nuisance? I think not. But I do intend to win you back, like I said. Then we can move on with our lives. I see marriage and babies in our future."

She laughed. "You've got to be kidding. Didn't you hear what I said? We won't be getting back together, so we don't have a future."

"And you're willing to throw away the last three years?"

"What I've done is make it easy for you."

He lifted a brow. "To do what?"

"Go back to your womanizing ways. You seemed to

be enjoying yourself so much at your birthday party I wouldn't think of denying you the opportunity."

He crossed his arms over his chest. "I gave up my so-called womanizing ways when I fell in love with you."

"Could have fooled me with your lap dancer and all those strippers waiting their turn."

"Like I said, I didn't invite them."

"But you could have asked them to leave."

He shrugged. "Yes, I could have. But you're going to have to learn to trust me, Jillian. I can see where my attitude leading up to that night might have been less than desirable, but at no time have I betrayed you with another woman. Do you intend to punish me forever for one night of a little fun?"

"I'm not punishing you, Aidan. I'm not doing anything to you. I didn't invite you on this cruise. You took it upon yourself to…"

Her words trailed off and she gazed at him suspiciously before saying, "Paige and I were supposed to go on this cruise together and she had to back out when she had a conflict, which is why I came alone. Please tell me you had nothing to do with that."

He'd known she would eventually figure things out but he had hoped it wouldn't be this soon. "Okay, I won't tell you."

She was back in his face again. "You told Paige about us? Now she knows I was duped by a womanizer."

Her lips were mere inches from his again. Evidently, she'd forgotten his earlier warning. "I am not a womanizer, and I didn't tell her anything about us. She figured things out on her own. Ivy told Paige about the lap dance and Paige told me. And I appreciate her doing so."

From Jill's expression he could tell that although he

might appreciate it, she didn't. "I am so upset with you, right now, Aidan. You are—"

Suddenly he pulled her into his arms. "You were warned."

Then he captured her mouth with his.

Push him away. Push him away. Push him away, a voice inside of Jillian's head chanted.

But her body would not obey. Instead of pushing him away, she leaned in closer, wrapping her arms around his neck.

Had it been a year since she had enjoyed this? A year since she'd had the taste of his tongue inside her mouth? Doing all those crazy things in every nook and cranny? Making liquid heat she'd held at bay shoot straight to the area between her legs?

How could any woman deal with a master kisser like him? She would admit that during the past year she had gone to bed dreaming of this but the real thing surpassed any dream she'd ever had.

The sound of voices made them pull apart. She drew in a deep breath, turning her back to him so she could lick her lips without him seeing her do so. That had been one hell of a kiss. Her lips were still electrified.

She turned back around and caught him tracing his tongue across his own lips. Her stomach clenched. "I think you have it all wrong, Aidan," she managed to say.

"After that kiss, I'd say I got it all right."

"Think whatever you like," she said, walking away.

"Hey, where're you going? The Madrid Room is this way."

She stopped and turned. "I'll order room service."

Jillian continued walking, feeling the heat of his gaze on her back.

Aidan watched her walk away, appreciating the sway of her hips. He drew in a deep breath. He loved the woman. If there was any doubt in her mind of that— which there seemed to be—he would wipe it out.

Turning, he headed toward his own cabin, thinking room service sounded pretty good. Besides, he had shocked Jillian's senses enough for today. Tomorrow he planned to lay it on even thicker. She had warned him not to be a nuisance. He smiled at the thought. He wouldn't be a nuisance, just totally effective.

Tonight they had talked, although he seemed to annoy her and he'd found her somewhat infuriating. But at least they knew where they both stood. She knew he was aware of the real reason she'd ended things between them. He had to convince her that his life as a woman-izer was definitely behind him, that he had no desire to return to that life again.

He would admit getting rid of the lap dancer that night hadn't been easy. Somehow she'd figured it would be okay to hang around after the party was over. She'd been quick to let him know there wouldn't be an over-time charge. He had countered, letting her know he wasn't interested.

When Aidan reached his suite, he saw the elephant made of hand towels on his bed. Cute. But not as cute as the woman he intended to have back in his arms.

Jillian checked the time as she made a call to Paige. It was around ten in the morning in L.A., so there was no reason her sister shouldn't answer the phone. Paige was definitely going to get an earful from her.

"Why are you calling me? Aren't rates higher on the high seas?" Paige asked, answering on the fourth ring.

Jillian frowned. "Don't worry about the cost of the rates. Why didn't you tell me you knew about me and Aidan?"

"Why hadn't you told *me* so I wouldn't have to tell you? And don't say because it was supposed to be a secret."

"Well, it was. How did you figure it out?"

"Wasn't hard to do. Both of you started getting sloppy with it. Aidan slipped and called you Jilly a couple of times, and I caught you almost drooling whenever he walked into the room."

"I did not."

"You did, too. Besides, I knew you had a crush on him that first time we met the Westmoreland family at Pam's engagement party. You kept me up all night asking, 'Isn't Aidan cute, Paige? Isn't he cute?'"

Jillian smiled as she remembered. She had been so taken with Aidan. Although he and Adrian were identical twins it had been Aidan who pushed her buttons. "Well, no thanks to you he's here and he wants me back."

"Do you want him to get you back?"

"No. You didn't see that lap dance. I did."

"Didn't have to see it because I've seen one before. I know they can get rather raunchy. But it was a birthday party. His. Thrown by his friends and the lap dancer and the strippers were entertainment."

"Some entertainment," she mumbled. "He enjoyed it. You should have seen the look on his face when the woman shoved her girls at him."

"Pleeze. He's a man. They enjoy seeing a pair of

breasts. Anytime or anyplace. Will it make you feel better if I get the Chippendales dancers for your next birthday party?"

"This isn't funny, Paige."

"You don't hear me laughing. If anything, you should hear me moaning. Can you imagine a lap dance from one of those guys? If you can't, I can. And my imagination is running pretty wild right now."

Jillian shook her head. "Before I let you go, there's one more thing. Did you really get a part in a Spielberg movie?"

"No."

"So you lied."

"I was acting, and I evidently did a great job. It sounds like you have some serious decisions to make about Aidan. But don't rush. You have fourteen days. In the meantime, enjoy the cruise. Enjoy life. Enjoy Aidan. He plans on getting you back. I'd like to be there to watch him try. I've got my money on him, by the way."

"Sounds like you have money to lose. Goodbye, Paige." Jillian clicked off the phone, refusing to let her sister get in the last word, especially if it would be a word she really didn't want to hear.

Regardless of what Paige said, her sister hadn't been there to witness that lap dance. She hadn't seen that salacious grin on Aidan's face while looking up at the half-naked woman sprawled all over him. There was no doubt in Jillian's mind that he'd enjoyed every minute of it. He had wanted those women there; otherwise, he would have asked them and his friends to leave. And although he claimed otherwise, how could she be certain one of those women didn't spend the night with him; especially since he didn't tell Jillian anything about the party, even when she had asked? She of all people knew what a healthy sexual appetite Aidan had, and they hadn't seen each other in more than three months. And at the time, that had been the longest amount of time they'd been apart.

Before getting in bed later that night, Jillian checked the ship's agenda. Tomorrow was a full day at sea and she refused to stay locked in her cabin. This was a big ship and chances were she might not run into Aidan. She knew the odds of that were slim; especially when he admitted his only reason for coming on the cruise was to win her back. Well, he could certainly try.

She could not deny it had felt good to be kissed by him tonight. Pretty damn good. But there was more to any relationship than kisses. Even the hot, raw, carnal kind that Aidan gave. And when he took a mind to kiss her all over…

She drew in a deep breath, refusing to let her thoughts go there. He would probably try using his sexual wiles to win her back. And she intended to be ready to disappoint him.

Twelve

"Good morning, Jillian."

Jillian glanced up from the book she was reading to watch Aidan slide onto the lounger beside her. She was on the upper deck near the pool. Why had she thought he would never find her here?

"Good morning," she grumbled and went back to her reading. Although she had gone to bed fairly early, she hadn't gotten a good night's sleep. The man stretched on the lounger beside her had invaded her dreams not once or twice, but all through the night.

"Had breakfast yet?"

She glanced away from her book to look over at him. "Yes." She remembered the pancakes and syrup she'd enjoyed. "It was tasty."

"Um, bet it wasn't tasty as you. Want to go back to my cabin and be my breakfast?"

His question caused a spark of heat to settle between her thighs. Something she definitely didn't need after all those erotic dreams she'd had. "You shouldn't say something like that to me."

"You prefer I say it to someone else?"

She narrowed her gaze. "Do whatever you want. At breakfast I happened to notice a group of women on the cruise. All appeared single. I think I overheard one say they're part of some book club."

"You want me to go check out other women?"

"Won't matter to me. Need I remind you that we aren't together?"

"And need I remind you that I'm working on that? And by the way, I have a proposition for you."

"Whatever it is, the answer is no."

He chuckled. "You haven't heard it."

"Doesn't matter."

"You certain?"

"Positive."

He smiled over at her. "Okay then. I'm glad. In fact, you've made my day by not accepting it. I'm happy that you turned it down."

She stared over at him and frowned. "Really? And just what was this proposition?"

In a warm, teasing tone, he said. "I thought you didn't want to hear it."

"I've changed my mind."

He nodded. "I guess I can allow you to do that." He shifted and sat up. She tried not to notice the khaki shorts he wore and how well they fit the lower half of his body. Or how his muscle shirt covered perfect abs.

He took her hand, easing her into the same sitting position he was in, as if what he had to say was something he didn't want others around them to overhear.

"Well?" she asked, trying to ignore the tingling sensation in the hand he touched.

"You're aware the only reason I came on this cruise was to get you back, right?"

She shrugged. "So you say."

A smile touched the corners of his lips. "Well, I

thought about a few of the things you said last night and I wanted to offer you a chance to make some decisions."

She lifted a brow. "Like what?"

"Like whether or not I should even pursue you at all. I don't want to be that nuisance you insinuated I could be. So my proposition was that I just leave you alone and wait patiently for you to come to me. I hope you know what that means since you just turned it down."

She would not have turned it down had she heard him out, and he knew it. Unfortunately, she could guess what the consequences would be and she had a feeling she wasn't going to like it. "What does that mean, Aidan?"

He leaned in closer to whisper in her ear. His warm breath felt like a soft, sensuous lick across her skin. "I want you so bad, Jillian, that I ache. And that means I'm not giving up until you're back in my bed."

She immediately felt a pounding pulse at the tips of her breasts. She leaned back to stare at him and the razor-sharp sensuality openly displayed in his gaze almost made her moan.

"And before you ask, Jillian, the answer is no. It isn't just about sex with me," he murmured in a low, husky tone. "It's about me wanting the woman I love both mentally and physically. You're constantly in my mind but physically, it's been over a year."

She drew in a deep breath and felt the essence of what he'd said in every single nerve ending in her body. It had been over a year. With Aidan she'd had a pretty active sex life, and although there were periods of time when they were apart, they always made up for any time lost whenever they were together.

"Your needing sex is not my problem," she finally said.

"Isn't it?" he countered. "Can you look me in the eyes

and say that you don't want me as much as I want you? That you didn't dream about us making love last night? Me being inside you. You riding me? Hard. My tongue inside your mouth…and inside a lot of other places on your body?"

She silently stared at him but her entire body flared in response to the vivid pictures he'd painted in her mind. Unlike Paige, Jillian wasn't an actress and couldn't lie worth a damn. But on that same note she would never admit anything to him. That would give him too much power. "I won't admit to anything, Aidan."

"You don't have to," he said, with a serious smile on his face. "And it's not about me needing sex but me needing you." He paused a moment as if giving his words time to sink in. "But this leads to another proposition I'd like to make."

She'd set herself up for this one. "And what is the proposition this time?"

He leaned in closer. "That for the remainder of the cruise you let your guard down. Believe in me. Believe in yourself. And believe in us. I want you to see I'm still the man who loves you. The man who will always love you. But that's something you have to believe, Jillian. However, at the end of the cruise, if for whatever reason, you still don't believe it or feel that the two of us can make a lifetime commitment, then when we dock back in Barcelona, we'll agree to go our separate ways."

She broke eye contact with him to glance out at the ocean. Today was a rather calm day outside but inside she was in a state of turmoil. He was asking a lot of her and he knew it. His proposition meant forgetting the very reason she broke up with him. That would definitely be easy on him if she did. Was that why he'd come up with this latest proposition?

Jillian turned her gaze back to him. "You want me to just forget everything that's happened, Aidan? Especially the incident that caused our breakup?"

"No, I don't want you to forget a single thing."

His answer surprised her. "Why?"

"Because it's important that the two of us learn from any mistakes we've made, and we can't do that if we safely tuck them away just because doing so will be convenient. We should talk about them openly and honestly. Hopefully, we'll be able to build something positive out of the discussions. You're always harping a lot on the things I did. What about you, Jillian? Do you think you were completely blameless?"

"No, but—"

"I don't want to get into all that now, but have you ever noticed that with you there's always a *but* in there somewhere?"

She frowned at him. "No, I never noticed but obviously you have." Was it really that way with her? As far as sharing the blame, she could do that. But she hadn't been the one getting a lap dance.

"My proposition is still on the table," he said. "I've been completely honest with you on this cruise, Jillian. I've been up-front with my intentions, my wants and my desires."

Yes, he had. Every opportunity he got. And she knew that he would have her on her back in a flash if she were to let him. Jillian inclined her head to look deeper into his eyes. "And you promise that at the end of the cruise if things don't work out the way we think they should that you will go your way and I'll go mine?"

He nodded slowly. "It would be difficult, but yes. I want you to be happy and if being happy for you means not having me in your life then that's the way it will be. It will be your decision and I would like to have that decision the night before we return to Barcelona."

She digested what Aidan said. He'd laid things out, with no fluff. She knew what, and who, she would be dealing with. But she also knew that even if she decided she didn't want him in her life romantically, he could never be fully out of it; their families were connected. How could they manage that?

"What about the family?" she asked. "Paige, Stern and Adrian know our secret. If things don't work out between us it might have an effect on them."

"We will deal with that if it happens. Together. Even if we're no longer lovers, there's no reason we can't remain friends. Besides, are you sure there aren't others in the family besides those three who know? It's my guess others might suspect something even if they haven't said anything."

She shrugged. "Doesn't matter who knows now. I had planned on telling Pam anyway."

Surprise flashed in his eyes. "You had?"

"Yes."

"When?"

"After I talked to you about it, which I had planned to do when I flew into Portland for your birthday."

"Oh."

She released a sigh. Evidently the one thing he hadn't found out was that she'd intended to release him from their secret. "Afterward, when things didn't work out between us, I saw no need for me to tell Pam anything.

In fact, I felt the less she knew about the situation, the better."

Aidan didn't say anything for a moment and neither did Jillian. She figured he was thinking how that one weekend had changed things for them. He finally broke the silence by asking, "So, what's your answer to my proposition?"

Jillian nibbled at her bottom lip. Why couldn't she just turn him down, walk away and keep walking? She knew one of the reasons was that her mind was filled with fond memories of the good times they'd shared. It hadn't been all bad.

Would it be so dreadful if she were to give his proposition a try? What did she have to lose? She'd already experienced heartbreak with him. And a year of separation hadn't been easy. Besides, she couldn't deny that it would feel good to be with him out in the open, without any kind of secrecy shrouding them. Whenever he'd come to Laramie, she'd always been on guard, looking over her shoulder in case she ran into someone who knew Pam. And he did have a good point about the remaining days on the cruise testing the strength of a relationship between them.

She met his gaze. "Yes. I accept your proposition and I will hold you to your word, Aidan."

Later that night, as Aidan changed for dinner, he couldn't help remembering Jillian's words.

"Fine, baby, hold me to my word," he murmured to himself as he tucked his white dress shirt into his pants. "That's the way it should be. And that's the way it will be."

Today had gone just the way he'd wanted. After she'd

agreed to his proposition he'd been able to talk her into going with him to the Terelle Deck so he could grab breakfast. She'd sat across from him while he ate a hefty portion of the pancakes and syrup she'd recommended. They had chosen a table with a beautiful view of the ocean, and he liked the way the cool morning breeze stirred her hair. More than once he'd been tempted to reach across the table and run his fingers through it.

After breakfast he had talked her into joining him in the Venus Lounge where a massive bingo game was under way. They had found a table in the back and she'd worked five bingo cards while he worked three. In the end, neither of them had won anything but the game had been fun.

Later they had gone to the art gallery to check out the paintings on display and after that they'd enjoyed a delicious lunch in the Coppeneria Room. After she mentioned her plans to visit the spa, he'd taken a stroll around the ship. The layout was awesome and the entire ship was gorgeous. Tomorrow morning before daybreak they would arrive in Monte Carlo, France, and from there, Florence, Italy. He'd never been to France or Italy before but Adrian had, and according to his twin both countries were beautiful. Aidan couldn't wait to see them for himself.

He smiled as he put on his cuff links. Being around Jillian today had reminded him of how much she liked having her way. In the past he had indulged her. But not this time. While on this cruise he had no intention of letting her have her way. In fact, he planned to teach her the art of compromising. That was the main reason he had suggested she drop by his cabin to grab him for dinner instead of the other way around. Although she hadn't said anything, he could tell she hadn't liked the idea.

He turned from the mirror at the sound of a knock on his door. She was a little early but he had no problem with that. Moving across the suite, he opened the door, and then stood there, finding it impossible to speak. All he could do was stare at Jillian. Dressed in a red floor-length gown that hugged every curve, her hair wrapped on top of her head with a few curls dangling toward her beautiful face, she looked breathtaking. His gaze scanned the length of her—head to toe.

Pulling himself together, he stepped aside. "Come in. You look very nice."

"Thank you," she said, entering his suite. "I'm a little early. The cabin steward arrived and I didn't want to get in his way."

"No problem. I just need to put on my tie."

"This suite is fantastic. I thought my suite was large but this one is triple mine in size."

He smiled over at her. "It's the owner's personal suite whenever he cruises."

"Really? And how did you get so lucky?"

"He's a friend. You remember my cousin Quade who lives in North Carolina, right?"

"The one who has the triplets?"

"Yes, he's the one. Quade and the ship's owner, Dominic Saxon, are brothers-in-law, married to sisters—the former Steeles, Cheyenne and Taylor.

Jillian nodded. "I remember meeting Cheyenne at Dillon and Pam's wedding. The triplets were adorable. I don't recall ever meeting Taylor."

"I'll make sure you meet Taylor and Dominic if you ever come to visit me in Charlotte." He'd deliberately chosen his words to make sure she understood that if a meeting took place, it would be her decision.

After putting on his tie, he turned to her, trying not to stare again. "I'm all set. Ready?"

"Whenever you are."

He was tempted to kiss her but held back. Knowing him like she did, she would probably expect such a move. But tonight he planned to keep her on her toes. In other words, he would be full of surprises.

"Hi, Aidan!"

Jillian figured it would be one of those nights when the group of women sharing their table chorused the greeting to Aidan. It was the book-club group. She should have known they would find him. Or, for all she knew, he'd found them.

"I take it you've met them," she whispered when he pulled out her chair.

"Yes, earlier today, while taking my stroll when you were at the spa."

"Evening, ladies. How's everyone doing?" Aidan asked the group with familiarity, taking his seat.

"Fine," they responded simultaneously. Jillian noticed some were smiling so hard it made her wonder how anyone's lips could stretch that wide.

"I want you all to meet someone," Aidan was saying. "This is Jillian Novak. My significant other."

"Oh."

Was that disappointment she heard in the voices of the six women? And what happened to those huge smiles? Well, she would just have to show them how it was done. She smiled brightly and then said, "Hello, everyone."

Only a few returned her greeting, but she didn't care because she was reflecting on Aidan's introduction.

My significant other.

Before their breakup they had been together for three years and this was the first time he'd introduced her to anyone because of their secret. It made her realize that, other than Ivy, she'd never introduced him to anyone, either.

The waiter came to take their order but not before giving them a run-down of all the delectable meals on the menu tonight. Jillian chose a seafood dinner and Aidan selected steak.

She discreetly checked out the six women engaging in conversation with Aidan. All beautiful. Gorgeously dressed. Articulate. Professional. Single.

"So, how long have the two of you been together?" asked one of the women who'd introduced herself earlier as Wanda.

Since it appeared the woman had directed the question to Aidan, Jillian let him answer. "Four years," he said, spreading butter on his bread. Jillian decided not to remind him that one of those years they hadn't been together.

"Four years? Really?" a woman by the name of Sandra asked, extending her lips into what Jillian could tell was a plastered-on smile.

"Yes, *really*," Jillian responded, knowing just what the chick was getting at. After four years Jillian should have a ring on her finger. In other words, she should be a wife and not a significant other.

"Then I guess the two of you will probably be tying the knot pretty soon." It was obvious Wanda was dig-

ging for information. The others' ears were perked up
as if they, too, couldn't wait to hear the response.

Jillian tried not to show her surprise when Aidan
reached across the table and placed his hand over hers.
"Sooner rather than later, if I had my way. But I'll be
joining the Cardiology Department at Johns Hopkins in
the fall, and Jillian's just finished medical school, so we
haven't set dates yet."

"You're both doctors?" Sandra asked, smiling.

"Yes," both Aidan and Jillian answered at the same
time.

"That's great. So are we," Sandra said, pointing to
herself and the others. "Faye and Sherri and I just finished Meharry Medical School a couple of months ago,
and Wanda, Joy and Virginia just completed pharmacy
school at Florida A&M."

"Congratulations, everyone," Jillian said, giving all
six women a genuine smile. After having completed
medical school she knew the hard work and dedication
that was required for any medical field. And the six had
definitely attended excellent schools.

"And congratulations to you, too," the women said
simultaneously.

Jillian's smile widened. "Thanks."

Aidan glanced down at the woman walking beside
him as they left the jazz lounge where several musicians
had performed. Jillian had been pretty quiet since dinner. He couldn't help wondering what she was thinking.

"Did you enjoy dinner?" he asked.

She glanced up at him. "Yes, what about you?"

He shrugged. "It was nice."

"Just nice? You were the only male seated at a table

with several females, all gorgeous, so how was it just nice?"

"Because it was," he said, wondering if this conversation would start a discussion he'd rather not have with her. But then, maybe they should have it now. They *had* agreed to talk things out. "So what did you think of the ladies at our table tonight?"

She stopped walking to lean against a rail and look at him. "Maybe I should be asking what you thought of them."

He joined her at the rail, standing a scant foot in front of her. "Pretty. All seven of them. But the prettiest of them all was the one wearing the red dress. The one named Jillian Novak. Now, she was a total knockout. She put the *s* in sexy."

Jillian smiled and shook her head, sending those dangling curls swinging. "Laying it on rather thick, aren't you, Aidan?"

"Not as long as you get the picture."

"And what picture is that?"

"That you're the only woman I want. The only one who can get blood rushing through my veins."

She chuckled. "Sounds serious, Dr. Westmoreland."

"It is." He didn't say anything for a minute as he stared at her. "Do you realize that this is the first time you've ever referred to me as Dr. Westmoreland?"

She nodded. "Yes, I know. Just like I realized tonight at dinner that it was the first time you'd ever introduced me during the time we were together."

"Yes. There were times when I wished I could have."

But you couldn't, she thought. *Because of the secret I made you keep.*

"But I did tonight."

"Yes, you did fib a little. Twice in fact," she pointed out.

He lifted a brow. "When?"

"When you said I was your significant other."

"I didn't fib. You are. There's no one more significant in my life than you," he said softly.

Jillian couldn't say anything after that. How could she? And when the silence between them lengthened, she wondered if he was expecting her to respond. What *could* she say? That she believed him? Did she really?

"And what was the other?" he asked, finally breaking the silence.

"What other?" she asked him.

"Fib. You said there were two."

"Oh. The one about the amount of time we've been together. You said four years and it was three," she said as they began walking again.

"No, it was four. Although we spent a year apart it meant nothing to me, other than frustration and anger. Nevertheless, you were still here," he said, touching his heart. "During every waking moment and in all my dreams."

She glanced away from him as they continued walking only to glance back moments later. "That sounds unfair to the others."

"What others?"

"Any woman you dated that year."

He stopped walking, took her hand and pulled her to the side, back over to the rail. He frowned down at her. "What are you talking about? I didn't date any women last year."

She searched his face and somehow saw the truth

in his words. "But why? I thought you would. Figured you had."

"Why?" Before she could respond he went on in a mocking tone, "Ah, that's right. Because I'm a womanizer."

Jillian heard the anger in his voice, but yes, that was the reason she'd thought he'd dated. Wasn't that the reason she had ended things between them as well, so he would have the freedom to return to his old ways? She drew in a deep breath. "Aidan, I—"

"No, don't say it." He stiffened his chin. "Whatever it is you're going to say, Jillian, don't." He glanced down at his watch and then his gaze moved back to her face. "I know you prefer turning in early, so I'll see you back to your cabin. I think I'll hang out a while in one of the bars."

She didn't say anything for a moment. "Want some company?"

"No," he said softly. "Not right now."

Suddenly, she felt a deep ache in her chest. "Okay. Don't worry about seeing me to my cabin. You can go on."

"You sure?"

She forced a smile. "Yes, I'm sure. I know the way."

"All right. I'll come get you for breakfast around eight."

If you can still stand my company, she thought. "Okay. I'll see you in the morning at eight."

He nodded and, with the hurt she'd brought on herself eating away at her, she watched Aidan walk away.

Thirteen

Aidan forced his eyes open when he heard banging coming from the sitting area.

"What the hell?" He closed his eyes as sharp pain slammed through his head. It was then that he remembered last night. Every single detail.

He had stopped at the bar, noticed it was extremely crowded and had gone to his room instead. He'd ordered room service, a bottle of his favorite Scotch. He'd sat on the balcony, looking out over the ocean beneath the night sky and drinking alone, nursing a bruised heart. He didn't finish off the entire bottle but he'd downed enough to give him the mother of all headaches this morning. What time was it anyway?

He forced his eyes back open to look at the clock on the nightstand. Ten? It was ten in the morning? Crap! He'd promised Jillian to take her to breakfast at eight. He could only imagine what she'd thought when he was a no-show. Pulling himself up on the side of the bed he drew in a deep breath. Honestly, did he care anymore? She had him pegged as a player in that untrusting mind of hers, so what did the truth matter?

"Mr. Aidan," called the cabin steward, "do you want me to clean your bedroom now or come back later?"

"Come back later, Rowan."

When Aidan heard the door close, he dropped back in bed. He knew he should call Jillian, but chances were she'd gotten tired of waiting around and had gone to breakfast without him. He could imagine her sitting there eating pancakes while all kinds of insane ideas flowed through her head. All about him. Hell, he might as well get up, get dressed and search the ship for her to put those crazy ideas to rest.

He was about to get out of bed when he heard a knock at the door. He figured it was probably the guy coming around to pick up laundry, so he slipped into his pajama bottoms to tell the person to come back later.

He snatched open the door but instead of the laundry guy, Jillian stood there carrying a tray of food. "Jillian? What are you doing here?"

She stared at him for a moment. "You look like crap."

"I feel like crap," he muttered, moving aside to let her in. She placed the tray on his dining table. His head still pounded somewhat, but not as hard as the way his erection throbbed while staring at her. She was wearing a cute and sexy shorts set that showed what a gorgeous pair of legs she had. And her hair, which had been pinned atop her head last night, flowed down her shoulders while gold hoop earrings dangled from her ears. Damn, he couldn't handle this much sexiness in the morning.

She turned around. "To answer your question as to why I'm here, you missed breakfast so I thought I'd bring you something to eat."

He closed the door and leaned against it. "And what else?"

She lifted a brow. "And what else?"

"Yes. What other reason do you have for coming here? Let me guess. You figured I brought a woman here last night and you wanted to catch me in the act? Right? Go ahead, Jillian, search my bedroom if you like. The bathroom, too, if that suits your fancy. Oh, and don't forget to check the balconies in case I've hidden her out there until after you leave."

Jillian didn't say anything for a long minute. "I guess I deserved that. But—"

He held his hand to interrupt her. "Please. No buts, Jillian. I'm tired of them coming from you. Let me ask you something. How many men did you sleep with during the year we weren't together since you think I didn't leave a single woman standing?"

She narrowed her gaze at him. "Not a single one."

He crossed his arms over his chest. "Why?"

She lifted a chin. "Because I didn't want to."

"Why didn't you want to? You had broken things off with me and we weren't together. Why didn't you sleep with another man?"

Jillian knew she'd screwed up badly last night and she could hardly wait until morning to see Aidan so she could apologize. When he didn't show up at eight as he'd promised, she would admit that for a quick second she'd thought he might have been mad enough to spend the night with someone else. But all it had taken to erase that thought was for her to remember how he'd looked last night when he told her the reason why he'd introduced her as his significant other.

There's no one more significant in my life than you.
And she believed him. His reason for not sleeping

with another woman during the year they'd been apart was the same reason she hadn't slept with another man.

"Jillian?"

She met his gaze. He wanted an answer and she would give him one. The truth and nothing but the truth.

"Sleeping with another man never crossed my mind, Aidan," she said softly. "Because I still loved you. And no matter what I saw or imagined you did with that lap dancer, I still loved you. My body has your imprint all over it and the thought of another man touching it sickens me."

She paused and then added, "You're wrong. I didn't come here thinking I'd find another woman. I came to apologize. I figured the reason you didn't come take me to breakfast was because you were still mad at me. And after last night I knew that I deserved your anger."

"Why do you think you deserve my anger?"

"Because everything is my fault. You only kept our affair a secret because I asked you to, begged you to. Last night when I got to my room, I sat out on the balcony and thought about everything. I forced myself to see the situation through someone else's eyes other than my own. And you know what I saw, Aidan?"

"No, what did you see, Jillian?"

She fought back tears. "I saw a man who loved me enough to take a lot of crap. I never thought about what all the secrecy would mean. And then the long distance and the sacrifices you made to come see me whenever you could. The money you spent for airplane fare, your time. I wasn't the only one with the goal of becoming a doctor. It's not like you didn't have a life, trying to handle the pressure of your dual residency."

She paused. "And I can just imagine what your

friends thought when all of a sudden you became a saint
for no reason. You couldn't tell them about me, so I can
understand them wanting to help get your life back on
track with those women. That was the Aidan they knew.
And unfortunately that was the Aidan I wanted to think
you missed being. That night I showed up at the party,
I should have realized that you were just having the fun
you deserved. Fun you'd denied yourself since your involvement with me. I should have loved you enough and
trusted you enough to believe that no matter what, you
wouldn't betray me. That I meant more to you than any
lap dancer with silicone boobs."

He uncrossed his arms. "You're right. You do mean
more to me than any lap dancer, stripper, book-club
member or any other woman out there, Jillian," he said
in a soft tone. "And you were wrong to think I missed
my old life. What I miss is being with you. I think we
handled things okay that first year, but during those
second and third years, because of trying to make that
dual residency program work and still keep you at the
top of the list, things became difficult for me. Then in
the third year, I was the one with focusing issues. It became harder and harder to keep our long-distance affair
afloat and stay focused at work. And the secrecy only
added more stress. But I knew if I complained to you
about it, that it would only stress you out and make you
lose focus on what you needed to do.

"You were young when we started our affair. Only
twenty-one. And you hadn't dated much. In all honesty, probably not at all, because I refuse to count that
dude you dated in high school. So deep down I knew
you weren't quite ready for the type of relationship I
wanted. But I loved you and I wanted you and I figured

everything would work out. I knew how challenging medical school could be and I wanted to make your life as calm as possible. I didn't want to be the one to add to your stress."

He paused. "But it looks like I did anyway. I tried to make the best of it, but unfortunately sometimes when we talked, I was in one of my foul moods because of stress. I would get an attitude with you instead of talking to you about it. At no time should I have made you feel that you deserved my anger. I apologize. I regret doing that."

"It's okay," Jillian said, pulling out a chair. "Come sit down and eat. Your food is getting cold."

She watched him move away from the door. When he reached the table, she skirted back so he could sit down. When he sat, he reached out, grabbed her around the waist and brought her down to his lap.

"Aidan! What do you think you're doing?"

He wrapped both arms around her so she wouldn't go anywhere. "What I should have done last night. Brought you back here and put you in my lap, wrapped my arms around you and convinced you that I meant everything I said about your value to me. Instead I got upset and walked away."

She pressed her forehead to his and whispered, "Sorry I made you upset with me last night."

"I love you so much, Jillian, and when I think you don't believe just how much I love you, how much you mean to me, I get frustrated and wonder just what else I have to do. I'm not a perfect man. I'm human. I'm going to make mistakes. We both are. But the one thing I won't do is betray your love with another woman. Those days are over for me. You're all the woman I'll ever need."

She leaned back from him to look in his eyes. "I believe you, Aidan. I won't lie and say I'll never get jealous, but I can say it'll be because I'm questioning the woman's motives, not yours."

And she really meant that. When he hadn't come down for breakfast she had gone into the Terelle Dining Room to eat alone. She ran into the book-club ladies and ended up eating breakfast with them and enjoying herself. Once Aidan had made it clear last night that he was not available, they had put a lid on their man-hunter instincts. Jillian and the six women had a lot in common, since they were all recent medical-school graduates, and they enjoyed sharing their experiences over breakfast. They invited her to join them for shopping at some point during their two days in Rome and she agreed to do that.

She shifted in Aidan's lap to find a more comfortable position.

"I wouldn't do that too many times if I were you," he warned in a husky whisper.

A hot wave of desire washed over her. He was looking at her with those dark, penetrating eyes of eyes. The same ones that could arouse her as no man ever had... or would. "Why not?"

If he was going to give her a warning, she wanted him to explain himself, although she knew what he meant.

"Because if you keep it up, *you* might become my breakfast."

The thought of that happening had the muscles between her legs tightening, and she was aware that every hormone in her body was downright sizzling. "But you like pancakes and syrup," she said innocently.

A smile spread across his lips. "But I like your taste better."

"Do you?" she asked, intentionally shifting again to lean forward so that she could bury her face in the hollow of his throat. He was shirtless and she loved getting close to him, drinking in his scent.

"You did it again."

She leaned back and met his gaze. "Did I?"

"Yes."

She intentionally shifted in his lap when she lowered her head to lick the upper part of his chest. She loved the salty taste of his flesh and loved even more the moan she heard from his lips.

"It's been a year, Jillian. If I get you in my bed today it will be a long time before I let you out."

"And miss touring Monte Carlo? The ship has already docked."

"We have time." He suddenly stood, with her in his arms, and she quickly grabbed him around the neck and held on. He chuckled. "Trust me. I'm not going to let you fall." He headed for the bedroom.

"Now to enjoy breakfast, the Aidan Westmoreland way," he said, easing her down on the bed. He stood back and stared at her for a long moment. "I want you so much I ache. I desire you so much I throb. And I will always love you, even after drawing my last breath."

For the second time that day, she fought back tears. "Oh, Aidan. I want, desire and love you, too. Just as much."

He leaned down and removed her shoes before removing every stitch of her clothing with a skill only he had perfected. When she lay there naked before him, he slid his pj's down his legs. "Lie still for a minute. There's something I want to do," he instructed in a throaty tone.

That's when Jillian saw the bottle of syrup he'd

brought into the bedroom with them. She looked at the bottle and then looked up at him. "You are kidding, right?"

"Do I look like I'm kidding?" he asked, removing the top.

She swallowed. No, he definitely didn't look as if he was kidding. In fact he looked totally serious. Too serious. "But I'm going to be all sticky," she reasoned. All she could think about was how glad she was for the bikini wax she'd gotten at the spa yesterday.

"You won't be sticky for long. I plan to lick it all off you and then we'll shower together."

"Aidan!" She squealed when she felt the thick liquid touch her skin. Aidan made good on his word. He dripped it all over her chest, making sure there was a lot covering her breasts, around her navel and lower still. He laid it on thick between her legs, drenching her womanly core.

And then he used his tongue to drive her insane with pleasure while taking his time to lick off all the syrup. The flick of his tongue sent sensuous shivers down her spine, and all she could do was lie there and moan while encased in a cloud of sensations.

He used his mouth as a bearer of pleasure as he laved her breasts, drawing the nipples between his lips and sucking on the turgid buds with a greed that made her womb contract. She wasn't sure how much more she could take when his mouth lowered to her stomach. She reached down and buried her fingers in his scalp as his mouth traced a hungry path around her navel.

Moments later he lifted his head to stare at her, deliberately licking his lips. They both knew where he was headed next. The look on his face said he wanted her to know he intended to go for the gusto.

And he did.

Jillian screamed his name the moment his tongue entered her, sending shockwaves of a gigantic orgasm through her body. His hot and greedy tongue had desire clawing at her insides, heightening her pulse. And when she felt another orgasm coming on the heels of the first, she knew it was time she took control. Otherwise, Aidan would lick her crazy.

With all the strength she could muster she tried to shift their bodies, which was hard to do since his mouth was on her while his hands held tight to her hips. When she saw there was no way she could make Aidan budge until he got his fill, she gave in to another scream when a second orgasm hit.

He finally lifted his head, smiled at her while licking his lips and then eased his body over hers. "I told you I was going to lick it all off you, baby."

Yes, he had. Then his engorged erection slid inside of her. All she recalled after that was her brain taking a holiday as passion overtook her, driving her over the edge, bringing her back, then driving her to the edge again.

He thrust hard, all the way to the hilt and then some. He lifted her hips and set the pace. The bed springs were tested to their maximum and so was she. She released a deep moan when he pounded into her, making her use muscles she hadn't used in a year. And then he slowed and without disconnecting their bodies, eased to his knees. He lifted her legs all the way to his shoulders and continued thrusting.

"Aidan!"

He answered with a deep growl when the same explosion that tore through her ripped through him, as well. She could feel his hot, molten liquid rush through her body, bathing her womb. But he didn't stop. He kept going, enlarging inside her all over again.

She saw arousal coiling in the depth of his eyes. They were in it for the long haul, right now and forever. And when his wet, slick body finally eased down, he pulled her into his arms, wrapped the strength of his legs over hers and held her close. She breathed in his scent. This was where she wanted to be. Always.

Hours later, Jillian stirred in Aidan's arms and eased over to whisper in his ear. "Remind me never to let you go without me for a full year again."

He grinned as he opened his eyes. "One year, two months and four days. But I wasn't counting or anything, mind you."

She smiled. "I'll take your word for it." She eased up to glance over at the clock. Had they been in bed five hours already? "We need to shower."

"Again?"

She laughed out. "The last time doesn't count."

"Why?"

She playfully glared over at him. "You know why."

He'd taken her into the shower to wash off any lingering stickiness from the syrup. Instead he ended up making love to her again. Then he'd dried them both off and had taken her to the bed and made love to her again several times, before they'd both drifted off to sleep.

"I guess we do need to get up, shower and dress if we want to see any of Monte Carlo."

"Yes, and I want to see Monte Carlo."

"I want to see you," he said, easing back and raking

his gaze over her naked body. "Do you know how much I missed this? Missed you?"

"The same way I missed you?"

"More," he said, running his hand over her body.

She couldn't ignore the delicious heat of the fingers touching her. "I doubt that, Dr. Westmoreland."

"Trust me."

She did trust him. And she loved him so much she wanted everyone to know it. "I can't wait until we return to Denver for Adrian's wedding."

He looked down at her. "Why?"

"So we can tell Pam and Dillon."

He studied her expression. "Are you ready for that?"

"More than ready. Do you think they already know?"

"It wouldn't surprise me if they did. Dillon isn't a dummy. Neither is Pam."

"Then why haven't they said anything?"

He shrugged. "Probably waiting for us to tell them."

She thought about what he'd said and figured he might be right. "Doesn't matter now. They will find out soon enough. Are you ready?"

"For another round?"

"No, not for another round. Are you ready to take a shower so we can get off this ship for a while?"

He pulled her into his arms. "Um, maybe. After another round." And then he lowered his mouth to hers.

Fourteen

"I hope you're not punishing me for what happened the last two days, Jillian."

Jillian glanced up at Aidan and smiled. "Why would I do that?" she asked as they walked the streets of Rome, Italy. She'd never visited a city more drenched in history. They would be here for two days and she doubted she could visit all the places she wanted to see in that time. She would have to make plans to come back one day.

"Because it was late when we finally got off the ship to tour Monte Carlo, and the same thing happened yesterday when we toured Florence. I have a feeling you blame me for both."

She chuckled. "Who else should I blame? Every time I mentioned it was time for us to get up, shower and get off the ship, you had other ideas."

He smiled as if remembering several of those ideas. "But we did do the tours. We just got a late start."

Yes, they had done the tours. For barely three hours in Monte Carlo. They had seen all they could in a cab ride around the city. Then yesterday, at least they had ridden up the most scenic road in Florence to reach Piazzale Michelangelo. From there they toured several palaces and museums before it was time to get back to the ship.

She had made sure they had gotten up, dressed and were off the ship at a reasonable time this morning for their tour of Rome. Already they had walked a lot, which was probably the reason Aidan was whining.

"What's the complaint, Aidan? You're in great shape." She of all people should know. He hadn't wasted time having her belongings moved into his suite where she had spent the night...and got very little sleep until dawn. But somehow she still felt energized.

"You think I'm punishing you by suggesting that we walk instead of taking a taxi-tour?" she asked as they crossed one of the busy streets.

"No. I think you're punishing me because you talked me out of renting that red Ferrari. Just think of all the places I could have taken you while driving it."

She chuckled. "Yes, but I would have wanted to get there in one piece and without an accelerated heart rate."

He placed his arms around her shoulders. "Have you forgotten that one day I intend to be one of the most sought-after cardiologists in the world?"

"How could I forget?" she said, smiling. She was really proud of him and his accomplishments. Going through that dual residency program was what had opened the door for him to continue his specialty training at Johns Hopkins, one of the most renowned research hospitals in the country.

Last night, in between making love, they had talked about their future goals. He knew she would start her residency at a hospital in Orlando, Florida, in the fall. The good thing was that after a year of internship, she could transfer to another hospital. Because he would be working for at least three years at John Hopkins, she would try to relocate to the Washington, D.C., or Maryland area.

A few hours later they had toured a number of places, including the Colosseum, St. Peter's Basilica, the Trevi Fountain and the Catacombs. While standing in front of the Spanish Steps, waiting for Aidan to return from retrieving the lace fan she'd left behind in the church of Trinità dei Monti, she blinked when she saw a familiar man pass by.

Riley Westmoreland? What was Aidan's cousin doing in Rome?

"Riley!" she yelled out. When the man didn't look her way, she figured he must not have heard her. Taking the steps almost two at a time, she hurriedly raced after him.

When she caught up with him she grabbed his arm. "Riley, wait up! I didn't know you—"

She stopped in midsentence when the man turned around. It wasn't Riley. But he looked enough like him to be a twin. "I'm so sorry. I thought you were someone else."

The man smiled and she blinked. He even had Riley's smile. Or more specifically, one of those Westmoreland smiles. All the men in the family had dimples. And like all the Westmoreland men, he was extremely handsome.

"No problem, signorina."

She smiled. "You're Italian?" she asked.

"No. American. I'm here on business. And you?"

"American. Here vacationing." She extended her hand. "I'm Jillian Novak."

He nodded as he took her hand. "Garth Outlaw."

"Nice meeting you, Garth, and again I'm sorry that I mistook you for someone else, but you and Riley Westmoreland could almost be twins."

He chuckled. "A woman as beautiful as you can do whatever you like, signorina. No need to apologize." He grasped her hand and lifted it to his lips. "Have a good day, beautiful Jillian Novak, and enjoy the rest of your time in Rome."

"And you do the same."

He turned and walked away. She stood there for a minute, thinking. He was even a flirt like those Westmorelands before they'd married. And the man even had that Westmoreland sexy walk. How crazy was that?

"Jillian?" She turned when she heard Aidan call her name.

"I thought you were going to wait for me on the steps," he said when he reached her.

"I did but then I thought I saw Riley and—"

"Riley? Trust me, Riley would not be in Rome, especially not with Alpha expecting their baby any day now."

"I know, but this guy looked so much like Riley that I raced after him. He could have been Riley's twin. I apologized for my mistake and he was nice about it. He was an American, here on business. Said his name was Garth Outlaw. And he really did favor Riley."

Aidan frowned. "Outlaw?"

"Yes."

"Um, that's interesting. The last time we had our family meeting about the investigation Rico is handling, I think he said something about tracing a branch of the Westmoreland roots to a family who goes by the last name of Outlaw."

"Really?"

"That's what I recall, but Dillon would know for sure. I'll mention it to him when we return home. That information might help Rico," Aidan said as they walked back toward the Spanish Steps.

Rico Claiborne, a private investigator, was married

to Aidan's sister Megan. Jillian was aware that Rico's PI firm had been investigating the connection of four women to Aidan's great-grandfather, Raphel Westmoreland. It had been discovered during a genealogy search that before marrying Aidan's great-grandmother Gemma, Raphel had been connected to four other women who'd been listed as former wives. Rico's investigation had confirmed that Raphel hadn't married any of the women, but that one of them had given birth to a son that Raphel had never known about. Evidently, Jillian thought, at some point Rico had traced that son to the Outlaw family.

"Ready to head back to the ship?" Aidan asked, interrupting her thoughts.

She glanced back at her watch. "Yes, it's getting kind of late. You can join me and the book-club ladies when we go shopping tomorrow if you'd like."

He shook his head. "No thanks. Although it's a beautiful city, I've seen enough of Rome for now. But I will bring you back."

She lifted a brow. "You will?"

"Yes."

"When?"

"For our honeymoon. I hope." Aidan then got down on one knee and took her hand in his. "I love you, Jillian. Will you marry me?"

Jillian stared at him in shock. It was only when he tugged at her hand did she notice the ring he'd placed there. Her eyes widened. "Oh, my God!" Never had she seen anything so beautiful.

"Well?" Aidan asked, grinning. "People are standing around. We've gotten their attention. Are you going to embarrass me or what?"

She saw that people had stopped to stare. They had heard his proposal and, like Aidan, they were waiting for her answer. She could not believe that here in the beautiful city of Rome, on the Spanish Steps, Aidan had asked her to marry him. She would remember this day for as long as she lived.

"Yes. Yes!" she said, filled with happiness. "Yes, I will marry you."

"Thank you," he said, getting back to his feet and pulling her into his arms. "For a minute there you had me worried."

The people around them cheered and clapped while a smiling Aidan pulled Jillian into his arms and kissed her.

Aidan walked down the long corridor to his suite. Jillian had sent him away an hour ago with instructions not to return until now because she would have a surprise waiting for him when he got back. He smiled thinking she had probably planned a candlelit dinner for their last day on the cruise.

It was hard to believe their two weeks were up. Tomorrow they would return to Barcelona. After two days in Rome they had spent two days at sea before touring Athens, Greece. While there they had taken part in a wine-tasting excursion and visited several museums. From there they had toured Turkey, Mykonos and Malta. Now they were headed back to Barcelona and would arrive before daybreak.

He couldn't help the feeling of happiness that puffed out his chest when he thought of being an engaged man. Although they hadn't set a date, the most important thing was that he had asked and she had said yes. They talked every day about their future, and although they still had at least another year before she could join him in Maryland, they were okay with it because they knew the day would come when they would be together.

They decided not to wait until they went home for Adrian's wedding to tell the family their news. Some would be shocked, while others who knew about their affair would be relieved that their secret wasn't a secret any longer. They would head straight to Denver tomorrow when the ship docked.

He chuckled when he thought about Jillian's excitement over her engagement ring. The book-club ladies had definitely been impressed as well, ahhing and ooing every night at dinner. Jewelry by Zion was the rave since Zion was the First Lady's personal jeweler. Jillian hadn't known that he knew Zion personally because of Aidan's friendship with the Steele family, who were close personal friends of Zion. Zion had designed most of his signature custom jewelry collection while living in Rome for the past ten years. Thanks to Dominic, Aidan had met with Zion privately on board the ship in the wee hours of the morning while Jillian slept, when they first docked in a port near Rome. Zion had brought an attaché case filled with beautiful rings—all originals hand-crafted by Zion. When Aidan had seen this one particular ring, he'd known it was the one he wanted to put on Jillian's finger.

When Aidan reached his suite's door, he knocked, to let her know he had returned.

"Come in."

Using his passkey, he opened the door and smiled upon seeing the lit candles around the room. His bride-to-be had set the mood for a romantic dinner, he thought, when he saw how beautifully the table was set.

Closing the door behind him he glanced around the dimly lit suite but didn't see Jillian anywhere. Was she in the bedroom waiting on him? He moved in that direction and then felt a hand on his shoulder. He turned around and his breath caught. Jillian wore a provocative black lace teddy that showed a lot of flesh. Attached to the teddy were matching lace garters and she wore a pair of stilettoes on her feet. He thought he hadn't seen anyone as sexy in his entire life and he couldn't help groaning in appreciation.

She leaned close, swirled the tip of her tongue around his ear and whispered, "I'm about to give you the lap dance of your life, Aidan Westmoreland."

The next thing he knew he was gently shoved in a chair. "And remember no touching, so put your hands behind your back."

He followed her instructions, mesmerized beyond belief. Her sensual persona stirred his desire. His pulse kicked up a notch, followed immediately by a deep throbbing in his erection. "And just what do you want me to do?" he asked in a low voice.

She smiled at him. "Just enjoy. I plan to do all the work. But by the time I finish, you will be too exhausted to move."

Really? Him? Too exhausted to move? And she would be the one doing all the work? He couldn't wait for that experience. "Now will you keep your hands to yourself or do I need to handcuff you?" she asked him.

He couldn't help smiling at the thought of that. Did she really have handcuffs? Would she be that daring? He decided to find out. "I can't make any promises, so you might want to handcuff me."

"No problem."

The next thing he knew she'd whipped out a pair of handcuffs slapped them on his wrists and locked them with a click to the chair. *Damn.* While he was taking all this in, he suddenly heard music coming from the sound system in the room. He didn't recognize the artist, but the song had a sensual beat.

While sitting there handcuffed to the chair, he watched as Jillian responded to the music, her movements slow, graceful and seductive. She rolled her stomach and then shimmied her hips and backside in a sinfully erotic way. He sat there awestruck, fascinated, staring at her as she moved in front of him. He felt the rapid beat of his heart and the sweet pull of desire as his erection continued to pulsate.

Although he couldn't touch her, she was definitely touching him—rubbing her hands over his shirt, underneath it, through the hair on his chest, before taking her time unbuttoning his shirt and easing it from his shoulders.

"Have I ever told you how much I love your chest, Aidan?" she asked him in a sultry tone.

"No," he answered huskily. "You never have."

"Well, I'm telling you now. In fact, I want to show you just how much I like it."

Then she crouched over him and used her tongue to lick his shoulder blades before moving slowly across the span of his chest. He would have come out of his chair had he not been handcuffed to it. She used her tongue in ways she hadn't before and he heard himself groaning out loud.

"You like that?" she asked, leaning close to his mouth, and licking there, as well. "Want more? Want to see what else you've taught me to do with my tongue?"

He swallowed. Oh, yes, he wanted more. He wanted to see just what he'd taught her. Instead of answering, he nodded.

She smiled as she bent down to remove his shoes. Reaching up, she unzipped his pants and he raised his hips as she slid both his pants and briefs down his legs. She smiled at him again.

"You once licked me all over, Aidan, and you seemed to have enjoyed it. Now I'm going to do the same to you and I intend to enjoy myself, as well."

Moistening her lips with a delicious-looking sweep of her tongue, she got down on her knees before him and spread his legs. Then she lowered her head between his thighs and took him into her mouth.

As soon as she touched him, blood rushed through his veins, sexual hunger curled his stomach and desire stroked his gut. Her mouth widened to accommodate his size and she used her tongue to show that with this, she was definitely in control. He watched in a sensual daze as her head bobbed up and down while she fanned the blaze of his desire.

He wanted to grab hold of her hair, stroke her back, caress her shoulders but he couldn't. He felt defenseless, totally under her control but he loved every single minute of it. When he couldn't take any more, his body jerked in one hell of an explosion and she still wouldn't let go.

"Jillian!"

He wanted her with an intensity that terrified him. And when she lifted her head and smiled at him, he knew what it meant to love someone with every part of your heart, your entire being and your soul.

While the music continued to play, she straightened and began stripping for him, removing each piece of clothing slowly, and teasing his nostrils before tossing it aside. Sexual excitement filled his inner core as he inhaled her scent. When she was totally naked, she began dancing again, touching herself and touching him. He'd never seen anything so erotic in his entire life.

When she curled into his lap and continued to dance, the feel of her soft curves had him growling, had his erection throbbing again, harder. "Set me free," he begged. He needed to touch her now. He wanted his hands in her hair and his fingers inside her.

"Not yet," she whispered in a purr that made even more need wash over him. Then she twisted her body around so her back was plastered to his chest then she eased down onto his manhood and rode him.

Never had she ridden him this hard and when she shifted so they faced each other, the feel of her breasts hitting his chest sent all kinds of sensations through him.

"Jillian!"

He screamed her name as an orgasm hit him again, deep, and he pulled the scent of her sex through his nostrils. He leaned forward. Although he couldn't touch her, he could lick her. He used his tongue to touch her earlobe and her face. "Uncuff me baby. Please. Uncuff me now."

She reached behind him and he heard the click that released him. When his hands were free he stood, with her in his arms, and quickly moved toward the bedroom.

"You're the one who was supposed to be exhausted," she mumbled into his chest.

"Sorry, it doesn't quite work that way, baby." And then he stretched her out on the bed.

He straddled her, eased inside her and thrust, stroking her, wanting her to feel his love in every movement. This was erotic pleasure beyond compare and her inner muscles clenched him, held him tight and tempted him to beg again.

His thrusts became harder, her moans louder and the desire he felt for her more relentless than ever. And when he finally exploded, he took her along with him as an earth-shattering climax claimed them both. They were blasted into the heavens. Jillian Novak had delivered the kind of mindless pleasure every man should experience at least once in his lifetime. And he was glad that he had.

Moments later, he eased off her and pulled her into his arms, entwining her legs with his. He kissed the side of her face while she fell into a deep sleep.

Their secret affair was not a secret any longer and he couldn't wait to tell the world that he'd found his mate for life. And he would cherish her forever.

Epilogue

"So, you thought you were keeping a secret from us," Pam said, smiling, sitting beside her husband on the sofa as they met with Aidan and Jillian.

"But we didn't?" Jillian asked, grinning and holding Aidan's hand.

"For a little while, maybe," Dillon replied. But when you fall in love with someone, it's hard to keep something like that hidden, especially in *this* family."

Jillian knew exactly what Dillon meant. It seemed the bigger secret had been that she and Aidan had wanted to keep their relationship a secret. No one in the family knew who else knew, so everyone kept their suspicions to themselves.

"Well, I'm glad we don't have to hide things anymore," Aidan said, standing, pulling Jillian up with him and then wrapping his arms around her shoulders.

"You mean you don't have to *try* and hide things," Pam corrected. "Neither of you were doing such a good job of pretending. And when the two of you had that rift, Dillon and I were tempted to intervene. But we figured if it was meant for the two of you to be together, you would be, without our help."

Jillian looked down at her ring. "Yes, we were able to get our act together, although I will have to give Paige some credit for bailing out of the cruise. Aidan and I needed that time together to work things out."

"And I guess from that ring on your finger, the two of you managed to do that," Dillon said.

Aidan nodded as he smiled down at Jillian. "Yes, we did. The thought of a year-long engagement doesn't bother us. After Jillian's first year at that hospital in Orlando, Florida, she'll be able to transfer to one near me. That's when we plan to tie the knot."

"Besides," Pam said, smiling. "The year gives me plenty of time to plan for the wedding without feeling rushed. These Westmoreland weddings are coming around fast, but trust me, I'm not complaining."

Dillon reached out and hugged his wife. "Please don't complain. I'm elated with each one. After Adrian gets hitched next month and Aidan is married in a year, all we'll have to be concerned with is Bailey and Bane."

The room got quiet as everyone thought about that. Only two Westmorelands were left single, and those two were known to be the most headstrong of them all.

"Bay says she's never getting married," Aidan said, grinning.

"So did you and Adrian," Dillon reminded him. "In fact, I don't think there's a single Westmoreland who hasn't made that claim at some point in time, including me. But all it takes is for one of us to find that special person who's our soul mate, and we start singing a different tune."

"But can you see Bay singing a different tune?" Aidan asked.

Dillon thought about the question for a minute, drew in a deep breath and then shook his head. "No."

Everyone laughed. When their laughter subsided Pam smiled and said, "There's someone for everyone, including Bailey. She just hasn't met him yet. In other words, Bailey hasn't met her match. But one day, I believe that she will."

The following month

"Adrian Westmoreland, you may kiss your bride."

Aidan, serving as best man, smiled as he watched his twin brother take the woman he loved, Dr. Trinity Matthews Westmoreland, into his arms to seal their marriage vows with one hell of a kiss. Aidan spotted Jillian in the audience sitting with her sisters and winked at her. Their day would be coming and he couldn't wait.

A short while later, Aidan stole his twin away for a few minutes. The wedding had been held in Trinity's hometown of Bunnell, Florida, at the same church where their cousin Thorn had married Trinity's sister Tara. The weather had been beautiful and it seemed everyone in the little town had been invited to the wedding, which accounted for the packed church of more than eight hundred guests. The reception was held in the ballroom of a beautiful hotel overlooking the Atlantic Ocean.

"Great job, Dr. Westmoreland," he said, grinning at Adrian.

Adrian chuckled. "I intend to say the same to you

a year from now, Dr. Westmoreland, when you tie the knot. I'm glad the cruise helped, and that you and Jillian were able to work things out."

"So am I. That had to be the worst year of my life when we were apart."

Adrian nodded. "I know. Remember I felt your pain whenever you let out any strong emotions."

Yes, Aidan did remember. "So where are you headed for your honeymoon?"

"Sydney, Australia. I've always wanted to go back, and I look forward to taking Trinity there with me."

"Well, the two of you deserve a lifetime of happiness," Aidan said, taking a sip of his champagne.

"You and Jillian do, as well. I'm so glad the secret is a secret no longer."

Aidan's smile widened. "So am I. And on that note, I'm going to go claim my fiancée so you can go claim your bride."

Aidan crossed the span of the ball room to where Jillian stood with her sisters Paige and Nadia, and his sister Bailey. He and Jillian would leave Bunnell in the morning and take the hour-long drive to Orlando. Together they would look for an apartment for her close to the hospital where she would be working as an intern. He had checked and discovered that flights from the D.C. area into Orlando were pretty frequent. He was glad about that because he intended to pay his woman plenty of visits.

Aidan had told Dillon about Jillian's chance meeting with a man by the name of Garth Outlaw while in Rome and how she'd originally thought he was Riley.

Dillon wasn't surprised that any kin out there would have the Westmoreland look due to dominant genes. He had passed the information on to Rico. The family was hoping something resulted from Jillian's encounter.

"Sorry, ladies, I need to grab Jillian for a minute," he said, snagging her hand.

"Where are we going?" Jillian asked as he led her toward the exit.

"To walk on the beach."

"Okay."

Holding hands, they crossed the boardwalk and went down the steps. Pausing briefly, they removed their shoes. Jillian moaned when her feet touched the sand.

"What are you thinking about, baby?" Aidan asked her.

"I'm thinking about how wonderful I feel right now. Walking in the sand, being around the people I love, not having to hide my feelings for you. And what a lucky woman I am to have such a loving family and such a gorgeous and loving fiancé."

He glanced down at her. "You think I'm gorgeous?"

"Yes."

"You think I'm loving?"

"Definitely."

"Will that qualify me for another lap dance tonight?"

Jillian threw her head back and laughed, causing the wind to send hair flying across her face. Aidan pushed her hair back and she smiled up at him.

"Dr. Westmoreland, you can get a lap dance out of me anytime. Just say the word."

"Lap dance."

She leaned up on tip toes. "You got it."

Aidan then pulled her into his arms and kissed her. Life couldn't get any better than this.

* * * * *

"Sometimes," he said softly. "Families just happen."

Cole's hand was warm, strong. He didn't immediately let her go, and a strange feeling surged up her arm, pushing into her chest.

Time seemed to stop. She stood still and drank in his appearance. He was such a gorgeous, sexy man. His smoke-gray eyes were dark with emotion. She noticed once again that his shoulders were broad, arms toned, chest defined. He seemed to radiate a power that was more than just physical.

She fought another urge to go to him. It couldn't happen...not this time.

* * *

The Missing Heir
is part of the No.1 bestselling series from
Mills & Boon® Desire™—
Billionaires and Babies: Powerful men...
wrapped around their babies' little fingers.

THE MISSING HEIR

BY
BARBARA DUNLOP

Published in Great Britain 2014
by Mills & Boon, an imprint of Harlequin (UK) Limited,
Eton House, 18-24 Paradise Road, Richmond, Surrey, TW9 1SR

© 2014 Barbara Dunlop

ISBN: 978-0-263-91488-7

51-1214

Harlequin (UK) Limited's policy is to use papers that are natural, renewable and recyclable products and made from wood grown in sustainable forests. The logging and manufacturing processes conform to the legal environmental regulations of the country of origin.

Printed and bound in Spain
by CPI, Barcelona

Barbara Dunlop writes romantic stories while curled up in a log cabin in Canada's far north, where bears outnumber people and it snows six months of the year. Fortunately she has a brawny husband and two teenage children to haul firewood and clear the driveway while she sips cocoa and muses about her upcoming chapters. Barbara loves to hear from readers. You can contact her through her website, www.barbaradunlop.com.

For Mom

One

Cole Henderson propped himself against a workbench in Aviation 58's hangar at the Juneau, Alaska, airport and gazed at the front page of the Daily Bureau. He realized news of the Atlanta plane crash deaths should make him feel something. After all, Samuel Henderson had been his biological father. But he had no idea what he was supposed to feel.

A nearby door in the big building opened, letting in a swirl of frigid air and blowing snow. At ten o'clock in the morning, it was still dark outside this far north.

His business partner, Luca Dodd, strode in, crossing the concrete floor alongside the sixty-passenger Komodor airplane that was down for maintenance.

"You looking at it?" Luca asked.

"I'm looking at it," said Cole.

Luca tugged off his leather gloves and removed his wool hat. "What do you think?"

"I don't think anything." Cole folded the paper and tossed it on the bench behind him. "What's to think? The guy's dead."

A drill buzzed on the far side of the hangar, and the air compressor started up, clattering in the background as two maintenance engineers worked on the engine of the Komodor.

"He was your father," Luca pointed out.

"I never met him. And he never even knew I existed."

"Still…"

Cole shrugged. His mother Lauren's marriage to billionaire Samuel Henderson, whose family owned Atlanta-based Coast Eagle Airlines, had been short-lived and heartbreaking for her. She'd never hidden Cole's heritage from him, but she'd certainly warned him about the Henderson family.

"Eight dead," said Luca, spinning the paper so the headline was right side up.

"Sounds like it all went to hell in the final seconds." As a pilot, Cole empathized with in-air emergencies. He knew the pilots would have been fighting to safely land the airplane until the very end.

"Early speculation is a combination of icing and wind shear. That's freakishly rare for Atlanta."

"We all know how bad that can go."

"An Alaskan pilot might have helped," said Luca.

Cole didn't argue that point. Pilots in Alaska had more experience than most in icy conditions.

He glanced over his shoulder at the headline once again. On a human level, he felt enormous sympathy for those who'd lost their lives, and his heart went out to their friends and family who had to go on without them. But for him personally, Samuel Henderson was nothing but a stranger who'd devastated his mother's life thirty-two years ago.

By contrast, when his mother, Lauren, had passed away from cancer last year, Cole had mourned her deeply. He still missed her.

"They put up a picture of the baby on the website," said Luca.

The article had mentioned that Samuel and his beautiful young wife, Coco, had a nine-month-old son, who, luckily, hadn't accompanied them on the trip. But Samuel's aging mother and several company executives had been on board when the family jet had crashed into the Atlanta runway.

"Cute kid," Luca added.

Cole didn't answer. He hadn't seen the picture, and he had no plans to look at it. He wasn't about to engage in the Henderson tragedy on any level.

Luca leaned forward, putting his face closer to Cole's. "You do get it, right?"

"What's to get?" Cole took a sideways step and started walking toward a hallway that led to the airline's offices. November might be Aviation 58's quietest month, but there was still plenty of work to do.

Luca walked beside him. "The kid, Zachary, is the sole survivor of that entire family."

"I'm sure he'll be well cared for." For the first time, Cole felt an emotional reaction. He wasn't proud, but it was resentment.

Immediately after their secret marriage in Vegas, Samuel had succumbed to his parents' pressure to divorce Lauren. As a young woman, she'd walked away, newly pregnant. With only a few thousand dollars to her name, she'd boarded a plane for Alaska, terrified that the powerful family would find out about her baby and take him away from her.

Hidden in Alaska, she'd scraped and saved when Cole was young. Then he'd worked night and day to put himself through flight school and to build his own airline. Zachary, by contrast, would have an army of nannies and protectors to ensure he had everything a little boy could need—from chauffeurs to private schools and ski vacations in Switzerland.

"He's all alone in the world." Luca interrupted Cole's thoughts.

"Hardly," Cole scoffed.

"You're his only living relative."

"I'm not his relative."

"You're his half brother."

"That's just an accident of genetics." There was nothing at all tying Cole to Zachary. Their lives were worlds apart.

"He's only nine months old."

Cole kept on walking across the cavernous hangar.

"If the Hendersons are as bad as Lauren said they were…" Luca's voice trailed off again, leaving the bangs and shouts of the maintenance crew to fill in the silence.

Cole picked up his pace. "Those Hendersons are all dead."

"Except for you and Zachary."

"I'm not a Henderson."

"You looked at your driver's license lately?"

Cole tugged the heavy hallway door open. "You know what I mean."

"I know exactly what you mean. The jackals in Atlanta might very well be circling an innocent baby, but you'd rather walk away from all this."

"I don't *have* to walk away from this. I was never involved in it to begin with."

Cole's operations manager, Carol Runions, poked her head out of her office. "One seventy-two has gone mechanical."

Cole glanced at his watch. Flight 172, a ninety-passenger commuter jet, was due to take off for Seattle in twenty minutes. "Is maintenance on board?" he asked Carol.

"They're on their way out there now. You want me to prep Five Bravo Sierra?"

"What's the problem?" Luca asked her.

"Indicator light for cabin pressure."

"Probably a faulty switch," said Cole. "But let's warm up Five Bravo Sierra."

"You got it," said Carol, heading back into her office.

"If we take the Citation, we can be there in four hours," said Luca.

Cole stared at his partner in confusion. "There are ninety passengers on 172." The Citation seated nine.

"I meant you and me."

"Why would we go to Seattle?" And why did Luca think it would take them four hours to get there?

"Atlanta," said Luca.

Cole's jaw went lax.

"You gotta do it," said Luca.

No, he didn't. And Cole was done with talking about the Henderson family. Without answering, he turned to walk away, shaking his head as he went.

"You gotta do it," Luca called after him. "You know as well as I do, the jackals are already circling."

"Not my problem," Cole called back.

The Atlanta Hendersons had gotten along perfectly well without him up to now. He had no doubt their *i*'s were dotted and *t*'s crossed for every possible life or death contingency. They didn't need him, and he didn't want them.

Amber Welsley folded her hands on the top of the massive inlaid-maple table in the formal dining room of the Henderson family mansion. She was one of a dozen people riveted on Max Cutter at the table's head. Max's suit was well cut, his gray hair neatly trimmed and his weathered expression was completely inscrutable as he drew a stack of papers from his leather briefcase.

From the finely upholstered chair next to hers, Amber's friend Destiny Frost leaned in close. "Six lawyers in the same room. This is not going to end well."

"Seven lawyers," Amber whispered back.

Destiny's glance darted around. "Who'd I miss?"

"You. You're a lawyer."

"Yeah, but I'm the good guy."

Amber couldn't help flexing a tiny smile. She appreciated the small break in the tension.

Max was about to read Samuel Henderson's last will and testament. The others gathered in the room had an enormous amount at stake—about a billion dollars and control of Coast Eagle Airlines. But the only thing that mattered to Amber was Zachary. She hoped whatever arrangements Samuel and her stepsister, Coco, had made for the baby's guardianship would allow Amber to stay a part of his life.

Amber was ten years older than Coco, and the two had never been close. But Amber had been instrumental in her stepsister meeting Samuel at a Coast Eagle corporate function two years ago, and Coco's pregnancy had brought them closer together for a short time. Since then, Amber had felt a special kinship with Zachary.

Across the wide table from her, vice president of operations Roth Calvin shifted in his seat. Since the day the company's president, Dryden Dunsmore, had been killed in the plane crash, the three vice presidents had been running the show. Now Samuel's will would reveal who would get control of Coast Eagle.

Whoever it was would control Roth Calvin's future. Much further down the corporate ladder, as assistant director of finance, Amber didn't much care who took over the helm of the company. Her day-to-day job as an accountant wasn't about to change.

"My personal apologies for the delay in scheduling this reading," Max opened, his gaze going around the room. "But there were several complexities to this case due to the number of deaths involved."

Amber's throat thickened. She quickly swallowed to combat the sensation. Poor Coco had only been twenty-one.

"I'll start with Jackie Henderson's will," said Max. "I'll follow that with her son, Samuel's, which was written jointly with his wife, Coco. In addition, there is a small codicil, executed by Coco alone. I would caution you all to draw no conclusions until I've finished reading all three."

Max straightened the papers. "Aside from some small bequests to friends and long-time staff members, and a generous donation of ten million dollars to the Atlanta arts community, Jackie Henderson has left her estate to her son, Samuel, including her twenty-five percent ownership of Coast Eagle Airlines."

Nobody in the room reacted to Max's statements, and they gave only a cursory glance to the list of bequests handed around. That Samuel was Mrs. Henderson's heir was completely expected. And though Mrs. Henderson had been an exacting and irritable old woman, she had long been a patron of the arts.

"As to the last will and testament of Samuel Henderson…" said Max.

Everyone stilled in their seats.

Max looked down at a page in front of him. "Mr. Henderson has also left a list of small, specific bequests, and has made several charitable donations, also ten million dollars to the Atlanta arts community, along with an additional ten million dollar scholarship to the Georgia Pilots Association."

Max took a sip of water. "As to the bulk of Mr. Henderson's estate, I'll read directly from the document. 'My entire estate is left in trust, in equal shares, to my legitimate children. So long as my wife, Coco Henderson, remains guardian of my children, and until they reach the age of majority, business decisions pertaining to the children's interest in Coast Eagle Airlines will be made by Dryden Dunsmore.'"

There was a collective intake of breath in the room, followed by murmured sidebar conversations.

"Well, there's a complexity," Destiny whispered to Amber.

It was obvious Samuel had not contemplated Dryden Dunsmore dying along with him.

Max cleared his throat, and everyone fell silent.

"'Should my wife predecease me,'" he continued, "'guardianship of my minor children will go to Roth Calvin.'"

The room went completely silent, and a dozen gazes swung to Roth. He held his composure for a full ten seconds, but then an uncontrollable smile curved his thin lips, gratification glowing in the depths of his pale blue eyes.

A buzz of conversation came up in the room.

Roth turned to the lawyer on his right. His tone was low, but Amber heard every word. "With Dryden out of the picture, do I have control over the shares?"

The lawyer nodded.

Roth's smile grew wider and more calculating.

"The codicil," Max interrupted the various discussions.

People quieted down again, and Roth's expression settled into self-satisfaction.

"To give some context to this…" said Max. "And I do apologize for being so direct on such an emotional matter. Samuel Henderson was pronounced dead at the accident scene, while Coco Henderson was pronounced dead during the ambulance ride to the hospital."

Amber's stomach tightened. She'd been assured Coco had not regained consciousness after the crash, but she couldn't help but be reminded of the fear and horror her stepsister must have experienced in those final seconds while the plane attempted to land in the storm.

"As such, Samuel is deemed to have predeceased his wife." Max held a single sheet of paper. "Given that fact, Coco Henderson's codicil is legal and valid. It modifies the joint will in only one way." He read, "'I leave guardianship of my child or children to my stepsister, Amber Welsley.'"

Amber could feel shock permeate the room. Jaws literally dropped open and gazes swung to her. Roth's glare sent a wave of animosity that nearly pushed her backward.

Beneath the table, Destiny grasped her hand.

"What about business decisions?" Roth barked. "That woman is in no position to run the company. She's an assistant."

"Assistant *director*," Destiny corrected.

Amber was in a management position, not a clerical one.

Roth sneered at them both. "Samuel clearly wanted someone qualified in charge of business decisions on behalf of his son."

"It's a valid question," said Max. "For the moment, Amber Welsley has guardianship over Zachary, including all rights and responsibilities to manage and safeguard his ownership position in Coast Eagle."

"But—" Roth began.

Max held up a hand to forestall him. "For any changes to that, you'll need a decision from a judge."

"You can bet we're going to a judge," spat Roth.

Amber whispered to Destiny, "What does this all mean?"

"It means we're going to court to duke it out with Roth. And it means he just became your mortal enemy. But right now, it also means you get Zachary."

Amber's chest swelled tight. Zachary would stay with her. For now, nothing else mattered.

Walking through the entrance of the Atlanta hotel ballroom, Cole gazed at the crowds of people attending the Georgia Pilots Association annual fund-raiser. Tonight was the formal recognition of the new Samuel Henderson Memorial Scholarship, so he knew the who's who of Coast Eagle Airlines would be in the room.

Luca was beside him, dressed in a formal suit. "You'll be glad you came."

"I'll mostly be glad if it shuts you up."

Cole had told himself a thousand times that the Hendersons of Atlanta were none of his business, and he still believed it. But Luca had kept after him for three long weeks. Finally, Cole had given in and checked out a picture of Zachary on a news site.

The baby was cuter than he'd expected, and his face had seemed strangely familiar. But Cole chalked it up to the power of suggestion. When you started looking for a family resemblance, everything took on new meaning. Sometimes gray eyes were simply gray eyes.

But once he'd scratched the surface, he'd ended up reading the rest of the article, learning there was a court challenge for guardianship. He didn't necessarily agree with Luca that everyone involved was a jackal out to get the kid's money. But he did find himself analyzing the players.

In the end, his curiosity won out, and he agreed to make the trip to Atlanta. He had no intention of marching up to the front door and introducing himself as a long-lost relative. He was staying under the radar, checking things out and returning to Alaska just as soon as he confirmed Zachary was safe.

"Right there," said Luca. "In the black dress, lace sleeves, brown hair, kind of swooped up. She's at the table below the podium. She's moving right now."

As Cole zeroed in on Amber Welsley, she turned, presenting him with a surprisingly pretty profile.

Her diamond jewelry flashed beneath the bright lights, accenting her feminine face. Her dress was classic, a scooped neckline, three-quarter-length lace sleeves that blended to a form-fitting bodice and a narrow skirt that emphasized her trim figure.

From this distance, she surprised him. She wasn't at all what he'd expected. She was younger, softer, insidiously captivating. While he stared at her, the wholly inappropriate thought that she was kissable welled up in his mind.

"You want to go over and say hi?" asked Luca.

The true answer was no. Cole wanted to get on an airplane and fly back to Alaska.

He might as well get this over with. Checking out Amber and all the other characters in this family drama was his purpose in being here. There wasn't any point waiting.

"Let's do it," he said.

"Roth Calvin's at the next table," said Luca as they walked. "He's facing us, talking to the guy with red hair, in the steel-gray jacket."

"I think you missed your calling as a spy."

Luca grinned. "I'm calling dibs on the one named Destiny."

"Who's Destiny?"

"She was in a couple of the photos with Amber Welsley. She's hot. And with a name like that, I'm definitely giving her a shot."

Cole shook his head. "She's all yours, buddy. I just want to make sure the kid's okay." Then any duty he might have as a blood relative would be done.

"By kid, you mean your baby brother?"

"Yeah, that's not a phrase we'll be using."

"Boggles the mind, doesn't it?"

"You're going to have to be boggled all by yourself. I won't be here long enough."

"You want a wingman for the intro?"

"Sure. But don't use the name Henderson."

"Undercover. I like it."

"I'll use Cole Parker. My middle name."

"Right behind you, Cole Parker."

The closer they drew to the Coast Eagle tables, the more beautiful Amber became. Her hair wasn't brown, but a rich chestnut with highlights that shimmered under the bright stage lights. It was half up, half down in a tousled bundle with wisps flowing over her temples and down her back. The scalloped neckline of her dress showed off an expanse of creamy skin, while the lace across her shoulders played peekaboo with his imagination.

Her eyes were deep blue, fringed with dark lashes. Her full lips were dark red, her cheeks enticingly flushed. He had a sudden vision of her clambering naked into his bed.

She turned as he approached, caught his stare and gave him an obviously practiced smile. He realized hundreds if not thousands of people must have introduced themselves and offered their condolences in the past weeks.

"Amber Welsley?" he asked her, offering his hand.

"I am."

"I'm Cole Parker from Aviation 58. My condolences on your loss."

"Thank you, Mr. Parker." She shook his hand.

The soft warmth of her palm seemed to whisper through his skin. He felt a ripple of awareness move up his arm and along the length of his body. Her expression flinched, and for a second he thought she'd felt it, too. But then her formal smile was back in place, and she was moving on.

Cole quickly spoke again to keep her attention. "This is my business partner, Luca Dodd."

"Please call me Luca."

"And I'm Cole," Cole put in, feeling like an idiot for not having said it right away.

"Aviation 58 was looking to contribute to the Samuel Henderson fund," said Luca.

Cole's stomach twisted, and he shot Luca a glare of annoyance.

Where had that come from? There was no way on earth Cole was contributing to something with Samuel's name on it.

"It's a very worthy cause," said Amber. But then she caught Cole's expression. "Is something wrong?"

"No," he quickly answered.

"You look upset."

"I'm fine."

She canted her head to one side, considering him. "You don't agree that the pilot scholarship is a worthy cause?"

"I believe what Luca meant is that we're thinking of setting something up in parallel. With Georgia Pilots, but not necessarily…" How exactly was he going to phrase this?

"Not necessarily in honor of Samuel Henderson?" Amber finished for him.

Cole didn't know how to respond to the direct challenge. He didn't want to lie, but he didn't want to insult her, either.

"You have a spare ten million hanging around to match Coast Eagle?" she asked.

"Ten million is a little out of our league," Cole admitted.

Her blue eyes narrowed ever so slightly. "Did you know Samuel?"

"I never met him."

The suspicious expression didn't detract at all from her beauty, and Cole experienced an urge to sweep back her hair and kiss the delicate curve of her neck.

"So you disliked him from afar?" she asked.

"I didn't..." This was getting worse by the second. Cole gave himself a mental shake. "I knew people who knew him."

"Amber?" prompted a man at her elbow.

Cole clenched his jaw at the interruption.

"Five minutes to introductions," said the man.

"Thanks, Julius." She glanced at Luca for a moment before settling her attention back on Cole. "It looks like I need to take my seat. It was a pleasure to meet you, Cole Parker."

"Are you always this polite?"

"Do you want me to be rude?"

Cole was the one who'd been rude. "This conversation didn't go the way I expected."

"Maybe you could try again some other time."

"What are you doing later?" He hadn't intended the question to sound intimate, but it did.

She didn't miss a beat. "I believe I'm eating crab cocktail and chicken Kiev, giving a short, heartfelt speech on behalf of the Henderson family, then relieving the nanny and going to sleep."

"Zachary?" Cole took advantage of the opening.

"He'll be having his bath about now. He likes splashing with the blue duck and chewing on the washcloth."

"Are you staying for the dance?"

"I doubt it."

"*Will* you stay for the dance?"

She hesitated. "You think you'll do better if we're dancing?"

"I'll try not to insult the evening's deceased honoree."

"You set a high bar."

"Underpromise and overdeliver."

The man named Julius returned, touching Amber's arm. "Amber?"

"Goodbye for now," she told Cole with a smile.

Though her expression was more polite than warm, he decided to take the words as encouraging.

"What the hell was *that?*" Luca muttered as she walked away.

"Contributing to his *scholarship?*" asked Cole. "Where did you expect me to go from there?"

"You choked."

"We are *not* contributing to his scholarship."

"You made that much clear."

They turned to wind their way between tables.

"She's not what I expected," said Cole as they returned to the back half of the big ballroom.

"She has two arms, two legs, speaks English. What did you expect?"

"I don't know." Cole struggled to organize his thoughts. "Snobbish, maybe, polished and conniving."

"She looked pretty polished to me."

"She's beautiful, but that's not the same thing."

"She's a knockout. Do you actually think she'll dance with you?"

"Why not?"

"Because you choked, and I'm sure she has other offers."

"I'm staying optimistic."

As the lights went dim and the applause came up, Cole made up his mind to approach her as soon as the dinner was over. This was by far his best chance to mingle with the Hendersons and Coast Eagle without revealing his identity, and he wanted to get it done and over with.

Two

Amber couldn't wait to get out of the ballroom. Her first choice on a Saturday night was to stay home with Zachary, tucked in her jammies with a cup of hot chocolate and an old movie. But she was the closest thing there was to a member of the Henderson family, and somebody had to graciously accept the pilots association's thanks.

Unlike her sister, Coco, Amber never attended highbrow events. Consequently, everything she wore tonight was new. Her feet were killing her in the ridiculous high heels. Her push-up bra was digging into her ribs, the lace scratching her skin. And the tight dress, chosen by Destiny, who insisted it was perfect, was restricting her movements so that she couldn't even cross her legs under the table.

The MC ended a string of thank-yous with a request for applause to compliment the catering staff. As the clapping died down, the music came up, signaling the start of the dance.

Amber breathed a sigh of relief. All that was left was to politely make her way toward the exit, find a cab and get home. She stood, tucking her tiny purse under her arm.

A fiftysomething woman she vaguely recognized grasped her hand to shake it. "Lovely speech, Ms. Welsley. Lovely speech."

"Thank you."

The woman's expression turned serious. "Even in such tragic circumstances, the Henderson family is having a positive impact on the community."

"Samuel was a very generous man," Amber responded by rote, though she had her own private thoughts on Samuel's character, most particularly his decision to marry her beautiful, impetuous, nineteen-year-old stepsister.

Amber had initially kept her distance from the couple, regretting many times the decision to bring Coco to the company party where the two had met. But then Coco had become pregnant, and Amber had been drawn back into the drama of Coco's life.

"Excuse me, Ms. Welsley," came a male voice.

The woman seemed reluctant to step back to give way.

"Good evening." Amber smiled at the new man, taking his offered hand, mentally calculating how long it would take her to run the gauntlet to the exit. It would be an hour or more at this pace. She truly didn't think she could stand that long in these shoes. For a nonsensical moment, she pictured herself toppling over onto the ballroom floor.

"I'm Kevin Mathews from Highbush Unlimited. I wonder if I might give you my card."

Amber kept her smile in place. "Certainly, Mr. Mathews."

He dug into his inside pocket for a business card. "We're a charitable organization, focused on environmental rehabilitation, primarily in the northwest. I know a lot about Mr. Henderson and Coast Eagle, and I can't help imagining that he would have been a supporter of the environmental rehabilitation."

Amber doubted that Samuel had given much thought to the environment, since he flew around in a private jet, air-conditioned the heck out of his mansion and owned several gas-guzzling luxury cars.

But she took the card the man offered. "I'd be happy to pass this along to Coast Eagle's Community Outreach Unit."

His expression faltered. "If you have some time now, I could outline for you our—"

"There you are," came a deeper male voice. "I believe it's time for our dance."

Cole Parker appeared by her side, his arm held out, a broad smile on his face.

Amber couldn't tell if he was rescuing her or about to pitch something himself. But she quickly estimated that the dance floor was more than halfway to the exit. That was progress. She returned his smile and took his arm.

"Please excuse me," she said to Kevin.

Kevin's expression faltered, but he had little choice but to let her go.

Cole guided her through the crowd, keeping their pace brisk enough to discourage the people who looked as though they might approach. It was hard on her feet, particularly her baby toes, but there was no option but to keep walking. Gradually, the crowd thinned near the dance floor.

"Am I out of the frying pan and into the fire?" she asked him.

"I'm not hitting you up for a donation, if that's what you mean."

"Good to hear." She wasn't sure what he wanted, but he was persistent enough that he had to be after something.

"I brought you a gift," he told her.

"Bribery? That's a bit blatant, don't you think?"

"I believe in getting straight to the point." He lifted his palm.

She glanced down, squinting. "You bought me a pair of… socks?"

"Dancing slippers. I got them from a vending machine in the lobby." He glanced down at her black-and-gold four-inch heels. "Unless I miss my guess, those are two-hour shoes."

She grimaced. "Is that what they call them?" It was an apt name.

She knew she should be suspicious of his motives, but she couldn't help but feel grateful.

"Over here." He pointed to a couple of empty chairs at the edge of the dance floor. "Have a seat."

She eased down, deciding to accept the gift and remove the torture chambers from her feet. How much could she possibly be indebted to him for a pair of vending-machine dancing slippers?

She unbuckled the straps and slipped her feet free.

"I went with medium." He handed her the black-satin, ballet-style slippers.

Slipping them onto her feet, she nearly groaned out loud. "They're so soft."

He bent to pick up her shiny heels, dangling them from his fingertips for a moment before setting them down. "These are ridiculous."

She rose with him. "This is an important event for Coast Eagle. And Destiny says they make my calves look longer."

"Your calves are already the perfect length." He set the shoes on the chair.

"You're not even looking at them."

"I can tell by your height." He offered his arm again. "Shall we?"

"I suppose it's the least I can do, since you saved my feet. But you have to make me a promise."

"Sure."

She took his arm. "After the dance, walk me to the exit." She glanced discreetly around. "For some reason, nobody's bothering me when I'm with you."

"Were they bothering you before?"

"All evening long." She'd never experienced anything like it. "Donations, jobs and pictures. Why on earth would anybody want their picture taken with me?"

"Because you're beautiful?" He drew her into his arms.

"Ha, ha." Coco had been beautiful. Amber was, well, sensible. She was very sensible.

Not that sensible was a bad thing. And she truly didn't mind her looks. Her eyes were a pleasant shade of blue. Her nose wasn't too big. Her hair was slightly curly and had its good days and bad days. Today it had been tamed by a team of professionals, so it looked pretty good. She had to say, though, she wasn't crazy about the sticky feeling from all the products they'd used at Chez Philippe.

"I wasn't joking," said Cole.

"We both know you've got a lot of ground to make up for from earlier," she said, settling into the rhythm of the music.

"True," he agreed.

"So anything you say or do is suspect."

"You're pretty tough to compliment, you know that?"

"There's no need. I'm over the fact that you didn't like Samuel."

He paused as if weighing his next words. "You're a very good dancer."

She couldn't tell if he was mocking her or not. She'd certainly never spent much time perfecting dance steps. Was he trying to kowtow, or was he simply making small talk? Or maybe he was just getting off the topic of Samuel.

"So are you," she answered neutrally. "I can't remember where you said you were from."

"Alaska. Are you changing the subject?"

"From me to you? Yes. You're about out of things to compliment. Unless you like my hair."

"I like your hair."

"Good. It cost a lot of money to get it this way. Now back to you."

"Aviation 58 is in Juneau. The state capital. It's on the panhandle."

"You're a pilot?"

"I am. I'm also one of the owners of the airline."

"I've never heard of it."

Coast Eagle flew to Seattle and California, but they didn't venture into the north. "We're regional."

She tipped her head back to look at him. "And what brought you to Atlanta, Cole Parker?"

He gave a small shrug. "It's December. Have you seen a weather report for Alaska?"

"Not recently. Maybe never."

"It's cold up there."

"So you're on vacation?"

"For a few days, yes."

For the first time, she allowed herself to take a good look at his face. She realized he was an astonishingly handsome man, deep gray eyes, a straight nose, square chin, all topped with thick, dark hair, cut short and neat. She couldn't detect aftershave or shampoo, but there was something fresh and clean about his scent.

He was probably six-two. His shoulders were square, body fit and trim. And his big, square hands seemed strong and capable where they held her. In a flash, she realized she was attracted to him.

"Amber?" His deep voice startled her. That sound was another thing she liked about him.

"Yes?"

"I asked if there was anything in particular we should see." Had he? How had she missed that?

She quickly corralled her thoughts. "The botanical gardens are beautiful. Or you can do outdoor ice-skating. My favorite is Atlantic Station. A little shopping, a little Christmas-light gazing, some hot chocolate." She couldn't help thinking about Zachary and the Christmas events he might enjoy as he got older.

She'd easily come to love seeing him every day. He was a bit fussy in the evenings, but the poor little guy had been through a lot. His mother and father were both gone, and he had no way of knowing why it was happening.

She was doing her best to substitute. And she'd wrapped her head around the possibility of raising a baby. Though she couldn't yet imagine her life with a child, a school-age child, then a teenager, then a young man. When she thought that far ahead, she feared she wasn't capable of pulling it off. But she knew she had to come through for him. She was all he had.

She felt a sudden urge to rush home and hold him in her arms, reassure him that she'd figure it out.

"Are we close to the exit?" she asked Cole, thinking she could slip out and get herself home.

"I'll dance you over there," said Cole. "Tired?"

"Partly. But this isn't exactly my thing."

"I thought the über-rich thrived on fresh crab, Belgian torte and champagne."

"I'm not über-rich." Though she could understand how he would make that mistake. Lately, everybody seemed to assume that guardianship of Zachary made her an instant billionaire. It was far more complicated than that.

"Right," he drawled.

She didn't want to have this debate. "Thank you for the dance, Cole."

His expression turned serious. "I did it again, didn't I? Stuffed my foot in my mouth?"

"Not at all. I am tired, and I really appreciate you escorting me across the ballroom. It was going to take hours at the rate I was going."

"I'll get you to the front doors," he offered.

"That's not necessary."

"It's my pleasure." His hand dropped to the small of her back. "I'll glower at anyone who tries to talk to us along the way."

She couldn't help but smile at that. And, to be truthful, it did seem like a prudent course of action. The lobby and foyer were full of people. Her name and face had been in the news for the past three weeks, so she was easily recognized.

"Then, thank you," she told him.

"Let's go."

He picked up the pace, drawing her across the mezzanine floor lobby and down two sets of elevators. People stared as they passed but didn't approach them. For a fleeting moment, she wondered if he'd consider a permanent gig as her escort. This was certainly more pleasant than her trek into the event.

"The doorman will get me a cab," she told Cole as they came to the glass front.

"No need. I have a car right here."

"Cole—"

"And a driver," he finished, moving through the front door. "I'm not plotting to get you alone. I'll get you home safe and sound, nothing else."

As she stepped onto the sidewalk, she felt its cold hardness through the dancing slippers, and her memory kicked in. "My shoes." She turned. "I left my shoes upstairs."

"I'll go back for them," he offered. "You don't need to walk all that way again."

"Taxi, sir?" the doorman inquired.

"I've got a car waiting," Cole answered, handing the man a tip. "A sedan for Aviation 58."

"I'll have it brought around," the doorman answered.

"I can't take your car," said Amber. How had this gotten so complicated?

"Where are you going?" asked Cole.

"Fifth Avenue and Eighty-Ninth."

"It'll only take ten minutes to get you there."

A black car pulled up in front of them and Cole opened the door.

Amber decided to go with the flow. The sooner she got going, the sooner she'd be home with Zachary. She climbed in, and Cole shut the door behind her.

But before they pulled away, he surprised her by hopping in the other side.

"I thought you were going back for my shoes."

"I'll do that after we get you home. Fifth Avenue and Eighty-Ninth," he said to the driver.

"That's ridiculous."

She couldn't understand why he'd make the round trip for nothing. Unless he was worried she'd commandeer his car for a joyride. Though she doubted the driver would let her do that.

As they pulled out of the turnaround and onto the street, she clicked through other possibilities. He'd been intensely persistent, awfully complimentary and easy to get along with, and he'd stuck to her like glue. What could he be after?

And then it came to her. The man owned an airline, a small regional West Coast airline that was likely looking to expand. She instantly realized the vacation story was a cover. Cole was here to do business.

She angled herself in the seat, facing him. "You're after our Pacific routes."

"Excuse me?"

"I figured it out. You're thinking Samuel's death makes Coast Eagle vulnerable. You're hoping we'll be looking to downsize, and you think you can get your hands on the Pacific routes to expand Aviation 58."

He stared at her for a long moment.

"You've been way too friendly," she elaborated. "You overplayed your hand."

"Maybe I'm simply attracted to you."

She gazed down at the fancy dress. She did look better than

usual, but Cole was still out of her league. "There were far more beautiful women at the event tonight."

"I didn't see them." The sincerity in his expression was quite impressive.

"Nice try. It's the routes."

"You see that as the only possible explanation?"

"I do."

"Then, I admit it. It's the routes. Will you sell them to me?"

She leaned back in the seat. "I don't know why everybody thinks I have so much power. I'm the assistant director of finance. There's still a board of directors in place, and the vice presidents are in charge of operations until they name a new president."

"But as Zachary's guardian, you control board appointments."

"Theoretically."

If she kept custody of Zachary, that would be true. But before that could ever happen, she had a big fight with Roth on her hands.

"There's nothing theoretical about it," said Cole. "The board answers to the shareholders, and the president answers to the board, and everyone else answers to the president. You can do anything you want."

"But I won't. I have my own job at Coast Eagle, and I'm not about to muscle in on anyone else's."

"It's your responsibility." There was an unexpected hardness to Cole's tone. "It's your responsibility to Zachary to take control of the company."

She turned to look at him again. "It's my responsibility to Zachary to ensure the company is well run. That doesn't mean I make any particular decision."

His dark eyes were implacable. "Yes, it does."

"Well, Mr. Cole Parker, owner of Aviation 58 in Alaska, you are certainly entitled to your opinion. And I'm more than entitled to ignore it."

He opened his mouth but then obviously thought better of speaking.

The car came to a halt at the curb.

"The Newmont Building?" the driver asked. "Or are you in Sutten's Edge?"

"This is it," said Amber, feeling anxious to get away. "Joyce Roland is the director of planning," she said to Cole. "You can ask her about the Pacific routes, but she may not take your call."

The driver had come around and now swung open her door.

"Thank you for the ride. Good night, Cole."

A small smile played on his lips. "You're very polite."

"So I've been told."

"Good night, Amber. Thank you for the dance."

A sudden rush of warmth enveloped her, and she found her gaze dropping from his eyes to his lips. For a fleeting second, she imagined him kissing her good-night.

She shook away the wayward feeling and quickly exited the car. Zachary was upstairs waiting, and Roth was in the wings with a team of high-priced lawyers. Amber didn't have time for kisses or fantasies or anything else.

Cole advanced through the hotel lobby, heading for the escalators that would take him back to the ballroom.

It didn't take him long to spot Luca coming the other way, a pretty blond woman at his side.

"There you are," said Luca as they met. "I wondered what had happened to you."

"I left something in the ballroom," said Cole.

"This is Destiny Frost. Turns out, she's a friend of Amber Welsley." Luca's expression was inscrutable.

Cole played along, pretending Luca hadn't planned to meet Destiny. "Nice to meet you." He offered his hand.

She shook, and hers was slim and cool. "It's a pleasure."

"I offered Destiny a ride home," said Luca. "You coming with us?" His expression told Cole a third wheel would not be particularly welcome.

Cole tipped his chin toward the escalator. "I have to grab something upstairs. Can you swing back and get me later?"

Luca gave a satisfied smile. "Will do."

"Luca says you're from Alaska?" asked Destiny.

"We are," Cole replied.

"I've never been there."

"It's beautiful, magnificent."

"It must be cold."

Luca stepped in. "I've already offered to keep her warm."

Destiny smiled and shook her head. "He's shameless."

"But harmless," said Cole, intending to be reassuring, but also being honest. Luca was a perfect gentleman.

"I'll text you on the way back?" asked Luca.

"Sounds good." With a nod to both of them, Cole headed for the escalator.

He was going against the crowd, most people on their way out of the event. So he easily made it to the ballroom and headed for the chair where they'd parked Amber's shoes.

To his surprise, they were gone.

"Seriously?" he muttered out loud.

He glanced around at the departing crowd. At an event this highbrow, somebody was going to steal a pair of shoes?

Then he caught a glint of gold in one of the waiter's hands. He squinted. It was definitely Amber's shoes. The man was headed toward a side exit.

Cole made a beeline after him, feeling better about human nature. The waiter obviously thought they'd been abandoned and was taking them to the hotel's lost and found.

Cole wound his way through the tables and took the same exit, coming out into a long dim hallway. One direction obviously led to the kitchen, the other down a narrow flight of stairs. It seemed unlikely that the lost and found was in the kitchen, so he took the stairs.

At the bottom, he spotted the guy about thirty yards away. He called out, and the man turned.

"The shoes," called Cole.

Before he could say anything more, the man bolted, running a few steps before shoving open a side exit.

"Are you kidding me?" Cole shouted, breaking into a run.

He burst through the side door, finding himself in an alley.

He quickly scanned the area and spotted the guy at a run. He sprinted after the man. When he caught up, he grasped the guy's left arm and spun him around, bringing him to a sliding halt.

"What's going on?" Cole gasped. "You're stealing a pair of *shoes?*"

"They're my girlfriend's." The man was gasping for breath.

"They're *my* girlfriend's." As he spoke, Cole couldn't help but take note of the man's unshaven face, and the rather wild look in his eyes. "You're not a waiter."

The man reached in his pants pocket and pulled a knife, flicking open a six-inch blade and holding it menacingly out in front of him.

"They're *shoes,*" said Cole, adrenaline rushing into his bloodstream. Admittedly, they were nice shoes. And given the Hendersons' wealth, they were likely ridiculously expensive. But what could they possibly bring this guy on the black market?

The man snarled. "Do yourself a favor and walk away."

No way was that happening. Cole was returning Amber's property to her. "Give me the shoes."

"You want to get *hurt?*"

Suddenly, a low growl sounded next to Cole. His skin prickled, and he glanced cautiously down. But the mangy dog was staring at the man with the knife. It didn't seem to be threatening Cole.

"He'll go for your throat," Cole lied.

The man glanced furtively at the dog.

The dog growled again.

"Drop the knife, or he'll attack."

The man hesitated, and the dog took a step forward. The knife clattered to the ground, along with the shoes, and the man took two rapid steps backward. Then he spun around and ran.

Cole took in the medium-size dog that was now wagging its tail, obviously feeling proud of himself.

"Good job," he told the mutt, patting its head, finding sticky, matted fur.

He looked closer and realized the animal was painfully thin.

It had a wiry, mottled coat, mostly tan, but black on the ears and muzzle. Its brown eyes looked world-weary and exhausted.

"You a stray?" Cole found himself asking.

He moved to pick up the shoes. When he straightened, the dog was watching him patiently.

"You probably want a reward for all that."

The dog blinked.

"I don't blame you." Cole blew out a breath. He supposed the least he could do was buy the animal a burger.

"Come on, then." He started down the alley toward the brightly lit street. The dog trotted at his heels.

At the front of the hotel, Cole reported the incident to one of the doormen, who sent someone to retrieve the knife. Cole learned that they'd had previous trouble with a thief impersonating a waiter at large events. If the knife had fingerprints on it, they might be able to catch the guy. It seemed likely he'd stolen more than just the shoes tonight.

Duty done, Cole and the dog then made their way down the street until they came to a fast-food restaurant.

Thinking it was a fifty-fifty shot the mutt would wait, Cole left it outside while he purchased two deluxe hamburgers. He was hungry after the fancy little portions at the pilots association event, and a burger didn't seem like the worst idea in the world.

When he returned to the street, the dog jumped to attention. It wolfed down the burger in two bites, so Cole gave it the second one, as well.

His phone chimed, and a text message told him Luca was sending back the empty car. Luca and Destiny were stopping for a nightcap.

Cole smiled at his friend's luck, tossed the wrappers in the trash and headed back toward the hotel. Predictably, the dog followed along. It was sure to be disappointed when a meal didn't appear at their next stop.

Cole took the animal back to the alley at the edge of the hotel property and pointed. "Go on, now," he told it.

It looked up at him uncomprehendingly.

"Go home," Cole commanded.

It didn't move.

He made his voice sterner. "Go on."

The dog ducked its head, eyes going sad.

Cole felt a shot to his chest.

He tried to steel himself against the guilt, but the effort didn't pay off. He crouched down in front of the dog, scratching its matted neck and meeting its eyes. "I don't know what you expect here."

It pushed forward, nuzzling its nose against Cole's thigh.

"Those are rented pants," said Cole.

It pushed farther forward.

"I live in Alaska."

Its tail began to wag.

"Crap."

"Mr. Parker?" The driver appeared in Cole's peripheral vision. "Are you ready to go, sir?"

Cole stood, drawing a deep sigh. "We're ready."

"We?"

"The dog's coming, too."

The driver glanced down at the scruffy animal. He hesitated, but then said, "Of course, sir."

"Do you have a blanket or something to protect the seat?"

"I'll get a newspaper from the doorman."

"That'll work," said Cole. He looked to the dog. "You want to go for a car ride?"

Its head lifted. Its brow went up. And its tail wagged harder.

"I'll take that as a yes." Cole knew he was making a stupid, emotional decision, one he'd likely regret very quickly. But he couldn't bring himself to leave the animal behind.

He closed his eyes for a long moment. All this for a pair of shoes.

Three

The next morning, Cole headed for the Hendersons' penthouse apartment to return Amber's shoes. He took the dog with him, thinking maybe he'd stop by the shelter on his way back and drop it off. He told himself they were in the business of finding stray animals good homes.

The dog looked much more appealing since Cole had given him a bath in the hotel's carwash bay. He smelled better, too, considerably better. And he'd probably put on five pounds between the room-service steak last night and the bacon and sausage breakfast.

The animal had been meticulously well behaved, and now stood quietly by Cole's side while Cole rang the bell.

A minute later, Amber answered the door. She was dressed in faded blue jeans, bare feet poking out at the bottom. A stained T-shirt stretched across her chest, and she had what looked like oatmeal smeared in her hair. Zachary was bawling in her arms.

"The doorman said it was a delivery," she told Cole over Zachary's cries.

Cole held up the shoes. "It is a delivery."

She focused on the shiny creations while struggling to hold the wiggling, howling Zachary. "Honestly, I'd hoped somebody might steal them."

"You have got to be kidding." Cole didn't know whether to laugh or cry.

"Only partially kidding," she admitted. "They cost a lot of money, but I don't ever want to have to wear them again." She glanced down. "You have a dog?"

"I have one now," he said.

"Okay." She seemed to digest that while Zachary continued to wriggle. It was clear she had her hands full. "Could you maybe just bring them in and toss them down?" She glanced around the foyer.

"Sure." Cole moved through the doorway, spying a closet door. He opened it and placed them inside.

The baby's cries faded to whimpers behind him.

He turned back. "I'll have you know I practically risked my life to rescue these."

Zachary suddenly stiffened. He twisted his head to stare at Cole in what looked like amazement.

"The party got that wild?" Amber asked.

Zachary's silver-gray eyes focused on Cole like lasers. He went silent and stared unblinking, seeming to drink in Cole's appearance.

Then, suddenly, he lunged for Cole.

"Hey." Amber grappled to keep hold of him.

Zachary's own arms were outstretched, reaching almost desperately for Cole. He started to howl again, hands clasping the air.

"This is weird," said Amber.

Cole didn't have a clue how to respond.

"Do you mind?" She moved closer, glancing meaningfully at the baby.

"I guess not." Who would say no?

Taking Zachary from her arms, he cautiously brought him into his chest. Zachary instantly wrapped his arms around Cole's neck, squeezing tight. He nuzzled his sticky, tear-damp face against Cole's skin. Then he sighed, and his entire body went limp against Cole's chest.

Through his shock and surprise, Cole's heart started to pound, bringing a strange tightness to his chest. For some bizarre reason, his baby brother trusted him. How was a guy supposed to react to that?

"You're magic," Amber whispered. "Whatever it is you're doing, just keep it up."

"I'm only standing here."

"He's been crying for over an hour. He gets like that sometimes."

"He probably exhausted himself before I got here."

"I think he misses his parents," Amber said softly, her expression compassionate as she gazed at Zachary. She reached out to stoke the baby's downy hair. "But he doesn't understand what he's feeling, and he certainly can't put it into words."

Then she gave Cole a sweet smile. "You should come inside for a minute."

The dog seemed to understand the invitation. It padded gamely into the living room.

Amber's cute, disheveled appearance, the mutt's claws clicking on the hardwood and the baby powder scent of Zachary's warm body curled in his arms brought a sense of unreality to Cole.

"Sure," he answered, and followed her through the archway.

It took only seconds for him to realize this was a perfect opportunity to learn more about her.

"It was either this or the mansion." She seemed to be apologizing for the opulent surroundings. "We thought it would be less disruptive if Zachary kept his nanny, Isabel. She occasionally sleeps over, so there was no way we'd all fit in my apartment. It's one bedroom with a tiny kitchen. This place belonged to Samuel."

The furnishings were obviously expensive, but they were strewn with baby blankets and rattles, the floor decorated with colorful plastic toys.

"Sorry about the mess," she said.

"You don't need to apologize."

"And me." She looked ruefully down at herself. "Well, this is me. This is what I normally look like. Last night was the anomaly."

"Seriously, Amber. You have nothing to apologize for. You look great."

She coughed out a laugh of disbelief.

"Okay, you look normal. How formal do you think we get in Alaska?"

She seemed to consider that. "Can I get you something?"

"I'm fine."

He didn't want to put her to any work. Then again, judging by Zachary's even breathing and relaxed body, his excuse for hanging around had just fallen asleep. Maybe refreshments weren't such a bad idea.

"Do you happen to have coffee?" he asked.

"Coming up. Take a seat anywhere." She gestured to the furniture as she exited through another archway that obviously led to the kitchen.

Cole took in the massive living room. In one corner, a plush sofa and a couple of leather armchairs bracketed a gas fireplace. Another furniture grouping was set up next to a bank of picture windows overlooking the city. The room was open to a formal dining room at one end and a hallway at the other that obviously led to the bedrooms.

He decided to follow Amber into the kitchen. No point in wasting valuable conversation time here by himself.

The kitchen was also huge, with high ceilings, a central island, generous granite counter spaces, stainless-steel appliances of every conceivable description and maple cabinets interspersed with big windows that faced the park. There was a breakfast nook at one end, stationed beside a balcony door, and an open door at the other, leading to a big pantry.

"This is very nice," said Cole.

"I'm still getting used to the size." She closed the lid and pressed a button on the coffeemaker. "It's weird moving into someone else's stuff—their furniture, their dishes, their towels. It's crazy, but I miss my pepper mill." She pointed to a corner of the counter. "You practically need a forklift to use that one."

Cole found himself smiling. "You should move your own stuff in."

For some reason, her expression faltered.

"I'm sorry," he quickly put in. "It's too soon?"

She paused, seeming to search for words. "It's too something. I won't pretend I was close to my stepsister, and I barely knew Samuel. Maybe it's the court case. Maybe I don't want to jinx anything. But I'm definitely keeping my own apartment intact until everything is completely finalized."

Cole perched on a stool in front of the island. Zachary was

quiet and comfortable in his arms and surprisingly easy to hold. "Tell me about the court case."

"You haven't read the tabloids?"

"Not much."

"I'm in a custody battle with Roth Calvin. He's a vice president at Coast Eagle and Samuel's stated choice for guardian."

"I'd heard that much."

"Coco named me as guardian, and I won on a technicality, but Roth's fighting it."

"Is Roth close to Zachary?"

Amber pulled two hunter-green stoneware mugs out of a side cupboard. "Roth's close to Coast Eagle. You were right last night in the car. The person who controls Zachary ultimately controls the company."

"So you *can* get me my Pacific routes." Now that Cole had thought it through, he realized the cover story was perfect. It gave him an excuse to ask all kinds of questions without anybody growing suspicious.

"I have no intention of micromanaging Coast Eagle."

"We had a fight last night, didn't we?" Cole had become so focused on the shoes, and then the dog, and then on Zachary, he'd forgotten she'd left the car mad at him.

"You call that a fight?"

"I believe I questioned your commitment to Zachary's inheritance."

"My commitment is to Zachary. I want the company to stay healthy for him, sure. But I can tell when I'm not the smartest person in the room. There are a lot of committed, hardworking managers and employees at Coast Eagle. They need to continue running the company."

"Don't sell yourself short."

"I'm an assistant director, Cole."

He liked it when she said his name. "You're responsible for the well-being of the company owner."

Her gaze rested on Zachary, and her tone went soft. "Poor thing."

"Poor little rich boy?" It came out more sarcastic than Cole had intended.

"I honestly wish he'd inherited a whole lot less. That way nobody would fight me for him."

"So you're afraid you might lose?"

Her expression faltered, and she focused on pouring the freshly brewed coffee. "I try not to think about it." She turned back with both cups in her hands. "I can't believe you got him to sleep."

"I'm just sitting here breathing. You wore him out."

"Maybe he likes the sound of your voice."

"Maybe," Cole agreed.

Cole didn't like to think Zachary's behavior had anything to do with the genetic connection. But Cole supposed it was possible he sounded like Samuel. Maybe Zachary was subconsciously picking it up.

"You can probably get away with putting him down in his bed," said Amber.

"He's fine here."

Oddly, Cole didn't want to put Zachary down, at least not right away. This vulnerable little baby was his brother. And for some reason, the kid had instantly trusted him. Cole was suddenly acutely aware that there were two of them in the world. He could not have imagined how that would make him feel.

Amber's boss, Herbert Nywall's, expression was stern as he rose from the table in her compact office on the seventh floor of the Coast Eagle building.

Max Cutter was the company's chief lawyer, so Herbert had had no choice but to acquiesce to his request to speak privately with Amber. But it was obvious Herbert was becoming frustrated with the increasing interruptions of Amber's day-to-day duties.

She didn't blame him.

"Can this wait, Max?" she asked, earning a look of shock from Herbert.

"I'm afraid not. Sorry, Herbert."

"Not at all," Herbert responded with false cheer. "She's all yours."

"We're pretty busy today," Amber told Max as Herbert closed the door behind him.

"You can't pretend this isn't happening." Max took the chair across from her at the two-person meeting table. It was wedged between her desk and a bookshelf in the windowless room.

"Believe me, I'm not pretending anything isn't happening." In the past three weeks, her life had been turned completely upside down.

Nothing was remotely normal, and now Cole Parker had appeared, somehow insinuating himself into the circumstances. She didn't quite know what to make of him. He was opportunistic, that was for sure. And he had definite designs on Coast Eagle.

But Zachary's reaction to him had been astonishing. And her own reaction was just as bizarre. Yesterday, she'd fought a ridiculous urge to throw herself into Cole's arms and trust him completely.

Max got straight to the point. "Roth's pressuring the board to appoint him president."

The news surprised Amber. It also worried her. "I thought they were going to wait to choose a president."

"That was the agreement. But he wants it bad, and half of the board members are convinced he'll win the custody battle. If he does, he'll be the guy deciding who stays on the board. They want to ingratiate themselves now while they have a chance."

Amber understood their dilemma. She even sympathized. If Roth obtained custody of Zachary, he'd be ruthless in his revenge on board members who'd stood against him.

"Plus," Max continued, "they see strength in him, decisiveness and intelligence. They think he'll make a good president."

"I don't like him," Amber blurted out. "And I don't think he'd make a good president."

Max sat back in his chair. "That was definitive." He seemed to be considering her words. "Is it because of the situation with Zachary? Because that would certainly be understandable."

"It's because he recklessly spends company money. He wants to refurbish or replace the entire fleet with no regard whatsoever for the debt load. He's a shopaholic on a massive scale."

Max quirked a smile. "Interestingly put, but not inaccurate from what I've seen."

"They can't make him president."

"The board's deadlocked. We need to appoint another board member to break the tie."

Amber shook her head. Max had broached the subject of board appointments with her two weeks ago.

"You know I don't want to do that."

"I know you don't."

"I don't want to run Coast Eagle." She knew she wasn't qualified to take the helm of the company.

"Well, you're the only one who doesn't."

Amber came to her feet, taking the three steps that brought her flush against the front of her desk. She turned back. This was a terrible office for pacing.

Max spoke again. "If you appoint the right person, a majority will agree on a different interim president and Roth will have to back down. If you don't appoint anyone, MacSweeny will flip. It's only a matter of time. And then Roth's in."

Amber spoke more to herself than to Max. "And the spending spree begins."

For some reason, her thoughts turned back to Cole Parker. In the car Saturday night, he'd said it was her responsibility to take control of the company for Zachary. She'd disagreed with him at the time, but the advice stuck with her.

She let the memory take shape, and his image came clear in her mind. The streetlights had played across his handsome face. He was sexy in a suit, sexier still in his blue jeans the next morning at the penthouse. And the memory of him holding Zachary? The tenderness had touched a chord deep down inside her. It shouldn't have turned her on, but it did. The truth was, everything about Cole turned her on.

All that probably meant she *shouldn't* take his advice.

She looked at Max, bringing herself back to the present. She had to agree that letting Roth plunge the airline into debt wasn't in Zachary's best interest. Any thinking person could see that. And what Max said was true. At the moment, she was the only person who could legally appoint a new board member.

If she didn't do it, no one could.

"Who?" she found herself venturing. "If I was to appoint someone, who would that be?"

It had to be someone they could trust. It also had to be someone who didn't have to fear Roth if he won the custody battle. It had to be someone who understood the airline, who brought true value to the board and who could be strong in the face of divided loyalties, uncertain times and extraordinarily high stakes.

She couldn't think of a single person who fit the bill.

"You," Max told her softly.

"No." She gripped the back of her chair and shook her head. "No." It was unthinkable. *"No."*

"You underestimate yourself, Amber."

"Coco chose me because she knew I would love Zachary. She had no idea it would put me in this position with the company."

"Coco had no idea about anything," said Max.

Amber didn't know how to respond to that. Her sister wasn't the most analytical person in the world. It was fair to say that Coco had operated on emotion rather than logic. It was also fair to say that Coco had never really grown up. She'd wanted what she'd wanted, and she'd usually wanted it right away. She'd never spent much time worrying about the impact on others.

"There's no one else," said Max, spreading his palms.

"There has to be."

"It's one vote. You take the appointment. You go to one meeting. You vote. You leave. And the new president takes over the reins." He glanced around her small office, all but wrinkling his nose. "You can come back here an hour later and take over your regular duties."

"There's nothing wrong with my job."

"Nobody's saying there is. Though not many new billionaires would keep working in this particular office."

"I'm not a new—"

"Amber, please. I can see that your instinct is to be humble. But you're Zachary's guardian. Anytime you want to exercise it, you have control of a billion-dollar company."

"Temporarily."

"Maybe. But maybe not."

She slid back into her chair, propping her elbows on the table. "It's not that simple."

"It's very simple."

She couldn't, wouldn't, didn't dare let her head run away with any aspect of the situation. There was too much at stake for her to let her guard down.

She tried to explain her feelings to Max. "I can't let myself think it's real until it's really real. You know?"

"Amber, this is no time to be superstitious."

"I can't jinx custody of Zachary. I can lose anything else, but not him."

"Coast Eagle needs you to step up."

Her stomach went hollow, and her pulse began to pound. It wasn't exactly what Cole had said, but it was close. Two apparently smart men were telling her the same thing.

"How long do I have to decide?"

"Twenty-four hours. After that, we may lose MacSweeny."

"Let me think about it."

Max gave a sharp nod. Then he rose. "I'll be back tomorrow."

"I'll be here."

"Max is a very intelligent lawyer," said Destiny over Zachary's cries.

They were in the penthouse kitchen, Amber jostling Zachary and Destiny doling out linguini and salad.

"You're a smart lawyer, too," said Amber.

"Sure, but I'm looking after your interests. Max is looking after the interests of Coast Eagle. From the perspective of what's in the best interests of the company, you should absolutely take the board appointment."

"And from the perspective of me?"

"You'll make a lifelong enemy out of Roth."

"I've done that simply by breathing."

Destiny grinned, while Zachary's cries increased.

Amber jiggled harder. She was growing exhausted. "I swear, if I had Cole Parker's phone number, I'd call him up and beg him to come over."

"He's the other Alaska guy?"

"Yes, the one who put Zachary to sleep Sunday morning without lifting a finger." Amber knew she should feel miffed by that, because it sure didn't seem fair.

Destiny picked up her phone. "I've got Luca's number."

"Yeah, right," Amber chuckled.

But Destiny raised her phone to her ear. "Luca? It's Destiny."

"Don't you dare," said Amber.

Destiny stopped talking and smiled. "Thanks."

Amber shook her head in warning.

"That's not why I'm calling," said Destiny. "No. It's really not. I'm looking for Cole."

Amber shook her head more frantically, moving closer.

"Not even close," said Destiny. "Tell him Amber needs him to put Zachary to sleep."

"She's joking," Amber called out, causing Zachary to cry louder. She turned away, walking toward the living room. "Shh, shh, shh," she whispered in his ear. "I'm sorry, baby. I didn't mean to scare you."

"Hi, Cole," said Destiny from behind her. "Yes, Amber needs the baby cavalry. Can you come?"

Amber couldn't believe this was happening. Cole was a stranger. You couldn't ask a stranger to drop everything, drive over and soothe your baby. The world didn't work like that. With any luck at all, he'd be bright enough to say no.

"They're on their way," called Destiny.

"You've lost your mind."

Destiny set down her phone and moved to the wine rack recessed in the kitchen wall. "How's Zachary been doing with the nanny?"

"Sometimes he's good with Isabel, sometimes not. Evening

is always the worst. We're been helping each other, but tonight's her night off."

Perusing the shelves, Destiny chose a bottle. "Do you think maybe we could give him a little of the merlot?"

"I wish. But definitely pour me a glass."

Destiny located the corkscrew, peeled the foil and opened the bottle. She moved two glasses to the center of the island and poured, placing them next to the two plates of linguini.

Then she slid onto a stool while Amber jiggled her way back to the island.

Amber knew there was no point in sitting down. Zachary had a built in altimeter. His preferred height was precisely five feet off the ground, not four feet, not four and a half. And his preferred swaying arc was approximately nine inches. Any deviation from the pattern brought an immediate vocal protest.

Luckily, Amber had become adept at simultaneously standing, swaying and eating. She lifted her fork and swirled a bite of the seafood linguini.

"Say I was to appoint myself to the board," she ventured.

"Say you were."

"Would it hurt my custody argument? I mean, would it look like I was the kind of person who used Zachary to gain power in Coast Eagle?"

Destiny thought for a moment. "Maybe. I mean, we'd spin it that you were willing to step up and look after Zachary's interests."

"Would a judge believe that?"

"Maybe. It's a fifty-fifty shot. Then again, a judge might just as easily take you *not* joining the board as a sign you weren't a suitable guardian."

"Problem is we can't separate the two." Amber set down her fork to free her hand for a drink of wine.

Zachary batted his arm out, nearly knocking the glass from her hand. She gave up on the drink.

"If you do it," said Destiny, "Roth will spin it that you're power hungry. If you don't, he'll spin it that you're incapable. But Coco wanted you, and that's important."

"But Samuel wanted Roth."

"He did," Destiny agreed.

"And in a character and intellect debate, Samuel is going to win out over Coco every time."

Destiny took a drink, and Amber couldn't help but feel envious. She settled for another bite of the linguini.

A knock sounded on the door.

"That was fast," said Amber, starting for the path through living room.

"They're staying at the East Park."

With a tired and tearful Zachary on her shoulder, Amber crossed to the entry hall. She checked the peephole and opened the door to Cole and Luca.

She couldn't help but smile at the sight of the dog at Cole's heels. He'd told her about the shoe altercation, and his decision to take the animal back to the hotel. She also knew he'd been planning to drop the scruffy dog at a shelter. He hadn't done it yet, and that was somehow endearing.

His expression was sympathetic as he gazed at the pathetically sobbing Zachary.

"I hear you've got trouble?" he said.

Zachary instantly perked up. He straightened in Amber's arms, turning to Cole and blinking his watery eyes. Then he lunged for him.

Cole reflexively reached out, stepping forward to catch the baby. "Hey there, partner."

"It's hard not to take this personally," said Amber, even though her arms and shoulders were all but singing in relief as the weight was removed.

For some reason, Luca was grinning ear to ear as he took in the sight of Cole and Zachary. "Nice to see you again, Amber."

"Hello, Luca. I'm really sorry that Destiny called you guys. It wasn't a fair thing to do."

"No problem at all," said Luca. "She in here?" He brushed past Amber.

The dog kept his position next to Cole.

"In the kitchen," Amber called to Luca's back.

Cole moved into the entry, and Amber shut the door behind him. Zachary heaved a shuddering sigh and laid his head on Cole's shoulder.

"Do babies always react to you like this?" she couldn't help asking.

"I don't know. I'm not usually around them. Mostly, they ignore me."

"Do you mind if I have something to eat while you hold him?"

"Not at all." Cole shrugged out of his jacket, draping it over the brass coat tree. "Do whatever you want. Have a bath. Take a nap."

"Tempting," Amber admitted. "But I've got a glass of merlot in there with my name on it."

Cole and the dog followed her into the kitchen, where Destiny had dished up some linguini for Luca.

"Peace and quiet," she noted, taking in Zachary's posture.

His little hand was stroking one side of Cole's neck, his face buried in the other.

"Hungry?" Amber asked Cole.

"You go ahead. But I'd pour myself a glass of wine." He took the remaining of the four stools, and the dog curled up at his feet.

Amber took a satisfying sip of wine and another bite of linguini. It was wonderful to have the use of both hands.

"What's his name?" Destiny nodded to the dog as she poured wine for the men.

"I don't know," said Cole, looking down. "We met in the alley after the dance, and I wasn't really planning to keep him."

"I think he's planning to keep you," said Amber.

"That's because I fed him a burger that first night."

"Cole's got plenty of room in Alaska," said Luca.

"You're taking him home with you?" asked Destiny.

Cole glanced down and seemed to contemplate. "I suppose I am. I'm not liking his chances stacked up against those adorable puppies at the shelter. I don't know who would choose him."

"He's not that homely." Amber sized up the square, tan muzzle, the floppy, uneven ears and wiry, mottled coat. "Okay, maybe Alaska's not such a bad idea."

"You're so diplomatic," Cole said with a smile.

"He'll need a name," said Amber.

"Rover?" Cole asked the dog.

It didn't react.

"Spot?"

Nothing.

Amber smiled as she ate and drank.

"Lucky? Butch? Otis?"

The dog glanced sharply up.

"Seriously?" asked Cole. "Otis?"

The dog came up on its haunches and lifted its chin.

"Otis wins," said Destiny.

"Otis it is," said Cole, reaching down to pat the dog's head.

It sniffed at Zachary's bare foot.

Zachary looked down with curiosity, and the two stared at each other for a long moment.

"Sizing up the competition?" said Destiny.

"Which one?" asked Amber.

Zachary looked suspicious of Otis, and Otis looked suspicious of Zachary. The adults all chuckled at the picture.

Amber quickly polished off her dinner, knowing it wasn't fair to take continued advantage of Cole.

She moved her plate to the sink. "I should give this little guy his bath."

"I'm guessing you mean Zachary and not Otis," said Luca.

"Definitely Zachary." She couldn't help but picture Coco's reaction to Otis in her expensive bathtub.

Cole shifted Zachary on his lap. "Otis had a bath in the hotel car wash the first night I found him."

"Did he mind?" asked Amber.

"Didn't seem to. He smelled pretty bad, so I bribed the valet."

She couldn't help admire his ingenuity.

"Smells a little like Showoff Gold now, but it's a big improvement."

Zachary reached for Otis, grabbing a handful of his ear.

"Careful there," said Cole, gently pulling Zachary back. But Otis just gazed at Zachary, not seeming the slightest bit concerned.

Much as Amber hated to disturb Zachary when he seemed so happy, it was getting late. She moved toward him.

"Time for a bath?" she asked, a lilt to her voice as she smiled brightly, trying to send him the message that something fun was about to happen.

She held out her arms. "Bath?"

Zachary shrank against Cole, his face scrunching up in discontent.

"I can come with you," Cole offered.

"That seems like a cop-out," said Amber. She was already feeling a bit inadequate as a guardian.

Cole rose. "It's a bath. No big deal. Sometimes it's good to just go with the flow."

She couldn't deny she was tempted. "Okay, maybe just this once. But I'm supposed to be convincing a judge that I'm the best guardian for Zachary. I'd hate to have to tell him it was you instead."

"Definitely just this once," Cole answered. "I can hardly give the kid a bath from Alaska."

"In that case, let's make my evening easier."

She led the way down the hall to the main bathroom.

It was easy to tell which of the rooms had been redecorated by Coco. The living room and kitchen were luxurious, with the finest appliances and handcrafted furnishings. But they were subdued and sophisticated, with the obvious touch of a professional decorator.

The master bedroom and the three bathrooms were in stark contrast. They were bright and flamboyant, every feature an extravagance of brilliance and color.

"I should probably prepare you for this," she told Cole.

He was behind her in the wide hallway, followed by Otis.

"I don't mind a mess," he answered.

Amber couldn't help but laugh. "I wish I was talking about a mess."

The bathrooms were very well cared for. Samuel had employed the same housekeeper at the penthouse for nearly a decade, and Amber had no intention of letting the efficient woman go. She paused with her door on the handle.

"What's wrong?" Cole asked.

"It's purple."

"Okay?"

"Very purple." She pushed the door wide and pressed the light switch, watching for his reaction.

The floor tiles were a deep, mottled violet. The wallpaper was mauve with violet pinstripes. Two ultramodern sinks were purple porcelain on clear glass.

The skylight glowed with perimeter lighting, while spotlights twinkled above the shower, sinks and tub. In addition to the complex purple tile work, the walls were decorated with pink-hued abstract paintings, while violet-scented candles and whimsical figurines were placed on glass tables.

"This is very purple," Cole agreed, moving inside as he gazed around in obvious amazement.

She followed. "The tub in here is a relatively manageable size."

She pushed up the sleeves of her sweater and twisted the taps on the oval tub. "The one in the master bedroom is nearly a pool."

Cole grinned. "I guess if you've got the money, you can do whatever turns your crank."

Straightening, Amber retrieved a couple of thick towels and a facecloth from a recessed cabinet, balancing them next to a pink porcelain cat. For all its size, the room was hopelessly impractical. There was only one small cabinet, and the counter space was minimal, most of it taken up with decorations.

"It was pretty interesting to see what Coco did when she was suddenly presented with money," said Amber.

"Did you offer your opinion?" Cole asked, shaking his head at the outlandish decor.

"I didn't see this room until after she died."

Cole perched himself on the edge of the tub and began to

pop the snaps on Zachary's one-piece suit. "But you don't think your stepsister handled money very well?"

"I think it overwhelmed her. She grew up in downtown Birmingham without a lot of advantages. She was nineteen when she met Samuel."

"He must have been fifty."

"At least."

There was an edge to Cole's voice. "Nice."

"She was pretty, stunningly beautiful, actually. She was outgoing and fun loving, and she seemed to idolize Samuel. I'm sure a psychologist would have a field day with the relationship."

"I'm sure," Cole agreed.

Amber knelt down and tested the water temperature with the inside of her wrist. She shut off the taps. Then she suction cupped Zachary's bath safety ring to the bottom of the tub and dropped a couple of brightly colored plastic fish into the water.

"Based on my single college psychology elective," said Amber as Cole lowered the naked Zachary into the ring, "I would say Samuel was everything Coco's father was not. Conversely, I suspect Samuel secretly feared he'd never have children and saw Coco as someone he could care for and protect."

"And sleep with," said Cole.

"He did marry her. I have to give him credit for that."

Zachary grabbed for the green fish, sending splashes of water over the edge of the tub, dampening Amber's sweater and jeans.

"To be fair," she continued, "from what I saw, he genuinely loved Zachary. I think he'd have had more children if Coco was willing."

Cole had gone silent, his attention fixed on the baby.

After a long moment, he spoke. "You liked Samuel?"

"Not really. I mean, I barely knew him, but it's hard to admire a fiftysomething man who marries a nineteen-year-old. Especially one who…" Amber tried to reframe her thought, but there was no way to put it that wasn't insulting to Coco.

She stretched to retrieve the facecloth, dampening it in the bathwater then squirting some rose-scented soap from a china dispenser.

"So how is it that you and Coco became stepsisters?" Cole asked.

Amber started to wash Zachary's back, relieved that he'd let her blow past the nonanswer. "My mother died when I was a baby. When I was seven, my father remarried. But shortly after, he was killed by a drunk driver, and then it was just Tara and me."

"I'm sorry to hear that."

"Thank you." At first, Amber had been inconsolable over the loss of her father, while Tara had seemed overwhelmed by the responsibility of Amber. So Amber had grown up fast, accepted the situation and learned to be strong.

She continued with the story. "Shortly after he died, Tara remarried and got pregnant with Coco."

"Did you and Tara have a good relationship?"

Zachary splashed happily, cooing in the tub while Amber washed him.

"We didn't fight or anything. She worked as a waitress. I was in after-school care. She made sure I was fed and had clothes. Meanwhile I was a pretty good kid, and stayed out of her way."

"That sounds lonely."

Amber shrugged. "It was okay. I didn't really know any different until Coco came along." She dampened Zachary's soft hair and rubbed in a dollop of baby shampoo.

"What happened?"

"I saw a different approach to parenting."

"Let me guess, Coco was the golden child."

"She was the princess of the family. She was their biological baby. While I was ten and didn't belong to either of them."

"I'm so sorry, Amber."

She gave herself a mental shake as she removed Zachary from the bath ring. "It was a very long time ago. I don't know why I'm even going into it."

"Because I asked."

Crouched over the tub, she leaned Zachary along her arm to rinse his hair. He squirmed but didn't cry.

"I never knew my father," Cole said from beside her.

"Divorce?" she asked.

"Yes. Before I was born."

"Did you have a relationship with him?"

"None."

"Why not?"

"My mother wanted nothing to do with him, and neither did I."

"Do you still feel the same way?"

"I do. But it wouldn't matter."

Amber guessed at what Cole meant. "He passed away?"

"He did."

She stood Zachary up, checking to make sure he was squeaky-clean. "Any regrets?

"Not a one. He never knew about me. My mom was absolutely fantastic. It was just the two of us, but she was hardworking, loving, supportive."

"That's nice to hear." Amber lifted Zachary from the tub, wrapping him in a fluffy mauve towel.

He cooed happily, but then spotted Cole. He wriggled in her lap, reaching out and whimpering.

"This is definitely insulting," she said.

"You're great with him."

"I'm not sure about that." She was honest. "But I'm what he's got, and I do love him."

Cole rose from the edge of the tub, reaching out to take Zachary in one arm and then helping her to her feet. It took him a minute to speak.

"Sometimes," he said softly, "families just happen."

His hand was warm and dry beneath hers, broad, strong and slightly callused. He didn't immediately let her go, and a strange feeling surged up her arm, pushing into her chest.

Time seemed to stop. She stood still and drank in his appearance. He was such a gorgeous, sexy man. His smoke-gray eyes were warm with emotion. She noticed once again that his shoulders were broad, arms strong, chest deep. He seemed to radiate a power that was more than just physical.

She fought another urge to throw herself into his arms.

"Amber," he breathed.

He lifted his hand to brush her damp hair from her cheek.

His touch was featherlight, but she felt herself sway toward him.

He leaned in, slowly, surely.

Then he touched his lips to hers.

He tasted like fine wine, his lips warm and firm. The scented steam rose between them while his fingers slipped back, delving into her hair.

The kiss deepened, and her desire skyrocketed.

"Gak," called Zachary, his hand smacking her ear.

She jerked back in shock.

"Gak," Zachary repeated, pressing his feet against her as if he needed space.

"All right, partner," said Cole. "You have my attention." But his gaze stayed fixed on Amber.

Embarrassment flooded her. "I don't know what happened there."

"I do," said Cole. He held her gaze for a long beat. "And I've never taken a single psychology course."

Then he backed away to the bathroom door, leaving her awash in arousal and confusion.

Four

Cole sat across from Luca at a small table in the festively decorated lobby lounge in the East Park Hotel. A blue-and-silver Christmas tree towered thirty feet above them. Lit reindeer bracketed the entrance. Strings of garland and clusters of icicles cascaded from the high ceilings, while the windows were frosted with scenes of ice and snow.

Carols played softly in the background as guests enjoyed the breakfast buffet.

"There's not a doubt in my mind that Amber is the right guardian for Zachary," said Cole.

He couldn't help but worry about Amber's description of her stepsister, and how Roth's legal team might use Coco's background and reputation. Amber was definitely going to have a fight on her hands in court.

"This is what I'm talking about," said Luca, seeming not to have heard Cole's comment as he swiveled his laptop around to face Cole. "That's Samuel at the age of thirty-three, a year older than you are now."

Cole focused on the picture of his biological father. The eyes were similar, but Samuel's hair was lighter, his chin narrower and his nose had a bit of an upturn.

"It's only there if you're looking for it," he said. "And nobody's looking for it."

"You've been outed by a nine-month-old baby."

"Yeah, well, I think we can count on him to keep quiet."

"He'll learn to talk someday."

"Not before I leave town."

"And listen to this." Luca turned the laptop and punched another key. "It's Samuel giving a speech twenty years ago."

"…once the plan is fully implemented, the new routes will take us to Britain, France and Germany…"

"Okay, that's a bit uncanny," Cole had to admit. He'd heard

his own voice recorded on numerous occasions, and Samuel's was very, very close.

"The kid knows you're family."

"At least that explains why he's latched on to me."

Luca took a sip of his coffee. "But you're still just going to walk away?"

"No."

Luca drew back in clear astonishment. "You're not?"

"First, I'm going to make sure Amber wins custody. Then I'm going to walk away. Involving myself in the Henderson family was never part of the plan."

Cole was heading back to his life in Alaska just as soon as things were under control here. Showing up in Atlanta was about him doing his duty. It wasn't some family reunion, and he wasn't about to upend his and Zachary's lives by acknowledging their biological connection.

Kissing Amber last night might have momentarily thrown him off track. He still couldn't believe he'd done it—in a purple bathroom of all places, with Zachary in his arms. How ridiculous was that?

His plan was to keep complications to a minimum. Not that a single kiss had added some huge complication. In fact, he'd already put it into perspective.

Sure, Amber was pretty. She was sweet and kind and compassionate. And she'd had a rough time of it growing up. Her stories had engaged his sympathies.

But lots of people had a less-than-stellar upbringing. She was fine now, and she loved Zachary. And Cole was right to leave the two of them to get on with it.

"You're sure that's what you want?" asked Luca.

"I'm positive it's what I want." Cole pulled his thoughts back to his earlier point. "Roth will try to prove that Coco was unfit to name either a guardian for Zachary or the person to control Coast Eagle."

"On the bright side," said Luca, "I don't think many wills are overturned because they're foolish."

"I hope not." Just then, Cole wished he knew more about the law.

"So what do you think of Destiny?" he asked Luca. "I mean, other than she's hot. Can you see past the fact that she's hot? Because you should declare a conflict of interest if you can't be objective." Cole wanted to be sure Amber was getting the best possible legal advice.

Luca was all but laughing as he cut into his waffle. "I don't need to declare a conflict of interest. I know she's smart."

"Are you sure? How do you know?"

"I asked her a few questions last night."

"And?"

"And she had a ton of technical information at her fingertips. But she wouldn't tell me anything about Amber specifically."

"You didn't make her suspicious, did you?"

"No. I pretended I was curious about what I'd read on social media. There's a lot out there on social media." Luca set down his cutlery and pressed a few more keys on the laptop. "For example, this, here. There are new rumors that Roth Calvin will be named interim president of Coast Eagle."

Cole reached out to turn the laptop to face him again. "I thought Amber was in charge?" Letting Roth step up as interim president couldn't be a good move for her.

"It's a board decision," said Luca.

"Which tells us Roth has the ear of the board." Cole didn't like the thought of that.

"It does seem like he's got the power at least temporarily."

Cole dropped his napkin onto the table and stood. "I need to get a handle on the guy."

"Where are you going?"

"Coast Eagle's corporate headquarters. I want to look Roth Calvin in the eyes."

"Right now? Without an appointment?"

"I'll talk my way in. I'm a fellow airline owner."

"You want some help?"

Cole considered the offer. But then he shook his head. "He's less likely to have his guard up if it's just one guy."

"Whatever you want."

Cole shrugged into his jacket. "See what else you can find out about the law."

"Can I talk to Destiny again?"

"As long as you're oblique."

Luca's eyes lit up. "Covert operations. Roger that. This is kind of fun."

Cole couldn't help but grin in return. "Seduce her if you have to."

"I'm all in for you, buddy."

Cole skirted the Christmas tree, made his way past the reindeer and exited to the sidewalk. It was easy to hail a cab, and it was a short ride to Coast Eagle.

He took a few fast steps across the lobby, purposefully blending in with a group of employees to pass unnoticed by the security counter. Then he entered the elevator, pretending he knew exactly what he was doing. Taking the chance that Roth's office would be on the top floor, he pressed the button.

The rest of the group exited on twelve. Cole continued up to a big, brightly lit reception area. It had gleaming hardwood floors, a bank of windows overlooking the city and a pair of immaculate saltwater fish tanks bracketing a long reception counter staffed by one woman.

"Good morning." She was immaculately dressed and thirty-something, and she smiled as she greeted him.

Cole strode forward and held out his hand. "Good morning. I'm Cole Parker, owner of Aviation 58. We're a midsize commercial airline out of Alaska. I was told Roth Calvin was the man to speak with at Coast Eagle."

"Do you have an appointment, sir?"

"I'm afraid I just got into town."

The woman's smile faded a little. "I'm sorry, but Mr. Calvin doesn't have any openings today."

Footfalls and male voices rose up behind them. The woman's surreptitious, worried glance to the group told Cole one of them was likely Roth Calvin.

He quickly turned, talking the man in the middle of the group to be the guy in charge. It had to be Roth.

Again, Cole strode forward, offering his hand. "Roth Calvin. I'm Cole Parker."

Roth's expression was guarded, and his critical glance flicked to the receptionist. Cole figured it was only a matter of moments before security arrived on the scene.

"I was speaking with Amber Welsley the other day. She suggested you were the person to discuss Coast Eagle's Pacific routes? I'm Cole Parker, Aviation 58 out of Alaska."

"Amber told you to see me?" Roth asked.

"She did," Cole lied. "She speaks very highly of you."

Roth's eyes narrowed, and Cole feared he might have gone too far. He was trying to arouse Roth's curiosity, and maybe put him off guard with the mention of Amber.

Roth looked at Cole. Then he looked to the receptionist. "Sandra, push the Millsberg meeting by fifteen minutes."

"Yes, sir," the receptionist answered.

"Right this way, Mr. Parker." Roth gestured to a doorway off the reception area.

"Please, call me Cole." Cole entered an airy meeting room that housed a round table for four with leather and chrome chairs, coffee service on a marble side counter and a sofa grouping near the picture windows.

Roth gestured to one of the chairs at the round table, then took the one opposite. "How can I help you, Cole?"

"I understand you're about to be named interim president," Cole opened.

A smug smile formed on Roth's face. "You've been listening to rumors."

"I find, more often than not, rumors tend to be based on some truth. I'll be honest, Roth, Aviation 58 is looking to expand along the West Coast. With the shakeup at Coast Eagle, I wondered if you might be interested in discussing some of your less-profitable routes in the West."

"All of our routes are profitable."

Cole had checked out Coast Eagle's public information on

the ride over, and now he made some assumptions and guesses. "Seattle to Vancouver is barely break-even. You've been losing market share in Portland. And your passenger load is low on anything northbound out of LA. Entering into a lease or code-share deal with Aviation 58 could boost your cash flow and profits considerably."

"You've done your homework, I see."

"I have," said Cole. "And it tells me Amber Welsley is a short-term play. You're the guy with the ear of the board."

Roth didn't answer, but he did nod.

"I haven't seen the actual will, of course. But I can guess where that's going. A trophy wife is all well and good, but no-body's under any illusions. Samuel would never have allowed a situation where Coco's decisions could run Coast Eagle into the ground."

Roth chuckled, and his expression relaxed. "You strike me as an intelligent man, Cole Parker."

"I'm also a patient man. I get that your attention has to be on the home front for a few months."

Roth gave a shrug. "These things can be expedited."

"That's good to hear."

"A word here, a conversation there. It's all about who you know, and who knows you."

"I understand," said Cole. "The sooner you get custody of the kid, the better." He paused. "I mean, the better for Coast Eagle, of course."

"Once the big question is settled, we will be looking for an early cash influx," said Roth, coming to his feet.

Cole rose with him. "That's good to hear, I'll—"

Suddenly, the meeting room door flung open, and Amber burst in. She glared at Cole, cheeks flushed, nostrils flared. "You went behind my back?"

"Amber." Roth's voice was stern and patronizing.

"You suggested I follow-up," Cole said to Amber, purpose-fully mischaracterizing their conversation.

"This is a private meeting, Amber." Roth's tone grated on Cole's nerves.

Amber ignored Roth and spoke to Cole. "I suggested you follow up with Joyce Roland."

"Amber," Roth all but shouted. "Can you please *excuse us?"*

Cole had to steel himself from demanding that Roth shut up.

The receptionist appeared in the doorway. "Mr. Calvin? They're waiting. The Millsberg meeting?"

Roth looked to Cole. "I do apologize."

"No problem. Thank you for seeing me. I'll be in touch."

Roth looked to Amber, obviously waiting for her to leave.

She folded her arms across her chest, standing her ground. Cole wanted to applaud.

Roth gave in and left the room, followed by the receptionist.

"How dare you," Amber whispered.

Cole wished he could tell her he was on her side. "It was an initial courtesy call. Nothing sinister. I told you up front that I was interested in the Pacific routes."

"And what were you doing last night? Pumping me for information? Are you actually using Zachary's trust to gain an inside advantage?"

"You called *me* last night," he reminded her.

"And you were only too happy to show up."

"To help with Zachary."

"That's how you played it, all right." There was something in her eyes, a veiled hurt that made him think of their kiss.

He took a step forward. "Amber, I'm sorry."

"For lying to me?"

"I didn't lie to you. Last night was all about Zachary." He paused. "I mean, it was *mostly* all about Zachary."

She gave her hair a little toss. "You don't need to explain."

But he did need to explain. He wanted to explain. "I like you, Amber."

"Well, I don't like you."

He moved closer anyway. "Yes, you do."

"Go away."

He shook his head. "I understand that it's complicated."

"It's not complicated."

"It's Zachary. It's business. It's you, and it's me." Even as he spoke the words, he asked himself what on earth he thought he was doing. He needed to leave this alone, not ramp it up.

"There is no you and me." But her expression instantly shifted, telling him otherwise. Her lips parted, her blue-eyed gaze going bedroom soft.

Cole glanced at the open door, debating pushing it closed and pulling her into his arms again. But that would be a stupid move. The receptionist, Sandra, would certainly report the closed door to Roth. It would complicate things even further for Amber.

But she was so enchanting, and his memory of kissing her was so incredibly strong, he couldn't stop himself. He reached past her and gave the door a shove. Her eyes went wide as it clicked shut.

Without giving her a chance to protest, Cole pulled her into his arms, bringing his thirsty lips down to hers and kissing her soundly. She gasped, but she didn't pull away. After a moment, her lips softened. She kissed him back, and her arms wound around his neck.

He pressed their bodies close together, feeling the sweet heat of her thighs and the softness of her breasts. He teased her lips with his tongue, and she responded, parrying with him, a small moan burbling in the back of her throat.

His hand went to her cheek, cradling the soft skin, holding her in place while he plundered her mouth. He forgot where they were, forgot everything except the sweet taste and scent of Amber. His other hand moved to her waist, sliding beneath her linen blazer, along her silk blouse, feeling the heat of her skin through the thin fabric.

Suddenly, she pushed back. "We can't."

Cole sucked in a breath. Of course they couldn't. What was he thinking? They were in her place of business.

"I'm sorry," he said.

But she shook her head. "My fault, too." Then she glanced at her watch. "I have to go. There's a board meeting." She stopped talking. Inhaled a deliberate breath and took a step back. "That was foolish. I don't know what got into me."

"Amber—"

"Goodbye, Cole." She moved for the door.

"Can I call you later?"

"No." She shook her head and pulled open the door.

From behind her desk, Sandra's sharp gaze went to Amber, then to Cole. He tried to look casual, innocent, as if nothing more than a brief conversation had taken place between them.

But it was hard to put his finger on the exact expression and posture that would convey those things. So he simply left the room, bid a brief goodbye to Sandra and took the elevator back to the lobby.

Smoothing back her hair and mentally pulling herself together, Amber reached for the door handle to Coast Eagle's main boardroom.

She couldn't believe she'd kissed Cole again. She couldn't believe she'd done it in the office. And she sure couldn't believe she'd enjoyed it.

She tugged open the door.

"There you are," said Max, rising from his seat at the head of the long boardroom table.

The other eight members of the board nodded politely, their gazes fixed on her. They were all men, fortysomething to sixtysomething, longtime members of the Atlanta business community and the aviation industry. She knew most of them by sight, but she'd shared little more than a passing greeting with any of them.

Max moved away from the head chair, gesturing for her to sit down in it. "Please, Ms. Welsley."

She hesitated over the bold gesture, but Max gave her an encouraging smile.

She told herself she could do this. For Zachary, she could do this. She lifted her chin, walked forward and took the power chair.

Max took the chair to her right.

She stared down the center of the table, fixing her vision on the photograph of a red-and-white biplane at the far end of the room. She had no idea what to say.

Luckily, Max opened for her. "Per article 17.9 of the Coast Eagle Articles of Incorporation," he said, "Ms. Welsley is exercising her right as majority shareholder—"

"She's not the majority shareholder," said Clint Mendes.

Max peered at Clint. "According to the State of Georgia, she represents the majority shareholder."

"But that's under appeal," said Clint.

"And until that appeal is settled, Ms. Welsley represents the interests of Zachary Henderson. Now, as I was saying—"

The boardroom door swung abruptly open, revealing Roth in the threshold, his eyes wide, face ruddy, and his jaw clenched tight.

"Mr. Calvin," said Max, a clear rebuke in his tone. "I'm afraid this is a private meeting."

"Is this *a coup?*" Roth demanded.

A hush came over the room as everyone waited to see what Amber would do.

She immediately realized she had to step up. She couldn't let Max defend her against Roth. She was going to be a board member, and she had to stand her ground.

If she lost the court case, Roth would have her fired within seconds. He would have done that anyway. She had nothing left to lose.

She came to her feet, turning and squaring her shoulders. "Please leave the meeting, Roth."

The silence boomed around her.

Roth's jaw worked, his face growing redder. "Are you out of your—"

"Please leave," she repeated. "This meeting is for board members only."

"You're not a board member," Roth all but shouted.

"I'm the majority shareholder, Roth. That's as much as you need to know. *Now leave.*"

Nelson MacSweeny coughed, but said nothing.

Roth glared at the man.

Then he fixed a biting, narrow-eyed stare on Amber.

But he seemed to understand that he'd lost the round. He stepped back, banging the door shut.

Knees shaky, Amber sat down. Everyone was still looking down the table at her. But something in their expressions had changed.

It might have been her imagination, but there seemed to be a level of respect in their eyes. She gazed levelly back. Her heart was pounding and her palms were sweating, but she wasn't about to let anyone know that Roth had rattled her.

"Ms. Welsley is exercising her right to appoint herself as a board member," said Max. "As current majority shareholder, she will sit as chair. As chair, she will break any tie over the appointment of an interim president."

"So not Roth," said Clint.

"Then who are we talking about?" Nelson asked.

"Are we taking nominations?"

"I've given it a lot of thought," said Amber. "I'd like to discuss Max Cutter as the interim president."

Max drew back in his seat. "I can't—"

"Turns out you can," said Amber. "I spoke to a lawyer this morning."

"You'll have to leave the room for the discussion," Nelson said to Max.

Max fixed his shrewd gaze on Amber. She didn't flinch. If she could sit as chair of the board, then he could sit as president. There was no one else she'd trust.

"Very well," said Max. He rose and gathered his briefcase.

As he passed, he paused behind her and leaned down. "I guess we'll go down together."

She turned her head to whisper. "Then I guess you'd better help me win."

"I was always going to help you win." He gave her a friendly pat on the shoulder as he walked away.

The door closed behind him and another board member spoke up. He was Milos Mandell, a former commercial pilot and internet entrepreneur.

"Can we speak freely?" asked Milos.

"I would think we'd better," said Amber.

"You seem like you understand what you just did."

She couldn't help flexing a small, resigned smile. "I believe I know what I just did."

"He's going to come after you," said Nelson, clearly referring to Roth.

"He's right to go after her," said Clint, glancing around at his fellow board members. "This *is* a coup."

Milos sat forward. "The coup would have been Roth taking over as president without the support of the major shareholder."

Clint stared hard at Amber. "You're jumping the gun, and it's going to cost you."

"While Roth will know you sided with him, so I guess you're safe." She let her words sink in for a moment.

Clint was smart enough to realize the opposite was also true. Amber now knew he was in opposition to her.

His jaw dropped a fraction of an inch. "I don't mean… That is, I'm not…"

"Any discussion on Max?" Amber asked the group.

She didn't have time to worry about Clint. She needed to get Max settled in as president, then she needed to focus on the court case, do justice to her day-to-day work and make sure Zachary stayed clean, fed and as happy as possible. The alliances, machinations and power plays at Coast Eagle were going to have to take a backseat.

On the staircase in front of Coast Eagle headquarters, Cole appeared and fell into step beside Amber. It was six o'clock. She was exhausted, and he was the last person she wanted to see.

Ironically, he was also the person she most wanted to see. The conflicting reactions were due to the kiss they'd shared in the meeting room.

"I read the press release," he opened, turning right along with her as she headed down the crowded sidewalk toward the transit station.

"I think that was a good move," he continued. "There's an

element of risk, but there's nothing about this situation that's not risky."

She stopped to turn on him, forcing the flow of people to part around them. The man had gone behind her back, kissed her senseless, and now he wanted to analyze her business decisions? "Is that really what you want to say to me?"

Her words seemed to catch him off guard and he hesitated. Horns honked and engines revved on the street as cars breezed past.

"Yes," he answered.

"Well." She coughed out a chopped laugh. "It's so *very* nice of you to approve of my decision."

"Are you still upset?"

"I'm also tired, and I'm busy, and I'm going to miss my train."

"Then you should get moving."

He was right. She turned abruptly to march toward the station.

He kept pace. "I have a hard time believing the Hendersons don't have cars and drivers."

"Are you going to pretend it didn't happen?"

"That you joined the board of directors?"

She rolled her eyes.

"That I kissed you?" he asked.

"That you betrayed me."

"I didn't betray you. I told you I was after the Pacific routes."

"Don't pretend you're stupid, Cole. And don't pretend I'm stupid, either."

"You're not stupid."

"I know."

"Except when it comes to transportation. Can I offer you a ride home?"

"You cannot."

"Why?"

Because he had her rattled. The memory of his kiss had taunted her all afternoon long, messing with her concentration. She wanted to know the kiss had rattled him, too.

"It'll get you home faster," Cole offered reasonably. "You'll be able to spend more time with Zachary."

"Go away." She fixed her sights on the train platform.

"Not what I was planning."

"What were you planning?" The question was automatic, and she instantly regretted asking it.

She didn't care about his plans. She wanted him out of her life. At least, a part of her wanted him out of her life. The other part wanted him to kiss her again. She nearly groaned in frustration.

"You're having a tough week," he said. "You need to have some fun."

She dodged her way around a group of pedestrians, then skirted a trash can and a stroller. "What? This doesn't look like fun?"

"Well, I'm having fun."

"What do you want, Cole?"

"To take you on a date."

His words shocked her to a halt.

He took her arm and drew her under a shop awning, next to a brick wall and out of the flow of pedestrians. "I can only guess at how hard you're working and how tired you must be. I want to help you take a break. Come out with me tonight. Let's walk through Atlantic Station, see the lights, drink hot chocolate. Or we can go skating. You said skating was your favorite."

"I don't like you, Cole."

"To be fair, you don't know me."

"I know enough."

"You only think you know enough." His gaze captured hers again, and the noise and commotion of the sidewalk seemed to fade.

"I'll sweeten the pot," he said. "We'll go to the penthouse. I'll work my magic and put Zachary to sleep. Can Isabel stay for the evening?"

"You're bribing me?"

"Absolutely."

"Why, Cole? The jig is up. I know you were using me to worm your way into Coast Eagle."

"Amber, I don't need you to worm my way into Coast Eagle. I walked through the front door and got a meeting with the soon-to-be president without an appointment."

"Roth's not going to be president."

"Good decision."

"You just switch your opinion on a dime, don't you?"

"I never thought he should be president."

She didn't know what to say to that. She didn't care what Cole thought. Still, for some reason she was glad to hear him agree with her.

"You need to get out for a while," Cole continued. "Take a break. Forget about everything."

She fought a smile at the absurdity. "What I want to forget is you."

His expression faltered, and she felt a stab of guilt.

"I'm sorry to hear that, Amber."

She was sorry she'd said it.

Wait, no, she wasn't. No good could come of her attraction to him. A date? The idea was absurd. He lived in Alaska, and her life was a mess.

The best they could hope for was a one-night stand. Which, when she thought about it...

Hoo, boy. She reached out to grip the brick wall.

"You okay?"

"I'm perfectly fine." She paused. "No, make that confused. Why do you want to go out with me? And why do you still want to help me with Zachary?"

It took him a moment to shrug. "Why not? I like you, Amber. I like Zachary."

"That's too simple an explanation." Amber raked her hand through her hair to tame it in the freshening wind.

"I'm not complicated."

"I am."

"It's ice-skating, Amber. What could be simpler than ice-skating?"

"You're trying to get your hands on our Pacific routes."

"Only if you want to sell them."

"I don't."

"Fair enough. Did you know you missed your train?"

It was pulling smoothly away on the tracks. He really was the most infuriatingly distracting man.

"My car is only a block away. What do you say?"

She wanted to say yes. She suddenly, desperately wanted to leave her troubles behind for a few hours and go ice-skating with Cole.

She gave in. "Okay."

He grinned, and she couldn't shake the feeling she'd been outmaneuvered.

Five

As they passed by the lit trees that lined the outdoor skating rink, Cole turned backward so that he was facing Amber. She wore a short white puffy jacket, blue jeans and bright yellow knit hat.

"Impressive," she told him with a smile.

He was grateful that she seemed relaxed. "Hockey."

Since it was barely below freezing, he'd gone with a windbreaker and a bare head. The fresh air felt good in his lungs.

"You're a hockey player?"

"Snow and ice sports are big in Alaska. I also snowboard and ski cross-country." He glanced over his shoulder to make sure the path was still clear as they rounded a corner.

"I swim," she said.

"Competitively?"

"At resorts, usually in the leisure pool, sometimes on the lazy river."

He brought up a mental image. "Impressive."

"Yeah, I float with the best of them."

"I was picturing you in a little yellow bikini. It was very impressive."

"That's just mean."

"Why?"

"Because I'll never live up to your imagination."

"Sure you will." His gaze took a reflexive tour of her trim figure. "Wait a minute. Do you intend to try?"

She laughed, and he loved the sound.

"Not this time of year," she singsonged.

"If I come back in June?"

"Maybe." She twirled neatly around.

"You're pretty good yourself."

"Flatterer." But her smile was bright.

"You're beautiful, too."

"I'm not interested in a one-night stand."

The statement took him by surprise. "Excuse me?"

"Just so you know. I wouldn't want you to get to the end of the night and be disappointed."

"Is that what you think this is about?"

He didn't know whether to be insulted or just plain disappointed. He hadn't invited her out to get her into bed. But he didn't deny he'd give pretty much anything for an unbridled night of passion in her arms.

"You're not staying in Atlanta," she said.

"True," he agreed, even though he kind of now wished he was.

"And you're putting in an awful lot of effort flirting with me."

"Also true." But only because flirting with her was so much fun.

"So the options are limited."

"Maybe I'm trying to romance the Pacific routes out from under you."

"You know that will never work."

It was true. Cole couldn't imagine her falling for something so simplistic. Then again, he wasn't remotely interested in the Pacific routes.

He and Luca were following a carefully planned and meticulously orchestrated expansion scheme for Aviation 58. It was on track, and he had no intention of deviating from it for the next few years. He'd never make a knee-jerk decision based on random availability.

"You're great with Zachary, you know." Cole didn't want to talk business.

"*You're* great with Zachary. I'm mostly treading water." Then she frowned. "But if you're ever called to testify, the correct answer is that Amber is *fantastic* with Zachary."

"I've never seen such incredible natural mothering instincts," he said.

Her frown deepened. "I'm not his mother."

"I didn't mean that," Cole quickly corrected the innocent comment. "I only meant that it's obvious that you love him."

She skated in pensive silence for a moment, the lighthearted music and bright lights suddenly seeming out of place.

"I'm sorry," he offered, moving back to her side, reminding himself that she had grown up without the love of either of her natural parents.

"He's so young," she said softly. "He won't remember either of them."

Cole reached out and took her hand. "He'll remember you."

"It's not the same thing."

There was a deep sadness in her eyes, and it wasn't at all what he'd planned for her tonight.

"Hot chocolate?" he asked, nodding toward the strip of shops and cafés. "I'll spring for whipped cream and orange brandy."

Her expression relaxed again. "Sure."

They coasted to a stop, exchanged their skates for boots and made their way through the colored lights and happy crowds. It felt natural to take Amber's hand again as they strolled along the pedestrian street. He helped her pick out a stuffed dog and a soft rattle for Zachary. They waited while the clerk gift wrapped the toys, and Cole slung the package over his shoulder.

"That looks nice." He pointed across the street to a fenced restaurant patio with padded chairs and glowing propane heaters.

"Sold," said Amber.

They crossed through the crowds and were shown to a table near a festively lit garden.

He glanced at his watch. "I read there were fireworks at ten."

"Perfect timing." She glanced around. "I love it down here at Christmas."

"There's nothing like this in Juneau."

"Too cold?"

"During the holidays, yes. We do fireworks on the Fourth of July, but they lose something since it doesn't get completely dark at night."

"Not at all?"

"A sort of twilight look around 2:00 a.m. But you can golf at midnight on the solstice."

"I can't even picture it. Do you like living there?"

"I love living there. Juneau has a great sense of community."

"Tell me about your mother."

Cole brought up fond memories. "She was very pretty. She was kind and cheerful. She worked hard. Looking back, I realize just how hard she had to work when I was young."

"She never went after your father for support?"

"She didn't want him to know I existed."

The statement clearly piqued Amber's interest. "Why not?"

Cole immediately realized his mistake in letting Samuel get into the conversation. He purposely kept the rest of his answer casual. "She thought he'd be more trouble than he was worth."

Amber nodded her understanding. "I hear you."

How she said it made him wonder if she'd had bad experiences with men. He wanted to ask, but just then, the waitress arrived with magnificent mugs of hot chocolate, decorated with whipped cream and chocolate sprinkles.

"Dessert in a cup," said Amber with a happy smile.

Cole took the opportunity to shift the conversation away from his father. "Tell me about your dad."

She thought for a moment while she spooned a dollop of the whipped cream into her mouth. "He was tall. He had this booming, infectious laugh. I remember him flipping pancakes in the air, and how he used to trot around the yard, whinnying like a horse, with me on piggyback."

"Little girls like that?"

"I did."

"My mom baked bread on Friday nights," said Cole. "I'd hear her in the kitchen after I went to bed. She'd let it rise all night, then bake it in the morning. Best breakfast of the whole week."

"I'm trying to picture you young."

An image of Zachary came to his mind, and he hoped she wasn't trying to picture back that far. He'd hunted the internet for more photos of Samuel, found many and he realized there was a significant family resemblance. Then he'd had a friend back in Alaska send him some of his own baby pictures to compare to Zachary. They were all but identical.

Amber took another spoonful of the whipped cream. "I can't picture it. You must have always been old."

"Old? Thanks a lot."

"How old are you?"

"Thirty-two. You?" He already knew, but it seemed logical to ask.

"Thirty-one. So I guess you're not so old."

"Gee, thanks."

She grinned. "But I'm surprised you're not married, or at least in a relationship."

"There's no current or likely future Mrs.—" He caught himself. "Mrs. Parker. You?"

"Married?" she scoffed.

"I meant in a serious relationship?"

"Nope."

"What about in the past?"

"These questions are getting quite personal."

"They are, aren't they?" He didn't apologize or retract it.

She wrapped her hands around the mug. "Nobody of note." After a pause, she kept talking. "I left home right after high school, worked days, went to school at night to get my accounting designation. I might not be a vice president, but my job at Coast Eagle is significant."

He stirred the whipped cream into his hot chocolate. "I never doubted it was."

"I oversee six branch offices and several dozen staff members."

"Have I said something wrong?" He couldn't figure out what had made her defensive. He had nothing but admiration and respect for what she'd accomplished in her professional life.

She took a sip. "Not you. Roth, I guess. And some of the other executives. Sometimes I think they assume I'm just like Coco. They all knew her, while most of them had barely met me before the crash. They seem to have forgotten that I was at Coast Eagle before she met Samuel. I sometimes get the impression they think Coco got me the job."

He could imagine that would be frustrating.

"I decided the best defense was to ignore it," she continued. "And to do a good job, hard work and success would prevail and all that."

"Did it work?"

"Not really. And then the plane crashed. And now everyone thinks there's a ditz at the helm."

"They're wrong."

"They don't know that."

"Fair enough. But you know what I think?"

Her expression seemed to relax a little. "What do you think, Cole Parker?"

"I think they'd better learn. They'd better learn to respect your intelligence and your tenacity."

Anyone could see she was the perfect guardian for Zachary. The judge was going to see that, too. And soon she was going to be in charge of all of their lives.

"You're good for my ego, Cole."

"I'm trying."

"But, wow, did I ever get off topic." She took another sip. "That was a very roundabout way of explaining that I didn't have time for boyfriends. It's not that I never had offers."

"Of course you had offers." He couldn't figure out what made her so insecure. "You're amazing. And you're gorgeous. And I never meant for a second to hint that men didn't seek you out. I meant… Okay, I was fishing around for the competition."

She drew back. "Competition for *what?*"

"That didn't come out right. I'm attracted to you, Amber. I know I'm not staying in Atlanta. But I think of this as a date. And I guess it's a reflex for guys to wonder about who else might be out there in the wings."

"There are no wings. I mean, I have no wings. At least none with guys waiting in them." She closed her eyes and shook her head. "I'm making this worse and worse, aren't I?"

Cole struggled not to smile. "You're making it better and better."

"Tell me some more about you instead."

"Sure. What do you want to know?"

She settled back into the chair. "Women."

The first volley of fireworks burst in the night sky, and Amber laughed.

"Timing," she said.

"I *wish* my love life was that exciting."

"Give."

"Marcy Richards," he said.

"She is?"

His memory was warm. "My high school sweetheart. Tall, lanky, long red hair, a few freckles. She was captain of the girls' basketball team."

"What happened?"

"Tragic story, really. Senior year, she met a guy from Skagway. He was in town for a tournament. He kissed her. I punched him. She cried. But then four months later they both went off to U of Alaska. They're married now with two kids."

"Do you miss her?"

"Not really. She's my accountant, so I see her every week. She's great. And so, it turns out, is her husband, Mike."

"You're saying you're over the heartbreak?"

"I went off to flight school and had a series of short but satisfying relationships. Turns out, women can't resist a pilot."

"How short?"

"Hours, sometimes days."

"That's appalling."

"I was recovering from heartbreak. I was young and vulnerable."

"*Vulnerable* isn't the word I'd use."

He grinned. "You'd be right."

"And now?" she asked, brandishing her nearly empty mug.

"A few dates here and there, nothing that's ever turned into anything but a friendship. I'm pretty busy with Aviation 58, and Juneau's population is not that huge. A lot of the women my age have moved on."

"You ever think about moving on?" she asked.

He shook his head. "I love it there. And given how much Aviation 58 has grown, my roots are pretty deep."

"Maybe you can find a nice girl in Atlanta and take her home with you." There was a glow in her blue eyes that seemed to reach right down to his soul.

"Good idea. You doing anything for the next thirty or forty years?"

She set down the empty mug. "I know you're joking, but that's a pretty good line."

He wished he was certain it was a line. He pointed to her mug. "You want another?"

"I need to get home so Isabel can leave."

Six

As Isabel left the penthouse, Amber made her way down the hall to where Cole had gone in search of Otis. The dog had apparently plunked himself down in Zachary's open doorway and gone to sleep.

She found Otis there, with Cole inside the bedroom, tucking a blanket over the sleeping Zachary. Cole rubbed a gentle hand across Zachary's forehead before turning away from the crib. In the doorway, Amber stood to one side, her chest strangely warm.

"Sound asleep," Cole whispered as he stepped over Otis.

The dog opened one eye but didn't lift his head.

"Isabel said he slept right through," Amber whispered in return.

"Good for him." Cole stopped right in front of her.

He was close, too close, but she didn't want to move. Instead, she inhaled deeply, letting his fresh, masculine scent fill her lungs. It was a fight to keep from reaching out to touch him.

"Hi," he breathed.

She lifted her chin to gaze up at him, wishing he would kiss her, but knowing any more intimacy was a very bad idea. Her life was complicated, and he was leaving, and she needed to keep her focus on the court case. But the temptation to lean into his arms and forget everything for just a little while was almost overwhelming.

He brought his palm to her cheek, and the warmth of the contact seemed to flow through her entire body. Her breasts tingled and she parted her lips, subconsciously inching toward him.

His free arm slipped around her waist, and he slowly dipped his head to meet hers. "Is this just a kiss good-night?"

"I don't know." She grasped the sleeves of his shirt, anchoring herself.

"Fair enough." His soft lips captured hers.

His kiss was everything she remembered and more. It was

more than his lips, more than his tongue, more than his taste. Every pore on her body drank in his essence. Her heart rate increased. Her blood heated. She pressed herself against him, nipples beading against his hard chest, thighs molding to his, hands twining around his neck, into his hair then back again, tracing the planes and angles of his face.

She wanted to memorize his skin. She wanted to touch him everywhere, imprint every contour onto her brain.

Arousal swiftly pushed away reason.

Needing to get closer still, she worked her hands between them, struggling in the tight space to release the buttons on his shirt. In answer, his hands slid down her back, across her waist, cupping her rear, pulling her tight against his body, letting her know how strongly he desired her.

She stripped off her sweater. Her tank top followed. And she was before him in a white lacy bra.

He drew back and his pupils dilated, his breathing labored. He swore under his breath, then stripped off his shirt and backed her tight against the cool wall. He lifted her there, bringing her legs around his waist.

He flicked the catch on her bra, pulling it from between them, and they were skin to skin. She was in heaven.

His voice was a rumble against her mouth. "Amber?"

It was a struggle to speak. "Yes?"

"This is more than just a good-night kiss."

"Yes," she rasped. "Yes."

He worked his way down her neck, kissing the curve of her shoulder, then the swell of her breast. His lips fastened onto her nipple, and her body bucked, fingertips curling hard into his muscular shoulders. He switched sides, and her head tipped back, legs going tight around him.

"Which way?" he asked.

"Left," she rasped. "My left. End of the hall."

He scooped her into his arms and paced to the bedroom door, pushing it open and crossing to the big bed.

There he tossed back the covers and set her down. In a split second, he was with her, covering her body with his, kissing her deeply, his hands roaming her skin.

She went on an exploration of her own, following the hard definition of his shoulders and biceps, to his pecs and his washboard stomach. She unsnapped his jeans. He immediately did the same.

Then he pulled back to look into her eyes.

Without a word, he dragged down her zipper.

She followed suit, the backs of her knuckles grazing him as she went.

He sucked in a tight breath, eyes as dark as coal while they watched her.

She tugged down his jeans, and he kicked them off.

He pulled off her pants, palms skimming across her silk panties, back and forth, until she twitched in reaction. She moaned his name.

He kissed her breasts, and her arms stretched out, hands clenching into fists. And then her panties were gone. His boxers disappeared, and he had a condom. Thank goodness he had a condom.

He was on top of her, pressing into her, so slowly, so exquisitely. She arched against him, wrapping her arms and legs around him. She'd never felt anything that came close to Cole Parker.

He smelled of fresh air and wide-open spaces. He tasted like chocolate and brandy. His callused fingertips were rough and hot as he caressed every intimate spot on her skin. His body was shifting iron beneath her hands.

His weight felt good. His thrusts were focused, and her body reflexively adjusted its angle to accommodate him. He whispered her name. Then his arm braced the small of her back, pressing them tighter and tighter together.

Everything else was forgotten except the sensations cresting endlessly through her body as she climbed higher and higher. Colors glowed behind her eyes while white noise roared in her ears. Her world contracted to their joined bodies, tighter and tighter, until the dam exploded. The colors turned to fireworks, and sound boomed like a symphony as Cole called out her name.

Her pulse was in overdrive, and she was dragging in oxygen. Her limbs lost all feeling as she sank deeper and deeper into the soft mattress.

"You still with me?" Cole asked from what seemed like a distance.

"I think so. I'm not sure. Are we in Kansas?"

He chuckled. "I was *definitely* over the rainbow."

Reality floated its way back. "Oh, my."

"Don't second-guess," he warned.

"That was a lot more than just a kiss."

He brushed back her hair and looked into her eyes. "It felt kind of inevitable."

She knew what he meant. Every second they spent together seemed to draw them closer and closer.

"Maybe it was good to get it over with," she ventured.

"At least we're not wondering anymore."

"Were you?" she couldn't help asking. "Were you wondering?"

"Absolutely. From the first second I laid eyes on you. That's why I botched it so bad that night at the dance."

"It was a rocky start," she agreed. "But you rescued me. Then you rescued my shoes."

"You hate those shoes."

"True. But you do get points for trying."

He skimmed the backs of his fingers along her side. "Are those points redeemable?"

His touch was distracting, and his eyes were taking on that dark glow again.

"For valuable prizes," she told him.

He traced the curve of her hip. "What do I get?"

"What do you want?"

He seemed to hesitate for a moment. "To stay."

A shimmer of anticipation warmed her chest at the thought of sleeping in Cole's arms, waking up next to him, having breakfast together with Zachary.

"Are you serious?"

"Absolutely."

"Okay."

Cole awoke to the feel of Amber spooned in his arms and the realization that he had to tell her the truth. Up until last night, he'd been prepared to breeze into town, make sure Zachary was settled and breeze back out again. But things had changed. She had changed them.

She rolled onto her back, blinking her eyes in the dim light from the window.

"Morning," he said softly.

A pretty smile grew on her face. "Morning."

Otis whimpered at the door.

Then Zachary let out a cry down the hall.

"Is Isabel in yet?" Cole asked.

Amber craned her neck to look at the bedside clock. "Not for an hour."

Otis whined more insistently and Zachary's cries grew steady.

Cole grimaced. "I'll walk the dog if you feed the baby."

"Sorry," said Amber.

"Not your fault at all." He sat up, shaking off sleep. "We jumped from a one-night stand to an old married couple in the blink of an eye."

"Not the morning you had in mind," she asked from behind him.

He turned, already smiling. "Oddly, it feels like the perfect morning. Shall I pick up some bagels while I'm out?"

She rose from the other side of the bed, gloriously naked and indescribably beautiful. "Make mine blueberry."

"You got it." He forced himself to look away and pulled on his jeans.

Otis's leash was at the front door, along with Cole's jacket. They took the elevator, and once they were on the sidewalk, they headed to the park.

Cole let the fresh air clear his brain. While they walked, he formulated and discarded several versions of a speech to Amber. Should he plunge in with the fact that he was Samuel's long-lost son? Or should he go about it chronologically, outline his motivation and rationale before hitting her with his real identity?

He didn't want to upset her. He didn't want to worry her. And he certainly didn't want to make her distrust or dislike him any more than she already had. But last night had been too amazing for anything less than complete honesty.

He and Otis ended up on the opposite side of the park. They made their way down the block to a bakery Cole had found a couple of days ago. He left Otis outside and chose a variety of bagels, then they started back to the penthouse.

He found himself wondering what Zachary ate. Would he like to try a bit of bagel? Or did he stick to pureed foods?

Cole knew absolutely nothing about babies or toddlers. All he knew was that Zachary was adorable, and that he was curious about the stages of development to come. He hoped once he told Amber the truth, she'd be willing to send him pictures and videos. Maybe he could even come back occasionally and check up on Zachary.

The more he thought about it, the more he realized acknowledging their blood relationship was the right thing to do. He wasn't sure why he waited so long.

Nearly an hour had gone by before he returned to the penthouse. Amber had given him her spare key, so he let himself in, wondering if Zachary would have finished his bottle and might be having a morning bath. He hoped he wasn't being fussy for Amber.

When Cole opened the door, he did hear Zachary's cries. But they were interspersed with adult voices. At first he assumed Isabel had arrived. But it was a man speaking, then another answering.

Cole and Otis rounded the corner to the living room to see Roth Calvin and four other men standing with Amber in the middle of the room. Two of the men were on cell phones, while Amber was holding a crying Zachary. Cole reflexively moved forward to take the baby.

"What's going on?" he asked, worried that something had gone wrong in the court battle.

"Thank you," whispered Amber as Zachary's cries quieted. "Isabel's running late, and we've got a problem."

Cole glanced at the other four men. "What's wrong?"

"A Coast Eagle flight is in trouble," said one of them.

Cole went instantly on alert. "What kind of trouble?"

"Hydraulic failure," said the shortest of the three. "The landing gear won't come down."

"What's he doing here?" Roth demanded, ending his call, seeming to have just recognized Cole.

"I brought bagels," said Cole.

"Zachary likes him," said Amber.

"What kind of plane?" Cole asked.

"We've got work to do here," said a large, rotund, fiftysomething man with gray hair and a bulbous nose.

"Cole," said Amber. "This is Max Cutter. He's our interim president. This is Sidney Raines and Julius Fonteno, both vice presidents. You know Roth."

"What kind of plane?" Cole repeated. The size of the plane dictated the scale of the problem.

Julius, the large man, frowned. "Shouldn't you go change a diaper or something?"

Cole braced his feet apart. "It'll be faster if you just answer the question."

"Boonsome 300 over LAX," said Sidney, the shorter, younger man, glancing up from the screen of his phone. "They're reporting twenty minutes of fuel left."

Cole's stomach sank. A Boonsome 300 was a passenger jet. There were up to two hundred souls on board.

Max Cutter ended his own call. "The pilot's leaving the holding pattern and bringing her in."

Cole looked to Amber. She was still and pale.

"Are you a pilot?" he asked Sidney.

"Yes."

"They've checked the pump circuit breakers?" Cole knew

the answer would be yes. But he couldn't help going through the diagnostics in his mind.

Sidney gave a nod.

"Any visible leaks?"

"None," said Sidney. "Foam's down on the runway."

"They'll cycle the gear again?"

"They will."

Cole stepped closer to Amber, wishing he could reach out and take her hand. A belly landing in a plane that size was incredibly risky.

"Gear's down," said Sidney, grasping the back of the sofa even as he uttered the words. "They cycled the gear one last time. They've got hydraulic pressure back."

Relief rushed through Cole.

Amber dropped into an armchair, a slight tremor in her hands. "Thank goodness."

"They're on short final," said Sidney, putting his phone to his ear. "Tower's patched me in."

They all waited, watching Sidney closely until he gave the thumbs-up. "Wheels down. It's all good."

"Yes," hissed Max.

"Relief valve, do you think?" Cole posed the question to Sidney.

"They'll have to go through the whole system."

Roth spoke up. "Amber, get the communications director on the phone."

Cole bristled at Roth's abrupt tone, but Amber moved to the landline.

Roth continued talking. "We'll call it a minor delay in the deployment of the landing gear. All safety procedures were followed, and it was an isolated incident."

Amber stopped, looking back over her shoulder. "An isolated incident?"

"Yes."

"We know this how?"

"Because we've been flying the Boonsomes for nearly ten years, and it's never happened before."

"I don't like the word *isolated,*" said Amber.

Roth's eyes narrowed.

"I'd suggest replacing that clause with everyone on board is safe, and there were no injuries. Once we've confirmed that's the case."

Roth squared his shoulders. "The whole point of a press release is to reassure the public—"

"I agree with Amber," said Max.

"Of *course* you agree with Amber," said Roth. "You're her appointee."

"I agree with Amber, too," said Sidney.

Roth set his jaw.

"I have to side with Roth on this," said Julius. "The more reassurance we can give our passengers, the better."

"It's early days," said Cole. "Better to mitigate your words until the investigation is complete."

"Who let this guy in here?" asked Julius.

"I'm an airline pilot," said Cole. He might not be a Coast Airlines employee, but he knew the industry.

"Bully for you," said Julius.

"It might be better if you excused us," Roth said to Cole.

Cole looked to Amber. He could go or he could stay, but he was taking his cue from her, not from Roth.

"What about the other Boonsome 300s in service?" asked Max. He was scrolling through the screen on his phone. "Here. Midpoint Airlines just grounded theirs."

"That was fast," said Sidney.

"Kneejerk," said Julius. "It's not like there's a pattern."

"They've got a total of three Boonsomes," said Roth. "It's an easy decision for them to make."

"It puts pressure on us," said Sidney.

"We're not caving to pressure," said Roth. "We've got twenty-four Boonsomes. It's a quarter of our fleet."

Amber's hand was resting on the telephone. "We could have lost two hundred passengers."

"We didn't," said Julius.

"We're *not* considering this," said Roth with finality. "Unless the federal regulator orders us, we are *not* grounding twenty-four airplanes."

"It's a publicity grab from Midpoint," said Julius.

Cole couldn't help jumping in. "Depending on the problem."

"We'll find the problem," said Roth. "And we'll fix it. Nobody's suggesting we send that particular plane up again without a thorough overhaul."

"And if something happens with another Boonsome?" asked Sidney.

"Nothing's going to happen," said Roth.

"You're playing the odds," said Amber.

"I play the odds every time I get out of bed," said Roth. "You want one hundred percent certainty? We lose a million dollars a day with those planes on the ground. *That's* a certainty. It'll take two weeks minimum to get any answers on an investigation. Anybody want to do the math?"

Max looked to Amber. "What are your thoughts?"

"That's a lot of money," she said. "But it's a lot of lives to risk, too." Her gaze moved to Cole.

Julius gestured to Amber, disdain in his tone. "*This* is our leader?"

"She's looking for input," said Max. "I'm looking for input, too."

Roth's face twisted into a sneer. "My input is don't bankrupt the company while you're temporarily in charge."

Cole clamped his jaw to stop himself from speaking.

"The plane is at the gate," said Sidney. "And the terminal is full of reporters."

"We have to put out a statement," said Roth.

"We have to make a decision," Amber told him.

"We don't have a choice," said Julius. "Nobody's giving up a million dollars a day."

"Say that again after we lose a plane full of passengers," said Sidney.

"Do you want my opinion?" Cole asked Amber.

"Yes."

Roth let out an inarticulate exclamation.

Cole ignored him. "Ask yourself this. Before the inspectors identify the problem, would you risk putting Zachary on a Boonsome 300?"

Amber shook her head.

"We ground the planes," said Max.

"Have you *lost your minds?*" asked Julius.

Amber squared her shoulders and gave Max a sharp nod of agreement.

Pride swelled up inside Cole's chest.

"This is amateur hour," Roth spat. "Believe me, you haven't heard the last of it."

"We'll request an expedited investigation," said Max. "But for now the decision is final."

Amber focused in on Cole, moving closer to speak in an undertone. "I have to go to the office."

"I know." He realized their conversation about Samuel would have to wait.

"Can you stay with Zachary until Isabel gets here? She thought maybe noon."

"Don't worry, I'll stay."

Relief flooded her eyes. "Thank you."

"No problem. Talk to you later?"

"I'll call you."

"Good luck."

"Everyone's safe. That's a whole lot of luck already."

The group moved toward the door, Amber grabbing her purse and throwing a coat over her slacks and sweater. When the last of them left and the door latched shut, Cole turned his attention to Zachary.

The baby was sucking on the sleeve of his stretchy one-piece suit.

"You like bagels?" Cole asked.

"Gak haw," said Zachary, grabbing at Cole's nose.

Amber's day went from frightening to stressful to downright infuriating. At six o'clock, Destiny was sitting across from her at her compact office meeting table.

"*That's* how Roth spent his day?" she asked Destiny.

Destiny pushed a sheaf of papers across the table. "I don't know how they did it, but they got an emergency court date. The custody hearing starts at nine tomorrow morning."

"I thought we'd have weeks to get ready." Amber gave the paperwork a passing glance, but she trusted Destiny's assessment.

"We have hours to get ready."

"Can we do it?"

"Not as well as I'd like. But we can work hard tonight. And Roth's side is under the same deadline."

Amber's cell phone rang.

"Remember," said Destiny, "the fundamentals remain the same. Coco's codicil is legal and valid. They have to prove you're not a fit guardian."

Amber didn't recognize the calling number. "Hello?"

"Amber, it's Cole."

She glanced to Destiny, feeling a small spike of guilt about last night. "Hi, Cole."

Destiny's interest obviously perked up.

"I need to talk to you about something."

"Is it Zachary?"

"No, no. He's fine. At least, he was fine when I left him with Isabel this afternoon. Can you meet me for dinner?"

She wished she could. "I'm afraid not. Destiny and I are going to be busy."

There was silence on his end. "It's kind of important."

"I'm sorry."

"Maybe later?"

"Tonight's not going to be good. We'll be working really late."

"Is everything okay?"

"Yes." She hesitated. "No." She knew she shouldn't share, since she barely knew him. But she felt like she owed him an explanation. "It's actually not okay. Roth's convinced the judge to hold an emergency hearing tomorrow morning. He's going after custody."

"Tomorrow morning?"

"He's going to use my decision on the Boonsome 300s as proof I'm unfit to control Coast Eagle."

"He'll lose, Amber."

"I hope so." Her stomach was already beginning to cramp up.

"Is there anything I can do?"

"Ask me out again in a few days?"

Destiny's brows went up.

"Happy to," he answered. Then his tone changed. "I really wish I could see you now. Even for a short time."

"That would be nice. But we're pretty much pulling an all-nighter here. I'm about to call Isabel and arrange for her to stay over."

"I could stay at your place, wait for you there."

"Not necessary." She wasn't going to let herself presume any more on Cole's good graces. He didn't come to Atlanta to be a babysitter.

He was quiet again. Then he blew out a breath. "Okay. A couple of days, then."

"Thanks."

"Nothing to thank me for. Good luck."

"Thanks for that." She'd take every scrap of luck she could get. "Bye, Cole."

"Bye."

She pressed the end button and set down the phone.

Destiny spoke. "We're going to take thirty seconds of our valuable time here, and you're going to tell me what's going on with Cole. Then I'm putting it completely out of my mind until after the hearing." She glanced at her watch. "Go."

"I like him. He likes me. We went skating last night, then we drank killer hot chocolate. We went back to my place, slept together, which was pretty killer, too. Then he stayed over, went out for bagels and then all hell broke loose. He wanted to see me again tonight, but…" She spread her arms.

"Holy cow," said Destiny in obvious awe. "We are definitely going to talk more about this. But right now we've got a whole lot of work to do."

Seven

Cole and Luca slipped into the back of the courtroom. Word had obviously gotten out about the hearing, because the room was packed with reporters and onlookers. He couldn't help but feel bad for Amber. It was stressful enough to have Zachary's custody on the line without an audience of one hundred.

Predictably, Roth's side attacked Coco. They started by disparaging her motivations in marrying an older, wealthy man, then they called witness after witness, painting an unflattering picture of her intellect. Cole knew from conversations with Amber that Coco was emotional and sometimes erratic, but the witnesses made her sound unstable, unprincipled, even dishonest.

Luca tipped his head closer to Cole. "How much do you think is true?"

"She did marry a billionaire nearly three times her age. And I don't think she was a rocket scientist."

Cole imagined a lot of what was being said about Coco's temper and her behavior at parties was accurate. Then again, if she'd been at a frat party like most nineteen-year-olds, instead of at a posh charity function or the opening of an art museum, nobody would have raised an eyebrow.

"Doesn't mean she wasn't a good mother," said Luca.

"And it doesn't mean her wishes shouldn't be respected." Nothing Cole had heard so far would indicate mental incompetence on the part of Coco.

Roth took the stand, and the gallery's attention seemed to heighten. Cole guessed most people here knew the pivotal players in the drama.

Roth's own lawyer questioned him first.

"Did you and Samuel Henderson ever discuss his future plans for Coast Eagle Airlines?" the lawyer asked.

"Extensively and on many occasions," Roth answered.

"Did he ask your advice?"

"Yes, he did."

"To your knowledge, did he ever ask his wife, Coco Henderson's, advice on Coast Eagle Airlines?"

Roth smirked. "Never."

"You're certain?"

"Positive."

"Objection," said Destiny.

"Sustained," said the judge.

"I'll rephrase," said the lawyer. "Did Samuel ever say anything directly to you regarding his opinion of his wife's advice on Coast Eagle?"

"He told me she knew nothing about business. He said he never discussed it with her."

The lawyer gave a satisfied nod. "Did Samuel Henderson indicate to you that he wanted his son to one day take over the business?"

"Yes. Samuel loved his son deeply. I've never seen him so happy as when Zachary was born. He talked about keeping the airline in the family for another generation. It was his fondest wish that Coast Eagle be protected and preserved for his son."

Destiny rose again. "Objection. The witness is not in a position to know Samuel Henderson's fondest wish."

"That's what he said to me," said Roth.

"Overruled," said the judge.

"Did Samuel ever speak to you about his wife having any kind of a hand in running Coast Eagle Airlines in the event of his death?"

"He did," said Roth, and an odd expression flicked in his eyes.

Cole found himself doubting Roth's honesty on the question.

Roth answered, "He said the only people he trusted with Coast Eagle and with his son were Dryden Dunsmore and me. He said someone needed to control Coco because she had the decision-making ability of a twelve-year-old."

"He said that directly to you? Those were his words?"

"Yes. And they're supported by his will, which included

both Dryden and I in guardianship or controlling positions in Coast Eagle."

"A little too convenient," Cole whispered to Luca.

"I can't tell if the judge is buying it or not."

Destiny cross-examined but wasn't able to poke holes in Roth's story. Cole and Luca slipped out at the lunch break, picking a restaurant several blocks away to avoid being seen by Amber or Destiny. By late afternoon, Amber was the only witness left.

Roth's lawyer started with Amber's competence at Coast Eagle. It went as expected. There was no getting around her lack of experience, but Cole thought she held her own, particularly on yesterday's decision to ground the Boonsome jets. Yes, it was a financial loss, but risking passenger lives was too dangerous.

Unfortunately, it then came to light that their closest competitor had not grounded their Boonsomes, and Amber's decision had, at least in the short term, put Coast Eagle at a competitive disadvantage. The lawyers successfully framed her decision as emotional and even brought Cole into the equation, accusing Amber of taking advice from a competitor on a confidential corporate matter.

It wasn't going well for Amber's side.

"You were ten years older than your stepsister?" the lawyer then asked her.

The question obviously surprised Amber, and it seemed to take her a moment to regroup. "Yes."

"And you left home when she was eight years old?"

"I did."

"How often did you see her after that?"

"Not often."

"Once a week, once a month, once a year?"

"Maybe once a year," Amber admitted, causing a small flurry of whispers in the courtroom.

"Until you introduced her to Samuel Henderson."

"Yes," said Amber.

"And why did you introduce them to each other?"

"Coco was in town. When I mentioned the corporate Christmas party at Coast Eagle, she asked to go with me."

"She asked to go with you?"

"Coco enjoyed parties."

"Yes, I think we've established that already."

"Objection," said Destiny.

"I withdraw the comment," said the lawyer. "After she began dating Samuel Henderson, would you say you and your stepsister grew closer?"

"We did."

"And you saw each other how often then?"

"A couple of times a month. She was busy. And she was newly married. And she had a lot of obligations."

Cole wanted to tell Amber to stop talking. She was sounding defensive, as if she was embarrassed that they weren't closer.

"Tell me, Ms. Welsley, how did Coco feel about her baby?"

"She loved Zachary very much."

"As mothers do."

Amber didn't answer.

Cole applauded that decision.

"What about before he was born?"

She went still, and her face paled a shade. "I don't understand."

"I don't like this," Cole muttered beneath his breath. Something was clearly wrong.

"Before Zachary was born. How did Coco feel about being pregnant?"

"She was healthy. There were no particular problems, morning sickness or anything."

"I'm not talking about her physical health, Ms. Welsley. I'm talking about her emotional health."

Again, Amber stayed silent.

"Was your stepsister happy to be pregnant with Zachary?"

Cole got a cold feeling in the pit of his stomach.

"She was surprised," said Amber. "She hadn't planned on it happening so soon."

"Surprised or upset?"

Amber paused. "She was upset at first."

"Upset enough to get an abortion?"

Amber's hesitation said it all.

"Damn it," Cole ground out.

"She didn't get an abortion," said Amber.

"Did she want an abortion?"

"Objection," said Destiny.

"I'll rephrase," said the lawyer. "Did she ever tell you she wanted an abortion?"

The silence was unfortunately long.

"Once," Amber admitted.

"Did you talk her out of getting an abortion?"

"I gave her my opinion."

"Which was?"

"That babies were always good news. And that she was going to be a wonderful mother."

"Is it fair to say you changed her mind?"

Amber didn't answer.

"Ms. Welsley? Is it fair to say you changed your stepsister's mind, talked her out of getting the abortion she desired?"

"She wasn't serious," said Amber. "She was upset. She was newly married, and being pregnant came as a shock to her."

"Did she make an appointment at an abortion clinic?"

"No."

The lawyer waited.

"She didn't."

"Perhaps not to the best of your knowledge. But I can tell you she *did* make an appointment at an abortion clinic."

A collective gasp went up in the gallery, followed by whispered comments.

The judge pounded his gavel, and the room returned to quiet.

The lawyer returned to his table, lifting a piece of paper with a flourish. "I have here a copy of an appointment card for Coco Henderson for the Women's Central Health Clinic."

"Where did you get that?"

"From the Women's Central Health Clinic."

"Coco obviously did not have an abortion."

"Because you talked her out of it. Like so many of your step-sister's childish, ill-informed impulses, had you not been there to persuade her otherwise, the consequences would have been catastrophic. She would have had an abortion, and Zachary would never have been born."

The sick feeling of defeat was written across Amber's face. Cole fought an urge to go to her. He wanted to pull her into his arms and tell her everything was going to be okay. But he couldn't. And it wasn't.

"That was a body blow," said Luca.

There was nothing Destiny could do to counter the revelations. Both lawyers walked through closing arguments, but there wasn't a single person in the room who trusted Coco's judgment, nor was there anyone who truly believed she had her son's best interests at heart.

Samuel had been shown to be a loving father, thrilled from minute one that they were expecting a baby. Coco looked selfish and petulant, her intelligence and judgment suspect.

Destiny sat down and put an arm around Amber's shoulders.

"You have to do it," Luca whispered.

"Do what?"

"Tell them who you are."

Cole shot Luca a look of astonishment. *"What?"*

"Now. Right now. Put in a bid for custody. You're a blood relative."

"Custody?" Had Luca lost his mind?

"At the very least, it'll throw a wrench in it, slow things down. If you don't, if the judge rules on this—and it looks like he's about to rule—then it's done."

Adrenaline shot into Cole's system, and his stomach clenched. How could he do it? How could he not?

"Ms. Welsley," said the judge, "I have no doubt as to the love you feel for Zachary. However—"

"Do it!" Luca hissed.

Cole shot to his feet. "Your Honor."

The judge drew back in obvious shock. "You're out of order, sir."

"Go, go, go," said Luca.

Cole moved into the aisle and walked forward.

Amber and Destiny both turned to stare. But he didn't dare look at them.

"Bailiff," called the judge.

Cole knew he had only seconds. "My name is Cole Parker Henderson. I'm Samuel Henderson's son."

Amber felt her world dissolve beneath her.

Cole continued walking to the front of the courtroom. He continued talking. He didn't even bother to look her way.

"I want to petition the court for custody of my half brother," his voice boomed.

"He's a competitor," Roth cried out, coming to his feet.

"Order," called the judge, bringing down his gavel.

The bailiff seemed uncertain of what to do.

Destiny whispered in an undertone, "What the—?"

"I'm *such* an idiot," said Amber.

"Can it possibly be true?"

Cole came to a stop at the little gateway.

Amber took in Cole's expression. "That's no bluff."

He was firm and resolute. She realized he had to have planned this all along. And she'd let him in. She'd trusted him. She'd armed him with all kinds of information. She'd left him alone in the penthouse, alone with Zachary.

"This is preposterous," said Roth. "It's a stalling tactic."

Cole glared at him. "It's easy enough to prove. DNA, for example."

"That'll take time. And we're losing money by the hour. Your Honor, this can't possibly be legal."

Roth's lawyer stood. "Your Honor, you were about to rule."

A voice came from the back of the room. "We have a DNA test."

Cole spun.

Luca came to his feet. "Your Honor, I have the results of a DNA test by Central Laboratories, proving Samuel's paternity."

"What do we do?" asked Amber, panic beginning to build deep in her stomach.

"Wait," said Destiny, watching the judge closely.

The judge finally spoke. "I'm not persuaded that a genetic relationship alone alters the merits of this case. Samuel Henderson could have any number of illegitimate children—"

"They were married," Cole's deep voice intoned.

Silence followed the pronouncement.

"My mother and Samuel Henderson were married." He shot a sharp look to Roth. "Again, very easy to prove."

Luca spoke. "I have a copy of the marriage certificate and the divorce decree."

Cole turned to stare at Luca for a long moment.

Destiny leaned close to Amber. "*This* is a whole new ballgame. Hang tough."

Destiny came sharply to her feet. "Your Honor, we ask for a recess."

Roth's lawyer jumped in. "*We* ask for a ruling."

But Destiny wasn't finished. "Under the terms of the will, as a legitimate child of Samuel Henderson, Cole Henderson is entitled to half of Samuel's estate."

The courtroom erupted.

"Order, order," the judge called over the din. "Court is in recess until such time as Samuel Henderson's will can be reviewed." He looked to Cole. "Mr. Henderson, if you do not already have a lawyer, I suggest you get one."

Everybody left their seats, and the courtroom turned into a mob scene. Cole stood still, the crowd jostling around him. He was nearly chest to chest with the bailiff guarding the low gate.

"Get me out of here," Amber said to Destiny. "I can't see him. I can't talk to him."

"We can take the side door." Destiny grabbed her briefcase.

All Amber wanted to do was get back to Zachary. For a horrible moment there, she'd known she was about to lose him. Zachary had almost been ripped from her care and given over to Roth. She was still shaking with reaction.

"Amber," called Cole.

She refused to look at him. "Go away."

"I wanted to tell you. I tried to tell you."

She let out a short, high-pitched laugh. "When? *When?* It's not like you lacked opportunity."

"We need to talk."

"We've talked enough. I've told you enough." She turned away.

"Amber," Cole tried again.

Luca's voice interrupted. "Destiny, we need a copy of the will."

"Not *now*," said Cole.

Destiny's tone was sharp. "As if you haven't already read it."

"We haven't," said Luca.

"Why the theatrics?"

"You were about to lose," said Luca.

"Amber?" Cole tried again.

Destiny appealed to Cole. "This is not a good time."

"I don't particularly care. You can't ignore this."

Amber glared at him. She wanted to yell at him. He'd deceived her. He'd slept with her. He'd let her think he cared about Zachary.

But before she could do anything stupid, she forced herself to turn and walk away.

She left the courtroom and all but ran down the hallway to the foyer. It was full of reporters, but she ignored their questions. She ignored everything, striding blindly for the exit.

Destiny caught up. "You're doing great. Just keep walking. My car's to the left, one block up."

"I remember. I need to see Zachary."

"We'll go there first."

"Ms. Welsley, did you have any idea Samuel had another son?"

"Did your sister know Samuel had another wife?"

"Did Coco have any other abortions?"

Destiny hit the unlock button and pulled open the passenger door for Amber. Amber climbed inside and slammed the door, not particularly caring if she smashed someone's camera.

And then Destiny was inside, too. She started the car, and the reporters finally backed off.

"You okay?" she asked, reaching out to touch Amber's shoulder.

"I'm terrible," Amber answered.

She felt trapped, desperate. For a wild moment, she thought about sneaking Zachary out of the country, hiding out on a beach somewhere where nobody could find them.

"What happens now?" she asked, her voice shaking.

"First, we comb through the will."

"Does Cole really get half?"

"Unless there's something I'm remembering wrong, yes, he does."

Amber's voice broke over the next question. "Will he get Zachary?"

"I don't know, honey. I honestly don't know."

Amber's mind scrambled, zipping from Zachary to Coast Eagle, to the Boonsome 300, and then to Cole.

"I have to talk to Max," she told Destiny. "I have to get back to the office."

"Do you want to go home first?"

Amber shook her head. "I'll call Isabel. Roth will go straight to Coast Eagle, and who knows what move he'll try to make next." She realized in a rush that despite everything, she feared Roth more than she feared Cole.

Back at the office, Roth had fought with Max. Julius had argued with Sidney. Each of the board members had called to express their concern. Though, thankfully, all had agreed that Max should stay in place for now as interim president.

Destiny had reviewed Samuel's will and was now on her way to the penthouse to meet Amber. It was nearly ten by the time Amber finally made it through the door, exhausted and starving.

She kicked off her shoes, shrugged out of her steel-gray blazer and dumped her purse on a table in the living room. Destiny had promised to bring a large pepperoni and mushroom, while Amber was in charge of margaritas.

She called out to Isabel, then, without stopping, she went directly to the kitchen and dumped a tray of ice cubes, lime juice, tequila and orange liqueur into the blender and set it on high.

The doorbell rang, and she padded through the living room to greet Destiny.

"Extra cheese?" she asked hopefully as she eyed the large cardboard carton.

"You bet."

"Come on in."

While Destiny settled the pizza on the kitchen island and retrieved the plates, Amber poured the margaritas into two large glasses.

"I've been seriously thinking about strapping Zachary into his car seat and heading for the border," said Amber.

"Which border?"

"Does it matter? I can't help but think we'd be better off if nobody could find us."

"You might be better off, but I'd have a legal nightmare to unravel."

"I suppose."

The fight suddenly went out of Amber, and exhaustion set in. She climbed onto one of the stools and helped herself to a slice of the gooey pizza.

"You could try to make a deal with Cole," Destiny suggested. She started with a sip of the slushy drink. "It's pretty clear he's after Coast Eagle."

"Do you think Samuel knew about him?" In her few spare moments this evening, Amber couldn't help but wonder if Samuel had shunned Cole and kept him a secret or had been oblivious to his existence.

"Interesting wording in the will," said Destiny. "Either Samuel knew, or at least suspected he had a child with his first wife, or he was planning more children with Coco."

"He definitely wanted more children," said Amber.

There was more silence.

"An abortion?" asked Destiny.

"I almost couldn't talk her out of it."

"For future reference, that's the kind of thing you want to share with your lawyer."

"I had no idea it would ever come out."

"Everything always comes out eventually."

"I didn't know she'd made an appointment. She didn't tell me that. It was one night—one long, horrible night where we argued. And then she changed her mind. I don't remember any of the staff being around. I thought nobody knew but me."

"She might have told Samuel."

Amber gave her head a decisive shake. "She knew how much he wanted children. If she'd had an abortion, it would have been in secret. She'd never have admitted to him she'd had doubts."

They both fell silent, chewing their way through the pizza slices.

"We were about to lose, weren't we?" Amber asked.

"We were about to lose big-time. Roth knows how to run Coast Eagle, and Samuel was way out front in the character debate."

"Just because Coco was self-centered doesn't mean she was wrong to choose me."

"I agree," said Destiny, helping herself to another slice. "We need to figure out Cole's plan. I can guess at Roth's next move. Between Samuel and his mother, the Hendersons controlled sixty-five percent of Coast Eagle. The other shareholders are minor, mostly companies, none with more than seven percent. But Roth still has a play. If he gets custody, therefore half of the Henderson family shares, and if he can bring the other shareholders on side, he'll control the board and get himself appointed as president."

"He doesn't care anything about Zachary."

"True, but all but impossible to prove," said Destiny. "Samuel named him guardian for some reason."

"If Cole gets custody, he controls all sixty-five percent. He's invincible." Amber paused. "But why the ruse?"

"He was obviously looking for information, solidifying his position. That has to be why Luca was cozying up to me."

"Did you tell Luca anything?"

"Nothing that wasn't already public. Cole obviously saw you as his primary rival rather than Ross. I'm guessing he was either going to co-opt you or take you out."

"He must have been shocked when it went in Roth's favor."

"And had to suddenly change the game plan. I don't think they planned it like that."

"They did have DNA and a marriage certificate at the ready."

"True," said Destiny.

Amber took a drink, appreciating the hit of alcohol warming her system. "What do we do now?"

"We need more information on Cole."

"Maybe I could seduce it out of him. No, wait. I already tried that."

Destiny gazed at her for a moment, the tone of her voice going softer. "How was it?"

"Seriously?"

Destiny gave a helpless shrug. "What can it hurt to tell me now?"

Amber set down her half-eaten slice of pizza, regret enveloping her. "It was great. He was funny, romantic, totally into me." She swiped back her hair. "At least he seemed totally into me. Too bad he was faking the whole thing." Every time she thought about their night together, the humiliation returned. "I'm not sure I can face him again."

"I could talk to Luca instead. He might give me something we can use."

"Did you sleep with Luca?"

"Almost. He tried pretty hard."

Amber held up her glass in a toast. "You're a stronger woman than me. And you've still got that as leverage."

"I'd have said yes eventually."

"But you won't anymore, right?"

"I won't anymore," said Destiny. "Well, unless I think it'll make him talk. Then, well, okay, I'd be willing to take one for the team."

Eight

"I know she's here," Cole said to Luca as he pulled open the steel door of the Coast Eagle hangar. "And she'll have to be polite."

He knew Amber wouldn't dare step out of line at the Coast Eagle children's Christmas party. She'd have to listen to him.

He walked inside.

Carols chimed from unseen speakers, while soap bubbles drifted around them like snow. White lights and colored balls domed over the ceiling, swooping down in swirls and shapes to meet the concrete floor, which was covered in artificial snow.

There was a giant Christmas tree in the center of the hangar and a forest full of lighted trees and friendly elves. A cookie-decorating station took up one big corner of the room. Another group of elves painted Christmas shapes on the children's faces. And, of course, Santa was in his castle, posing for pictures and handing out presents.

The festive scene jarred with the frustration swirling inside Cole's head. In the three days since the hearing, a group of lawyers had poured over Samuel's will. This morning, they'd all agreed that Cole was a beneficiary, entitled to half of Samuel's estate.

Cole didn't want an inheritance. When he'd come forward and announced himself, he hadn't the slightest inkling he'd be included in the will. He wasn't here to take anything away from Zachary. Still, he'd use the position if it gave them leverage.

"There she is," said Luca. "Beside the Christmas-tree forest."

Cole spotted her. As always, he was immediately struck by her beauty. She wore a bright red dress with white piping. It clung to her slender curves.

He was here to talk. But talking was far down on his wish list. For starters, he wanted to haul her off somewhere and kiss her senseless.

"Mr. Henderson," Sidney Raines greeted him cheerfully, shaking his hand. "I heard the estate was settled this morning in your favor."

"Call me Cole. It's nice to see you again, Sidney."

Of all the vice presidents, Sidney was easily the more savvy and most reasonable. Cole also liked Max. He was less impressed with Julius, and he was prepared to fight long and hard against Roth.

"It's probably early on to broach the subject," said Sidney, glancing around the huge building, "and I realize this isn't the time or the place, but have you given any thought to what role you'll take on in the company?"

"It isn't the time or the place," said Cole. "But you're right to ask the question. Would you be able to meet over the weekend?"

"Absolutely. You just name the time and place."

Cole took out his cell phone. "If you give me your cell number, I'll call you later on."

Sidney dictated his phone number, then bowed out.

"It's a good question," said Luca.

"I know," said Cole as the two men started toward the brightly lit forest.

"Do you have any idea what you are going to do?"

Cole's thinking hadn't made it past the first couple of moves. "I'm going to find a permanent president."

He worked fourteen-hour days taking care of Aviation 58. He had to get back there as soon as possible. But he'd accepted that he now had a role in protecting Zachary's inheritance.

The closer they got to Amber, the more beautiful she became. No surprise to Cole.

Zachary was in her arms, also dressed in red and white, a goofy little hat on his head. Cole couldn't help but smile at how Zachary reached for the twinkling lights of the closest tree. He'd really missed the little guy.

But then Amber saw him.

Her smile instantly disappeared, and her blue eyes went cold. She took a step, and it was obvious she was going to flee.

Cole quickly crossed the space between them, wrapping a hand around her arm and keeping her close.

Luca wisely hung back.

"Everybody's watching," he cautioned her in a low tone. "Smile. Pretend it's all good between us."

"Go away."

"Not a chance. Smile."

Zachary zeroed in on Cole.

"Gak baw," he called, lurching toward Cole.

Cole reflexively reached for him. His arm brushed her breast, and the contact sent a surge of energy through his body.

He ordered himself to calm the heck down. "You heard the decision on the will?"

Amber put a brittle smile in place, but her tone was flat. "Congratulations."

"We have to talk."

"I don't have time. I promised Zachary we'd decorate some gingerbread." She reached for the baby, but he turned his head, clinging tighter to Cole.

"It'll be easier if I come with you," said Cole.

"No, it won't."

"I'm on your side."

She scoffed out a laugh. "Is that a joke?" Then she held out her arms to Zachary. "Come on, pumpkin."

The baby stayed firmly latched to Cole.

Cole couldn't help feeling sympathetic. "As much as I hate to think about it, I must look like Samuel. Or maybe I sound like him, or smell like him."

"Zachary loves me, too, you know."

"Of course he does."

"He's known me since birth."

"It's a case of mistaken identity," said Cole. "Somewhere in his subconscious, he sees me as family."

"You are family."

Cole was growing more and more conscious of the interest in their conversation. Nobody had dared come within hearing distance, but there was a lot of pointing and whispering going on amongst the staff.

"Let's go decorate some gingerbread."

"Why can't you just leave?"

"If I give him back, he's going to make a scene."

"Was that your plan? I mean today's plan—use Zachary against me?"

"There was no plan."

"Do I strike you as stupid?"

"Amber, please. Gingerbread. Let's just do the gingerbread."

There must have been a note of desperation in his tone that got her attention because she glanced around, seeming to become aware of the onlookers.

"Right," she agreed. "Let's go."

They moved casually to the rear corner of the hangar. People eyed them speculatively as they did so, but held back. Luca disappeared, obviously understanding that Cole needed to speak with Amber alone.

"Mr. Henderson, Ms. Welsley, Merry Christmas!" called a middle-aged woman as they passed.

"Merry Christmas," Cole automatically returned.

"Notice you got top billing," Amber muttered.

"I'm carrying the little rich kid."

"You are the little rich kid."

The greeting seemed to break the ice, and they were bombarded with well-wishers all along their route.

Amber was right. While the employees were completely polite and respectful to her, Cole was getting the lion's share of the attention.

Finally, they came to the cookie-decorating station. The attendants quickly cleared a stand-up table for them, spreading out a new paper cover and bringing an assortment of gingerbread, sugar-cookie shapes, icing and colorful candies.

"Go for it," said Cole. "Pretend you're completely absorbed in the cookies, and maybe people will stay away."

She stared at the tabletop without moving.

"The tree," Cole prompted. "Decorate the tree with the green icing."

Amber picked up a plastic knife.

He focused on keeping his expression agreeable as he spoke. "I'm going to need your support."

She gave another strained smile as she iced the sugar cookie tree. "Like that's going to happen."

"I didn't know about the will."

"Yes, you did."

"How would I know? Tell me how I would know."

"There were ten people in the first reading. Obviously someone leaked the details to you."

"None of them knew I existed."

"So you say."

His voice rose. "I don't just say. It's true."

"The red candies?" she asked him sweetly. "Or the blue and white?"

He took a calming breath. "The red."

"I like the blue and white."

"Seriously? You want to argue about candies?"

"I don't want to argue about anything. I want you to go away. Preferably far away. I hear Alaska's nice this time of year."

Cole shifted Zachary in his arms. Happily, the baby was fascinated by the lights, the sounds and the people moving around.

"If you'll listen to what I have to say, you'll understand why you need to help me."

"No, Cole. If I believed what you had to say, I might be inclined to help you. But that's never going to happen. I'm never going to trust you again."

"I want what's best for Zachary."

"You want what's best for Cole. And congratulations, you're halfway there."

Cole regrouped. "Roth can still take control of the company."

She dropped a handful of blue and white candies on the freshly iced tree and pressed them firmly down with her palm.

For a moment, he thought she'd crush the cookie.

"I can see you've done the math on the share ownership," she said.

"Do you have any influence with the minor shareholders?"

She flashed another phony smile. "None whatsoever. I'm the lowly assistant director of finance and the stepsister of a flaky trophy wife. Why would anyone listen to me?"

"We can still help each other."

"Have a cookie, Cole. It's all you're ever going to get from me."

She suddenly scooped Zachary out of his arms.

It took the baby a second to realize what had happened. Then he immediately opened his mouth and let out a cry.

If not for the staff members surrounding them, Cole would have gone after her. Instead, he watched her march away and disappear into the crowd.

Zachary's cries were soon swallowed by the cheery carols and happy shouts of the other children.

Luca appeared beside him. "Didn't look like that went too well."

"She has *got* to be the most stubborn woman on the planet." Cole's gaze fell to the slightly mangled cookie. He picked it up and took a bite.

"Fighting with Amber makes you hungry?"

"It makes me something, that's for sure."

He crunched down on the sweetness. Fighting made him want to grab her and squeeze her tight, kiss her hard and press their bodies together. It didn't matter what insanity swirled around them, he couldn't forget the night they'd made love, and he couldn't quell the overriding urge to do it all over again.

Amber wasn't going to crack.

It was nearly ten o'clock at night. Zachary had barely napped during the afternoon. He'd fussed through dinner and pouted through his bath. She'd even given him an extra bottle, going through their entire bedtime routine a second time in the hope he'd catch on.

Now he was in his crib, kicking his feet and sobbing. His

covers were on the floor. His head was sweaty, and his hands were wrapped tightly around the painted bars.

Her phone rang over the noise, and for a crazy second she hoped it was Cole. If he called her and asked to come over, it wasn't the same as giving in, was it?

Unfortunately, the number was Destiny's.

She moved into the hallway, and Zachary's cries increased behind her.

"Hi," she said into the phone.

"How're you doing?"

"Not great."

"Is that Zachary?"

Amber leaned against the wall of the hallway, sliding down to sit on the plush carpet. "He doesn't want to settle."

"I'm sorry."

"Not your fault. Not even his fault. Honestly, I feel like sobbing right along with him."

"Luca said you saw Cole today?"

Amber knew she should remember his annoying behavior, her anger and his new set of lies. But instead she remembered his touch, his voice and those now-familiar gray eyes.

"At the kids' party," she answered Destiny. "Wait, when did you see Luca?"

"Earlier tonight."

"Why?" What was going on?

"Nothing's going on. I like Luca, Amber. I'm not giving him any information. He's not even trying to ask. We both know we have to be circumspect."

Amber clunked her head back against the cool wall. "I'm sorry. You're entitled to a personal life."

"He did say something, though."

"What's that?"

"He said that by not helping Cole, you're de facto helping Roth."

Amber gave a slightly hysterical laugh. "I thought you were going to say something much more personal. Like you had beautiful eyes or he wanted to see you naked."

"Oh, he definitely wants to see me naked."

Amber firmly pushed her own problems away. "You should let him."

"Excuse me?"

"You want to. I can hear it in your voice."

"There's nothing in my voice that says—"

"Go for it. Your celibacy won't help me. In fact, it'll probably distract you from helping me."

"You want me to have a one-night stand?"

"I had one." The memories rose one by one in Amber's mind.

Into the silence, Destiny's tone turned reflective. "You think you're the better for it?"

"Not at all. But I'm stuck in the middle of a preposterous circumstance. You'll be fine."

"You want some company? Need some reinforcements?"

"You don't need to come all the way over here."

Not that Amber wouldn't welcome the support. Maybe Destiny could take a turn holding Zachary. He was still crying, and it was all but impossible to steel herself against his sadness.

"I'm five minutes away," said Destiny.

"You are?"

"Just left a meeting at Bacharat's. You know, that private lawyers' club? You're on my route home."

"Then, yes, sure. Stop by."

"Sounds good. It might take me a few minutes to park."

"See you then." Amber disconnected the call.

Feeling a bit lighter, she headed back into Zachary's bedroom. He had pulled up on his feet and was gripping the top of the crib rail. His cheeks were flushed red and damp with tears.

"Oh, sweetheart," she said out loud, lifting him into her arms. "How can I help?"

He cried harder.

She racked her brain. "What about some music? Want to watch videos?"

Zachary seemed to have a fondness for country and western, especially the drawling male singers.

With no better ideas, she carried him to the living room and tuned in the country station. It didn't fix the problem, but at least it gave something to blend with his cries.

Then the knock came on her door.

"I know you're too young to understand," she said to Zachary as they crossed the living room, "but my arms are about to get a rest, and that's a very good thing."

She swung open the door.

Cole stood in front of her, Otis at his heels.

She was stunned. "You're supposed to be Destiny."

"I saw her in the lobby."

At the sound of Cole's voice, Zachary swung around.

"She said she'd give me ten minutes," said Cole.

"Destiny sent you up?" Amber didn't want to believe it.

Zachary reached for Cole.

"You want me to take him?"

Amber caved. "She'll be up in ten minutes?"

Cole cracked a smile. "I bet he's asleep by then. He looks exhausted."

Amber was weak. In fact, she was defeated. "He's the one and only reason I'll let you in."

"I'll take it." Cole gathered Zachary against his shoulder and moved into the foyer.

"What's goin' on here, partner?" Cole rumbled.

Zachary laid his head onto Cole's shoulder and his cries turned to shuddering breaths.

She couldn't resist. She smoothed the sweat from Zachary's forehead, brushing her fingers across his downy, fine hair. "Poor little guy."

"You're very patient," said Cole.

"Not always."

There were times when she couldn't help feeling frustrated and resentful. She was doing everything she could for Zachary, but it wasn't enough. Sometimes she thought he was being miserable just to make her jump through hoops. But in her saner moments, she knew he was far too young to be manipulative.

"You need to do anything?" he asked her as they walked to the living room. "Hungry, thirsty?"

"Don't be nice."

A smirk appeared on his face. "Okay."

"You know what I mean. Don't try to ingratiate yourself by helping me with Zachary. It won't work."

Otis picked a spot beside an armchair and flopped down.

"Then do you think you could whip something up for me?" asked Cole. "Maybe a dry martini and a few hors d'oeuvres?"

"Shut up and mind the baby."

Cole grinned. "He's doing fine."

"I hate that you can do that, you know." It wasn't fair at all.

"Accident of genetics." Cole lowered himself into an armchair.

It was yet another thing that ticked her off. When she was soothing Zachary, she couldn't sit down. She had to stand and sway or he'd cry his head off.

"This whole thing is an accident of genetics," Cole repeated.

"You want some hot cocoa?" she asked. She couldn't help remembering the last time they'd shared that particular beverage, but she needed something soothing right now.

"I was just messing with you. Don't go to any trouble."

But it wasn't any trouble. "It'll only take a minute, and I'm having some."

He hesitated. "In that case, sure."

She left for the kitchen.

"You need any help?" he called behind her.

"You're already helping."

"Points for that?" he asked.

The question stopped her cold. She couldn't help remembering the last time they'd joked about points. He'd asked to spend the night, then they'd slept curled together in her bed. If only they could go back to that moment, even just for a little while. Because what she really needed right now was a broad shoulder to lean on. Unfortunately, leaning on Cole's shoulder was out of the question.

She heated up the cocoa and returned to the living room.

"Sorry," he told her.

"For what?" She set a steaming cup down on the small table beside him and took the end of the sofa opposite to where he sat.

"For making that points crack."

He obviously remembered the last time.

The sweetened air seemed to still around them. Her mouth went dry, and her heartbeat thudded thickly in her chest. She braved a look at his face, and their gazes held. The ticking of the clock seemed to grow louder.

Cole broke the silence. "The reason I'm here…"

She was half afraid, half excited about what he might say. She distracted herself with a sip.

"The reason I'm here," he began again, "is because we can't let Roth win, and that means I need your help."

She didn't want Roth to win. But she didn't want Cole to win, either. Her throat closed up, and her chest pierced with pain.

She had a desperate urge to rip Zachary from his arms. She didn't care if he cried. She didn't care if she never slept again. She wanted to hold him every second of every day from now until someone forced her to stop.

"I…" she tried. "How can…" To her mortification, a tear slipped out.

She rose from her chair, surreptitiously swiping the tear away. "He's asleep. We can put him in his crib now."

"Sure," Cole agreed easily, rising with Zachary in his arms, watching her closely.

She walked down the hall to the nursery. There, she straightened the rumpled sheets and folded a fresh blanket onto the mattress.

A yellow nightlight glowed in the corner, highlighting the cartoon giraffes, elephants and lions on the wall. Soft stuffed animals decorated every surface.

Cole moved beside her and eased Zachary down onto the white flannel sheet. He pulled his arm from beneath Zachary and stepped back. The baby didn't stir. Amber covered Zachary with a knit blanket and a patchwork quilt. Then she stroked her palm over his warm forehead.

"Good night, sweetheart," she whispered.

She straightened, her heart aching all over again. She gripped the top of the crib rail, struggling to draw a breath.

Cole's strong hand came down on her shoulder. "Are you okay?" he asked softly.

She swallowed. Her voice came out on a pained whisper. "I'm so frightened."

"I know."

She shook her head. "No, you don't. You can't possibly understand."

She was going to lose Zachary, and there wasn't a thing she could do about it.

He gently turned her. She didn't stop him as he drew her into his arms. It didn't seem to matter that he was one of the enemies; she accepted the strength he offered.

His voice was deep and steady. "I know you can't let yourself believe anything I say. But I want what's best for Zachary. I promise I'll do what's best for Zachary."

She tipped her chin to gaze up at him. She wanted so badly to believe it was true. She needed some hope to hang on to.

Minutes ticked slowly past.

He reached up to brush her chin, his voice low and sexy. "You are amazing."

She knew she had to pull away. She had to shut this down before it went any further. His eyes were smoldering, his desire completely obvious. His hand crept into her hair. His gaze zeroed in on her lips, and he bent his head.

He was going to kiss her.

She wasn't going to stop him.

His lips touched hers, warm, soft and gentle.

She stretched up, leaned in, let her arms twine around his neck as he took the kiss deeper. She'd missed him. She couldn't believe how much she'd missed him.

Her world was dissolving around her, and he felt like the only anchor point. His hand splayed her back, pressing her close. A moan rose up from her chest, and she met his tongue. Flicking flames of desire rose up inside her, heating her body, sensitizing every nerve ending. She needed to get closer, to feel his skin.

But suddenly, he drew back. "We can't do this."

She was mortified. What was she thinking? What was she doing, throwing herself into his arms?

He braced his hands around her upper arms, putting a few inches between them. "We need to talk."

"Talk," Amber managed to agree.

He put a hand lightly on the small of her back, guiding her from the nursery, down the hall, back to the living room.

She went straight to the far corner of the sofa, struggling to pull her dignity around her.

She could feel Cole's gaze on her from where he sat in the armchair. But she couldn't bring herself to look at him. She couldn't imagine what he thought of her. He'd deceived her, used her to gain information about Coast Eagle, Samuel and Zachary. And yet she'd been willing to leap into bed with him a second time.

There was something terribly wrong with her.

"What will Roth do?" Cole asked into the silence. "If he wins custody, what will he do?"

Amber struggled to move past emotion to logic. "I expect he will hire a nanny. I hope he keeps Isabel, but I don't know that he will." She had to stop for a breath. "Then he'll use the power of his guardianship to get appointed president of Coast Eagle."

"He won't want to be chairman of the board?"

"He wants to be hands-on. He wants to run the company day-to-day. His first plan is to update or replace the entire fleet. He thinks he'll be able to increase our market share enough to cover the debt."

"You doubt that?" asked Cole.

"His projections are dangerously optimistic."

Cole gave a contemplative nod.

Amber forced herself to ask the burning question. "What will you do?"

His gaze was level and honest. "I don't know."

"How can I trust you?"

"You can't. You shouldn't."

She scoffed out a laugh at that.

He took a sip of his now-cool cocoa. "All you can do right now is go on what's certain. Roth's got the advantage over me, and he cares about Roth, first, last and always."

"You're saying you're the lesser of two evils."

"I know you can't bring yourself to trust me yet. But you know for certain you can't trust Roth."

"That's not at all comforting."

"I know. But it's all you've got."

Amber knew he was right. She hated it. But it was true.

Nine

As a significant shareholder in Coast Eagle, no matter how things turned out in the long term, Cole knew he needed to understand the company. He and Luca had both been in daily contact with Aviation 58 since arriving in Atlanta, but Luca now offered to take over as much as possible on the Alaska operation.

Luckily, even leading into the busy holiday travel season, things seemed well under control at Aviation 58. There were no unexpected maintenance issues, passenger load was as predicted and the Alaskan weather was cooperating surprisingly well.

Cole entered the Coast Eagle building and was immediately recognized. Security greeted him and called up to the executive floor to announce his arrival.

As he exited the elevator, he was greeted by the receptionist, Sandra, who was exceedingly welcoming and polite this time. She introduced him to Samuel's personal assistant, a fiftyish man named Bartholomew Green. Bartholomew had a British accent and was dressed in a dark formal suit, a matching vest, crisp white shirt and a gold tie.

Samuel's office was also ostentatious, with a huge, ornately carved cherrywood desk, and a massive credenza with cut-glass decanters. A sofa and two armchairs had diamond tufted, dark leather upholstery, while expensive oil paintings hung on the walls. Cole couldn't help wonder how his down-to-earth mother had fallen in love with the man he was learning about.

"Will you be moving into the office today, sir?" asked Bartholomew.

"I will," said Cole.

The last thing in the world he wanted to do was step into his father's shoes. But he needed to make a statement. Roth, the judge and everybody else had to see he was taking the reins—even if it was only temporary.

He took in Bartholomew's attire once more. He supposed

he'd have to update his own wardrobe, and he was going to make the same recommendation to Amber. She was next on his list of things to deal with at Coast Eagle.

"Can you set up a meeting with Max and the vice presidents for this afternoon?" Cole asked Bartholomew.

"Do you have a preferred time, sir?"

"Two o'clock." Cole couldn't have cared less about the time, but he needed to be the guy making the decisions.

"The east boardroom?"

"Sounds fine. Can you direct me to Amber Welsley's office?"

"She's in accounting. That's on the seventh floor. Shall I show you the way?"

"Is it overly complicated?"

Bartholomew seemed to allow himself a small smile. "Left when you get off the elevator, first hallway on your right."

"I think I can manage. No need for a tour guide."

"Very good, sir."

"Anything else I should know?" Cole asked, curious to know where Bartholomew's loyalties would lie.

"What would you like to know?"

Cole paused to gauge the man's expression. "What do you think is important?"

An intelligent light came into Bartholomew's eyes. "Mr. Henderson had a lot of faith in Sidney. I believe that was appropriate. He also had a lot of faith in Roth. I believe that faith may have been misplaced. He also understood the need to deploy Julius in certain situations."

"Such as?"

"Would you like me to be blunt?"

"Always."

"Julius is a pit bull. But he's Coast Eagle's pit bull."

"What about Max Cutter?"

"Max Cutter will be completely up front and honest with you. If I had to guess, I'd say he can't wait to get out of the president's role and back to the legal department."

Cole agreed with that assessment. Max had said as much himself.

"And Amber Welsley?" Cole asked.

"I knew Mrs. Henderson a lot better than I knew Ms. Welsley."

"Impressions?"

"She has always struck me as hardworking but below the radar. I'm not certain she thought very highly of Mr. Samuel Henderson."

"He married her baby sister."

"Indeed. Though I'm not certain she was a fan of Mrs. Henderson, either."

"May I rely on your discretion, Bartholomew?"

"You may."

"Good to know." Cole was impressed with the man so far.

"If I may, sir?"

"Yes?"

"You haven't asked about Samuel Henderson."

"That's because I don't want to know."

Bartholomew was silent for a moment. "Very good."

"Is that a problem for you?"

"Not at all."

Cole looked through the doorway to the outer office and Bartholomew's desk. "Give me the lay of the land here."

Bartholomew moved to stand beside him. "You've seen reception, and my desk is right there. The office to your right is the president's. Max isn't using it, because he already has an office on this floor. Around the corner to your left is Roth, next to him is Julius, and Sidney is around the corner from the president's office. The east boardroom is next to Sidney, and the west meeting room is next to Julius. After that, you're through reception to the director's offices and the executive lunch room."

"Is everyone in today?"

"As I understand it, yes."

"Thank you, Bartholomew." Cole exited the office and made his way to the elevator in the reception area.

Under Sandra's veiled curiosity, he pressed the button for seven. He could well imagine the conversations and speculation would start the second the door closed behind him. That was good. He wanted people to wonder.

On the seventh floor, he took a left then a right, quickly finding Amber's office.

Her door was open, and he was taken aback by the small size. She sat at her desk, head down, writing on a financial sheet.

"There's an adding error on report sixteen," she said without looking up, obviously hearing him arrive. "I know we have to pull the soft commitments in manually, but we need to make sure the formulas are—"

She spotted Cole in the doorway. "Sorry." His presence seemed to fluster her. "I assumed you were my assistant."

"Nope." He walked in.

She sat up straight and set down her pen. "You're here."

"I'm here." He glanced around. "More to the point, you're *here*."

"I'm usually here."

"This is your office?"

"It is."

"So the office of the assistant director of finance?"

"That would be me."

He braced himself on the desk across from her. "Not anymore."

She drew back. "Have I been fired?"

"Promoted. Or haven't you been paying attention?"

"Being temporarily nominated as guardian is not a promotion."

"You're chair of the board."

"For the next five minutes."

"If you want people to take you seriously, you need to look the part."

"Pretending I'm the real chair of the board would be embarrassing for everyone involved."

He straightened. "I don't get you."

"I'm not that complicated."

"Yes, you are. But that's not my point. We need to use every weapon at our disposal. One of the strongest, if not *the* strongest we have is the fact that, for now, we *are* in charge. Get up."

Her brows shot up. "Excuse me?"

"There's an empty office on the top floor—you're moving in. Right now."

"You can't order me to—"

"Amber."

She set her jaw.

He ignored the expression. "Your biggest weakness is that nobody can picture you at the helm."

"That's because I'm not capable of taking the helm."

"Who says?"

"Reason and good judgment?"

"They're wrong. And you're wrong." His tone hardened. This was too important to mess up. "And if you don't march yourself up to that corner office right now and start giving orders, then you haven't done your best by Zachary."

"I have done everything—"

"No, Amber. You haven't. Right now, between the two of us, we control sixty-five percent of Coast Eagle. Let's start acting like it. Let's let the world see us at the helm. That way, they'll know we can do it."

She glanced around her office, the three computer screens, the stacks of reports. "But—"

"First stop, your boss's office to give him permission to replace you."

"Give away my job?" The prospect clearly distressed her.

"Temporarily. Trust me, Amber. And if you can't trust me, trust Destiny. Phone her now. I know she'll agree."

Amber's lips compressed as she obviously thought through the situation.

"Being seen in charge is our best weapon," he reiterated. "Don't throw it away."

"Okay." She came to her feet, expression determined. "I'm willing to try anything."

Cole felt a surge of relief. He'd known she was stubborn. But he'd also known she was smart. Luckily, smart had won out.

* * *

"I've never even set foot in this store," Amber whispered to Destiny.

The next step in Cole's stated strategy was to deck both of them out in what he called a power wardrobe. From what Amber could see, that meant spending a whole lot of money.

"I've never shopped here, either," Destiny answered. "But I know some of the senior partners do. I've heard them mention the name."

"I don't dare look at the price tags," said Amber, glancing around at the gleaming floors, marble pillars and leather furniture groupings with complimentary designer water and champagne.

"What price tags?" asked Destiny. "If you have to ask, you can't afford it."

"I think I might break out in hives."

Cole and Luca entered the store behind them.

"This ought to do it," said Luca with obvious satisfaction.

Cole took in the high, brightly lit ceilings. "It's nothing like the Fashion Farm back home."

"Are you two going upstairs?" Destiny nodded to the sign for menswear.

"And miss the fun?" asked Luca.

"Let's get Amber decked out first," said Cole. "I want to make sure she doesn't hold back."

"You doubt my powers of persuasion?" asked Destiny.

"You'll make me self-conscious," Amber told Cole.

"What better means to cure you? If you can get comfortable in front of me, the rest of the executives will be easy." He pointed to a headless mannequin in a blazer and skirt combination. "What about that?"

The skirt was short and black, scattered with tiny white flecks. The blouse was white with a braided scooped neck. And the blazer was solid black, fitted, with the sleeves pushed up the forearms.

"I like the necklace, too," said Cole. "And the belt. Why not try on the whole thing?"

"You don't think the skirt's a little short?" Amber asked. Though she would admit, the outfit looked fun.

"Shows you have confidence," said Cole.

"I don't have confidence."

Cole turned to Destiny. "You see what I'm dealing with?"

"It would work with black stockings," said Destiny.

Cole opened his mouth, but Luca elbowed him in the ribs.

A sales clerk arrived. "Do you need any help?" she asked with a broad smile.

Amber couldn't help wondering what Cole had been about to say on the topic of black stockings. She also couldn't seem to stop a shimmer of sexual awareness.

"She needs a whole new wardrobe," said Cole, gesturing to Amber.

Amber shifted under everyone's scrutiny. "Oh, I wouldn't say I need an entire—"

"Shut up," Destiny interrupted. She gestured back to Cole. "He's buying, and we need her to look like a million bucks. Literally."

"Daywear, evening, office?" the clerk asked.

"Yes," said Cole.

"This is getting out of hand," said Amber.

She understood the principle behind his strategy. And now that she'd had a few hours to think about it, she agreed with it. But still, it wasn't necessary to go overboard.

"She's been appointed to chair the board of a billion-dollar company," said Cole.

Amber opened her mouth to disagree, but his look stopped her. Fine. Okay. She was going to stop telling people she was a fraud. She was still a fraud, but she could fake it for Zachary's sake.

"Bring it on," she said to the clerk. "I need to look good in the office. I have several evening meetings scheduled, and given the season, there are a few formal events, as well."

"She'll need shoes and purses," said Destiny.

"Don't forget jewelry," said Luca.

"Do we want to do something with her hair?" asked Cole.

Amber glared at him. "Careful. You're next."

"I'm perfectly willing to get a haircut."

"He's the…" Amber paused. "What is your title? You're going to need a title. I'm thinking a big, brass plate on the office door, Mr. Henderson."

"The Big Cheese?" joked Luca.

Destiny gave him a thumbs-down.

The clerk smirked as she began looking through the well-spaced racks.

"Grand Pooh-Bah," said Cole.

"I'm not joking," said Amber. "This is your plan. You need to buy all the way in."

"We've got a president. We've got a chair. Executive board member?"

"You can be the chair," said Amber. "I'll be an executive board member."

"Cochair," said Luca. He pointed to Amber. "Cochair of the board." Then he pointed to Cole. "Cochair of the board."

Amber and Cole looked at each other.

"Okay by me," she said. It would be better than doing it alone.

Cole shrugged. "I'll order the brass nameplates."

"What do you think of these?" asked the clerk, holding a gold dress and a black blazer in one hand, and a navy-and-white outfit with a nautical flair in the other.

"The stuff on the mannequin, too," said Cole.

Amber gave in. "Sure. Bring me whatever you think will work. I'm new at this."

The clerk showed her to an airy changing room with a settee and a triple mirror.

"Come out and show us," Cole called.

"I'm going in to help," said Destiny, slipping past the velvet curtain.

The professional outfits were easy to find. But once they switched to dresses, things bogged down. There were simply too many choices, and all of them were gorgeous. Once she made it past her cost worries, Amber actually began to enjoy herself.

After an hour, Cole headed to menswear. Once he was gone,

Destiny dived into the fun, trying on a few of the dresses herself. The women were close enough in size that they could swap back and forth. Destiny was a little bigger in the bust while Amber had the longer legs. Some of the swaps were quite comical.

Amber had accepted a glass of champagne, and now wandered over to where it sat on a glass table. She was trying on a flirty, strapless cocktail dress that was unlike anything she'd ever worn before.

The bodice was snug, wrapping her in silver beading and sequins. It had a high waist of deep jewel blue with a chiffon skirt that flowed to midthigh. Her back was mostly bare, crisscrossed in shiny, beaded straps, ending in a drop V waist. She'd also found a pair of high-heeled silver shoes that were surprisingly comfortable and seemed to go with a lot of outfits.

"*This* is a keeper," said Destiny from behind her.

Amber turned to see Destiny do a runway turn in a glimmering, full-length gold sheath with a slit up the leg.

Luca's voice drawled from the armchair where he'd stayed back to watch. "Have you got a month's pay to blow?"

"I was going to let Cole buy it," Destiny answered with an impish grin. "The man just inherited half a billion dollars. He's not going to notice one little dress."

"Sure," came Cole's unexpected voice. "Dresses are on me."

Amber turned to find him looking her up and down. "Buy that one."

She felt suddenly self-conscious, particularly knowing he'd had a good view of the back.

"I'm just messing around," she told him. "I've already picked out more than enough."

"Buy it," he repeated. "It looks good on you."

"I don't have anywhere to wear it."

"You will."

"I don't think you have a good feel for my social life."

"The Coast Eagle Christmas party is on Friday. It's formal."

She glanced down at herself. "You call this formal?"

"What do you call it?"

"Nightclubbing."

"Nobody's going to complain." He moved in a bit closer, his voice going low as Destiny and Cole engaged in their own conversation. "I'm sure not going to complain."

The familiar shiver of arousal teased her limbs. "Stop."

"You done?" he asked.

She nodded.

"Got shoes, purses, jewelry? Whatever else Destiny says you need?"

"I wouldn't trust Destiny if I was you."

"She's right. I did just inherit a ridiculous amount of money. And this is important." There was something in his tone, some combination of reluctance and tenacity.

"Are you okay?" she asked.

"I'm fine."

"Are you still wrapping your head around it?"

It took him a moment to speak. "I don't think I've started wrapping my head around it. I'm going one step at a time. You hungry?"

The question took her by surprise. "Hungry?"

"For tonight, I think that's the next step."

"I could go for a pizza," she admitted. It would feel nice to climb back into her jeans and be normal.

A grin spread across his face. "I like you, Amber. All this, and now you want to go out for pizza."

"Double cheese if you don't mind. And maybe a beer?"

Cole tipped his head to the sales clerk. "We'll take everything she liked, including the dress she's wearing." Then he nodded to Destiny. "Her, too. She's got an important court case coming up, and she needs to look good."

The clerk's eyes went round.

"*Cole,*" Amber protested, horrified to think that the woman might take him seriously and ring up everything.

He ignored her protest, instead speaking to Luca and Destiny. "We're going for pizza and a strategy session. Now that we look the part, we have to act the part. Amber and I need to make a decision. Something important, positive and significant, and we have to be able to implement it fast."

"You mean change company policy?" asked Amber.

"Absolutely," said Cole. "You two get changed, I'll pay the bill."

Amber renewed her protest. "Cole, you can't buy everything."

He slipped an arm around her shoulder. "I know this is hard for you. But we're doing it. And honestly, I'm through having this argument with you."

A spurt of anger jumped to life inside her. She opened her mouth to retort, but something in his eyes stopped her cold.

Fine. He wanted to blow his money? That was up to him. She was through trying to save him from himself.

In her new clothes, and at the head of the boardroom table, Amber looked fantastic. Cole had to struggle to keep from chuckling at how the vice presidents kept shooting surreptitious looks her way. She was wearing a steel-gray blazer and skirt set, with a white blouse underneath. Lace along the scooped neckline kept the outfit from being too severe.

She'd changed her hairstyle, too. Strands were braided at her temples and partially pulled back to a knot at the nap of her neck. She looked sophisticated and professional. She also looked sexy, and it made him want to kiss her.

Then again, pretty much everything made him want to kiss her these days. Last night, watching her bite into a slice of double-cheese pizza had turned him on.

He dragged his gaze away from her, focusing on business. He and Amber both looked the part now, and they were going to act it, too, starting with some small but definitive strategic directions for the company.

"Thank you all for joining us," Cole opened politely, although everyone in the room was fully aware their attendance at the senior management meeting had not been optional.

"Ms. Welsley and I realize this is a temporary situation," he continued. "However, our expectation is that the status quo will continue into the future."

"Excuse me?" Roth piped up.

Cole sent him a glare and kept speaking. "My interest in Coast Eagle is not in dispute, and I'll be relying on Ms. Welsley for continuity."

Roth opened his mouth, but Cole spoke right over him. "For the moment, Ms. Welsley has made a few decisions about passenger compensation."

"Thank you, Cole," said Amber, her tone crisp, her posture straight. "As most of you know, new guidelines on passenger compensation were developed by the U.S. Consumer Association in October of this year."

"Voluntary guidelines," said Roth.

"Roth," said Cole. "If you could please hold your comments."

Roth's eyes blazed at the rebuke while Max obviously fought a smirk. Sidney also looked like he was enjoying himself.

"Accounting has done a comparison between overbooked flights, passenger compensation and lost passenger revenue due to last minute cancellations. Bartholomew, can you put up the slides?"

Bartholomew, who also looked a bit smug, brought up the graphic slides on the side screen.

"As you can see," said Amber, "with a change in our policy on flight overbooking, actual monetary loss will be manageable, while the marketing and social media attention, not to mention the customer confidence and goodwill could be significant. Therefore, we'll immediately adopt the new guidelines on passenger compensation and suspend the policy that allows overbooking. That way, our customers can be completely confident in their travel plans."

She stopped speaking and looked levelly down the table.

Cole felt an immediate surge of pride. She was damn good at this.

"May we speak now?" asked Roth, sarcasm dripping from his tone.

"Yes," Amber answered, even though the question was directed at Cole.

Cole's pride in her increased.

"The monetary losses will be significant," said Roth.

"Loses will be compensated for in the long run," said Amber.

"Maybe in a best-case scenario. But passengers don't want certainty. They want low prices. If you drive our prices up by even ten dollars a ticket, they leave for the competition in droves."

"I'm not suggesting we change our prices," said Amber.

"You're living in fantasyland," Roth all but shouted. "Do you have any idea what kind of a mess you'll leave for me to clean up?"

Though he was trying to let Amber take the lead, Cole couldn't help himself. "You?"

Roth seemed to catch himself. "Us."

"Well, *us,*" said Cole, "is Ms. Welsley and me. And I agree with her assessment."

"I agree with it, too," said Max. He looked to Sidney. "Can you work up a marketing plan? We'll need to hit the ground running as soon as the announcement is made."

"I want to announce right away," said Amber with both clarity and confidence. "I want passengers to know their remaining holiday travel plans will not be disrupted by overbooking."

"The Friends and Family campaign is nearly finished," said Sidney. "We can easily incorporate this as a marquee element."

"Done," said Max.

"Hold on," said Roth. "We haven't heard from Julius."

Julius's chin came up. He looked a bit like a deer in the headlights. It was clear he didn't know where to jump.

"Julius reports to Max," said Cole. "Max has made his decision."

"That's not how it works," Roth shouted.

"That's how it works now," said Cole. "This meeting is adjourned." He turned his attention to the president, clearly dismissing everyone else. "Max, do you have a second?"

"I do," said Max.

Fury in his eyes, Roth rocked back from the table and stomped from the room.

With an admirably contained smirk, Bartholomew closed the door behind them all, leaving Cole, Amber and Max alone.

"At the risk of speaking out of turn," said Max, "that was fun."

Amber blew out a breath and slouched down in her chair. "That's not the word I would use."

Cole gave in to the urge to place a hand on her shoulder. "You did great."

"He is out for blood."

"He was always out for blood," said Max.

"You don't think he'd ever take it out on Zachary, do you?"

The slight tremor in her voice told Cole just how brilliantly she'd been acting while the vice presidents were in the room.

"He won't have the chance. Because we're going to win." Cole refused to contemplate anything else.

He turned his attention to Max. "They're resuming the custody hearing on the twenty-eighth."

"Next week?"

Cole nodded.

"Who's representing you?"

"Since Amber is supporting my petition for custody, Destiny has agreed to represent me. She knows the background and circumstances better than anyone else I could hire."

Max's brow furrowed. "She's not the most experienced choice."

"Her firm has assigned a senior partner for support. And they've earmarked their top research team. I'm guessing they want my future business."

"Then that's the best of both worlds," said Max, his expression relaxing.

"That's what we thought." Cole covered Amber's hand with his.

Hers was cold.

Max spoke up. "You know Roth's out there soliciting the support of the minor shareholders."

"He's got the advantage in that," said Amber, sliding her hand from beneath Cole's.

"He does," Max agreed. "They all know him. And Samuel's vote of confidence goes a long way. And, I'm sorry to be so blunt, Amber, but they all knew Coco. That doesn't work in our favor."

"We've got genetics on our side," said Cole.

Cole felt no admiration whatsoever for his father. But he'd quickly come to care about his half brother. And he cared more about Amber than he could have imagined. She was desperately trying to do the right thing, and the jackals were circling her now.

"Can you see any problem with the policy change?" he asked Max.

"None," said Max.

"Any questions?" asked Cole.

"Not yet." Max paused. "Anything else you need right now?"

Cole looked to Amber, and she shook her head.

"We're good," said Cole.

Max rose to leave, closing the door behind him and leaving them alone.

"You did it," said Cole.

"I sure hope it works."

"It will. And so will the others. This one was a good idea, a solid business decision. As the first airline to adopt the guidelines, you're going to get some really positive buzz. The policy change will garner loyalty—maybe not all of your passengers, but enough. And those passengers will be the frequent fliers. That's huge. It was a smart move you made."

"We made."

"It was a smart move, Amber. Don't sell yourself short. They know who's in charge now, and it'll spread around the building like wildfire."

"You think?" She seemed to ponder. "Sidney might tell someone. But Roth will never admit it. And Bartholomew doesn't strike me as a gossip."

"I'm willing to bet Bartholomew knows exactly when and how much to gossip."

"Phase three underway?" she asked.

"Phase three well underway." He jokingly held out his hand. She accepted it and shook.

The contact made him instantly recall what it was like to hold her close. He wished he could pull her in for a hug. He longed to kiss her. He longed to stroke her hair and feel the length of her body pressed up against his.

"Destiny will be here in an hour," she said, retrieving her hand once again.

Cole accepted her withdrawal, shaking off his wayward feelings. "Destiny's been looking up precedents for blood relatives being given preference in custody cases. Do you know if Roth spent any amount of time with Zachary?"

"Not that I heard about, but Coco didn't tell me everything."

"I've been trying to predict his thinking," said Cole. "With you, his best ammunition was that you were too inexperienced to run Coast Eagle. With me, he'll go after my capability as Zachary's guardian. I'm vulnerable there."

"Not if they ask Zachary."

Cole chuckled at that. "It is too bad that Zachary can't talk."

"It's too bad Zachary's not a puppy."

"Excuse me?"

"With a puppy, you put him down between the two people and both call him. Whoever the dog runs to wins."

Cole grinned. "I do like my chances with that."

"Sometimes the simplest solutions work best."

"Can we suggest it to the judge?"

"Only if you want him to order a psychological evaluation."

Ten

Christmas Eve, Amber and Destiny had settled down in a corner of the penthouse living room in front of the twinkling tree and the gas fireplace, cups of eggnog in their hands. Zachary was bathed and wearing red-and-white snowflake pajamas. They'd already snapped a few pictures of him looking so adorable, and now he was busy pulling himself up on pieces of furniture, trying to toddle from one handhold to the next, falling down on his diapered bottom with each attempt.

"At least he's tenacious," said Destiny.

"Stubborn," said Amber. "And not always in a good way."

But she had to admire him in this. He picked himself up again, gripped the coffee table, made it to standing, then set his sights on the ottoman.

"Is it just me," asked Amber, "or does he seem extraordinarily intelligent?"

"He seems extraordinarily intelligent."

"I thought so. I only had to tell him once to leave the tree alone."

"And here I thought the pine needles prickled his hands."

"Maybe," Amber allowed. "Do you mind very much that we're staying in tonight?"

Over the past few years, she and Destiny had always travelled somewhere fun for Christmas. Last December they'd gone snowboarding at a great resort in Switzerland. This year, travelling would have been a lot more complicated with Zachary along. Amber knew it would be better relaxing at home. She also wanted to keep him in his routine, since tomorrow would be such an exciting day.

She knew he had no concept of Santa and wouldn't even realize the presents had appeared overnight. Still, she found herself looking forward to the morning. She was certain he'd take to unwrapping just fine. And she hoped he'd like playing with the toys she'd picked out.

"Not at all. This is fun, too," said Destiny. "The eggnog's fantastic. And the view from here is great."

"What about Luca?" Amber asked. She'd been curious about their budding relationship for days now. But whenever she and Destiny were together, the court case had taken all of their attention.

"He's still in town," said Destiny.

"I *know* he's still in town. I see Cole every day at the office. What I'm asking is if anything has happened between you two?"

"Define *happened*."

"Have you kissed him?"

"A few times." Destiny covered a smile with a sip of eggnog.

"And?"

"And what?"

"And anything more than kissing?"

"Not yet."

"But soon?"

"I don't know. Something's holding me back. I guess I'm not the flinging kind. Who knew?"

"Turned out I was," said Amber. "Who knew?"

Destiny's attention perked up. "Again?"

"No, not *again*. The once. I haven't slept with him since I found out the truth."

"But you want to."

"Who wouldn't? But he deceived me, and he's trying to take Zachary away."

"He's trying to keep Zachary away from Roth. That's not quite the same thing."

"It's not," Amber agreed. "I suppose I should be grateful."

"Are you grateful?"

"He's a fascinating guy, Dest. He's incredibly strategic, and unbelievably bold. In less than a week, he's got the entire company in awe of him."

"Controlling the company will do that to people."

"Yeah, but it's more than just that. He's got a certain pres-

ence. You should have seen him shut Roth down." Amber remembered the expression on Roth's face. "If Roth ever gets a
chance, he's going to annihilate Cole."

"I don't think he'll get the chance," said Destiny.

Amber looked closely at her expression. "Are you really that
optimistic? Or are you trying to make me feel good on Christmas Eve."

"Both. But I am optimistic. There are a lot of precedents out
there for blood relatives winning custody."

Amber's gaze caught on Zachary. "Look!"

Zachary took a step, then another and another. He sort of
toppled into the ottoman, but stayed upright. Then he turned to
Amber with a massive, self-satisfied grin on his face.

"Good boy," said Amber, beaming with pride.

"There'll be no stopping him now," said Destiny.

A knock sounded on the door.

Destiny rose. "I'll get it. You keep watch in case he does
something else amazing."

Zachary slapped his hands against the leather ottoman.
Amber guessed he was gearing up for the next excursion.

Then, suddenly, his face broke into another grin. "Gak baw!"
He let go of the ottoman and toddled forward.

"Hey there, partner."

Amber twisted to see Cole entering the room, a couple of
brightly wrapped packages tucked under his arm.

Zachary made it three steps, then four, then his pace sped up.
A split second later, things got entirely out of control.

Cole shot forward to grab him before he could go head over
heels. Otis stayed a safe pace behind.

"Nice job," Cole praised Zachary.

"He just started doing that," said Amber. She found herself
ridiculously happy to have Cole share the moment.

"Merry Christmas," came Luca's cheerful voice.

He and Destiny emerged from the foyer, Luca's arm firmly
planted around her waist, a sappy grin on his face. Her cheeks
were slightly flushed, and her lips were slightly swollen. No

need to guess who'd come up with the idea of dropping by to-night.

"I brought you a present," Cole said to Amber.

Her glance went to the packages, instantly guilty because she hadn't bought anything for him. "Oh, Cole, you shouldn't have."

"Oh. Uh...no." He looked contrite. "These are for Zachary."

In his arms, Zachary was already plucking at the ribbons.

"I'm your present."

"Excuse me?" She couldn't believe she'd heard him right, or that he'd made such an outrageous statement in front of Destiny and Luca.

"I'm here to make sure Zachary gets to sleep tonight."

She felt relieved. Or maybe it was disappointed. Sure, it would be mortifying to have Cole show up and announce he wanted to sleep with her. Then again, it would be awfully exciting to have Cole show up and announce he wanted to sleep with her.

She realized everyone was staring at her.

She quickly reined in her wayward thoughts. "You didn't have to do that."

"No trouble. Can I put these under the tree?"

"Sure. Of course. But I can't guarantee Zachary will stay away from them."

Cole looked at the clock. It was coming up on eight.

"He can sit with me for a while," he said. "That should keep him out of trouble."

Otis selected a spot near the tree in front of an armchair and curled up to watch.

"Mind if I steal Destiny?" Luca asked. "We've got a car and a driver, and I want to take in the lights."

"Ask Destiny," said Amber.

"Do you mind?" Destiny asked her.

"Go, go. Have fun. I've got the baby whisperer here to make my life easy."

Luca tugged Destiny against his side. "Your chariot awaits."

Cole set the gifts under the tree while Destiny and Luca all but scampered out the front door.

"Did he drag you here?" asked Amber.

Cole rose, Zachary happily bopping him on the top of the head. "What? Who?"

"Luca. He was pretty single-minded about getting Destiny out the door. I'm assuming you're the sacrificial lamb."

Cole smiled as he lowered himself into an armchair. "I volunteered for the gig."

"You're a good friend."

"I am," he agreed. "Got any more eggnog?"

"I do."

"I can get it myself."

She scooped up Destiny's empty cup. "Oh, no, you don't. You're on baby duty. Just sit tight."

He lifted Zachary into a standing position on his lap. "Oh, I like this," he said to the baby. "You and I hang out here. Your auntie does all the work."

She poured a fresh glass of eggnog and added some spiced rum, stirring the concoction together.

When she returned to the living room, Zachary was sitting facing Cole, playing with the buttons on his denim shirt.

She handed Cole the glass. "Don't let him taste it."

Cole's eyes squinted down. "I wouldn't do that. I won't give him anything without asking you."

"There's rum in it. That's all I meant." She hadn't meant to sound picky and possessive.

Cole took a drink. "Good." Then he set the glass out of reach of Zachary.

The awkward moment passed.

"Nice pajamas this guy's got going on," Cole said easily.

"I couldn't resist them. They were so cute."

"Did you take some pictures?"

"I did."

"Will you take one of the two of us?"

The request surprised her, but she quickly recovered. "Sure." Her phone was on a side table, and she reached to retrieve it.

"How about in front of the tree?" Cole asked Zachary, sitting down on the floor. "Any chance you'll hold still and pose for the camera?"

"Gak baw."

"As always, I'm going to take that as a yes."

Amber lined up the camera, taking various poses from various angles. While she snapped the pictures, the family resemblance between the two became startlingly evident. She was half amazed, half afraid.

It was obvious they belonged together. It was just as obvious that she'd have little say in the matter. And a win for Cole still left her up in the air. Or maybe it was out in the cold.

"Did you get any good shots?" asked Cole, setting Zachary down on his feet.

Zachary clung to his fingers, teetering on his feet before letting go and taking a single step away.

Amber scooted toward Cole, settling beside him, scrolling her way through the pictures.

"Those are pretty good," said Cole.

"I can see now why he thinks you're familiar," she admitted. "It's absolutely there."

He turned to look at her. "You think?"

"I do."

Something clunked loudly on the floor, and they both looked up.

Zachary was clinging to the coffee table, slapping his palms against a puddle of eggnog while the glass rolled away.

"Oh, no," Amber groaned, quickly rising to her feet.

Otis immediately seized on the opportunity, jumping up to lap at the spilled eggnog.

"Otis, no," Cole commanded, following Amber. "This walking thing is going to take some getting used to."

The dog looked disappointed, but obediently went back to lie down.

Zachary stuffed his fingers into his mouth, breaking into a grin at the taste.

Amber reached for him, pulling the fingers free. "No rum for you, young man."

Cole gazed around. "You want me to take care of the baby or the mess?"

She felt a surge of gratitude for his offer. "Do you think you could give him a quick bath?"

"I'm on it." He took Zachary carefully into his arms, facing the messy parts away from his shirt and pants as he carried him down the hall. Otis followed along behind.

Sighing in resignation, Amber went to the kitchen storage room for paper towels and the mini steam cleaner.

Twenty minutes later, Cole's shirt was soaked through. But Zachary was clean and happy, tossing little plastic ducks around the tub. The kid had an arm, so some of the ducks flew across the purple bathroom. Cole wasn't about to leave Zachary's side, so they were running out of ducks.

"About done there, partner?" Cole asked, reaching forward to lift him.

Zachary grinned and kicked happily, sending a few final splashes toward Cole, one of them hitting him in the face and dampening his hair. Cole quickly wrapped Zachary's wiggly, wet body in a mauve towel, rubbing him dry before settling him on one hip. Then he leaned down to unplug the tub and used his free hand to gather up the errant ducks.

They made their way into the living room to find Amber on her hands and knees. The rumble and hiss of a steam-cleaning machine obscured the Christmas music. Her brow was sweaty, and her blouse was mussed as she pushed the appliance back and forth on the carpet.

She glanced up to see them. Then she rocked back, hitting the machine's off switch and swiping a hand across her forehead.

"I think I got it clean," she said.

Cole peeled his wet shirt away from his rib cage. "I'm not sure we've quite got the hang of this billionaire lifestyle."

She grinned. "He looks happy."

"He's happy. I'm soaking wet."

She came to her feet, dusting off her knees. "When it comes to babies, trust me, bathwater is the least of your problems."

"I'll keep that in mind."

"You want to take on diaper and pajama duty? Or do you want to put away the steamer?"

"Your choice. But after that, I want champagne and maybe some Belgium chocolate truffles sprinkled with gold flakes."

She shook her head in obvious confusion.

"Something billionaires would eat."

She moved to the wall to unplug the steamer. "That's a thing? Gold flakes on chocolate?"

"Real gold, apparently."

"And you eat it?"

"Well, I've never tried myself. But I hear tell it's expensive."

She coiled the cord. "Alright, Midas. You take diaper duty. I'll check the wine rack and pantry for things that are expensive."

"We can send out," he offered.

He didn't want her to go to any work. That was his whole point. Christmas Eve wasn't the time for cooking and cleaning.

"You're going to send out for gold chocolates?"

"For whatever you want."

"Let me see what we have first. And you might want to get the kid into a diaper before too long."

Cole glanced down at Zachary. "Right. Good advice."

Realizing the risk, he wasted no time in getting to the nursery. His diapering job was awkward but adequate, and he easily found a new pair of soft, stretchy pajamas.

Soon, they were back in the living room, then into the kitchen in search of Amber.

She turned from the counter, obviously hearing them arrive. "This brand comes in a wooden box and a gold bottle." She opened the lid of the champagne case to demonstrate. "It should be expensive enough to meet your standards."

"I was only joking."

She gave a shrug. "There's nobody around to drink it but us. And I don't think champagne keeps indefinitely."

The microwave oven beeped three times.

Amber pointed to the sound. "Zachary's Chateau Moo 2014 is in the microwave."

"Got it," said Cole, crossing the kitchen.

"We have fresh strawberries. And I found a few bars of dark chocolate. The label's in French, so I'm guessing they're imported. And this…"

Cole approached with the formula bottle in his hand.

"Gold-colored sugar sprinkles. Yellow, actually."

"You take me way too literally." But he couldn't help but be impressed by her ingenuity.

He perched himself on a stool, used his best guess on how to position Zachary and offered him the bottle.

Fortunately Zachary knew the drill. He snagged the bottle with both hands and relaxed into Cole's lap.

"I'm going to melt the chocolate, dip the strawberries and sprinkled them with gold."

"You clearly did not understand my point."

She blinked at him with a wide-eyed, ingenuous expression. "I thought you wanted gold-covered chocolate."

"Sure you did. I wanted luxury to come to us with no effort. That's how billionaires live."

She separated the halves of a double boiler, filling the bottom with water at the sink. "So far, for me anyway, the billionaire lifestyle is pretty much like any regular lifestyle. Except that it's a ridiculously long walk from the kitchen to the master bedroom. My tea is cold by the time I get there."

"You take tea to bed?"

"I sip jasmine while I read. It's very relaxing."

"I sip single malt while I watch the sports news. Very relaxing."

She lit a gas burner under the double boiler.

"You are actually making chocolate strawberries."

"It is Christmas Eve." Then a look of concern crossed her face. "Have you had dinner?"

"We grabbed a burger on the way over. You?"

"Late lunch."

"I really can order something in. You want a steak or some pasta? Or you seem to have a thing for pizza."

She pouted. "Okay, now you're making me hungry."

"Pizza it is." He paused, gazing down at Zachary. "I think this guy's out for the count."

Her expression softened, and she moved toward them. "I can take him if you'll watch the chocolate."

Cole extracted the bottle from Zachary's pursed mouth. He sucked a couple more times before sighing in his sleep.

"I've got him," he told her quietly. "I mean, if you're okay with me putting him to bed."

"Of course I'm okay with that." She brushed a hand across Zachary's forehead, then she followed it with a tender kiss.

Emotion tightened in Cole's chest. For the first time in his life, he actually got it. He'd seen men with their families, watched them care for their children. But he'd never had an inkling of the strength of those instincts, the flat-out intensity of the desire to protect.

"You sure?" he found himself asking.

He was little more than a stranger to Amber, and it suddenly seemed unfair to ask her to trust him with Zachary.

She smiled. "Go for it. Then order that pizza. We're going to need something that goes with five-hundred-dollar champagne."

"Is that seriously the price?" It struck Cole as ridiculous.

"That's what it says."

"How can any taste be worth twenty dollars a swallow?"

"You tell me. You're the billionaire."

Cole rose. "I guess we're about to find out."

He gently parked Zachary over his shoulder. Zachary's little body was warm and soft, molded trustingly in his arms.

Minutes later, he finished tucking Zachary into his crib, leaving Otis posted across the open doorway, and returned to the kitchen to find Amber with a dozen chocolate-dipped strawberries lined up on waxed paper. She was sprinkling "gold" on the sticky chocolate.

"I'm impressed," he told her, coming up behind her.

"They turned out pretty good." She sounded happy, and that made him smile.

The scent of chocolate and strawberries floated around them. Her hair brushed his arm. He knew he was standing too close, but he hadn't the slightest desire to move.

He wanted to touch her, to wrap his arms around her, kiss the back of her neck, then turn her around and kiss her mouth. Forget the strawberries, he wanted to strip her naked and make love to her all night long.

"I was thinking a pesto pizza," she said. "Maybe with mushrooms and dried tomatoes, nothing too overpowering."

"Whatever you want," said Cole, realizing he meant it in every sense of the word.

"And feta cheese?"

He could see the corner of her widening grin. "Why is that funny?"

"Makes it more expensive."

"Now you're catching on. We'll definitely get some feta."

It was time to step back. It was time for him to step back from Amber and call a pizza place. He drew a deep breath to brace himself, telling his feet to get a move on. But he inhaled her scent above the strawberries.

And then she turned. She turned, and she was right there, in front of him, her lips only inches away.

"Do you want to change out of your wet clothes?" she asked. "There might be something around here of Samuel's that—"

"No." The question was like a bucket of cold water. "I'm not wearing Samuel's clothes."

Amber looked slightly hurt. "Okay."

"I'm sorry. He wasn't good to my mother, but it's a long story." Cole extracted his phone. "I'll order the pizza."

"You don't want to talk about it."

He didn't. Then again, it wasn't some big, painful secret that he couldn't discuss.

Samuel was a jerk who never deserved Lauren's love. But Cole wasn't going to waste any emotional energy hating the man, either. He didn't care. And he hadn't cared for a very long time. There was no reason not to tell Amber the story.

"I'm fine to talk about it. But let's pour the champagne first."

Eleven

They were on their second glass of champagne, munching their way through the pizza before Amber asked him again.

"You don't mind telling me about Samuel?"

She was at one end of the sofa, Cole at the other. She'd turned sideways to face him, crossing her legs beneath her. His body was canted sideways, one leg up on the leather cushion.

"There's nothing much to tell. You know I never met him. All I know is what my mother told me."

"Did she hate him?" From what little Cole had said, Amber guessed his mother, Lauren, had gotten a very raw deal.

"She hated his weakness, that he caved to his family." Cole stretched an arm along the back of the sofa. "They fell quickly and deeply in love. But she didn't come from the right family, hadn't been to the right schools, didn't have the refined tastes and manners he knew his parents would look for in a daughter-in-law. So he married her without telling them, thinking once it was a done deal, his parents would be forced to accept her."

"They didn't," Amber guessed.

"They went ballistic. They ordered him to divorce her right away, and to never admit to anyone that she'd existed. If he didn't, they said they'd disinherit him. No surprise that he loved the family money more than he loved my mother."

"He didn't deserve her," Amber said softly.

"I must have said that to her ten thousand times."

Cole fell silent, looking sad, and Amber found her heart going out to him. "You don't have to talk about it."

"He was nothing to me. I mean, nothing. I was angry off and on, especially as a teenager. But then I realized he didn't even deserve my anger. As far as I was concerned, he might as well have not existed. When he died…"

Cole lifted the crystal flute and took a drink of his champagne. "This sounds terrible, but when he died, I didn't care. I knew I should. But I didn't. I wasn't sad. I wasn't glad. I didn't expect his death or anything about the Henderson family to be even a blip on my life. Things were going to carry on as normal."

"It didn't occur to you there might be an inheritance?"

"Not even for a second."

She set down her half-eaten slice of pizza, exchanging it for the glass of champagne. "So why did you come to Atlanta?"

"Luca kept after me. Then one day, I gave in. I looked at a picture of Zachary. I don't know. There was something about him, something in his eyes. I knew I had to at least make sure he was safe and secure."

Amber's chest tingled and went tight. "You came here to take care of your brother."

"And then I met you." The look in his eyes was tender. "And I knew Zachary was safe. It was just a matter of getting through the hearing without anyone figuring out who I was."

"But then I lost."

He nodded. "I didn't know what to do. I'd learned enough about Roth by then that I couldn't let him win."

"Thank you."

"There's no need to thank me. And I haven't defeated him yet."

"But you're trying. You really don't want Coast Eagle, do you?"

"I want what's best for Zachary. It's ironic, really. When I first heard about him, I resented him. All I could think was that he was going to have the easy life while Mom and I had struggled so hard to get by."

Amber set down her glass, impulsively shifting closer. "But now you care."

He gazed into her eyes. "It's pretty easy to care."

She reached for his hands and squeezed. "It's pretty easy to care about you, too, Cole."

She'd meant to be reassuring, friendly and comforting. But her tone had become breathy, and the atmosphere thickened between them.

Cole stroked his thumbs across the backs of her hands. Then he stroked the inside of her wrists, watching as he moved his way up her bare arm.

Arousal became a deep, base pulse in the center of her body.

He raised his head, and there was a tremor in his tone. "I know I have no right to ask."

She wanted him to ask. She desperately wanted him to ask.

"Just for tonight," he said. "Just for a little while."

She nodded.

"Can we stop fighting it?"

She nodded harder.

"Oh, Amber." He leaned forward, placing his lips against hers, tenderly at first, but then with unmistakable purpose. She came up on her knees, wrapped her arms around his neck, pulling forward to kiss him more deeply.

He turned her into his lap, his hand splaying across her stomach as his tongue teased hers.

Instinct took over, and her body arched reflexively toward him while their kiss continued.

"You are so beautiful," he breathed.

"You are so wet." She drew back to stare at his shirtfront. "You're still soaking wet."

He gave a soft chuckle. "I could take it off."

"Yes." She nodded, pretending it was merely a practical suggestion. "You should take it off."

He flipped the buttons open, making his way down the pale gray shirt. She glimpsed his chest, then his abs. Then he peeled the shirt away, revealing his muscular shoulders and arms. He was an incredibly magnificent man.

"You're the one who's beautiful," she told him.

She gifted a lingering kiss on his smooth chest, flicking out her tongue to leave a wetter spot on his skin.

"Do that again." His voice was tight.

She kissed him again, tasting the salt of his skin, feeling his heat through the tenderness of her lips.

"I got your shirt wet," he rasped.

"That's too bad." She kissed a slow path across his chest.

One of his hands bracketed her hip; the other undid the buttons on her shirt.

"Are you fixing it?" she asked, lips brushing his skin as she spoke.

"I'm fixing it."

"That's good." She shrugged out of the shirt, revealing her white lace bra.

"All good." He released the catch on her bra, peeling it off. "All very, very good."

She knew she should be self-conscious, even embarrassed by her nakedness in the well-lit living room.

"If Destiny and Luca come back, we're…" She moved up to kiss his neck, bracing her hands on his shoulders, absorbing the feel of their taut texture.

"Oh, darling," he drawled. "They're not coming back."

"They're not?" Not that she was truly worried. She wasn't about to stop undressing Cole.

"Did you see their expressions?" There was a chuckle in his voice. "They're not coming back."

She unsnapped the top of his fly. "Just as well."

His warm hand closed over her breast. "I like the way you're thinking."

She bit back a moan. "What am I thinking?"

"That you want me." He narrowed his attention to her nipple.

A zing of sensation flashed to the apex of her thighs, and this time she did moan. "I do want you."

"I want you, too, very, very badly."

She wrapped her arms around his neck, bringing her mouth to his. "Oh, Cole."

"Amber." He tunneled his spread fingers into her hair, kissing her deeper and deeper.

She fumbled with her pants, while he got rid of his.

Then she was lying back on the sofa, pulling him to her, impatient and anxious to become one. But he made her wait, feathering his fingertips along her thighs, circling and teasing as he went.

"Now," she begged.

"Yeah?" he asked, his voice husky, breathing deep.

"Right now." The anticipation was too much.

"In a hurry?"

She knew how to stop this game. She raked her fingertips down his stomach, going lower until she grasped him, wrapping her hand smoothly around his length.

His body convulsed. "Okay."

"In a hurry?" she managed.

"Yes." He disentangled her hand, drawing her arms up above her head. "I'm definitely in a hurry."

Moments later, he was inside her, swift and sure, and she gasped at the strength of the sensations. His movements were steady and deep. Her reaction more and more intense.

He kissed her mouth, his hand going to her breast. She was bombarded with pleasure over every inch of her body. Time seemed to stop while she drank in his taste, scent and touch. She never wanted it to end.

"You're amazing." His lips brushed hers as he spoke. "I've never...ever...ever..."

"Cole," she gasped. "Don't stop. Please don't stop."

"I'm never stopping. Not...ever."

But she could feel it. She could feel her climax shimmering. Her body climbed higher and higher, her nerves extending, muscles tightening, until it all crashed into an apex of pleasure.

She cried out.

He groaned her name.

And their bodies peaked as one.

She was weightless at first, then exhausted, her limbs too heavy to move.

"That was your fault," he muttered in her ear.

It took her a moment to muster up the energy to speak. "What was my fault?"

"You ended it."

"I did. You're just too good."

"Oh, darling. That was exactly what I wanted to hear."

She cautiously blinked her eyes open, the twinkling Christmas tree coming into focus, then the fireplace and the champagne bottle.

Cole's weight pressed her into the sofa. For the first time in what seemed like forever, she felt safe, content and at home.

Cole eased himself into the giant tub in the master bathroom, settling at the end opposite to Amber. He'd lit candles all around and set the champagne glasses and the rest of the bottle on the wide tiled edge. The water was steaming in billows toward the box window that overlooked the city, mingling with the scent of citrus that filled the air.

"This *is* practically a pool," he couldn't help but note, stretching his arms to each side, his legs brushing lightly against Amber's beneath the water.

Amber lifted her champagne flute. "Are we behaving like billionaires now?"

Her hair was swept up in a messy knot. Her cheeks were flushed, her lips dark red and her lashes thick against the crystal blue of her eyes. Her breasts bobbed ever so slightly beneath the surface of the water. She had the most beautiful breasts he'd ever seen.

"Close enough," he answered. "I've got everything in the world I want right here."

She smiled. "Plus gold chocolates in the kitchen."

"I forgot about those."

She gave a mock frown.

"I mean," he said, attempting to properly appreciate her efforts, "I can't wait to try one."

She raised her glass in a mock toast. "Now you're catching on."

He drank with her. "So tell me what you have planned for tomorrow."

She looked puzzled. "Tomorrow?"

"Christmas Day."

Her expression said that she'd completely forgotten the date. He was going to take that as a positive sign.

"Presents for Zachary," she said. "And Destiny's coming

over. Luca, too, maybe? And…" This time a flash of worry creased her face.

"What?" he asked.

She shook her head.

"Something upset you. What was it?"

"Uh, you guys didn't…"

He wasn't following, and he gave his head a little shake.

She gestured to her naked body. "Please tell me you two didn't plan…this."

The question shocked him so much, it took several seconds to form an answer. "No."

Admittedly, it wasn't the most comprehensive answer in the world. He tried again. "We didn't plan a thing. Okay, yes, I know that Luca likes Destiny. And I guess he knows I like you. But we never talked about sex, and we sure as hell didn't plan out some Christmas Eve seduction scenario." Frankly, he was a little insulted by her suggestion.

"You don't talk to Luca about sex?"

Her question was so genuine that Cole's annoyance disappeared. "I don't talk to him about sex with you."

"Oh." She shifted under the water, looking decidedly guilty.

Wait a minute. "You talked about *me* with Destiny."

Amber blushed. "She asked me."

"And you told her?" He pretended to be affronted, but it was a struggle not to laugh.

"Sorry," she offered faintly.

He polished off his glass of champagne. "I'm the one who's sorry. I'm just messing with you. Tell anybody you want."

"I only told Destiny."

He gave a shrug as he reached for the champagne bottle. "I honestly don't care. But I won't tell Luca anything that makes you uncomfortable."

He gestured with the bottle.

She held out her glass. "I know it seems like the double standard."

"It *is* a double standard. But me and the rest of the male population have come to terms with it."

"Now I feel guilty."

"Don't. Believe me when I tell you, guilt is the last thing I'm going for here."

She seemed to relax and leaned back against the edge of the tub. "What exactly are you going for?"

"I have to say, I enjoyed the part where you said I was too good at sex." He paused. "And I liked the expression on your face when you said it. And I liked that I was holding you in my arms at the time. And that you were naked."

Arousal reawakened as he spoke.

He couldn't seem to get enough of looking at her, talking to her, touching her. But it was close to midnight, and he knew this interlude had to end—likely very soon.

"Come here," he told her softly.

Her blue eyes went wide in obvious surprise.

He set his glass aside. "Come sit with me."

It took her a minute to react. But then she braced herself on the edge of the tub and slipped across, candles flickering in the mist as she settled between his legs. The glass of champagne was still in her hand.

He wrapped his arms around her stomach, holding her naked softness to his body and kissed the crook of her neck. Her supple warmth, smooth skin and the subtle scent of her shampoo brought back memories of their lovemaking. He wanted her all over again.

"Tell me about Alaska," she said, relaxing against him.

"It's cold."

"How incredibly informative."

"Lots of snow, mountains, wildlife. The people are amazing. There's no road access to Juneau, so there's a very close-knit sense of community."

"You have no roads?"

"We have roads in the city, of course. But the only way to get there from the mainland is by ferry, boat or airplane. Good for business at Aviation 58."

"Is there much there? Can you shop?"

"We have stores, groceries, clothes, hardware, even car dealerships, certainly everything you need for day-to-day life. There are over thirty thousand people living in Juneau."

"That's less than a football game."

"That's why we have such a great sense of community."

"What do you do up there?"

"Mostly, I run a business and fly airplanes."

"And for fun?"

"Ski, snowmobile, mountain climb, swim, soccer. There's plenty of outdoor recreation, but we also have plays, music, restaurants, movie theatres, even fashion shows."

"Just like a regular city."

"Exactly like a regular city. But with more snow and more bears."

"I'd be terrified of bears."

"They're not exactly walking down the main drag in Juneau." He paused. "Well, not often."

"Are you serious? Or are you messing with me again?"

"It's rare. But it can happen. You should come and check it out."

As soon as the words were out, he felt the shift in atmosphere. He could have kicked himself. He and Amber were, right this moment, a tiny oasis in the midst of their bizarre situation.

"I'm sorry," he offered.

"It's okay."

"No, it's not. I didn't mean to hint we were going somewhere as a couple. That's just insincere and misleading, even manipulative."

Her tone went cool. "Don't worry, Cole. I won't be dropping in on you in Alaska."

"That's not what I meant, either. I'd love to have you come to Alaska."

Her body was growing stiffer by the second. "Isn't this where we came into this conversation?"

"I'm so sorry."

He smoothed back her hair. He couldn't help himself, he kissed her dewy neck. When she didn't rebuff him, he kissed her jawline. Then he tipped back her head and kissed her mouth.

The second he tasted her, arousal hijacked his senses. He kissed her deeply, turning her in his arms until she was facing him, straddling his lap, her wet breasts sliding along his chest. He sat up straight. He cupped her bottom, pulling her tight to the V of his legs.

He was right where he wanted to be. But the water was cooling off, and they were going to have to leave soon.

"I don't want to hurt you," he whispered.

"You're not."

"I want the world to go away. I want to stay right here and forget everything else. I don't want to let you go."

She nodded.

"Amber. You're incredible." He cradled her face, kissing her all over again.

Then he drew back, and they gazed at each other for a long, long time.

"Can I stay tonight?" he dared ask.

"I want you to stay."

His heart swelled with satisfaction, and he folded her into his arms.

Christmas morning, it wasn't clear to Amber which delighted Zachary more, ripping into presents or walking across the room on his own. He had no interest at all in any of the toys, but wandered from chair to table to ottoman with ribbons and bows in hands.

Otis stayed off to one side, looking stoic and long-suffering when Zachary grabbed at his fur or ears or tried to decorate him.

A few hours ago, Cole had had the presence of mind to put his clothes through the laundry. So while he was dressed the same as last night, the clothes, at least, were fresh.

Amber had given her hair a blow dry this morning, put on a little more makeup than usual and dressed in a pair of skinny black slacks and a shimmering red blouse. She'd chosen a funky pair of Christmas-ball earrings and felt überfestive. She had to admit, it was nice to have Cole around to entertain Zachary while she had spent the extra time getting ready.

Destiny arrived with Luca midmorning, and neither seemed surprised to find Cole on the floor with Zachary.

A couple of wrapped gifts in his hands, Luca headed for the tree. Destiny grasped Amber's arm to hold her back.

"Tell me what happened," she whispered in Amber's ear.

Amber pretended she didn't understand the question. "When?"

Destiny rolled her eyes. "Last night."

"What happened with you last night? I thought you'd come back."

"We had a great time, that's what happened with me."

"Great?" Amber asked. "Or *great*?"

Cole offered Luca a cup of coffee, and the two, along with Zachary and Otis, headed for the kitchen.

"Both," Destiny answered as the men disappeared. "We toured the lights, had a few drinks and went back to his hotel."

Amber filled in the blank. "And that's all she wrote?"

"I'm hoping we'll write some more."

Amber grinned and gave Destiny a one-armed hug as they moved into the living room.

"And you?" Destiny asked, brows going up as they each took a seat.

"Cole stayed the night."

"So it's better? You've made up?"

"*Made up* is not the right phrase. We didn't, don't have a relationship."

"What is it you have?"

Amber thought back to Cole's words last night in the tub. "I don't know. A mutual problem?"

"That doesn't sound very romantic."

Maybe not, but Amber was determined to see it for what it was and enjoy it for what it was. Last night with Cole had been amazing, and this morning had been fun. There was no point in speculating beyond that.

"You want coffee?" she asked Destiny.

"Please."

As Amber rose, she heard a phone ring from inside the

kitchen and recognized it as Cole's. Destiny followed behind her into the kitchen and took a seat at the island counter, where Zachary was in his high chair playing with a little pile of breakfast cereal rounds.

"When?" Cole asked into the phone. His tone was serious, and he gave a sideways glance to Amber.

She instantly knew something was wrong.

She glanced reflexively at Zachary, grateful he was right here beside her where she could see he was fine.

"How many?" Cole asked.

Amber found herself moving toward him.

He reached out and put a hand on her shoulder.

"Are you sure?" He paused. "Hundred percent?" He breathed a sigh. "Yeah. I will. You've got it. Call me if you hear anything else."

"What is it?" Amber asked, holding her breath.

"There was another hydraulic problem with a Boonsome 300."

Her tone went hushed. "The same thing?"

Cole nodded. "Astra Airlines. The flight was coming into O'Hare."

"Has it landed?" She swallowed. She couldn't bring herself to use the word *crashed*.

"Belly landing onto foam. Everyone got out, but there was a fire. The plane's destroyed. The federal government has grounded the Boonsomes, and they need complete access to the Coast Eagle plane at LAX."

"Absolutely," said Amber. "Whatever they need."

She stopped speaking and sucked in gulps of air, her mind galloping to what-if scenarios. What if she hadn't grounded the Coast Eagle fleet? Her decision had been based on her gut feeling, not on any technical expertise. She was an accountant, not an aviation specialist. What if she'd made the wrong choice, and a Coast Eagle flight had crashed and killed the passengers?

She felt the room spin around her, and a wave of nausea cramped her stomach.

Cole's hand tightened on her shoulder. "Amber?"

She pushed him off and bolted for the living room.

She made it as far as the hallway, and gripped the corner of the wall to steady herself.

Cole was instantly behind her, his hands on her shoulders.

"They're all okay." His tone was soothing. "Bumps and bruises, maybe a couple of cracked ribs. The captain did a spectacular job on the landing."

She swallowed the lump in her throat. "What if I hadn't?" she managed.

"Hadn't what?" He came around to look at her.

"What if I hadn't grounded the Coast Eagle fleet?"

"But you did. You made exactly the right decision."

"Because I listened to you."

"You listened to everyone in the room, and then you made the call."

"I'm scared, Cole," she admitted, starting to shake. "I'm not qualified to do this. I shouldn't be cochair of Coast Eagle. Nobody should be listening to me."

He drew her into his arms and smoothed a hand over her hair. "If they'd listened to Roth, a Coast Eagle plane might very well have crashed."

Amber digested that thought. She knew there had to be a counterargument to it, but she couldn't come up with it right now.

"They'll find the problem," said Cole, the certainty in his deep voice making her feel unaccountably better. "They'll fix it, and nobody else is going to get hurt."

"I want to go back to my regular job."

He looked down at her and gave her a smile. "You'd abandon me?"

"You made the right decision, right off, because of your knowledge and experience."

"Amber, the single most important attribute of being a good decision maker is listening—listening to the right people and weighing all the evidence. Nobody is an expert in everything. That's Roth's downfall. He won't listen to anyone but himself."

She had to concede that was true.

"It's Christmas," said Cole, rubbing her upper arms. "Everyone is safe, and the right people are out there doing their jobs. Let's take one more day to forget about the chaos all around us. Can we have one more day for us?"

She forced herself to break away from him. He was right. This was Zachary's first Christmas, and there was nothing that needed her immediate attention.

"Yes," she told him.

"Good. We should get outside for a while. Do you think Zachary would like a walk in the park?"

Amber knew Zachary would love a walk in the park. And so would she. Cole's instincts seemed bang on when it came to the two of them.

Twelve

By the time the judge called a recess, Cole could feel his blood pressure pounding inside his ears. Over Destiny's continued objections, Roth's lawyer had painted Cole as a conniving, opportunistic fortune hunter who had deliberately kept himself hidden from the Henderson family until there was some profit for him. The man had scoffed at the idea that Cole hadn't known about the will. And he'd railed about the unfairness of placing Zachary in the care of a man that neither of his parents had ever met.

It had taken all of Cole's self-control to stay quiet and seated. Now he shot up from his seat and rushed from the courtroom, keeping his gaze straight ahead as he passed through the gallery. He needed to bring his anger under control before he spoke with anyone.

He took long strides through the foyer, out onto the sidewalk, turning down the block where he could disappear into the crowd. He drew long breaths of the crisp air, trying desperately to clear his rioting emotions.

"Mr. Henderson?" a voice called from behind.

Cole didn't turn. The last thing in the world he needed right now was another nosey reporter. He wove through the busy sidewalks, lengthening his stride to put some distance between them.

"Mr. Henderson?" the voice repeated.

Cole took two more paces then decided to put an end to the intrusion. He pivoted, spread his feet and clenched his fists by his sides. "Do you mind—"

"Sorry to bother you. I'm Kevin Kent, president of Cambridge Airlines." The fiftysomething man huffed as he caught up.

The introduction surprised Cole.

"We're based out of London, England," said the man, holding out a business card.

Cole didn't take it. He didn't want to talk to anyone, not a reporter, not an airline executive, not Destiny, not anyone.

"Is there something I can do for you?" he snarled.

The traffic rolled past them, echoing against the pavement, while groups of pedestrians parted to go around.

"I've been watching the proceedings in the courtroom."

Cole didn't respond to the statement. The courtroom had been packed for a day and half, with a lineup outside. It seemed most of the city was watching the proceedings.

"I know you're taking a beating, but my money's on you."

If Kevin Kent wanted a thank-you for the vote of confidence, he was going to be disappointed.

"I've spent some time looking into your Alaska holdings," he continued. "Do you have a second to talk?"

"Here? Now? You want to talk about *Alaska?*" Who cared about Alaska? Zachary's future was on the line.

The man glanced at the multistory buildings around them. "There's a coffee shop on the corner."

"I'm not on a coffee break."

"Right. Okay. I'll get to it. I know you have a thriving airline in Alaska. That you built it from the ground up, and you have a partner and friend in that business with you."

Cole was getting impatient. So Kevin Kent could do an internet search. Big deal.

"When this court case ends, if you win, you're going to have a big decision to make."

Cole crossed his arms over his chest. No kidding. What else had the man deduced?

"I'm banking on you winning," said Kevin. "And I'm banking on your loyalty to Aviation 58."

"Are you working up to a point, Mr. Kent?"

"Call me Kevin. Yes. My point is you may be in the market to sell."

Cole drew back. "Sell Aviation 58?" There wasn't a chance in hell he'd sell his airline.

"No," said Kevin. "Coast Eagle Airlines."

Cole felt the ground shift beneath him; he dropped his arms to steady himself. The bustle of the downtown street went momentarily still and silent. "Sell Coast Eagle?"

"To Cambridge Airlines."

Cole wasn't sure he'd heard right. He was trying to save Coast Eagle for Zachary's future.

"I'm not in the market to sell," he assured Kevin. "I won't *be* in the market to sell."

"Perhaps not." Kevin seemed to be watching Cole closely. "Though I'm not sure you've had an opportunity to think through the complexities of running two separate airlines."

"I'm not going to—" Cole caught himself.

He hadn't thought of it in those terms. But if he won the custody battle, who *would* run Coast Eagle? He wasn't staying in Atlanta. He'd never planned to stay in Atlanta.

Max had made it clear he was temporary as president, and he wasn't the right fit anyway. Roth was absolutely not going to be in charge. Sidney was smart, but new to the VP post. Cole's take was that he needed several years of mentoring before taking on more responsibility.

"We have the corporate depth," said Kevin. "And we have the expertise. You'd have the choice to remain as a minor shareholder, of course. I won't lie to you, I think that would be a good investment. But we'd prefer to buy you out. Have you looked into Coast Eagle's net worth?"

Cole had not. Things had been moving ahead so quickly that he hadn't focused any attention at all on what happened after the court case. And at the moment, he was a lot more worried about the possibility of losing than of winning.

"You need to think about it," Kevin told him softly. "I'm not being opportunistic, and I'd fully expect due diligence on your side. But my take is that you need to win this. And my take is that you're going to fight with everything you've got. And when you win, I want to talk. Because I think you're going to have to make a choice—Coast Eagle or Aviation 58."

He offered his card again. "Call me anytime."

This time, Cole took the card. Kevin Kent gave him a nod and walked away.

Afterward, Cole stood still for a full five minutes.

How could he possibly sell Coast Eagle? Then again, how on earth was he going to run it?

"Mr. Henderson?"

Cole gave himself a mental shake.

This time the man who approached him was a reporter. "Frank Hast, Atlanta Weekly. How do you respond to the accusation that you're using your half brother as a pawn to get your hands on the Henderson fortune?"

Cole stared at the man, wondering what would happen if he simply slammed him into a wall.

"I don't," he said instead and began walking away.

The reporter paced alongside. "Then what do you say to reports that you're using a relationship with Amber Welsley to undermine Roth Calvin?"

The word *relationship* stopped Cole in his tracks. He almost rose to the bait, but he checked himself just in time. "Roth Calvin needs to worry about the facts, not about anything I have to say."

"What *is* your relationship with Amber Welsley?"

"Ms. Welsley is the guardian of my half brother."

"For the moment."

Cole began walking again.

"One more question, Mr. Henderson."

"I have to get back to court."

"But—"

Cole lengthened his stride.

The man hustled to catch up. "Do you agree that Roth Calvin was wrong to put profit before passengers' lives?"

Cole was tempted to answer that one, but he held his tongue and kept going. He was saving his arguments for the judge. The reporter finally gave up.

Luca was on the steps of the courthouse as Cole approached. He quickly spotted Cole and came forward to meet him.

"You okay?" he asked, glancing around as if gauging their distance from possible eavesdroppers.

"Not really."

Luca nodded his understanding. "Destiny was looking for you."

"I needed some air."

"Yeah."

Their conversation ended, but Cole's mind was clicking its way through information and options.

"Have you given any thought to what happens after?" he asked Luca.

"If you lose?"

"If I win."

Luca cocked his head. "No. And honestly, I don't think that's what you need to worry about right now."

"Maybe not," Cole allowed. They were a very long way from winning. But Kevin Kent had gotten him thinking.

"You're the underdog," said Luca.

Cole blew out a breath, telling himself to focus. "What did Destiny want?"

"To talk strategy."

"Are we changing it?" Cole didn't think that was a bad idea. They had hoped Cole's blood connection to Zachary would be their trump card, since the courts overwhelmingly sided with family. But Roth's attack on Cole's motivations and character had clearly turned the tide against them.

"She wants to demonstrate that Roth's sole interest in Zachary is his stake in Coast Eagle."

"So far, he's the one doing that to me."

"He's never spent any time with Zachary."

"Neither had I until last week." Cole knew he was sounding pessimistic. But he was feeling pessimistic.

Luca glanced at his watch. "She thinks it's the best bet."

Cole didn't think it was a huge strength. But they were running out of time and out of options. "I wish I had something better."

"So do I," said Luca. "We have to go back."

"And after?" asked Cole.

"Don't think about it."

"I have to think about it."

"Let's get through today. Whatever happens, we'll face it tomorrow."

Cole gave a reluctant nod. The best thing he could do for Zachary was to remain focused for the rest of the afternoon. If they got a decision today, whichever way it went, they'd start working through their next options in the morning.

Though the courtroom was packed, it was surprisingly quiet. From the third row, Amber focused on Cole's posture. His shoulders were tense, his body completely still as Roth's lawyer gave his summation.

"Samuel Henderson made his final wishes clear," the man's voice boomed with authority. "He named Roth Calvin as his son and heir's legal guardian. Samuel Henderson has known Roth Calvin for over a decade. He has put his trust in Roth Calvin." He made a half turn and pointed to Cole. "Nobody, not this man or anybody else, has the right to undermine Samuel Henderson's wishes on such an important, intimate and fundamental decision of who would raise his son in the event of his death. There is no ambiguity here, Your Honor."

As his voice thundered on, Amber's heart thudded harder. Sweat broke out on her palms. This was hopeless.

They were going to lose.

She was absolutely positive they were going to lose.

The room seemed suddenly hot, and her stomach churned with nausea. She rose from her seat. She could feel Luca watching her as she rushed to the back of the gallery, bursting through the double doors and heading for the ladies' room.

The length of the lobby felt endless, but finally she made it into the cool quiet of the restroom. She gripped the counter, staring at her reflection in the mirror, tears stinging her eyes as she willed her stomach to calm down. She didn't have time to fall apart.

"Think," she ordered herself. *"Think!"*

The marble counter was cold and hard, and her hands started to ache from the pressure of her grip. She ran through every wild and crazy solution, including grabbing Zachary and making a run for it.

Then, in a rush, it came to her fully formed. It was crazy. And it was a gamble, a huge gamble that might very well backfire on her. But at least it was something.

She let go of the counter and retrieved her cell phone from her purse. Then she pressed the speed-dial button for the penthouse.

It was silent, then it clicked, then silence again.

"Come on, come on, come on."

Roth's lawyer was probably finishing up, and there was only so much Destiny had to say.

Finally, the call rang through.

"Welsley-Henderson residence."

"Isabel?"

"Amber? Did they—"

"No. Not yet. But I need you to do something for me. And I need you to do it right now. It's important, and you have to hurry."

"Certainly, ma'am."

"Bring Zachary to the courthouse."

"He's asleep."

"I don't care. Wake him up. Don't stop to change him or to feed him. Tell the driver to go as fast as humanly possible. I'll meet you out front."

"But—"

"Just do it. There's not a second to waste."

"Okay," said Isabel. "Yes. I will."

Amber shut off her phone and tucked it away. She took a final, bracing breath, staring back at her reflection. This might be the stupidest move she'd ever pulled. But she didn't see any other possible hope. If she didn't do something, they'd lose.

She settled her purse strap on her shoulder. Then she left the restroom and made her way back across the big foyer. Her footfalls echoed against the high ceiling and the marble pillars. Sunlight streamed through a wall of glass above the main doors.

It was far too early to go outside to meet Isabel, but she was too jumpy to sit back down in the gallery. She stopped outside the courtroom. She cautiously cracked the door open and saw Destiny come to her feet. All she could hope was that Destiny had a lot to rebut.

She let the door swing shut again and began pacing in the opposite direction. She took a curved staircase to the second floor, walked the perimeter, then took the staircase back down again. She wandered through a side hallway and found an ancillary exit. She took it and walked the three blocks around the complex to the front courthouse stairs.

There she stood, telling herself it was still too early to expect Isabel and Zachary, but scrutinizing every dark sedan that came into view from the south.

She checked her watch. Fifteen minutes had passed.

"Come on, Isabel."

Another five minutes, maybe three minutes, and she'd let herself call Isabel's cell.

And then she spotted the dark blue sedan with Harrison at the wheel. She rushed to the curb, meeting it as it came to a stop, grabbing the back passenger-side handle.

It was locked. Her hand snapped away, and she had to steady herself.

"Ms. Welsley?" Harrison called, rising to look at her over the top of the car.

"Unlock," she called. "I have to hurry."

"Of course, ma'am."

The lock clicked, and Amber pulled open the door. She went to work on the car seat harness, tugging it free, releasing Zachary's arms and legs.

He blinked up at her, sleepy, puzzled.

"Is something wrong?" asked Isabel.

"I'm in a rush," Amber answered, pulling Zachary against her shoulder and stepping back. "They're almost finished."

She turned.

"The diaper bag," Isabel called after her.

"No time," Amber tossed over her shoulder, running up the stairs.

Zachary whimpered in her ear.

She didn't blame him. Poor little thing, dragged unceremoniously out of his bed, probably tired and hungry, likely with a very wet diaper.

"I'm sorry, sweetheart," she whispered in his ear. "But I have to try. I *have* to try."

She pulled open the door, still at a jog as she crossed the far-too-large foyer.

Zachary's whimpers become more insistent as she swung open the courtroom door.

Destiny was on her feet, back to the gallery, talking to the judge. "The precedent Chamber versus Hathaway clearly applies and clearly demonstrates…"

Amber's footsteps slowed as she experienced a rush of unadulterated fear. Was this stupid? Was she making a mistake? But then she focused on the back of Cole's head and forced herself to move forward.

Zachary started to squirm in her arms. His whimpers were turning into whines.

Luca stared at her as she passed the third row. But she ignored him. She ignored the stares of the spectators, and even the curious brow raise from the judge. She moved rudely in front of three people in the front row.

"Cole," she hissed. "Cole?"

He turned, and his expression faltered. "What's wrong?"

At the sound of Cole's voice, Zachary instantly swung around. He howled and lunged for him. As Cole had done a dozen times, he neatly reached out and caught Zachary in his arms.

Destiny turned, and then everything focused on the commotion.

"Order," called the judge, banging his gavel.

Zachary's arms wrapped tight around Cole's neck, and he buried his sobbing face against the crook of Cole's neck.

Destiny moved toward the pair. "Your Honor, this is Zachary Henderson."

The judge peered over the top of his glasses. "I will not allow this hearing to turn into a circus."

But Zachary's sobs were already subsiding, his little body relaxing against Cole's chest.

Roth's lawyer came to his feet. "Objection, Your Honor."

The judge swung his attention to the defendant's table. "What grounds are you going to choose?"

"The plaintiff is not permitted to use props."

"Props?" asked Destiny, with exactly the right note of surprise and censure in her tone.

"Props," the man repeated. "The plaintiff clearly believes that holding Zachary Henderson will make him look to the court like the more capable guardian."

"Mr. Henderson is the more capable guardian." Destiny nudged Cole. "However, if Mr. Calvin would rather hold the prop himself, we have no objection." She looked hard at Cole.

Cole was quick to pick up on the message, walking straight over to Roth to offer Zachary.

Roth jumped to his feet.

"Here you go," said Cole, holding the soggy Zachary out toward him.

As Roth recoiled, Zachary shrieked in obvious terror, reaching desperately for Cole.

"No?" Cole said to Roth.

He pulled poor Zachary back against his chest.

Zachary clung there, breaths shuddering in and out while murmurs came up all across the courtroom.

Destiny jumped back in. "In the interest of peace and order, I'd suggest we let Mr. Henderson hold his brother."

The other lawyer glared at her.

The judge banged his gavel.

Destiny turned to Amber. "Give me your phone. Quick."

Amber scrambled for her phone, handing it over to Destiny.

Cole sat down, and Zachary went mercifully quiet.

"Excuse me, miss?" A woman whispered behind Amber.

Amber turned to find the woman had scooted down to make room on the bench. She patted the spot.

Amber smiled her thanks and sat down.

Nobody seemed certain of what to do next, but Destiny spoke right up, talking while she glanced up and down from the tiny screen on Amber's phone. "Since arriving in Atlanta," she spoke loud and clearly to the judge, "Mr. Henderson has forged a special and intimate bond with his brother."

"Objection," said the other lawyer. "Their purported relationship is no more than hearsay. And it's his half brother."

Destiny glanced meaningfully down at Zachary cuddled up to Cole, obviously letting everyone make up their own mind about the relationship between the two.

"I'll rephrase," she said. "Since arriving in Atlanta, Mr. Henderson has spent a great deal of time with his baby *half* brother. This includes babysitting, feeding, bathing, diapering, playing with him and many hours of cuddling Zachary. In fact, Mr. Henderson spent Christmas Eve and Christmas Day with his half brother."

She took three paces to a small computer table. "I'd like to introduce into evidence some photographs." She swiftly plugged a cord into Amber's phone.

Amber couldn't help but smile.

Immediately, the picture of Cole and Zachary under the Christmas tree came up. Zachary looked adoringly up at Cole as he grasped Cole's nose, grinning. The expression on Cole's face was tender and loving.

"Objection," said Roth's lawyer.

As Destiny turned to acknowledge the lawyer's request, she obviously pressed a button on the phone. A candid shot came up, Zachary and Cole romping with Otis. It was even better than the first.

"On what grounds?" asked the judge.

"The plaintiff is clearly using these photos as a tool of manipulation. They're staged."

"They're family Christmas photos," said the judge. "Since

Christmas Day took place last week, I have no reason to doubt the voracity of the photographs."

Destiny immediately brought up the next photo. It was Cole holding Zachary wrapped in a fluffy towel. The baby was clearly fresh from the bath, and gazed happily into Cole's eyes.

Amber's heart warmed at the memory.

"As these pictures will attest—and we can certainly add witness testimony as well—with the exception of providing advice to Coast Eagle airlines in order to save passenger lives, Mr. Henderson has spent virtually every day with his half brother since arriving in Atlanta."

"Objection," Roth's lawyer repeated. "This isn't a contest to see who can rack up more baby hours."

Destiny countered, "This hearing is to establish who is the most appropriate guardian for Zachary. Time spent with the baby is absolutely relevant to that question."

"Ms. Welsley has obviously inappropriately used her temporary guardianship over Zachary to undermine my client's—"

"Ms. Welsley's conduct is not at issue."

Cole came to his feet. "May I speak, Your Honor?"

The gallery's attention swung to Cole, and both lawyers turned, as well.

The judge considered the question for a long moment.

"Yes," he said. "I think it would be valuable to hear from Mr. Henderson."

Destiny withdrew toward the plaintiff's table, clearly yielding the floor to Cole.

Zachary was quiet on Cole's shoulder, gently fingering his gray-and-red tie.

Cole took a deep breath before beginning. "To be perfectly candid, I have to say that when I read Samuel Henderson had died, I wasn't sorry. I didn't feel much of anything. All I knew about the man was that he'd broken my mother's heart. At that point, I wanted nothing to do with any of the Hendersons."

Cole shifted a couple of steps sideways to come out from behind the table. "As I've already stated, I didn't know about the will. And even if I had, I wouldn't have cared about it. I have a growing, thriving business of my own."

He absently rubbed Zachary's back. "When I finally did come to Atlanta, it was incognito and with the sole purpose of ensuring Zachary would be properly cared for. But from the first moment I met him, my brother insisted I pay attention to him."

Cole smiled fondly down at Zachary. "I don't know whether it was the sound of my voice, the smell of my skin or that I looked something like our father. But from that point on, this little guy has done everything in his power to tell me that he needs me, that it's my responsibility to take care of him, to protect him and to love him. He may not be able to talk, but he's made his desire clear."

Amber's chest went tight, and her throat closed over.

There was a catch in Cole's voice. "And he is right. He's so very right. No matter what you decide here today, Your Honor, Zachary is my brother. He will always be my brother. He will always need me, and I will always be responsible for his welfare. Not because I have to be, or should be, but because I love him, and I will fight with every breath in my body to keep him safe."

Cole went silent. If a pin had dropped in the courtroom, it would have echoed.

He stood a moment longer, then he sat down and placed a kiss on the top of Zachary's head.

Zachary tipped his chin and grinned up at him, gently patting the side of Cole's cheek. "Gak baw. Gak. Gak."

Amber nearly burst into tears.

"I agree, partner," Cole whispered softly. "I agree."

Everybody looked to the judge.

Even Roth's lawyer seemed dazed.

Destiny put her hand on Cole's shoulder.

The judge cleared his throat. "I find…" He paused, adjusting his collar, then rearranging a few sheets of paper in front of him.

He glanced to the bath picture that was still up on the screen. "This is a very unique situation. And I recognize that there is a lot of money at stake. I understand that Coast Eagle Airlines needs to be run effectively. And I understand that guardianship of Zachary Henderson is pivotal to the operation of the company and therefore to the safety and livelihood of thousands of employees and passengers."

Destiny's hand tightened on Cole's shoulder.

He turned to glance at Amber, and the worried expression on his face made her stomach sink. She blinked against tears all over again.

"However," said the judge, "the purpose of this hearing is to determine the best guardian for Zachary Henderson. I cannot let any of the complicating factors impact his well-being and his future." He lifted the gavel. "Therefore, I find in favor of the plaintiff. I grant full and permanent guardianship of Zachary Henderson to Cole Henderson." The gavel came down.

Amber didn't hear a thing as she burst from her seat at the same time Cole turned to face her.

She rushed through the little gate and flung her arms around both of them, her heart overflowing with gratitude.

Cole chuckled as he held her tight. "I can't believe you did it."

"Did what?"

"Turned Zachary into a puppy."

She pulled back and grinned. "I was so scared. But he went straight to you."

"You're a genius."

"It was a big risk."

"It worked."

"Well done, you two," Destiny chimed in, clapping one hand on each of them.

"Well done, you," said Amber in return. "You were brilliant."

"That was a great idea."

"So was using the pictures on my phone."

Roth marched past them, stone-faced, staring straight ahead.

Cole watched his back for a few seconds. "It's going to be an interesting day at the office tomorrow."

"I'm going to worry about *that* tomorrow," said Amber.

Cole gave her a nod. "Agreed. Tonight, we celebrate." A trace of concern seemed to flit through his eyes. "Tomorrow, we figure out the rest."

Thirteen

Cole set the champagne bottle on the fireplace hearth, handing one flute of champagne to Amber and taking the other for himself. "It's very convenient to have a well-stocked wine cellar."

"It is. And I finally managed to figure out the code," said Amber.

She was sitting beside him on the thick carpet, leaning back against the sofa. Zachary was fast asleep in bed, Otis on guard in the hallway outside his door, and the lights were dimmed throughout the penthouse. The flickering gas fire blended with the tiny white lights of the Christmas tree.

"Some of the wine is locked up?" Cole asked.

"I mean the color code to the price and vintage."

"Yeah?"

She raised her glass. "Oh, yes. We are enjoying a very fine vintage."

He didn't have the heart to tell her that champagne all tasted the same to him. "We have a lot to celebrate."

"You were brilliant."

"No, you were brilliant. I just picked up the ball."

"And carried it across the goal line."

"You threw the hail Mary pass."

She grinned. "I did, didn't I? To us, then, and our mutual brilliance."

"Don't forget about Zachary." If they'd scripted the event, the kid couldn't have pulled it off any better.

"He was perfect." She took a sip. "Oh, this is a good one."

Cole followed suit. It tasted like sweet, bubbly wine to him. "It is."

"I guess you're the chair of the board now," she said, stretching her arms out as she leaned back.

Cole felt an uncomfortable pull in his gut. "We should talk about something else."

"Did you see the look on Roth's face? He is both furious and terrified."

"I don't see him at Coast Eagle for the long term."

"Are you going to fire him right away?"

Cole took a swig of the champagne, wishing it was something stronger and less sweet. "That's a complicated decision."

And it wasn't a decision he was in a position to make. He'd have to be willing to stay at Coast Eagle for weeks, maybe months before he could figure out the quagmire of the company's inner workings. Not that he held out hope for Roth, but a knee-jerk reaction wasn't in the best interest of the company.

"You'll have to hire a president. Max is anxious to get back to the legal department."

Cole finished the glass and set it aside, fighting an urge to grab Zachary and drag Amber with them to the Alaskan border. Nobody else mattered.

"Can we talk shop tomorrow instead?" he asked, easing over beside her. "You look beautiful in the firelight."

Her blue eyes softened. "You think?"

"I know." He touched his finger to the bottom of her chin, lifting it ever so slightly to give her a kiss.

The champagne tasted a lot better on her than it had in the glass.

"Thank you, Cole," she whispered against his lips.

He scooted closer still and framed her face with his hands. "I'd do anything for you."

Her smile was beautiful. She was beautiful. She was smart and strong and capable. And she was the sexiest woman he'd ever laid eyes on.

He kissed her.

Then he kissed her deeper, longing radiating through him, pushing everything out of his mind, everything but Amber and how much he needed her.

When he came up for air, he reached for her glass, setting

it aside. Then he lay back, easing her on top of him, loving the press of her soft body against his. He ran his hands along her back, down to her thighs, remembering the exquisiteness of her form.

He slipped his hand beneath her shirt, touching the hot, supple skin of her back, stroking his palms upward.

"You're distracting me," she told him.

"That's the idea."

"We have to talk."

"I know."

"There are a thousand decisions to make."

"Not tonight."

"But—"

"Shh. Give me tonight." He could hear a note of desperation in his own voice. "The world will come apart soon enough."

"It won't be that bad."

But Cole knew it would. It was going to get very, very bad. He was Aviation 58, and she was Coast Eagle. And now he had Zachary.

When his office door burst open, Cole looked sharply up from his desk. He wasn't a stickler for protocol, but the action seemed rudely abrupt.

Then he saw that it was Roth.

He set down his pen and sat back in his chair.

Roth advanced into the room. "I *want* an explanation."

"Of what?"

The only unexpected thing Cole had done so far was to *not* fire Roth. And that was only because he wanted to leave that option for whoever became the next president. And he doubted Roth would demand an explanation for keeping his job.

"You were talking to Kevin Kent," Roth announced.

Cole was forced to hide his shock. Only Luca and Bartholomew had known about this morning's call. He couldn't imagine either of them telling Roth.

He bought himself some time while he mentally calculated both the damage and his next move. "And?"

Roth braced his hands on Cole's desk, leaning forward. "And we both know what that means."

"Do we?" Cole asked. His tone was mild, but his brain was still scrambling.

"It means you're looking to sell. Are you going to liquidate your interest, Mr. Loving Half Brother? Do you care so little about the Coast Eagle legacy that you'd sell it off, maybe break it up, whatever it takes to free up the cash that kid got you?"

"Leave my office," said Cole.

"If you're holding a fire sale, the senior management team deserves an explanation."

Cole felt his blood pressure creep up. "The senior management team will deal with whatever the *owner* decides."

"So you're selling out and pocketing the windfall," Roth spat.

"Leave," Cole ordered.

"No regard for *anyone* or anything else?"

Cole heard a gasp.

He glanced past Roth to see Amber in the doorway. Her eyes were wide and her face was pale as she clung to the doorjamb.

He swore under his breath, even as he vaulted from his chair. She was quick to turn away, dashing down the hall toward the elevator.

He followed at a run. When he caught her, she was frantically stabbing the down button.

"Calm down," he told her in an undertone.

She didn't look at him. "Is it true?"

"I'm not having this conversation in the foyer."

In his peripheral vision, he caught the interested look of Sandra, the executive receptionist. He remembered how friendly she'd been with Roth the first day he'd visited. And it occurred to him that she had a phone number readout on her switchboard.

Amber turned, jaw clenched. "Just tell me if it's true."

"Come back to my office."

"Tell me the truth. Are you going to sell Coast Eagle?"

He scrambled for a way out of the conversation. "It's complicated. We need to talk. And we can't do it here."

She pressed her lips together, staring at him with disdain.

"Come back to my office, where it's private. You can hate me just as easily there."

She didn't answer.

"Amber," he prompted.

"Fine."

He turned and gestured for her to go first.

He let the distance grow between them. Then he stopped at Sandra's desk. He pinned the woman with a furious glare. "If you *ever* research my phone calls again and report them to *anyone,* I'll fire you on the spot."

The color drained from her face.

Leaving, he followed Amber into his office.

She was standing at the window, back to him, staring into the sunny Atlanta afternoon.

He closed the door, composing and discarding opening lines. "I was going to talk to you tonight."

She turned. "I can't believe I fell for it—hook, line and sinker."

He automatically moved toward her. "You didn't fall for anything. I've barely decided. I only decided this morning that selling is the best thing for everyone."

"You mean the best thing for you."

"No, not for me." He amended that statement. "Yes, okay, for me. But only because I could never do it. It's not humanly possible to run two airlines. I wanted to do it. I thought about doing it. Believe me, I came at doing just that from every angle I could."

"Over an entire two days?" she taunted.

"And before."

"Before? You'd planned to sell out *before* we even went to court?"

"I didn't *plan* to sell out. I considered the possibility that I might *have* to sell out."

"You don't *have* to do anything, Cole."

He hated the coldness in her eyes. "I have a plan."

"Clearly, you've had a plan all along. Do you have a conscience? Do you have a soul?"

"A plan for us," he explained. "I want you to come to Alaska as often as you can."

She reached out to grip the window ledge. Her voice was a rasp. "Alaska?"

"To see Zachary. And me, of course." He hoped she'd want to see him. She had to want to see him. He'd come to need her in his life.

She scoffed. "Last time you invited me to Alaska, you admitted you were being insincere and misleading, even manipulative."

It took him a second to remember his words. But he did, and he regretted them deeply. "That was a long time ago."

"The truth is the truth, Cole. Like I said back then, you don't need to worry. I won't be dropping by Alaska to bother you."

"Will you hear me out?"

"I don't think so."

"For Zachary's sake, will you *please* hear me out?"

"Are you taking him away from me?"

"I'm taking him to Alaska, yes. But—"

"Then there's nothing more to say, is there?"

There was plenty more to say. But he could see that this was pointless. Maybe they could talk in a few days. Or maybe he should be patient and let things settle.

Zachary had to be his priority just then. And the Cambridge deal needed his immediate attention. He also needed to get back to Aviation 58. He couldn't stay away any longer.

He didn't want to wait to square this with Amber, but maybe it was for the best. She wasn't going to listen to him right now.

"I'm trying hard not to hurt you," he told her.

She moved for the door, her voice stone flat. "So nice that you at least tried."

* * *

Amber was never going to forgive Cole Henderson, and she'd probably never forgive herself. He and Zachary had been gone for nearly a week, and she'd rehashed every minute of the past month inside her head trying to figure out where she went wrong, and how she could have so thoroughly misjudged him.

"I should have realized," she told Destiny.

"Realized what?" Destiny was across the table from her at Bacharat's. It was Friday night, and the last thing Amber wanted to do was go back to the empty penthouse.

"I should have realized that with this much money at stake, all men would be ruthless."

Destiny toyed with her martini for a moment. She started to speak then stopped herself.

"What?" Amber asked.

"Don't shoot the messenger."

"Are you actually going to defend him?"

"No. But do you think maybe you should have heard him out?"

"Absolutely not." Of that, Amber was certain.

"Why?"

"Because he'd only make up more lies. You can't trust a liar."

"To be fair, you don't *know* he was lying."

Amber's voice rose. "I thought you said you weren't going to defend him."

"I'm not defending him."

"The man had a billion-dollar deal lined up less than forty-eight hours after he won the court case. You don't think that required a little preplanning?"

Destiny didn't seem to have an answer for that.

"I hate to say this," Amber continued, and she really did, "but Roth's right when he says it all looks suspicious."

Destiny paused a beat before responding. "Does it bother you that you're siding with Roth?"

It did bother Amber. But, bottom line, Cole had breezed into town for three short weeks, romanced her, then left with her nephew and a billion dollars.

"I made a huge mistake," she said, swallowing. "What if I never see Zachary again?"

"That's simply not going to happen," said Destiny.

"He's in *Alaska*."

"You can go to Alaska."

Amber shook her head. "No. No, I can't."

Destiny stared hard. "You can. You *will*. Not tomorrow and not next week, but you *will* go see Zachary."

"I'm mortified that I fell for Cole's act."

"I've known you for five years. You are not going to let your embarrassment get in the way of doing the right thing for your nephew."

"You sound like you have faith in me." Amber wasn't sure she deserved anybody's faith.

"I have nothing *but* faith in you."

"Thanks." Amber polished off her martini, trying to feel some faith in herself. "I think I need another."

"I'm with you." Destiny signaled for another round. "Luca has been texting all day."

"I'm sorry it went bad with Luca."

"It didn't go bad with Luca." Destiny's tone was a little sharp.

"I didn't mean—"

"It was too *short* with Luca." Destiny's tone mellowed. "But it was all good. I really do miss him."

"I don't miss Cole."

"That's a big fat lie. You might be ticked off at him, but you have to miss him."

"I'm—"

Destiny spoke overtop her. "This sharing-our-feelings thing isn't going to work if you're just going to lie to me."

Amber tried to wrap her head around the jumble of her feelings for Cole. "I can't miss a man who didn't exist."

"Tell me something," said Destiny, propping her elbow on the tabletop and her chin on her hand. "If Cole was real, if the guy you met was authentic, would you be in love with him right now?"

"That's a pointless question."

"I saw you at the courthouse," said Destiny. "How you looked at him. How he looked at you. In that moment, you were a goner."

Amber remembered. And she experienced the feelings all over again—the intense rush of pride and respect for his strength and honesty, the knowledge that Roth had been vanquished and Zachary was safe, the certainty that she didn't have to worry anymore, that somebody else would help shoulder the burden, and the way he'd immediately turned toward her, the emotion in his eyes, her absolute certainty that nobody else in his world mattered, just her and Zachary.

"Amber?" Destiny prompted.

"Yes," Amber admitted. There really was no reason to lie to Destiny. "If that guy, the guy from the courtroom... If that guy truly existed, I'd be a goner."

Destiny's phone chimed. She looked at the number display and then put the phone to her ear. "Destiny Frost."

She listened for a moment, and her eyes narrowed.

Amber selfishly hoped that whatever it was wouldn't drag Destiny away tonight.

"What kind of paperwork?" asked Destiny. She sent a puzzled glance Amber's way.

Amber frowned.

"Is there a rush?" asked Destiny. "I've had a couple of martinis."

Amber couldn't help feeling disappointed. She didn't want Destiny to leave.

"We're at Bacharat's."

We? Amber glanced around the room, looking to see if she recognized anyone else from Destiny's firm. She didn't.

"Sure," said Destiny. "We'll be here."

As Destiny ended the call, Amber gathered her purse.

"What are you doing?" asked Destiny.

"Getting out of your way." Amber started to rise.

"Well, don't. That was about you."

Amber sat back down. "What about me? Am I being fired already?"

"No. Good grief, where did that come from?"

"Roth's still a VP."

"And Cole still owns the company."

"Only until the deal is finalized."

"Don't be paranoid. You're good at your job, and the new guys are going to see that. And this has nothing to do with your job." Destiny grinned.

"So who was that?" asked Amber.

"Fredrick Galloway of Galloway, Turner and Hopple."

"That means nothing to me."

"He's Cole's new Atlanta lawyer."

A wave of apprehension washed over Amber. "What does he want?"

"He was pretty cagey. Galloway's the top attorney at the top firm in the city."

"I'm sure Cole can afford the best." Though she didn't need it, Amber took another sip of her martini.

"He's got some kind of paperwork for you."

"I don't know what more I can give him. I've already given him—" Amber suddenly teared up. "Oh, damn."

Destiny reached for her hand. "It's going to be fine."

Amber looked into her friend's eyes. "Why did I go and fall in love with him?"

"I wish I could—"

"Ms. Frost?"

Amber looked up to see a sixtyish, fit, well-groomed man standing next to their table.

Destiny came to her feet, purely professional and polite. "Mr. Galloway. It's a pleasure to meet you."

Amber managed a smile.

"I'm sorry to interrupt your evening," said Mr. Galloway. "And, please, call me Fredrick."

"This is my client, Amber Welsley."

"Ms. Welsley." He gave her a nod.

"Amber," she automatically corrected.

Fredrick looked around. "Reception was able to provide us with a private meeting room on the fourth floor. Would you mind joining me there?"

"We'd be happy to," Destiny answered.

Amber took her purse and her coat, doing a double check behind her to make sure she hadn't left anything on the table.

They made their way to the reception elevator, going up one floor to the club's meeting rooms. Fredrick led them down a quiet hallway to a large boardroom. The lights had been turned on and coffee set out on a side table.

Destiny poured herself a cup, but Amber decided to let her stomach rest for a bit.

Fredrick took a seat near the end of a long table. Destiny and Amber sat across from him.

"As I said on the phone," he opened, "you're welcome to take the package with you to read over the weekend. I'd appreciate it if we could talk again Monday morning."

"We can make that happen," said Destiny.

Amber slid a sideways glance at Destiny, gauging her reaction. She seemed impressed by the man, and not overly concerned about the paperwork.

"In a nutshell," Fredrick continued, "Cole Henderson is setting up a trust fund for Zachary."

Amber couldn't hold her tongue. "How incredibly magnanimous of him."

Fredrick gave her a surprised look.

Destiny grabbed her knee under the table.

"What?" Amber looked at them both. "He steals a billion dollars from Zachary, and now he wants to set up a trust fund? What is it, for college or something?"

She wasn't clear on what it had to do with her. Maybe Cole wanted her to believe he was taking care of Zachary so she wouldn't go gunning for him.

Wasn't that a rule of a good con? Make sure the mark's not too angry with you when you leave? She was sure she'd seen that in a movie somewhere.

Fredrick cleared his throat. "My client has requested that Ms. Welsley, Amber, be named trustee with full power to make all decisions regarding the trust fund until Zachary Henderson reaches the age of eighteen."

"Sure," said Amber with a careless shrug. "I'll make sure he gets to college."

This time, Fredrick seemed to be fighting a smile. He slid a sheaf of papers across the table to Destiny. "The trust fund will also provide a salary for Amber."

"I'm not taking any of the money for myself," Amber scoffed. "Just because certain other people believe it is perfectly acceptable to—"

"Amber," Destiny interrupted.

"—use a defenseless baby as a means to—"

"Amber!"

Amber snapped her mouth shut. "What?"

"It says all proceeds from the sale of Coast Eagle Airlines." The words didn't mean anything to Amber.

Destiny spoke slowly, articulating each word. *"All* the proceeds from the sale of Coast Eagle go into the trust for Zachary."

Amber cocked her head sideways, struggling to make sense of Destiny's words. "I'm not following."

"Cole is putting the whole billion into a trust fund for Zachary."

"Dollars?" Amber asked in a dry whisper.

"To be managed by you, as accountant, and he's suggested me as legal counsel, but you have discretion over that." Destiny sent a glance to Fredrick.

Fredrick nodded his confirmation.

Destiny continued, "Until Zachary is eighteen, at which time an orderly and gradual dispersal will begin to move control to Zachary."

Amber swiped her hair back from her forehead. "I know I'm

a little tired. But I thought you just said Cole put me in charge of *all* of the money."

"He did," said Destiny, a grin nearly splitting her face.

"And unlimited trips to Alaska," said Fredrick. He leaned forward and pointed to a spot on the page. "You get an annual salary, benefits and he was *very* specific about the unlimited trips to Alaska."

Amber instantly woke up. Her mind flashed back to the fight they'd had in Cole's office. *I have a plan,* he'd said. *A plan for us. I want you to come to Alaska as often as possible.*

Her hand flew to her mouth. "Oh, no."

"This is good," said Destiny. "This is amazing. I'm…" She looked helplessly to Fredrick.

"Mr. Henderson's instructions are clear and specific," said Fredrick. "And Galloway, Turner and Hopple is pleased to be working with you. This file will have my personal attention."

"He wasn't a fraud," said Amber, as much to herself as to Destiny.

Cole wasn't a fraud, and that meant Amber was in love with him. And she'd made a horrible mistake.

Cole now knew where he'd gone wrong. He never should have left Amber in Atlanta. And he should have brought her in on the decisions around Zachary from the very beginning. He knew she'd seen the trust fund documents; Fredrick confirmed he'd delivered them Friday night.

Cole had expected to hear from her. He'd expected her to understand his logic and like his solution. But it was Monday morning and there hadn't been a single word. Luca had called Destiny, but even she didn't respond.

It was late last night when he'd had the epiphany. Amber didn't want to be brought in at the end of the discussion. She wanted, needed and deserved to be a part of any decision involving Zachary. She also needed to be part of any decision involving Cole.

He knew he was in love with her, completely and forever.

That meant they'd be partners, completely and forever. So long as he could convince her to forgive him.

He wheeled his SUV into the terminal parking lot at the Juneau airport and turned to Zachary strapped into the car seat behind him.

"Got another trip in you?" he asked.

"Gak," said Zachary.

Cole grinned. "I'm going to take that as a yes."

He extracted Zachary, opened the hatchback to retrieve the small duffel bag he'd thrown together this morning. They were catching a scheduled flight, a big, fast jetliner that would get them to Seattle and then Atlanta as quickly as possible.

He balanced Zachary on one hip and lifted the duffel bag with his other hand, elbowing the hatchback closed. "Let's go get her, buddy."

It was a short walk to the main terminal entrance.

Cole would normally just hop in the back of the plane, not particularly caring about amenities. But with Zachary in tow, he'd gone with a first-class ticket. He'd been up most of the night figuring out his problems, and he hoped both of them could sleep for a few hours on the way.

He crossed the lobby toward the check-in lineups.

"Cole?" came a soft, familiar voice.

He stopped dead, not believing it could be true.

But when he turned, there she was, less than five feet away. She was smiling and her blue eyes shone. His heart lurched in his chest.

"Amber." He was in front of her in two strides, dropping the duffel bag to the floor.

"I was coming to see you," she told him.

Zachary immediately lunged for her. She caught him and pulled him to her chest.

"I was coming to you," said Cole. "I was so wrong. I'm so sorry."

Zachary patted her cheek, and she laughed.

"I'm the one who is sorry." She sobered as she told Cole, "I never should have doubted you."

"You had plenty of reasons to doubt me. I hoped you'd understand when you got the trust fund."

"I did understand. That's why I'm here." She gave a little laugh. "Well, that, and it was included in my salary package."

"I was wrong," Cole repeated.

Her expression faltered.

"About selling Coast Eagle," he quickly clarified. "That's not my decision to make alone."

She looked confused. "But you said you couldn't run them both."

"I know. And I can't. But I didn't explore all the options. I have now. And we have another option. But I'm not making this decision without you." He took a breath, steadying himself, realizing he was trying to tell her too much and all at once.

He stopped talking and drew her into his arms, her and Zachary, holding them both close.

"I love you," he whispered in her ear. "I love you so much. And I need you. And Zachary needs you. And you have to marry me. And you have to be his mother, because that's the only way this works. It's the only way he gets what he deserves out of life." He was talking too much again, but he couldn't stop himself. "You and I both had to compromise, but Zachary doesn't. He can have it all, Amber. But only if you'll marry me. I'm sorry. That was too much to throw at you. But once I started talking—"

"Yes," she said, drawing back. "Yes, I love you. And yes, I'll marry you. And of course, *yes,* I'll be Zachary's mother."

He kissed her deeply, until Zachary squirmed between them. "Gak!"

Cole chuckled, and Amber laughed as he drew back to give Zachary some space.

"Can you handle another thing?" he asked her.

"Things like you love me and want to marry me? Those kinds of things? Bring them on."

"We can merge the airlines."

She looked confused.

"But only if you want to do it. This is a decision we're making together. We can still do the trust fund instead. But Luca and I sat up all night last night. He's on board. We merge the airlines and run them together."

"Coast Eagle expands to Alaska?" she asked.

"No." Cole shook his head. "Aviation 58 expands to Atlanta. The head office stays here, but we live in both places."

"Yes," she said again. "Oh, yes."

"Can you handle one more?" Cole asked, feeling as if he was on a roll.

"*There* you are!" Destiny appeared out of the throng. "Hey, Cole. How did you know we were coming in on this flight?"

"I didn't," said Cole. "I was heading for Atlanta."

Destiny grinned at that. She turned to Amber. "I told you so. Did I not tell you so?"

"You did," Amber agreed with a smile.

"Hey, Zachary," Destiny greeted him.

"Does Luca know you're here?" asked Cole.

"I just called him."

Cole glanced at his watch. "Then, I expect he'll be here in about two minutes."

The Aviation 58 offices were on the far side of the airport grounds, but Cole knew Luca wouldn't waste any time getting to Destiny.

"So how're you two doing?" asked Destiny, jiggling Zachary's little hand.

"He's not selling Coast Eagle," said Amber.

Destiny froze, looking worriedly at Amber. "So you're out of a job?"

"She just agreed to marry me," said Cole.

"I was gone maybe five minutes," said Destiny.

"I work fast," said Cole. "We're going to run it together, as a family."

Luca appeared at a run, laughing as he scooped Destiny into

the air, kissing her hard and twirling her around. "I hope you don't plan to leave anytime soon."

Cole drew Amber close again. "You're not leaving, *ever.*"

Fine by her. "I'm staying right here."

"I love you *so* much."

Zachary reached for Cole, and he lifted him from Amber's arms, settling him once more on his hip. Then he looped his arm around Amber's shoulder, realizing in a rush of happiness that he had a family. He had a perfect little family of his very own.

"That last thing?" he whispered into her ear.

"Yes?"

"Brothers and sisters for Zachary?"

"Just as soon as you're ready."

Cole was ready now.

* * * * *

MILLS & BOON®

Why not subscribe?
Never miss a title and save money too!

Here's what's available to you if you join the exclusive **Mills & Boon Book Club** today:

✦ *Titles up to a month ahead of the shops*
✦ *Amazing discounts*
✦ *Free P&P*
✦ *Earn Bonus Book points that can be redeemed against other titles and gifts*
✦ *Choose from monthly or pre-paid plans*

Still want more?
Well, if you join today we'll even give you
50% OFF your first parcel!

So visit **www.millsandboon.co.uk/subs**
or call Customer Relations on 020 8288 2888
to be a part of this exclusive Book Club!

SUBS_2014